After
a
Fashion

D0373710

Books by Jen Turano

JEN TURANO

BETHANYHOUSE

a division of Baker Publishing Group
Minneapolis, Minnesota

© 2015 by Jennifer L. Turano

Published by Bethany House Publishers
11400 Hampshire Avenue South
Bloomington, Minnesota 55438
www.bethanyhouse.com

Bethany House Publishers is a division of
Baker Publishing Group, Grand Rapids, Michigan

Printed in the United States of America

Library of Congress Cataloging-in-Publication Data is on file at the Library of Congress, Washington, DC.

ISBN 978-0-7642-1275-8

Cover design by Paul Higdon
Cover photography by Brandon Hill Photos

15 16 17 18 19 20 21   7 6 5 4 3 2 1

For Tricia

1

NEW YORK CITY, 1882

*M*iss Peabody, I do so hate to interrupt your work, but an urgent message has just arrived that requires immediate attention. Would you join me for a moment so we may speak privately?"

Setting aside the feather she'd been about to attach to a delightful monstrosity of a hat, Harriet Peabody rose to her feet and hurried after her employer, Mrs. Fienman, who'd disappeared through the office door. Realizing that what Mrs. Fienman needed to disclose was unlikely to be of a pleasant nature, Harriet stepped into the office and pulled the door firmly shut. After dodging numerous hats lying about the floor, she stopped in front of the desk and resisted the urge to fidget when Mrs. Fienman simply stared at her.

"Would you like a cup of tea, dear?" Mrs. Fienman finally asked, causing sweat to immediately bead Harriet's forehead.

Mrs. Fienman had never offered her tea, not once in all the time she'd worked for the lady.

"Thank you, but I'm not actually thirsty," she managed to get out of a mouth that had turned remarkably dry.

"I insist." Mrs. Fienman nodded toward a tea set.

"I'd love some tea." Harriet moved to the teapot and poured out a cup, wincing when droplets of tea splashed onto the table, a result no doubt of hands that had taken to trembling. Brushing the droplets aside with a corner of her sleeve, she picked up the cup, turned, and noticed the odd circumstance of Mrs. Fienman thumbing through a copy of the latest fashion magazine. She cleared her throat. "The urgent message, Mrs. Fienman?"

"Ah, yes, quite right." Mrs. Fienman stopped thumbing and nodded to a chair stacked high with hats. "Have a seat."

Harriet edged gingerly down on the very front of the chair, desperately hoping that no hats were being squashed by the fashionable bustle attached to her backside. It truly was unfortunate she had not yet perfected the collapsible bustle she'd been attempting to create. Such a bustle would have come in remarkably handy at that particular moment.

"Now then," Mrs. Fienman began, "I need you to make a delivery for me."

Pausing with the teacup halfway to her lips, Harriet frowned. "A delivery?"

"Indeed, and I must state most emphatically that it's a very important delivery, one that I wouldn't trust to just anyone."

Setting the cup aside, Harriet rose to her feet, taking a brief second to collect her thoughts before she dared speak. "I do hope you won't take offense at this, Mrs. Fienman, but I wouldn't be comfortable delivering anything of a . . . shall we say, shady nature."

Mrs. Fienman's jowls began to quiver, she turned an interesting shade of purple, and then, to Harriet's amazement, the lady gave a loud hoot of laughter. Mrs. Fienman chortled for a full minute before she finally gave a last hiccup of amusement and motioned Harriet back to the chair. "How amusing to learn you find me capable of 'shady' dealings, Miss Peabody, but I assure you, nothing could be further from the truth." She tapped a finger against one of her many chins. "Although, I have often thought that if I did possess a mysterious attitude—which again, I don't—it might be helpful for drumming up business."

Unable to summon up a suitable response to that peculiar remark, Harriet moved back to the chair, sat down, and immediately sucked in a sharp breath when she heard an ominous *crunch*. Knowing without a doubt she was sitting on top of what had to be a ruined hat, she couldn't help wonder how much Mrs. Fienman was going to insist she hand over to compensate for the damage done. Harriet did have a few extra dollars at her disposal, but they had been painstakingly saved with the intent of splurging on a lovely birthday dinner—not a crushed hat.

She didn't really *need* a savory steak to celebrate the day of her birth. No, enjoying the company of her friends would suffice, but . . . a steak would have added a nice touch of extravagance to the evening, and she hadn't savored a tasty piece of beef for months.

". . . so I need you to take the carriage and see to it that Mr. Addleshaw's fiancée is satisfied with the hats we've created for her."

All thoughts of tasty beef evaporated in a split second. "Am I to understand the urgent situation you're facing is due to your need for a delivery of hats?"

"Too right it is, and not just any hats, but hats specifically created for Miss Birmingham. She has only recently arrived in town, and is newly engaged to Mr. Oliver Addleshaw, one of the wealthiest gentlemen in America."

Mrs. Fienman sent Harriet a wink. "Word about the city has it he's made an obscene fortune through some manner of finance. It's my dearest hope to grab a piece of that fortune through return business from the gentleman's fiancée." She picked up a letter lying on her desk and began fanning her face with it. "This note from Miss Birmingham, while being somewhat hysterical in nature, states that the lady is concerned the hats she ordered might not complement some of the pieces of a wardrobe she had delivered to her this morning."

Harriet's mouth dropped open. In her world, *urgent* meant someone had died, the rent was overdue, or dinner could not be served due to lack of funds. It never meant one was anxious for a delivery of hats.

"I've sent Timothy off to get the carriage," Mrs. Fienman continued briskly, "and he'll be back directly. All you need to do is help Miss Birmingham sort through the hats, and soothe any ruffled feathers she might have if some of the styles don't exactly complement her gowns."

"I do beg your pardon, Mrs. Fienman, but I must inquire as to why you're not personally seeing to this situation, considering it seems to be of a delicate nature."

Mrs. Fienman's expression turned a little shifty. "I thought it was past time we got you out of the back room and mingling with clients."

"And you believe my 'mingling' should begin with the fiancée of one of the wealthiest gentlemen in America?"

"You, Miss Peabody, are made of stern stuff, which is why I've chosen you for this unpleasant . . . or rather, *delightful* task. I cannot send Gladys or Peggy because Miss Birmingham is possessed of a slightly tumultuous personality. She would have those two in tears within minutes. Why, I wouldn't imagine you'd even cry if your dog died."

"I don't have a dog."

"Well, no matter. I'm certain if you did own a dog and it tragically died, you wouldn't shed a single tear, would you?"

Harriet forced a smile. "While I certainly appreciate your

10

confidence in me, I must remind you that, when you hired me, you specifically told me I was to keep to the back room and not mingle with our clients. Because of that, I am not being modest when I say I'm not exactly equipped to deal with a member of the quality."

"My reasoning behind banishing you to the workroom was not because I ever doubted your ability to mingle with clients, Miss Peabody. It stemmed more from the fact that with your all-too-pretty face, unusual violet eyes, and luscious black hair, you'd cast our customers in the shade. However . . ." She released a dramatic breath. "Miss Birmingham is not one of our usual clients. She apparently took issue with my rather large figure, and has specifically requested her hats be delivered by a person possessed of a pleasant and slender appearance." Mrs. Fienman waved a hand at Harriet. "Since you're the only person available with those qualifications, you'll have to make the delivery."

Alarm began to ooze from Harriet's every pore. While she was perfectly aware she possessed a slender figure, brought on by a distinct lack of food on a regular basis, she was fairly sure she'd detected a faint trace of glee in Mrs. Fienman's voice. She had the sneaking suspicion the glee was a direct result of her employer hoping she would cast this Miss Birmingham in the shade, which certainly wasn't going to help her deal with the lady. Before she could voice a protest, though, Mrs. Fienman leaned forward.

"I must admit I've been most curious about where you obtained such stellar good looks. Do you take after your mother or your father?"

"I never met my parents, Mrs. Fienman. My mother died giving birth to me, and my father, well . . ."

Mrs. Fienman's eyes turned considering. "Do forgive me, Miss Peabody. I should know better than to ask questions of a personal nature, especially from a lady forced to make her own way in the world. But, ancestry aside, you're a lovely young lady, which is exactly what Miss Birmingham requested and exactly what I'm going to give her." She wrinkled her nose. "A word of warning, though, before you depart—Miss Birmingham seems to make a habit of throwing things when she's annoyed, so watch out for flying shoes."

A droplet of perspiration trickled down Harriet's back. "While this Miss Birmingham sounds like a *charming* sort, I honestly don't believe I'm equipped with the social rules and expected manners to deal with her."

"Your manners are perfectly adequate for this appointment. It's not as if you should expect Miss Birmingham to invite you to sit down and enjoy a cup of tea with her."

"What if she goes beyond shoe chucking and attacks me? Am I allowed to defend myself?"

"Certainly not." Mrs. Fienman shook a plump finger in Harriet's direction. "Defending yourself against a society lady would definitely sully the good name of my business. If that were to happen, I would terminate your position immediately."

"But . . ." Harriet began as she struggled to come up with a plausible reason not to take on what was surely going to be a daunting task. "What about Mrs. Wilhelm's hat? I've only put on ten of the fifty feathers she's requested, and she's expecting delivery of that hat tomorrow."

"You'll have plenty of time to finish Mrs. Wilhelm's hat after you get back from dealing with Miss Birmingham."

Harriet glanced at the clock, saw that it was after two, and felt a sliver of disappointment steal over her. By the time she got back from making the delivery *and* finished Mrs. Wilhelm's hat, there would be no time left to celebrate her birthday.

Drawing in a steadying breath, she decided to throw caution to the wind and appeal to what little kindness Mrs. Fienman might actually possess. "I wasn't going to mention this, not wanting anyone to feel compelled to make a fuss, but today is my birthday. While I normally don't mind working extra hours, I was hoping I wouldn't have to work those hours today, since my two best friends have made arrangements to have dinner with me."

"Ah, your birthday. How marvelous!" Mrs. Fienman exclaimed. "Why, I adore birthdays, and if I'd known today was yours, I would have ordered you a pastry." She rooted around the papers strewn across her desk and pulled out a crumbly piece of dough that might have, at one time, been a tart. "Here, have what's left of the pastry I got this morning."

For a second, Harriet remained frozen in place, but since Mrs. Fienman was now waving the pastry determinedly at her, she had no choice but to rise to her feet and accept the woman's offering. A sticky mess of frosting immediately coated her fingers. "Thank you. I'm sure this will be delicious."

Mrs. Fienman beamed back at her. "You're most welcome. Now then, you'd best be on your way." She put a finger to her jowl. "Tell you what, don't bother coming back to finish Mrs. Wilhelm's hat today. You can come in early tomorrow morning and finish the job. Won't that be lovely?"

Not giving Harriet an opportunity to respond, Mrs. Fienman gestured toward the door. "Timothy should be out front by now. Remember, be pleasant, and duck if you see shoes flying your way."

"Ahh . . ."

"No dawdling now, Miss Peabody. Unpleasant matters are best dealt with quickly. Enjoy your tart."

Harriet couldn't find the incentive to move. She looked at Mrs. Fienman, who was once again thumbing through the magazine, then at the mess of a pastry clutched in her hand, and swallowed a sigh when she remembered her prayer only that morning.

It was a tradition, her birthday prayer.

Every year—well, for the past six years—she'd asked God to send her something wonderful. He hadn't always sent what she asked for, but one year He'd sent her unexpected money to pay the rent when she'd thought she'd be out on the streets. Another year, He'd led her to Mrs. Fienman, which had given Harriet stable employment. Last year, when she'd turned twenty-one, she'd asked for a gentleman, and while she hadn't received that particular request, her aunt Jane had given her—rather grudgingly, of course—a gown that had once belonged to her mother. Since she'd never met her mother, had never even seen a portrait of her, the gown had afforded her a glimpse of her mother's slender figure. The fact that the silk was a delicate shade of violet had given Harriet no small sense of delight, given that violet was her very favorite color.

This year she'd decided to keep her prayer simple and had only asked God to send her something of His choosing, something she would find wonderful.

Surely His idea of wonderful couldn't constitute a half-eaten tart and dealing with an overly emotional society lady, could it?

"Miss Peabody!" Mrs. Fienman suddenly yelled, raising her head from the magazine and causing Harriet to jump. "Oh, you're still here . . . Good. Although I would have thought you'd gone to fetch your reticule, but . . . no matter. I almost forgot something."

She pushed aside some papers, extracted one and held it up. "I need you to present Miss Birmingham with the bill—unless, of course, Mr. Addleshaw is in residence. He wasn't in town when I met with his fiancée last week, but was off doing whatever it is important gentlemen do to earn their vast amounts of money. Make certain you make it clear that full payment is expected in a timely fashion."

"You want me to give this bill to either Mr. Addleshaw or Miss Birmingham *and* inform them to pay it promptly?"

"Neither one of them will take issue with the request, if that's your concern." She glanced at the bill, smiled, and then lifted her head. "Good heavens, you'll need to change that hat."

"Change my hat?"

"Indeed. Not that there is anything remotely wrong with the hat you're wearing, other than it's entirely too tempting a piece to be anywhere near Miss Birmingham. I wouldn't put it past the lady to snatch it right off your head, and we wouldn't want that, would we? Especially since it's your birthday." Her expression turned calculating. "I'll tell you what we'll do. You may give me your hat in exchange for the one you so carelessly sat on. That way, I won't be forced to extract your hard-earned money from you. You may think of it as yet another birthday treat."

Pushing aside the pesky notion that the day was quickly turning disappointing, Harriet turned and eyed what remained of the hat she'd squashed. "Are those . . . birds?"

"They were," Mrs. Fienman corrected, "before you sat on them. Now I'm afraid they resemble mice, and sickly looking ones at that."

"And you believe it would be for the best if I dealt with Miss Birmingham while wearing sickly looking mice on my head?"

"Miss Peabody, you're stalling again."

"Too right, I am," she muttered before she set down the remains of the tart on the edge of Mrs. Fienman's desk. Reaching up, she pulled out a few hat pins, lifted her hat off, handed it to Mrs. Fienman, and turned and scooped up what remained of the bird hat. Plopping it on her head, she made short shrift of securing it, refusing to shudder when a mangled bird dangled over her left eye, obscuring her view.

"I don't believe you'll need to worry about Miss Birmingham snatching that hat off your head," Mrs. Fienman said as she began twirling the hat Harriet had been forced to part with. "This really is a creative design, Miss Peabody. It's the perfect size for a lady who wants to look fashionable, yet it won't hinder a lady as she goes about her day. Tell me, would you happen to have other hats crafted in this particular style, ones that might be put up for sale here at the shop?"

"I'm afraid that even though I do have an abundant supply of hats at home, none of them would be appropriate to sell here. The materials I use are scavenged from hats society ladies have abandoned to the poor boxes in churches throughout the city."

"You take hats from the poor boxes?"

"I don't steal them," Harriet said quickly. "I have permission from the ministers to take whatever fancy hats or clothing I might have a use for because their donation bins were overflowing with far too many extravagant pieces." She shrugged. "Ever since gentlemen have begun to amass such huge fortunes, their wives and daughters have become somewhat fickle when it comes to their fashions and are abandoning those fashions faster than ever. Unfortunately for the poor, though, they really don't have any need for such luxurious items—which is why I'm permitted to take them." She smiled. "I redesign the gowns, cut out any stains that might be marring the fabric, and then I provide ladies with limited funds a nice outfit they can wear to a special occasion, but for only a small fee."

"Fascinating," Mrs. Fienman exclaimed, "and a topic I'd love to explore further with you, but for now you'd best get on your way." She waved toward the door. "Good luck to you, and don't forget your pastry, but more importantly, the bill."

Picking up the bill and then, reluctantly, the tart, Harriet walked out of the office, trying to ignore the broken bird bouncing back and forth against her cheek. She stopped at her work-table and took off her apron before sliding her hands into gloves. Scooping up her reticule, she stuffed the bill inside, picked up the pastry, and then nodded to the three ladies who worked with her before heading for the door.

Stepping outside, she moved to Mrs. Fienman's carriage, the one pressed into service whenever a good impression needed to be made. When she opened the door, her gaze traveled over the stacks and stacks of hatboxes crammed into the interior. One quick glance upward explained why they weren't attached to the carriage roof. It looked ready to rain, and since there was no room for her in the carriage, she was probably going to get wet.

She was beginning to get the unpleasant feeling that nothing wonderful was going to happen to her today.

God, it seemed, had forgotten all about her and her tiny birthday request.

"I've saved a spot up here."

Harriet smiled. Timothy, a young man who worked as a driver for Mrs. Fienman, was grinning back at her with his hand held out. She took a second to throw the mangled pastry to a hungry-looking mutt sniffing around the sidewalk, moved to the carriage, and took Timothy's offered hand. Settling in right beside him, she found her mood improving rapidly as Timothy began to regale her with stories about his new wife as they trundled down street after street.

". . . so I made the small observation that the soup my missus served me was cold, and she hit me upside the head with a soup bowl, one that was still filled to the brim with chilly soup."

Harriet laughed, but her laughter caught in her throat when Timothy steered the horses into a narrow alley. He pulled on the reins, and the carriage came to a halt, right in the midst of a large courtyard paved with brick, that brick leading up to the back of a formidable-looking mansion.

Craning her neck, Harriet took in the sight of four stories of superbly cut stone, inlaid with numerous stained-glass windows.

Her stomach immediately began to churn. She really *was* ill-equipped to deal with this particular situation, no matter that Mrs. Fienman seemed to think she'd handle it well. She wasn't even certain if she was supposed to curtsy when she met Miss Birmingham, or maybe she was only expected to incline her head, but . . . what *was* an acceptable response if shoes came flinging her way?

"That sure is something, isn't it—all that stained glass on a back of a house where hardly anyone will see it?" Timothy asked, pulling her abruptly back to the fact she was still sitting on the carriage seat while Timothy was on the ground, holding his hand out to her. She took the offered hand and landed lightly on the bricks.

"Good thing my Molly isn't here with us," Timothy continued with a grin. "She'd probably start getting ideas, but I'll never be able to afford anything more than a hovel."

Harriet returned the grin before she pulled the carriage door open. "I've always thought that hovels have a certain charm, whereas mansions . . . What would one do with all that space?" Turning, she stood on tiptoes and pulled out a few boxes, handing them to Timothy. She grabbed two more, wrapped her fingers around the strings tied around them, and headed toward the delivery entrance. She stumbled to an immediate stop, though, when a loud shriek pierced the air. Turning in the direction of the shriek, she blinked and then blinked again.

A young lady was storming around the side of the mansion, screaming at the top of her lungs. But what was even more disturbing than the screams was the manner in which the young lady was dressed.

A frothy bit of green silk billowed out around the lady's form, but it *wasn't* a gown the lady wore—it was a wrapper. Sparkly green slippers with impractical high heels peeped out from under the hem with every stomp the lady took, and a long, feathery scarf, draped around the lady's throat, trailed in the breeze behind her. Her brown hair was arranged in a knot on top of her head, but pieces of it were beginning to come loose from the pins, brought about no doubt from the force of the lady's stomps. The woman clutched an unopened parasol, and she was waving it wildly through the air.

"He's a beast, a madman, and I'll never have anything to do with him again," the lady screeched to an older woman scurrying after her.

"You're allowing your emotions to cloud your judgment, Lily," the older lady returned in a voice more shrill than soothing. "Mr. Addleshaw was simply surprised by our unexpected appearance in his home. I'm sure once we explain matters to his satisfaction, he'll be more than mollified, and then the two of you will be in accord once again."

The lady named Lily stopped in her tracks. "I have no desire to be in accord with that man."

"That's ridiculous," the older woman argued. "You know your father and I are determined to see a union between our families."

"*You* marry him, then, Mother, because I certainly never will," Lily railed as she shook the parasol in her mother's direction before plowing forward.

"If I were a few years younger and *not* married to your father, believe me, I'd consider it." Lily's mother hustled after her daughter, grabbing the young lady's arm when she finally caught up with her. "You need to be reasonable about this, dear. We have a lot at stake here."

"I'm not feeling in a reasonable frame of mind, Mother." Lily shrugged out of her mother's hold, whacked the poor woman with the parasol, and then charged forward again. She came to an abrupt halt when her gaze settled on Harriet. Her lips thinned, her nostrils flared, and her brown eyes turned downright menacing. "Who are you?"

Harriet summoned up a smile. "I'm Miss Peabody."

Lily's eyes narrowed. "Are you here to see Mr. Addleshaw?"

Harriet took a step back. "Certainly not. I'm here at Mrs. Fienman's request to deliver hats to Miss Birmingham."

Lily looked Harriet up and down. "*You're* a hat girl?" She let out a grunt as her attention settled on Harriet's hat. "You're obviously not a very good one."

Reminding herself she desperately needed to keep her job, Harriet continued smiling. "I am indeed a . . . ah . . . hat girl, although I didn't create the hat I'm . . . Well, never mind about that. All you probably want to know is that I'm here to help you sort through your purchases, if you are, in fact, Miss Birmingham."

"Of course I'm Miss Birmingham."

"Wonderful. May I say that it's lovely to meet you, and—"

"I don't exchange pleasantries with the help," Miss Birmingham interrupted as she moved closer and jabbed a finger at one of the hatboxes. "Show me what's in there."

Glancing up at a sky that was turning more threatening by the second, Harriet was about to suggest they seek out a drier place to inspect the hats, but before she could speak, a gentleman's voice distracted her.

"Miss Birmingham, you need to repair back into the house immediately. You're certainly not dressed in a manner acceptable for strolling around in the open."

Looking past Miss Birmingham, Harriet discovered a gentleman striding in their direction with a large hound of undetermined parentage loping at his side. Her eyes widened as she took in the man's height, the breadth of his shoulders, and . . . the careless cut of his jacket, which strained against his chest and certainly hadn't been cut to suit his powerful frame.

Strange as it seemed at that particular moment, she found herself contemplating who his tailor was and how much he'd given said tailor to create a jacket that fit him so poorly.

Shifting her attention to the gentleman's face, she took in

hazel eyes and a sharp slash of a nose that gave the gentleman the appearance of a hawk, that appearance heightened by the fact his hair was nearly as black as her own. His lips appeared to be firm—what little she could see of them, considering they were currently drawn in a straight line—and his jaw was strong but rigidly set, giving testimony to the fact he was livid.

She looked back at Miss Birmingham, expecting her to be trembling on the spot, but instead, the woman was fairly bristling with rage as she swept the feathered scarf over her shoulder and sent the gentleman a look of deepest disdain.

"You dare presume to order me about?" Miss Birmingham screeched. "You forget yourself, Mr. Addleshaw. I am Miss Lily Birmingham, daughter of the esteemed Mr. John Birmingham. And as such, I'll stroll around outside dressed however I please."

"You're in a wrapper," Mr. Addleshaw shot back. "Your father would hardly approve, and it's rich you bring up presumption, considering you took it upon yourself to move into my home without my knowledge. I told you and your parents I'd secure you more than adequate rooms at a reputable hotel."

Miss Birmingham lifted her pointy chin in the air. "This is exactly why I will no longer be marrying you. You're a complete boor."

"Forgive me, Miss Birmingham, but we're not engaged, nor did I ever suggest we were soon to be. I invited you to the city for the express purpose of attending a few society events in the coming weeks, and I was completely upfront with you when I told you why I needed you in New York. If you will recall, the Duke of Westmoore will soon be in town, and I requested your company so that you could help me entertain the gentleman while I go about the delicate matter of negotiating a business deal with him. The very idea that you took it upon yourself to arrive in the city earlier than we discussed *and* took up residence in my home boggles my mind."

Panic began pounding through Harriet's veins.

They were not engaged, had never been from what Mr. Addleshaw was saying. That meant the day was destined for disaster, since Harriet had the feeling neither of the two people arguing right in front of her was going to be receptive to her presenting them with a bill at this awkward moment in time.

". . . and you can forget about me helping you with the duke," Miss Birmingham howled. "You're mean and rude, and you've been yelling at me ever since you stepped foot in the house."

"Of course I've been yelling," Mr. Addleshaw said between lips that barely moved. "You converted my home office into your personal dressing room."

"The lighting suits my complexion better in that room than the dismal excuse for a room I was given by that dreadful housekeeper of yours."

Harriet watched as Mr. Addleshaw's mouth opened, closed, opened, and then closed again, as if he couldn't decide what he should say next.

She really couldn't say she blamed him.

It was quickly becoming clear Miss Birmingham was not a lady with whom one could reason with in a sensible manner.

"You! Hat girl!" Miss Birmingham suddenly snapped. "Make yourself useful and show me what you've got in those boxes you're holding."

"You want to look at hats right now?" was all Harriet could think to respond.

"That is why you're here, isn't it?"

"Well, yes, of course, but . . ."

"Stop being difficult, Miss Birmingham," Mr. Addleshaw interrupted before he nodded to Harriet. "You, my dear, may take yourself and your hats straight back to the shop you came from. Miss Birmingham will send for them once she gets settled into a hotel."

22

Before Harriet could respond, Miss Birmingham began screaming at Mr. Addleshaw—nasty, horrible accusations that really had no business spewing out of a lady's mouth. Realizing it would not serve her well to remain in the woman's presence another minute, Harriet decided to take Mr. Addleshaw's suggestion and return to the shop. She knew she'd be facing Mrs. Fienman's wrath once she arrived with no bill delivered and a carriage stuffed to the gills with expensive hats, but couldn't see any benefit staying there, especially since Miss Birmingham's screaming was escalating. She turned on her heel and had barely taken five steps when stars erupted behind her eyes. Her head began throbbing right before she felt what she thought was Miss Birmingham's parasol poking her in the back.

"You're not going anywhere with those hats," Miss Birmingham hissed. "They're mine, and I demand you give them to me."

Harriet wasn't afforded the simple courtesy of handing the boxes over to the obviously deranged Miss Birmingham. The woman took care of acquiring the hats on her own by ripping the boxes straight out of Harriet's hands as she thrust the parasol directly into Harriet's stomach. With her hands flapping wildly, Harriet tried to find her balance, but before she could get her feet firmly beneath her, a large furry form flew through the air, hit her squarely in the chest, and sent her tumbling backward. Hard bricks greeted her right before the sound of snarling settled in her ears.

2

Oliver Addleshaw preferred to manage his life exactly as he managed his many businesses. Calmly, organized, and with a sense of purpose. Unfortunately, due to the antics of an exasperating lady, he was smack in the midst of one of the most chaotic and dramatic situations he'd ever witnessed, let alone participated in.

"If it wouldn't be too much trouble, sir," the hat lady called, "I could use a bit of assistance over here."

Directing his attention back to the poor woman—whose face his unruly dog, Buford, was licking a little too enthusiastically—Oliver resisted a sigh. "My apologies, miss, of course . . . you need assistance." He trudged back into the chaos. "Buford, it's not good manners to knock a lady over, let alone slobber all over her face. Get down."

Buford, being Buford, barely paused in his licking, but before Oliver had a chance to grab him, the sound of heels tapping across the bricks captured his dog's interest. Buford raised his head and a second later bounded away, his enthusiastic yelps echoing around the courtyard.

Turning, Oliver winced when he discovered the source of Buford's latest fixation. With her mother scampering behind, Miss Birmingham was tottering away on her ridiculously high-heeled slippers, swinging her hatboxes victoriously, apparently having forgotten her vow to never enter his house again since she was tottering straight toward it. The fluffy piece of nonsense she'd thrown around her neck was fluttering behind her, the fluttering the source of Buford's fascination.

"Buford, no," he yelled, but Buford was already sailing through the air. When the dog landed back on the ground, Miss Birmingham's scarf was clamped between his large teeth.

"Give that back to me." Miss Birmingham drew back her arm and, to Oliver's dismay, swung a hatbox directly at Buford's head. Buford let out a whine, dropped the scarf, and then, because he was constantly craving affection, he lifted his paw and gave Miss Birmingham a look that should have melted her heart.

Miss Birmingham ignored the look as well as the offered paw, snatched up her scarf, looped it twice around her neck, and picked up the hatbox she'd dropped to the ground. With a huff of disgust toward Buford, she swiveled on a high heel and flounced away.

Crouching down, Oliver let out a whistle, and for a second, it seemed Buford was going to come to him, but then . . .

"Stupid mutt," Miss Birmingham tossed over her shoulder.

The hair on Buford's back stood straight up right before he lunged for Miss Birmingham again.

"Oh . . . dear," the hat lady muttered as the sound of ripping silk suddenly filled the air.

In the blink of an eye, Miss Birmingham was standing in the middle of the courtyard, dressed only in her unmentionables with her scarf still around her neck as Buford scampered away with the green wrapper.

"This is hardly the time to dither, Mr. Addleshaw," the hat

lady admonished as she pushed up from the ground in a surprisingly agile move and dashed past him.

"I'm not dithering," he argued under his breath. He began running after his dog right as the hat lady jumped at Buford with her arms spread wide.

Buford skittered to the right, her arms meeting nothing but air, and she tumbled to the ground as Buford galloped away, straight toward Miss Birmingham.

Oliver changed direction as Miss Birmingham began shrieking, but her shrieks came to a rapid end when Buford dropped the wrapper and grabbed onto the scarf, his tugging effectively cutting off Miss Birmingham's voice as the scarf tightened around the lady's throat.

Picking up his pace, Oliver made it to within a few feet of the mayhem but came to an abrupt stop when Miss Birmingham sent him a look filled with rage.

"Stay back," she rasped.

"Really, Miss Birmingham, this is not the moment for such nonsense, considering you're not properly clothed and obviously need some . . ."

"You're not helping matters," the hat lady interrupted before she darted past him and grabbed Buford by the collar. "Drop it."

To Oliver's surprise, the end of the scarf popped out of Buford's mouth. His dog then plopped down on the bricks and rolled over to his back, where he immediately began to whimper.

"Pathetic," the hat lady said, giving Buford a quick rub before she snatched up the wrapper.

Oliver was about to breathe a sigh of relief, believing Miss Birmingham was soon to be reunited with at least a bit of clothing—even though the wrapper was tattered and torn—when to his absolute horror, she suddenly did the unthinkable and hurled herself on top of the hat lady.

For the first time in his life, Oliver had no idea what to do.

How was he to intercede, especially since there was so much of Miss Birmingham's skin exposed?

It was hardly permissible to grab hold of a lady's . . . limbs.

"Miss Birmingham, let go of me," the hat lady yelled. "I'm trying to help you."

Miss Birmingham ignored the lady's words as she went about the business of ripping the hat right off the woman's head, before she grabbed hold of a hunk of inky black hair and pulled it.

Yells and grunts soon filled the air, but expelled by whom, Oliver couldn't actually say. Looking to Mrs. Birmingham, who was standing frozen in horror a few feet away, he moved forward rather reluctantly but shuffled to a stop when the hat lady broke free of Miss Birmingham's hold. She bent down and somehow managed to fling Miss Birmingham over her shoulder before he could so much as move another muscle. She immediately headed toward a carriage stuffed with boxes, lurching a little to the right when Miss Birmingham began thrashing around like a fish out of water. "Stop that," the hat lady ordered as she regained her balance and plowed forward.

"Timothy, make me some room," she called, and a man Oliver hadn't noticed nodded and began throwing boxes from the carriage over his head.

"Be careful with those, you idiot," Miss Birmingham shrieked right before the hat lady reached the carriage and unceremoniously tossed Miss Birmingham inside, slamming the door shut a second later, effectively cutting off the rest of Miss Birmingham's tirade.

"There," the hat lady said, dusting her hands together. "That should hold her for a moment." She nodded to Oliver. "She's all yours."

Oliver glanced at the carriage and found Miss Birmingham, strangely enough, not trying to escape but rummaging through the boxes. "What do you suggest I do with her, Miss . . . er . . . ?"

"Miss Peabody, and as for what you should do with her, well, that's really not my place to say. You might consider looking into the Long Island Home Hotel for Nervous Invalids. I've heard tell it's a wonderful facility and might be exactly what Miss Birmingham needs to get control of her—" Miss Peabody's lips snapped shut, as if she'd suddenly realized the inappropriate nature of her words.

Oliver grinned. "While that's an interesting suggestion to be sure, Miss Peabody, I highly doubt Mr. or Mrs. Birmingham would want to deposit their daughter in a sanitarium. That means I'm back to the quandary of what I should do with her in the here and now."

Miss Peabody lifted her chin before she marched over to where Miss Birmingham's wrapper was lying on the ground and snatched it up. She returned to his side and handed it to him. "I would have to imagine the most urgent order of business would be to get Miss Birmingham back into this, and then you'll need to get her into the house."

The last thing Oliver wanted was to have Miss Birmingham in his house again, because, quite frankly, he wasn't certain she'd ever leave it, at least not willingly, no matter that she'd made the claim she wanted nothing more to do with him.

He *was* Oliver Addleshaw after all, and once Miss Birmingham remembered that, he was fairly certain she'd miraculously turn back into the sweet and demure young lady he'd thought he'd invited to spend time with him in New York.

Ladies had been trying for years to capture his attention, doing outlandish things in order to win his favor, which is why he'd finally resorted to creating a list a few years back. He'd hoped that by writing down exact characteristics he demanded in a lady, he'd avoid situations of an unpleasant nature.

It was rapidly becoming clear that even though he'd written things like pleasing appearance and demeanor, ladylike behavior at all times, and socially acceptable birth, his list was not helping him in the least in selecting an appropriate lady, even one he only needed to briefly spend time with as he negotiated a business deal.

He obviously needed to come up with another plan, and now that Miss Birmingham was not going to be around to help him with the Duke of Westmoore, he was going to have to come up with that plan somewhat quickly.

Miss Peabody waved her hand in front of his face. "I do so hate to interrupt what must be a riveting conversation you're holding in your head," she exclaimed, "but if you've neglected to notice, Miss Birmingham is trying to get out of the carriage. If you've forgotten, she's not exactly modestly dressed." She lowered her voice. "Your servants are pressed against the windows, sir, and I doubt it will help the young lady's reputation if people get an eyeful of her in her current state of *dishabille*."

Unable to help but wonder how a hat lady came to use a word like *dishabille*, Oliver opened his mouth, but before he could question her, the sound of fists beating against the carriage door drew his attention and had him moving up to the carriage. Miss Birmingham glared back at him, her features a little blurry from the fog covering the window. The fog thickened when she began yelling at him through the glass.

"Miss Birmingham," he called through the door, "you will cease your tirade immediately."

"Or what?" she yelled back.

Several ideas immediately popped to mind, none of them remotely achievable, but before he could summon up a suitable response, Miss Peabody let out a small yelp and lurched out of his sight just as her spot was taken by none other than *Mrs.* Birmingham.

Settling his gaze on the older woman, he noticed that her face was mottled with rage, but that rage, strangely enough, was not directed at her daughter but at Miss Peabody, who was slowly inching away from them.

"Explain yourself!" Mrs. Birmingham demanded. "What possible reason could you have for laying your filthy hands on my daughter?"

Miss Peabody lifted a gloved hand, considered it briefly, and then looked Mrs. Birmingham directly in the eye. "Since your daughter was outside dressed only in her unmentionables, I thought it might be prudent to get her out of the open before she suffered irreparable harm to her reputation."

Mrs. Birmingham drew herself up. "It is not the place for someone like you to contemplate my daughter's reputation. You mark my words, girl, Mrs. Fienman will hear about your unacceptable behavior before this day is through. I guarantee you that after I've had my say, you'll no longer be in possession of a position."

Miss Peabody's shoulders sagged ever so slightly, but then she lifted her chin. "It is certainly your right to speak to Mrs. Fienman. You evidently believe I abused your daughter, although by the knot I currently have forming on my head, it's debatable who was actually abused."

Miss Peabody began to fiddle with the clasp of a reticule looped around her wrist. She extracted a piece of paper from it and extended it to Mrs. Birmingham. "Since you've stated you intend to seek out Mrs. Fienman today, allow me to present you with the bill for the hats your daughter ordered. Mrs. Fienman will appreciate prompt payment. In fact, she expects nothing less."

A small bit of admiration stole through Oliver as he regarded Miss Peabody. There were not many ladies he knew who would brave additional wrath from an irate mother in order to attempt to collect on a bill, but Miss Peabody seemed to have no qualms about what she was doing.

His admiration was immediately replaced with anger when Mrs. Birmingham reached out and slapped Miss Peabody's hand. The bill fluttered to the ground and landed in the midst of a puddle of water.

Oliver stepped forward, intent on rescuing the bill, but Miss Peabody beat him to it. She snagged the paper, gave it a vigorous shake, and then, as calm as you please, thrust it once again in Mrs. Birmingham's direction.

Mrs. Birmingham seemed to swell on the spot. "Put that away. I've no intention of paying that bill, especially not after your reprehensible behavior toward my Lily."

Miss Peabody's hand didn't waver. "My 'reprehensible behavior' has nothing whatsoever to do with this bill."

"Your impertinence is astonishing, and because of it, your employer won't see a penny from me. In fact, I do believe I'm going to demand Mrs. Fienman hold you responsible for the full amount of the bill."

Miss Peabody looked at the bill and began muttering what sounded like numbers under her breath even as her face began to pale. Oliver heard her whisper, "That would take about three years of my wages," before she squared her shoulders and nodded. "Fine, do that."

The very idea that the young lady was even contemplating accepting Mrs. Birmingham's outlandish suggestion had protective instincts Oliver hadn't been aware he possessed roaring to life. He stepped closer to Miss Peabody and held out his hand. "You may give the bill to me, Miss Peabody. I'll take responsibility for it."

Something warm and unexpected shot through him when Miss Peabody turned and smiled a lovely smile in his direction—one that, strangely enough, seemed to steal the very breath from him.

He felt her press the bill into his hand, her touch leaving him frighteningly devoid of air, but then Mrs. Birmingham rudely shoved her way between them.

His lungs immediately began working again, as annoyance replaced the odd feeling of a moment before.

"That will be quite enough of that," Mrs. Birmingham said, shaking her finger at Miss Peabody. "The behavior of you shop girls is truly appalling, which is why I'm going to demand you remove yourself from my presence at once."

Instead of complying with that demand, Miss Peabody lifted her chin. "I would love nothing more than to 'remove' myself, but your daughter is currently residing in my employer's carriage. Until you decide how to get her out of there, I'm afraid my ability to leave is severely limited."

Mrs. Birmingham stopped wagging her finger and turned to Oliver, surprising him when she smiled. "Mr. Addleshaw, would you be a dear and summon a servant to fetch Lily something decent to wear? Her gowns, as you know, are currently in what used to be your office. I'm certain after she's properly dressed and we find ourselves some tea, we'll be able to look at matters with the right perspective."

The only response Oliver seemed capable of making was allowing his mouth to gape open. Surely the woman couldn't still believe there was the slightest chance he'd want to spend additional time with her daughter, could she? It was rapidly becoming apparent that he might actually have to inquire at the Long Island Home Hotel for Nervous Invalids as to whether or not they truly did have any available beds, preferably two—one for Miss Birmingham and one for her mother, because—

"I'm not getting out of this carriage, Mother," Miss Birmingham said as she rolled down the window and tried to stick her head out, her attempt thwarted when the new hat she'd put on wouldn't fit through. Drawing back, she yanked the hat off and then pushed her head back through the window. "I have no wish to become parted from my hats because I wouldn't put it past Mr. Addleshaw to hold them from me simply out of spite. We'll just take this carriage to the Grand Central Hotel." She sent Oliver a glare. "That's the hotel we were intending to stay at, until I foolishly decided I'd be more comfortable in your home."

"You're not suitably dressed at the moment, dear, to travel to the hotel," Mrs. Birmingham pointed out.

"My current state of undress is another reason for not getting out of this carriage," Miss Birmingham said with a sniff. "I'm sure that rabid dog is still on the loose, and I have no doubt he'll go for my unmentionables next time I'm in his sights."

Mrs. Birmingham looked as if she longed to argue with her daughter but then spun around and pointed a bony finger at Miss Peabody. "You, girl, go fetch an overcoat from the butler for my daughter, and make sure you use the back door."

Oliver watched Miss Peabody hurry away before he turned to Mrs. Birmingham. "Don't you think you're being a little hard on her?"

"Absolutely not, but I don't care to talk about that dreadful woman at the moment." She stepped closer and patted Oliver's arm. "What time may I expect you to call on us today at the hotel so we may discuss matters further?"

"I wasn't aware there was anything left to discuss."

"Of course there is. Even though you and Lily are currently at odds, I'm sure that, once we sit down and talk this situation through, you'll come to the conclusion Lily is perfect for you." She patted his arm again. "I've always been of the belief summer is a lovely time for weddings, which means we'll have to start planning immediately, since it's June." She nodded to the carriage. "Lily will make a most beautiful summer bride."

Miss Birmingham stuck her head back out the window. "I'm not marrying him, Mother. He's impossible."

"All gentlemen are impossible at times, dear," Mrs. Birmingham returned. "But if you'll only remember how generous Mr. Addleshaw has been, I'm sure your attitude will change."

Oliver frowned. "I've been generous?"

Mrs. Birmingham, surprisingly enough, giggled. "But of course you have, my dear man. Why, it was *quite* generous of you to encourage Lily to secure herself a new wardrobe, and from Madame Simone no less, *and* agree to pick up the full cost for that wardrobe." She batted her lashes at him. "Before I forget, I left Madame Simone's bill on the very corner of your desk."

Oliver turned and arched a brow at Miss Birmingham. To his amazement, she didn't look chagrined in the least but actually had the nerve to smile back at him.

"You *did* mention that you expected me to be fashionably turned out while we went about the business of entertaining your duke. Surely you didn't think I was going to be responsible for the bill to see that happen, did you?"

Oliver felt his teeth grind together. "I would have been more than happy to purchase a few new items for you, Miss Birmingham. However, you should have spoken with me before you ordered an entirely new wardrobe."

"And here is yet another reason why I won't be marrying you. I have no intention of spending the rest of my life with a man who is mean, stingy, and . . . did I mention *mean?*" She looked to her mother. "It's time for us to leave."

"I have the coat," Miss Peabody called as she rushed across the courtyard, coming to a stop a few feet away from Mrs. Birmingham, probably because the woman was glaring at her again. She held out the coat and didn't even flinch when Mrs. Birmingham stalked her way and snatched it out of her hand.

Marching back to the carriage, Mrs. Birmingham wrenched opened the door, shoved the coat at her daughter, and threw a few hatboxes out. She held out her hand, sent Oliver a telling look, and then smiled ever so sweetly at him when he helped her into the carriage. Once she got settled, her smile disappeared right before she snapped her fingers in Miss Peabody's direction. "Make yourself useful and get those boxes up on top of the carriage."

"There's no need for that," Oliver said, summoning the young man who was standing off to the side of the carriage. "May I assume you're the driver?"

"I'm Timothy, sir, and yes, I'm Mrs. Fienman's driver."

Oliver drew out his billfold, extracted a few bills, and handed them to Timothy. "I would appreciate it if you'd see these two ladies safely delivered to the Grand Central Hotel for me."

"But what about Miss Peabody? If I put those boxes on the top, she won't have a place to sit."

"I'll send her along in one of my carriages."

Mrs. Birmingham sniffed, loudly. "That's completely unacceptable, Mr. Addleshaw. She's a mere hat girl. Besides, after the abhorrent assault on my daughter, I would imagine a long walk home is just what she needs. It'll give her time to . . ."

Her mouth snapped shut when Oliver sent a not so subtle nod at Miss Birmingham, a lady who'd behaved far more abhorrently than Miss Peabody. The carriage door closed a second later, and a few minutes after that, after loading the extra hatboxes on the roof, Timothy pulled the carriage away.

"Well, that was pleasant," Miss Peabody proclaimed.

"*Pleasant* is hardly the word I'd use to describe what just happened."

"True, but I thought it would be rude of me to say what I really thought about the situation, and . . ." Miss Peabody's words trailed off when Buford suddenly slunk into view, his ears drooping.

To Oliver's dismay, his dog had a lady's hat clamped between his teeth, one that resembled the hat Miss Peabody had been wearing before Miss Birmingham snatched it off her head. Buford skulked up to Miss Peabody, leaned against the fabric of her skirt, and dropped the hat at her feet.

Smiling, she gave him a scratch behind the ears before she picked up the hat. "I don't think I'll be wearing this again." Tucking it into the crook of her arm, she caught his eye. "While it was generous of you to offer me a way home, Mr. Addleshaw, I'm quite fond of walking, so I won't need to take you up on your generosity."

"It's about to rain."

"Then I suppose I should get on my way." She took a step back. "It was interesting meeting you, and I wish you well in your future encounters with the Birmingham family."

"As bad luck would have it, Mr. Birmingham and I are actually scheduled to meet here at my home later today. Originally, we were supposed to discuss matters of business, but now I'm afraid we'll need to delve into the personal. I'm hopeful he won't be too disappointed to learn I have no intention of moving forward with his daughter, although I expect her behavior won't affect our business plans."

"If I were you, I'd reconsider having *anything* to do with the Birmingham family, even matters of a business nature." She sent him a nod and then began walking away without another word.

For some inexplicable reason, the very idea that she didn't seem to want to linger in his company intrigued him. He started after her. "Miss Peabody, wait."

Miss Peabody slowed but didn't stop. "Was there something else you needed, Mr. Addleshaw?"

"I was wondering if you'd care to return to the house and perhaps enjoy a cup of tea with me."

"I don't believe that's necessary."

"It might settle your nerves."

36

"My nerves rarely get unsettled."

"Fascinating," he muttered, earning a widening of the eyes from Miss Peabody before she turned and quickened her pace.

He was left staring after her as the most unusual thoughts whirled around his head. She'd been abused quite thoroughly by Mrs. and Miss Birmingham—and Buford, for that matter—and yet she seemed remarkably unscathed from her unpleasant encounter with them. Granted, her hair was straggling down her back and her dress was smeared with dirt, but her head was held high as she marched down the street. That gave clear testimony to the fact she was a strong woman, probably self-sufficient, and completely different from any woman he'd ever known.

"Miss Peabody, please, I need another moment of your time," he heard pop out of his mouth, even though he had no idea why he needed more of her time—he simply wanted it.

Miss Peabody stopped, turned, and waited for him to join her. "Mr. Addleshaw, forgive me, but you were the one who pointed out it looks ready to rain. Since I have no desire to get soaked, I really must be on my way."

"Are you married?"

"I certainly have no idea why my marital status is of interest to you, but no, I'm not married, which is why I told you my name is *Miss* Peabody."

He wasn't exactly sure why it was of interest to him either. In all honesty, he wasn't even sure why he'd asked in the first place.

"Was that all you wanted?"

"Ah, no . . . I . . . ah . . ." He smiled. "I wanted to offer you compensation for the hat Buford destroyed."

"My hat wasn't worth much to begin with, so there's no need to compensate me."

"Then at least allow me to provide you with a comfortable ride home."

Miss Peabody blew out what was clearly an exasperated breath. "Mr. Addleshaw, thank you, but no. I prefer walking, and I'm perfectly capable of taking care of myself."

It was apparent that no truer words had ever been spoken. Miss Peabody had a very managing way about her, one not often seen in ladies, and certainly not seen in ladies who were so lovely. He felt his breath hitch ever so slightly as the full extent of her beauty began to sink in. Her face was made up of delicate hollows that drew attention to her unusual eyes, while her lips were full and her cheeks rosy—although some of that color was likely a result of her brawl with Miss Birmingham. His gaze skimmed down her figure, taking in the slightness of her form even though parts of that form were rounded in all the right places.

From out of the blue, an enticing idea began to brew.

He'd been approaching the whole lady business completely wrong.

The only reason he'd invited Miss Birmingham to come to New York from her home in Chicago was because of the Duke of Westmoore and the meetings they were soon to have. If he'd thought about it from a business perspective, he would have realized that he didn't need a lady by his side, he needed a business associate—who happened to be a lady. More specifically, he needed someone he could pay to be at his beck and call, someone who would not expect to be pampered with new wardrobes and hats or, worse yet, prettily said words so that a lady's tender feelings weren't hurt.

He had the strangest feeling the perfect lady to fit that particular role was standing right beside him.

Taking a step closer to her, Oliver smiled. "You're very well-spoken."

"I beg your pardon?"

"Your speech, it's very refined. Have you had some schooling?"

Miss Peabody's eyes began glittering. "That's none of your business."

"You're also very fetching."

"Ah . . . what?"

"You're quite lovely."

Miss Peabody began inching away from him. "Thank you, Mr. Addleshaw, for that bit of nonsense, but I believe it might be for the best if we parted ways now. Do make certain to settle up with Mrs. Fienman, won't you? Even though I know full well I'm going to be released from my position once Mrs. Birmingham has her say, I did promise Mrs. Fienman I'd deliver her bill *and* do my best to make sure it was going to be paid."

"Ah, you're conscientious. Another mark in your favor."

"Yes, well, again, *lovely* to meet you, and—"

"I have a business proposition for you."

She took another step away from him. "A . . . business proposition?"

"Exactly."

Miss Peabody looked at him and then looked down at the front of her dress, which had large paw prints all over it. One of her hands moved to her head, and she grimaced, leaving Oliver to believe she'd touched a sore spot, put there no doubt by Miss Birmingham's parasol. She glanced to Buford and finally returned her attention to him. "In the interest of self-preservation, I'm going to have to say . . . no. But thank you."

"You're being too hasty with your refusal to hear me out. What I'm about to offer is a wonderful opportunity for someone like you, and . . ."

"Someone like me?"

"Ah, well, yes, you know, a hat girl and not of my social station in . . ." He stopped speaking when she leveled a glare at him that appeared hot enough to melt the skin right off his face.

"Don't say another word," she said between clenched teeth.

39

"You have insulted me most grievously, and I will not be held responsible for my actions if you continue to speak." With that, she turned on her dainty heel, picked up her skirt, and bolted away from him.

Reluctant admiration caught him by surprise as he watched her flee.

Miss Peabody was *exactly* what he needed. She was lovely, intelligent, and didn't appear to be possessed of a hysterical nature, even if she did seem to have a bit of a temper. All that was left to do now was convince her it would be in her best interest to join forces with him. But first he was going to have to catch up with her.

3

Slowing her pace when she began developing a stitch in her side, Harriet tipped back her head and scanned a sky that had turned an ominous shade of black.

"I'm still waiting for the wonderful," she called, and right there and then, the heavens opened up and a torrent of water poured over her—almost as if God hadn't appreciated her snippy tone of voice.

Dropping her head, she pulled out the horrible hat she had tucked under her arm and jammed it over her hair. Plowing forward, her annoyance increased steadily, especially when a mangled bird on the hat kept poking her in the eye.

Thoughts of Mr. Addleshaw continued to plague her with every step she took. He, and other gentlemen of his ilk, explained to perfection why she didn't hold the wealthy in high esteem.

The sheer arrogance of the man as he'd blithely suggested she listen to a business proposition from him was enough to set her teeth on edge. He knew absolutely nothing about her, except that she was *fetching* and spoke in a *refined* manner, which made it difficult to comprehend what type of business arrangement he'd even been suggesting.

She stumbled to a stop. Perhaps Mr. Addleshaw simply needed a secretary, someone to record all the business ideas he had. If that was the case, she might have been a little hasty in her refusal. She was soon to be out of work and . . . No. There was no reason for a secretary to be fetching and well-spoken, not unless Mr. Addleshaw spent his time gazing and conversing with his secretary, which didn't make a bit of sense. Men of his station normally employed other men. Besides, Mr. Addleshaw had insulted her, and she needed to remember that.

She started off down the sidewalk again, her steps turning to stomps when the conversation she'd had with the infuriating Mr. Addleshaw—the part about a *"wonderful opportunity for someone like you"*—kept rolling over and over through her mind.

The man had actually been smiling when he'd said those unfortunate words, as if he expected her, the poor, desperate hat lady, to fall on her knees in gratitude and thank him for his generosity.

Unfortunately, given that Mrs. Fienman had warned her about sullying the good name of the business, she truly was going to be desperate in the not too distant future. Maybe, just maybe, she should turn around and at least hear Mr. Addleshaw out.

"Don't even think about it," she argued aloud, glancing around to see if anyone had heard her. To her relief, since she'd reached Fifth Avenue, the rain had increased and the sidewalk was currently free of people.

"He's enough to turn a person into a lunatic," she muttered, trudging through a deep puddle and then shivering when water began seeping into her undergarments and through her stockings. She pushed aside the discomfort, allowing temper to replace it.

Mr. Addleshaw had questioned whether or not she'd had any schooling.

An unladylike snort escaped through her nose.

Her education had been obtained through slightly irregular means and could never be considered normal by any stretch of the imagination, but she had received one.

She'd lived throughout her childhood with a woman who'd somehow become responsible for Harriet after her mother died in childbirth. Though the woman never spoke of Harriet's mother, Harriet had always called her Aunt Jane.

Aunt Jane disliked staying in a place for any length of time, and vigorously proclaimed her dislike for mothering. Because of that, Harriet most often found herself in the care of an odd assortment of complete strangers—their willingness to take her in brought about by Aunt Jane's willingness to pay them. These strangers would occasionally send her to school, but more often than not, given that the people her aunt left her with were usually educated, although eccentric, they simply shared their knowledge with her. She'd learned mathematics from an elderly man who'd once taught at Yale, science from another who'd lectured at Harvard, and literature from a man all the way from England who adored everything Shakespearian. Dancing instruction, along with deportment, came from numerous ladies, many of them aging wallflowers who'd never secured a match but knew, in theory, everything a lady needed to know to secure a gentleman and move about in society.

Harriet's love of fashion and talent with a needle and thread came about when she was twelve and found herself deposited rather abruptly with a lady by the name of Mrs. Brodie. Mrs. Brodie owned a small dress shop and lived above that shop. She hadn't exactly seemed thrilled to have Harriet thrust on her, but once she realized Harriet had an interest in clothing, she soon set her to work stitching hems and sewing on buttons. Harriet loved the feel of the fine fabrics and enjoyed perusing the latest fashion plates. She'd been more than distraught when Aunt Jane had shown up out of the blue months later to inform her they were moving on . . . again.

The next two years passed in a blur, with different cities every few months, and Aunt Jane growing more hostile toward Harriet with every city they left behind. Harriet had always instinctively known that Aunt Jane didn't care for her, but as she grew older, the woman's dislike seemed to turn more and more to outright hatred. Questions had begun consuming Harriet's every thought, and when she'd had the audacity to ask Aunt Jane how they were related and how she earned a living, she'd received a slap across the face, and her questions had remained unanswered.

Matters began to make sense a few months later when they were in Chicago and Harriet woke up in their rented rooms to the sound of Jane arguing with an unknown gentleman. That gentleman was yelling about confidence schemes and how he would see Aunt Jane behind bars. Harriet then heard a loud thud, and her aunt appeared moments later. After tossing Harriet's belongings into a carpet bag, Jane had cautioned her not to look at the motionless man lying on the floor before she hustled her out of Chicago. Aunt Jane then told her they needed a place to lay low for a while, that place turning out to be the circus.

Harriet had adored the circus—loved learning the art of tumbling, and loved the people who worked there. Her aunt encouraged her to participate in the shows, riding ponies and waving to the crowds while Aunt Jane took tickets and cozied up to the owner. Harriet had just begun instruction on how to walk across a wire when she was pulled from a sound sleep, dragged to the nearest train station, and informed by Jane, who possessed a reticule stuffed with bills, that they needed to go to a large city this time, one where they could lose themselves amongst the masses.

That city turned out to be New York City. They'd rented a

small house in a working-class neighborhood. Harriet had actually been provided with a governess, whose sole job seemed to be reviewing everything Harriet knew and filling in areas she deemed Harriet to be deficient in.

Her aunt was rarely at home, which was fine with Harriet, since their relationship had deteriorated even further. That relationship became downright horrific, though, when Harriet turned sixteen.

Aunt Jane arrived unexpectedly on Harriet's birthday, bearing gifts and a cake, which Harriet found peculiar but somewhat promising. All sense of promise disappeared in a flash after the cake had been consumed. Aunt Jane proceeded to explain exactly what was expected of Harriet from that point forward. Her explanation finally shed much-needed light on the reason she'd bothered to secure Harriet a complete education.

It turned out that Jane made a lucrative living through dishonest means. She traveled often, insinuating herself into wealthy circles, for the purpose of swindling people. Not bothering to address Harriet's sputters of disbelief, Jane then informed Harriet that it was past time she joined the "family business" and earned her keep. Jane wanted Harriet to use the education she'd acquired and her somewhat polished manners to hoodwink wealthy targets, convincing them she was an orphaned young lady, though of means, needing assistance as she tried to navigate the daunting world of society.

When Harriet learned Jane expected her to steal a priceless painting from one of the mansions on Park Avenue, she balked, causing Jane to fly into a rage, screaming horrible things about Harriet's mother before resorting to throwing anything at hand in the direction of Harriet.

Fearing for her life, Harriet barricaded herself in her room, quickly packed her belongings, and took off out the window, determined to never return.

She'd almost starved to death over the weeks she spent on the streets, until one night, out of sheer desperation, she'd stumbled into a ramshackle old church.

Stepping into a room lined with pews, she'd been greeted by an older gentleman who introduced himself as Reverend Thomas Gilmore. He'd taken hold of her arm, ushered her into his office, helped her into a wobbly chair, and poured her a bracing cup of strong tea.

He'd listened with barely a word spoken as she'd poured out the story of her life. When she finally finished her sad tale, Reverend Gilmore took hold of her hand, told her he was going to help her, and then began to speak about God.

God became a daily part of her life after that, and Reverend Gilmore became a dear friend. He helped her secure reputable employment, along with new lodging that eventually came with new friends, Miss Millie Longfellow and Miss Lucetta Plum.

Rain whipping into her eyes pulled Harriet abruptly from her memories. Blinking to clear her vision, she frowned at a mansion that in no way looked familiar. Realizing she had been walking in the wrong direction down Fifth Avenue, she turned and began splashing her way back the way she'd just come. Her splashing slowed when a large, and unfortunately familiar, figure materialized out of the rain.

"Ah, Miss Peabody," Mr. Addleshaw exclaimed with a charming smile as he stopped in front of her, blocking her way. "Had a change of heart, have you?"

Her first impulse was to dash in the opposite direction, but it was raining harder than ever, and she didn't want to waste time wandering around Fifth Avenue in an attempt to avoid Mr. Addleshaw. Lifting her chin, she sidestepped the gentleman, sending him a nod before she passed him and continued forward. To her annoyance, the man caught up with her all too quickly—although, to her satisfaction, his smile had dimmed.

"What you need is a nice fire to warm you up and dry you out," Mr. Addleshaw said as he matched her step for step.

"I'm not going back to your house, Mr. Addleshaw."

What little remained of his smile disappeared. "Why'd you turn around, then?"

"I was heading in the wrong direction."

"You really *don't* want to hear about my business proposal?"

"Unusual as this must seem to you, no, I don't."

"I assure you, it would be worth your time to hear me out."

Stopping in the midst of a deep puddle that sent water dribbling down her high-buttoned shoes, Harriet pushed the bird dangling in front of her eye aside. "You're very tenacious."

"It's what makes me a successful businessman."

"But I, after being the recipient of your inexcusable insult, have no desire to be a part of that business, successful or not."

"I have no idea what I said that insulted you so greatly."

"And that is exactly why I'm now going to bid you good day one last time." Picking up her drenched skirt, Harriet tried to continue forward but found her progress thwarted when Buford appeared out of nowhere and immediately took hold of her hem with his overly large teeth.

"Buford thinks you should hear me out as well."

"And I think you should call off your dog and allow me to be on my way," she countered.

"I'm certain you must realize by now that Buford rarely listens to me."

"Which begs the question why someone of your temperament would suffer his company."

"I do believe there's an insult in there somewhere, directed at me."

"Besides being tenacious, I see you're astute as well."

"And that quick wit is exactly why I believe you'll be perfect for what I have in mind."

Harriet crossed her arms over her chest. "Fine, since it appears I'm stuck here, due to the massive jaws of your beast, tell me, Mr. Addleshaw, what exactly do you have in mind? I'll give you sixty seconds to explain."

"Don't you think it would be more comfortable to discuss this in my nice, warm office?"

"You don't have an office at the moment. Miss Birmingham turned it into a dressing room, and you're down to forty seconds."

A vein began to throb on Mr. Addleshaw's forehead. "Very well, since you're obviously intent on being unreasonable, I'll explain while the two of us get completely drenched."

"You're obviously confusing me with Miss Birmingham. *I'm* never unreasonable."

"In all fairness, Miss Peabody, I do hope that little statement didn't take further seconds off my allotted time."

Seeing absolutely no point in arguing further with the man, Harriet tried her hand at releasing a sniff, just like Mrs. Birmingham had done numerous times during their ridiculous exchange. To her acute embarrassment, though, it turned out that sniffing was not actually advisable when it was pouring down rain, because water tended to immediately be sucked up one's nose. She sneezed, snorted, sneezed again, and finally managed a halfhearted wave in his direction. "Continue, if you please."

Mr. Addleshaw reached into the pocket of his ill-fitted jacket and retrieved a handkerchief, although it seemed to be a struggle for him to get it out of his pocket. He shook it out and handed it to her.

"Thank you," she mumbled as she sniffled into the handkerchief.

"You're welcome." He studied her for a moment. "Shall I continue?"

"I'm waiting with bated breath to hear what you'll say next."

"Ah, sarcasm, how refreshing," he said pleasantly. "But allow me to return to my proposition. I regrettably have to admit that, because of Miss Birmingham's behavior, I currently find myself in a bit of a quandary."

"That must be an unusual circumstance for *someone like you.*"

"I do believe I'm about to find that sarcasm of yours more annoying than refreshing, but . . . Oh! I think I understand now how I insulted you. Really, Miss Peabody, I wasn't trying to throw aspersions on your status in—"

"Your time's almost up."

He sent her a glare. "If you don't want to hear the rest of my apology, that's fine with me, however I did not—"

"You don't apologize often, do you?" she interrupted when it appeared Mr. Addleshaw was getting ready to launch into a full-scale tirade that would undoubtedly insult her further.

His jaw turned rigid. "You're beginning to try my patience, but getting back to the business at hand . . . I need a lady."

"A . . . lady?"

"Indeed, and I've decided you'll do nicely."

Harriet frowned. "I'm afraid I don't understand."

"It's simple. Gentlemen of business are expected to abide by certain unspoken rules. One of those rules has to do with having a lovely lady by our side while we entertain our associates. Since Miss Birmingham has proven herself unfit for that position, I'm in need of a replacement, a lovely bit of femininity, if you will, to hang on my arm *and* my every word as I go about the tricky business of negotiating a deal with a duke. I've come to the conclusion you would fit that role admirably."

For a moment, words were impossible to produce, but only

for a moment. "Am I to understand you believe *I'm* a 'lovely bit of femininity'?"

Mr. Addleshaw had the audacity to grin. "Well, not at the moment. You're more of a sodden mess than a lovely bit of anything. But I imagine with the proper clothing and a fashionable hairstyle, you'd be a charming asset, one the Duke of Westmoore would appreciate."

Harriet yanked on her skirt, effectively pulling it away from Buford, who'd been gnawing at the hem, before she bobbed a curtsy in Mr. Addleshaw's direction. "You're delusional, and no, I won't be accepting your offer." With that, she spun around and walked as quickly as she could through the stream that had once been the sidewalk.

"I'll give you five hundred dollars."

Pride warred with practicality as Harriet's steps faltered. Practicality won and had her turning. "Five hundred dollars?"

"Indeed, which, for someone . . ."

"If you finish that sentence, I assure you, Mr. Addleshaw, our conversation will be at an immediate end."

Mr. Addleshaw frowned. "You're very touchy, aren't you."

"And you're very insulting and condescending."

Waving her words away with a flick of his wrist, a motion that almost caused one of his jacket seams to come completely apart, Mr. Addleshaw stalked closer to her. "So will you do it?"

Harriet considered him for a moment. He seemed so sure of himself, so very arrogant in his belief that she'd accept his offer that, instead of nodding—something she knew she should be doing—she shook her head instead. "No."

"What do you mean—no?"

"I thought my answer was self-explanatory."

"You're being ridiculous. You're a hat girl, one who is soon to be without a position. I can't imagine opportunities like this come your way often."

Her hands clenched into fists. "Miss Birmingham was right. You, sir, are a complete and utter boor, and . . ." Her words trailed off when she noticed an elderly gentleman dressed in black hobbling toward them through the rain, clutching a large umbrella in his hand. He stopped a few feet away from her, bent over as he drew in a few gasping breaths, straightened, wheezed a few times, and then opened his mouth. "I say, I could not believe . . ." He stopped speaking as another wheeze racked his aging body.

The irritation that had been pouring through Harriet ever since she'd made the acquaintance of Mr. Addleshaw evaporated into thin air. Here was clear proof there were still good people in the world. The elderly gentleman had obviously witnessed her quarreling with Mr. Addleshaw and was coming to her aid. Moving closer to the man, her lips curved into a smile, until she caught his eye and found herself pinned under the man's beady glare. He released a sniff, one that, annoying enough, didn't cause him to erupt into sneezing, and then edged closer to Mr. Addleshaw, placing the umbrella directly over that insufferable man's head.

"Shall I summon the authorities, sir?"

Harriet's temper roared back to life. "There is absolutely no reason to summon any authorities," she snapped before Mr. Addleshaw could respond. "I've done nothing wrong, whereas Mr. Addleshaw . . . Well, I hardly believe now is the appropriate time to discuss all of his transgressions, since it does seem to be raining harder than ever."

The elderly gentleman somehow managed to look down his nose at her, even though they were of a similar height. "From what I just witnessed, you were about to assault Mr. Addleshaw."

"Just because I was thinking about it, doesn't mean I was planning on seeing it through to fruition."

"A lady should never contemplate slapping a gentleman, especially not one of Mr. Addleshaw's social standing."

"I wasn't thinking about *slapping* him," Harriet muttered. "He deserved much more than a simple slap for being under the misguided belief that, simply because he has deep pockets, everyone should cater to his ridiculous whims."

The elderly gentleman's expression turned confused. "I'm afraid I don't understand." He looked to Mr. Addleshaw. "What is she talking about?"

"Miss Peabody has evidently taken issue with the idea I'd like to hire her to stand in as my lady of choice as I negotiate my business deal with the duke."

The gentleman's eyebrow rose until it disappeared beneath a shock of white and dripping hair. "Lady of choice?"

"Surely after witnessing that scene with Miss Birmingham you can understand my reasoning, Mr. Blodgett. Hiring a companion is the perfect answer to my current dilemma of not being attached to a lady. Also, I won't have to leave matters to chance with a temperamental society lady, since I'll be paying Miss Peabody to behave appropriately."

Mr. Blodgett sent Mr. Addleshaw a look that had disapproval written all over it. "I'm afraid your reasoning is a little faulty, sir, since such things are never done, especially amongst the quality. Why, if you ask me, your idea sounds completely untoward."

"It's nothing of the sort," Mr. Addleshaw argued. "If anything, my idea should be looked upon as an act of charity since Miss Peabody is soon to lose her position and will benefit greatly through the funds I'm willing to give her." He completely ignored Harriet's huff of disbelief and continued speaking even when she began to mutter under her breath. "Why, accepting a position that will only require Miss Peabody to look lovely and act in a charming fashion will surely have to feel like a holiday to a young lady used to spending tedious hours assembling hats."

Mr. Blodgett considered Mr. Addleshaw for a moment before he moved away from him and toward Harriet, taking the umbrella as he moved and leaving Mr. Addleshaw standing in the downpour.

Harriet felt the rain stop beating against her hat as Mr. Blodgett angled the umbrella over her head, right before he pressed the handle of it into her hand.

"He's normally a very rational gentleman, Miss Peabody, but I fear the rain and his unfortunate interaction with Miss and Mrs. Birmingham have affected his mental capabilities at the moment."

Mr. Blodgett patted Harriet on the shoulder, shook his head at Mr. Addleshaw, and then began hobbling away without another word. She looked back to Mr. Addleshaw, finding him peering through the rain with a bemused expression on his dripping face.

"How very odd," Mr. Addleshaw muttered. "Mr. Blodgett has never questioned my mental capacities before. It's quite unlike the gentleman. However, my butler's peculiar attitude has nothing to do with the matter we were discussing. Would you agree to my offer if I upped the amount to one thousand dollars?"

Harriet barely managed to choke back the *yes* that had been on the very tip of her tongue. "I think not."

Mr. Addleshaw's brows smashed together. "I only need your services for a few weeks, a month at the most, just until I secure the duke's agreement to allow me to invest in his wool business."

Before she could swallow what little pride she had left and accept the offer, Mr. Addleshaw let out a very loud grunt.

"Fine, two thousand dollars, then, and an allowance for a few new garments."

She knew her eyes had to be as wide as saucers. The man was clearly insane. No one in their right mind would offer two thousand dollars *and* an allowance for clothing for a few weeks' work. "Ah . . . " was all she seemed capable of saying.

"Three thousand, but that's my final offer."

Harriet's mouth dropped open.

He really was insane, and it seemed she might be a little as well because . . . "Very well. You win, Mr. Addleshaw, because *that* is an offer I'm incapable of refusing."

4

The moment those unfortunate words slipped out of her mouth, Harriet desperately wanted to call them back. Agreeing to be Mr. Addleshaw's companion was sheer madness. No matter that the gentleman had just offered her a small fortune to attempt it, she knew perfectly well she wasn't up for the daunting task of mingling with society members.

Scuffing her shoe through the water that swirled around her feet, she lifted her chin and discovered Mr. Addleshaw watching her with what appeared to be a trace of surliness on his face. "Is something the matter?"

He grimaced. "What could possibly be the matter? I've gotten exactly what I wanted. You at my beck and call for the next few weeks with no expectations of a trip down the altar."

There was definitely an edge to his voice, that edge causing her lips to curl. "Were you not intending to offer me so much for my cooperation?"

"I would have paid twice what you agreed to."

Her lips curled up another notch. "Now you're just being sulky."

To her surprise, Mr. Addleshaw let out a grunt and then, strangely enough, smiled. "Perhaps you're right, Miss Peabody. If you must know—and it pains me to admit this—I'm unused to anyone, especially a lady, besting me in a business negotiation. You, my dear, have managed to do just that, and while speaking relatively few words in the process."

His admission took her aback, even as she found herself returning his smile. "Would it be churlish of me to gloat a little?"

"Gloating is not in your job description, but perhaps now you'll finally agree to accompany me back to my dry home, where we can delve into exactly what I expect of you during the coming weeks."

Reality returned to smack her in the face. "Forgive me, Mr. Addleshaw, but I must speak frankly. I rarely act impulsively, but I fear that is the case today. You should know that I'm not one who enjoys being at anyone's *beck and call*. I believe we're making a huge . . ."

The rest of her words got lost as a strong gust of wind blew out of nowhere, wrenching the umbrella out of her hand and her hat from her head. She turned to run after them, but rain began falling more heavily than ever right as a flash of lightning lit up Fifth Avenue, followed by a boom that almost had her jumping out of her shoes.

"We need to get out of the storm," Mr. Addleshaw yelled as he took hold of her arm.

The second his hand touched her sleeve, Harriet felt as if *she'd* been struck by lightning. A bolt of something incredibly disturbing traveled up her arm and then all over her body. Her feet remained rooted to the spot, even though Mr. Addleshaw was trying to tug her forward.

"Miss Peabody, whatever is wrong with you?" he shouted.

"Didn't you feel that?"

"Indeed I did, which proves the lightning is far too close for comfort."

Relief was immediate. It hadn't been Mr. Addleshaw's touch that had tingles still resonating all over her, it had been the lightning. Ducking her head when another gust of wind whipped around them, she clutched Mr. Addleshaw's arm and allowed him to hustle her down the sidewalk. As they approached his mansion, she stumbled when Mr. Addleshaw suddenly stopped moving. She squinted through the rain and found none other than Mr. Blodgett once again struggling their way. He was trying his very best to keep a grip on another umbrella, but the umbrella was turned inside out, not affording the poor man a single piece of protection against the storm.

"What are you doing, Mr. Blodgett?" Mr. Addleshaw called.

The elderly man pressed forward, hobbling faster than ever until he reached them. He angled the useless umbrella over his head and scowled at Mr. Addleshaw. "We have a slight problem back at the house, sir."

"And this problem forced you out into this horrid weather because it is grave enough that it couldn't wait until I returned?"

Mr. Blodgett shifted his attention to Harriet. "Well, no, sir. It couldn't wait—especially because *she's* still with you." The butler stepped closer to Harriet. "My dear, why haven't you taken your leave?"

"Miss Peabody and I have recently agreed to join forces," Mr. Addleshaw answered for her.

"Oh . . . dear, that's a troubling state of affairs." Mr. Blodgett drew in a wheezy breath and shook his head. "Well, she can't come into the house."

Hurt, mixed with indignation, stole through Harriet, even though she should have expected nothing less from Mr. Addleshaw's staff. She'd told Mr. Blodgett exactly what Mr. Addleshaw required of her, and it hardly spoke well of her character that she'd agreed to take on the role of a lovely bit of femininity. She ducked her head and hoped the color she knew was now staining her cheeks would go unnoticed.

"Honestly, Mr. Blodgett, I do believe this storm has rattled not my brain but yours." Mr. Addleshaw gave her arm a squeeze, sending additional pesky tingles up it. "Of course Miss Peabody is welcome in my home. I'm surprised you'd say differently."

"My apologies, Miss Peabody," Mr. Blodgett said, nodding at her when she lifted her head. "I meant you no disrespect, but you see, Mr. Birmingham has arrived early for his meeting with Mr. Addleshaw. I'm afraid he's a little put out that his daughter and wife are not still in residence but have removed themselves to a hotel." He stepped closer to her. "Since you've apparently agreed to whatever ridiculous plan Mr. Addleshaw proposed—replacing Miss Birmingham in the process, I might add—I don't believe it's in your best interest to step foot into Mr. Addleshaw's home at this particular time."

Mr. Addleshaw's brows drew together. "Mr. Birmingham's in my home. . . . now?"

"Indeed he is. He evidently decided to come early, believing there would be celebration news to enjoy before the two of you got down to business. However, now that he's come to the conclusion something is dreadfully amiss, I fear he's beginning to become agitated."

Harriet began backing slowly away. "I think I'll just be on my way now, and clearly our deal is going to have to come to a rapid end. I'd hate to think what would happen if we'd run into the Birminghams while I was trying to help you entertain your duke."

"That might be for the best," Mr. Blodgett agreed.

"No, it's not," Mr. Addleshaw argued, as he pulled Harriet back to his side. "The entire Birmingham family has been entirely too presumptuous. I never broached the subject of marriage to Miss Birmingham. I'm sure that after I bring that to Mr. Birmingham's attention, he'll be disappointed, of course, but then I expect he'll immediately repair back to Chicago, taking his wife and daughter with him. You and I, Miss Peabody, have agreed to form a business alliance. If I need remind you, it's one you desperately need, given you're soon to be dismissed from your position, and given it's one where you're going to earn an indecent amount of money in a relatively short period of time."

Mr. Blodgett's eyes widened. "Good heavens, sir, you really have lost your mind." Not giving Mr. Addleshaw an opportunity to respond, the butler turned to Harriet. "Now, I don't blame you, dear, for what can only be described as downright lunacy. An offer of an 'indecent amount of money' must seem all too tempting, especially to a lady about to lose her income. However, such arrangements never turn out the way one might expect. As the only reasonable voice in this insanity, allow me to point out that your reputation could suffer irreparable harm. Besides that, society is not kind to outsiders, which you clearly will be seen as, and—"

"She'll be fine," Mr. Addleshaw interrupted right as a heavyset lady wearing a cap hurried up to join them. "Mrs. Rollins, you shouldn't be out in this storm."

"Neither should any of you," Mrs. Rollins returned as she splashed through a deep puddle and came to stop. She leaned forward and peered at Harriet. "Oh dear. You're the hat lady, aren't you."

Harriet frowned. "Why do I get the distinct feeling I'm about to hear something of an unpleasant nature?"

"Probably because what I'm about to tell you cannot, in any way, shape, or form, be considered pleasant." Mrs. Rollins stepped closer to Harriet. "I'm Mrs. Rollins, dear, the housekeeper, and unfortunately, when Mr. Birmingham moved to Mr.

Addleshaw's office, he immediately took note of all the gowns his daughter left behind. In an attempt to explain why those gowns were left behind, I brought to his attention the . . . ah . . . altercation his daughter had been involved with. I fear I might have mentioned something about her pummeling a poor girl who was just trying to deliver some hats."

"And he didn't react well to that information?" Harriet asked slowly.

Mrs. Rollins drew herself up. "Indeed he did not. Instead of coming to the conclusion I'd hoped he'd come to—that his daughter had behaved badly—he immediately demanded to know your name—not that I had that information available to give him—and I'm afraid he's considering pressing charges against you."

The sound of yelling suddenly reached them from what seemed to be inside Mr. Addleshaw's house. Harriet flinched when Mr. Addleshaw's jaw clenched. His eyes turned cold and his posture stiffened, that stiffening causing the seam that had been pulling apart on his sleeve to lose that particular battle. Although Harriet found it impossible to look away from his rapidly deteriorating clothing, he didn't seem to notice.

"Mr. Blodgett, please go and try to calm Mr. Birmingham while I escort Miss Peabody to the stables." Mr. Addleshaw nodded to Mrs. Rollins. "I need you to go retrieve the small blue bag I keep in the lower left-hand drawer of my desk and then bring it to me. I have to get Miss Peabody into a carriage and on her way before Mr. Birmingham catches a glimpse of her and realizes she's the hat girl in question."

"But what about our discussion regarding what's expected of me?" Harriet asked.

"We'll have to have that at a later date."

Not giving her a chance to protest, Mr. Addleshaw dragged her down the sidewalk and around his house, prodding her quickly over the courtyard and into an impressive-looking build-ing that turned out to be the stables. Calling for a groom to ready a carriage, Mr. Addleshaw looked back at Harriet and frowned. "I don't know your given name."

"Which is somewhat strange, considering you've brought me on as an employee."

"True, but you must admit, we've been under somewhat ex-tenuating circumstances."

Harriet smiled. "My name is Harriet."

"Do your friends call you Harry?"

"Not if they want to remain my friends."

"Harriet it is, then, and since we have to convince everyone we're . . . attached, you must call me Oliver."

She tilted her head. "Do your friends call you Ollie?"

"Not if they want to remain my friends."

Harriet grinned and saw that Oliver was grinning back at her. Her heart, for some odd reason, began hammering in her chest, and she couldn't seem to tear her gaze from his. His grin faded and his eyes clouded with what appeared to be confusion, but the moment was broken when Mrs. Rollins came bustling into the stable, dripping wet and holding a blue bag that appeared to be made of velvet.

"The situation is taking a nasty turn inside," she exclaimed, thrusting the bag at Oliver. "Mr. Birmingham is demanding your attention at once, which means you really do need to wrap matters up with Miss Peabody." Mrs. Rollins crossed her arms over her ample chest. "Mr. Blodgett has filled me in about what you're up to, young man, and I must tell you right now, your grandfather would not approve."

"We'll leave my grandfather out of this, Mrs. Rollins," Oli-ver said before he turned to Harriet and handed her the bag. "You won't have time to have clothing made up for you, but I'm hopeful you'll be able to find a few ready-made items that will do in a pinch. Use this money to purchase three dinner dresses, one or two day dresses, and whatever accessories you need to complete those outfits."

The weight of the bag sent fresh apprehension rushing through Harriet's veins. "I don't think I'm comfortable accepting this much money, Mr. . . . er, Oliver."

He narrowed his eyes. "While I admit it's refreshing to meet a young lady who doesn't seem to want to spend my money, you *will* go out and buy yourself appropriate clothing, and you *will* use the money in that bag to pay for that clothing."

"I'm not very good at taking orders either, Oliver, especially when they're delivered in that particular tone of voice."

Mrs. Rollins sent a smile Harriet's way. "That's the spirit, dear."

Oliver arched a brow at Mrs. Rollins, then looked back at Harriet. "For three thousand dollars—money you'll be paid once my negotiations with the Duke of Westmoore are completed—I would think you'd be able to learn to take orders, and take them with a cheerful smile on your face."

"I suppose I could give that a try, but I'm not promising anything," Harriet muttered as a carriage pulled up next to her. Oliver practically shoved her into it and then surprised her when he pulled out a lap robe and wrapped it around her. She began feeling all warm and fuzzy inside until he stepped back and opened his mouth.

"We can't have you taking a chill. You'll be of little use to me if you get sick."

"Mr. Addleshaw," Mrs. Rollins admonished. "What a thing to say to the poor dear." She smiled at Harriet again. "He's normally very pleasant."

"No I'm not," Oliver argued. "And it would be in your best interest, Harriet, to remember that."

"Not pleasant," she repeated back.

"Exactly," he agreed. "Now then, I'll need your address so I can tell Darren, my driver, where to take you."

Harriet rattled off her address, and the more she rattled, the more the vein on Oliver's forehead throbbed.

"Am I to understand that you live on the Lower East Side?"

"Someone has to live there."

He scowled at her for a second, then turned and whistled. A moment later Buford bounded into the stable, tail wagging furiously as mud dripped from his fur. "You may keep Buford with you for protection." Oliver snapped his fingers, and Buford leapt into the carriage, splattering the beautiful green velvet upholstery with bits of muck when he shook himself before climbing up on the seat opposite her.

"There's no need for me to take your dog," she began. "I've lived on the Lower East Side for years, and nothing horrible has happened to me yet."

"I thought we agreed you'd start accepting my orders and do so cheerfully."

Harriet forced a smile she knew full well did not appear all that cheerful. "I said I'd try, but I didn't promise anything. But as you *are* paying me a fortune, I suppose it would be churlish of me to refuse to take your dog with me. You should know, though, that I've never owned a pet before, which means there's no guarantee Buford's going to be happy with me, so . . . how long should I expect to keep him?"

"I'll call on you two days from now, and we'll reassess your situation. If I feel you truly are safe in your home, I'll collect Buford at that time."

"That long?"

"I have business meetings for the rest of today and most of tomorrow. Two days from now is the soonest I can fit you into my schedule. And just so we're clear, I expect you to have at least a dress or two at that time for me to inspect."

Harriet stiffened. "There's absolutely no need for you to inspect anything I purchase. For your information, I have a keen sense for fashion." She glanced at his sleeve that was now only attached to his shoulder by a single thread. "If anyone needs inspecting, I would have to say it's you. Your jacket barely fits you, and it's so poorly tailored that it's falling apart right before my eyes."

"My tailor is the best in the city, and . . ." Oliver looked at his sleeve and blinked. "I'm sure the only reason my clothing is currently falling to pieces is because it wasn't meant to withstand such a ferocious storm."

"I've never had any of my garments disintegrate because of a little water, and—" She stopped speaking when Oliver suddenly shut the carriage door, effectively cutting her off. Narrowing her eyes at him through the window, Harriet considered jumping out of the carriage to finish her sentence, but a sharp rap on the side sent it into motion, ruining her plans. As she settled back against the comfortable seat, Harriet's fingers tightened around the bag.

"I've obviously lost my mind," she told Buford, who simply stared back at her with his tongue lolling out. "I mean, honestly, who possessed of all of their wits would have agreed to a business deal that's doomed for failure?"

Buford licked his lips and whined . . . loudly.

"Good heavens, I never thought to ask Oliver to send along something for you to eat, and . . . Oh dear, what are we going to do about Mrs. Palmer's little yippers? She's my landlady, and her dogs are constantly underfoot, and if you're hungry . . ." She tucked the lap robe more securely around herself. "Well, you're just going to have to promise not to eat them. Reasonably priced rooms are hard to come by these days, and I'd hate to get evicted because you got a taste for yappy little pooches."

To her dismay, Buford licked his lips again.

"Or perhaps I'll run right out to the butcher once we get to my home and buy you something to eat, and . . . I'll use just a little of what's in this bag to pay for it." Forcing fingers that seemed reluctant to untie the drawstring, she peeked inside and pulled out a slip of paper lying on top of far too many bills.

For incidentals, she read. Harriet wrinkled her nose. "Who keeps this much money lying about for incidentals? Most people have a few coins at their disposal, but . . ." She glanced into the bag again and felt her stomach turn queasy. "There is no possible way I'm going to be able to go through with this."

Closing the bag, she looked out the window, drawing in one steadying breath after another. Her thoughts jumped from one problem to the next until she realized her brow was soaking wet and not from the rain she'd recently experienced.

"This is the worst birthday I've ever had. Well, perhaps not as bad as the one where I learned my aunt was a swindler, but . . ." She pressed her lips together and considered the bag of money lying on her lap. "Unless . . ." She looked at Buford, who was watching her closely, his dark doggy eyes following her slightest movement. "You don't think this is my something wonderful God sent me, do you?"

Buford's only response was another licking of his lips.

"Right, I'm probably being fanciful, because I highly doubt God would approve of the disaster I've landed myself into. But what am I to do now? It would hardly be honorable to renege at this point, especially since Oliver is counting on me, but . . . I have no idea how to mingle in society."

Leaning her head against the window, Harriet watched the passing scenery, the queasiness becoming more pronounced the longer she contemplated the mess she'd gotten herself into. As they traveled out of the well-heeled part of the city and into her world, the ramifications of what she'd agreed to settled over her, and panic replaced the queasiness. Just as she was about to roll down the window and ask the driver to take her back to Oliver's house so she could explain she could not go through with his scheme, the carriage rumbled to a stop.

A moment later, the door opened and Darren stuck his head in. "I do beg your pardon, Miss Peabody, but I'm afraid Mr. Addleshaw gave me the wrong address."

Looking past the man, Harriet saw a four-story, extremely narrow boardinghouse. It looked rather forlorn with its sagging shutters, peeling brown paint, and general air of neglect. "There's been no mistake. This is where I live."

"Are you certain?"

"Aren't you certain where *you* live?"

Darren frowned but offered her his hand. Taking a second to stuff the velvet bag into her reticule, she took Darren's offered hand and stepped down from the carriage. She tried to pull her hand from Darren's, but oddly enough, the man seemed remarkably unwilling to let go of it. "I will need my hand, sir."

"I'm not comfortable leaving you here, Miss Peabody. I think you should get back into the carriage and I'll take you to Mr. Addleshaw's house."

"If you think you're uncomfortable now, just think how uncomfortable you'll be trying to explain to Mr. Addleshaw why another unwanted lady is trying to move into his house."

Darren immediately released his hold on her. "He does seem opposed to ladies moving in uninvited." He suddenly smiled. "Oh look, your grandmother is waiting for you on the stoop, which explains why you've chosen to live in this area."

Craning her neck, Harriet caught sight of Mrs. Palmer, her landlady, waving madly at her. Harriet raised a hand, but before she could do more than give a halfhearted wave, Mrs. Palmer was joined on the stoop by her four yappy little dogs. To her dismay, the chorus of excited yaps immediately drew Buford's interest. He bolted out of the carriage before Harriet had the presence of mind to grab his collar and took off toward the yippers, howling in a manner that stood the hair straight up on the back of Harriet's neck.

As she dashed forward to catch him, she could only pray that Buford wasn't too hungry.

5

ripping over the sodden skirt sticking to her legs, Harriet stumbled on the one and only step leading up to the boardinghouse. Regaining her balance, she heaved a huge sigh of relief when she discovered Buford, not enjoying a tasty treat of annoying yippers but rolled on his back as the four little dogs clambered around him.

"Hello, dear," Mrs. Palmer said. "That's quite the beast you've got. May I assume he belongs to that handsome young man over there?"

Harriet lifted her head and saw that Darren had resumed his seat on the carriage, although he hadn't urged the horses into motion yet.

"Everything all right?" he called.

"We're fine," Harriet called back before she turned to face her landlady. "Do forgive me, Mrs. Palmer. Buford must have scared you half to death when he charged up here."

Mrs. Palmer waved Harriet's apology away. "Don't give it another thought, Miss Peabody." She smiled. "I must say, I'm delighted to discover you've finally gotten a suitor." Her smile dimmed. "Having said that, I do feel compelled to offer you a small piece of advice. It really isn't advisable to accept a ride in such a fine carriage, especially since you're drenched to the skin. Why, your young man might get in horrible trouble if you've stained the upholstery *and* if the owner of that carriage discovers his driver has been squiring his ladylove as well as his muddy dog around in it."

"Those are excellent points, Mrs. Palmer, but that driver is not my suitor, nor is Buford his dog."

Mrs. Palmer drew herself up. "If he's not your suitor and that isn't his dog, who owns that fancy carriage and what were you doing in it, and . . . who is responsible for that dog?"

It really was unfortunate that Mr. Birmingham had descended on Oliver before they'd been able to talk everything through. As it stood now, she truly had no idea what story she was supposed to tell people. Harriet forced a smile. "An . . . ah . . . *acquaintance* of mine wanted me to watch Buford for a day or two, and that acquaintance kindly provided me with a means to get home."

Mrs. Palmer gestured to the carriage that was, thankfully, trundling off down the street. "That's a wealthy man's carriage, my dear, which means you've gotten yourself into some sort of mischief."

Heat, no doubt the result of Mrs. Palmer's speculation, spread over her cheeks. "I fear your imagination is getting away from you, Mrs. Palmer. I have not gotten into mischief, not exactly, and I assure you, there's no reason for you to be concerned about me." Pretending not to notice the clear doubt on Mrs. Palmer's face, she called to Buford, amazed when the dog actually lumbered to her side. "Now then, if you'll excuse me, I need to get Buford inside before it starts raining again."

"There's still time for you to come to your senses."

Since Harriet had been thinking the same thing on the ride from Oliver's house, she didn't see the point in arguing. Instead, she kept the smile firmly on her face and nodded at her landlady. "I'll keep that in mind, Mrs. Palmer, but I must get Buford inside and rummage up something for him to eat. I think he may be hungry." She lowered her voice. "We wouldn't want him to get tempted by those little darlings of yours, would we?"

"It doesn't speak well of this acquaintance of yours that he gave you his dog to watch over but didn't provide any food for it."

"I never said my acquaintance was a gentleman."

"You didn't have to, dear." Mrs. Palmer turned and began walking to the door. "Stay there. I'll get you something to feed the dog." She disappeared into the house, with her yippers scampering around her feet, and reappeared a moment later carrying a dented pot.

Buford moved closer to Mrs. Palmer and sniffed the air.

Mrs. Palmer smiled down at him before looking at Harriet. "Here are some scraps I got from the butcher. You're welcome to them."

Guilt stole over Harriet as she accepted the pot, knowing that even though Mrs. Palmer owned the house and charged all her tenants rent, she didn't charge much and was almost certainly short on funds. Recalling, however, that she had a fortune tucked away in her reticule, Harriet's guilt slipped away.

"Thank you, Mrs. Palmer. I do appreciate it, and I'll be certain to refill the pot tonight and drop it off if I see your light on when I get home from dinner."

"You're going out to dinner? With the gentleman who owns that carriage?"

"I'm not going out with him. I'm—"

"So it is a gentleman."

Harriet refused to sigh. "I'm going out to dinner with Millie and Lucetta. It's my birthday, you see, and we're going to Mort's, which means I'll certainly be able to refill your pot with leftover scraps from our meal."

"Where are you getting the money to splurge at Mort's?"

"I've been saving up."

"A likely story."

Realizing she was in the midst of a battle she couldn't win, Harriet stepped off the stoop. "I'll bring the pot back soon, Mrs. Palmer. Buford. Come on, boy."

Rounding the corner of the boardinghouse, even as Mrs. Palmer's dire predictions followed her, Harriet reached the rickety steps leading up to the small rooms she shared with her friends. Mindful of the slick surface, she began to climb. "Watch your paws," she said to Buford when they reached the second floor. She turned to check on his progress and found him standing perfectly still a few steps below her, trembling from head to tail.

Setting down the pot, she hurried back to him. "I know the climb seems slightly terrifying, but you really have to move along. It's going to start raining again any second now."

Buford let out a pitiful whimper and staunchly refused to budge.

Taking hold of his collar, she gave a hard tug, but that only resulted in increased whimpers. Releasing the collar, she scrambled up to the pot and extracted a revolting piece of grisly beef. She waved it in what she hoped was an enticing manner. "If you want this, you're going to have to come and get it."

Buford eyed the beef, let out a mournful yip, stepped up one step, then froze in place.

"It would have been less problematic if you'd discovered your fear of heights on the first floor. As it stands now, we're halfway up, which means we're also halfway down, and you're much too heavy for me to carry you in either direction." She sat down beside him on the narrow step and gave him the piece of beef, even though he'd done absolutely nothing to earn it.

He wolfed it down and nudged her with his nose.

"Harriet, why are you lingering on the steps, and . . . why are you trying to bring a pony up them?"

Tipping her head, Harriet found one of her roommates, Miss Lucetta Plum, peering at her from over the railing. "Buford isn't a pony, Lucetta. He's a dog. And unfortunately, I've just discovered he's a bit of a coward when it comes to heights."

"I'll be right down," Lucetta called, and a second later, Harriet heard the sound of bare feet padding down the steps. She wasn't surprised in the least that Lucetta wasn't wearing shoes. Her roommate was known throughout the city as one of the most beautiful actresses to ever grace the stage, but any care for her appearance disappeared the moment Lucetta left the theater. Lucetta preferred comfort over fashion when she wasn't in the spotlight, and when she came into view, Harriet saw that today was no exception. Her friend was wearing a ratty old wrapper that had seen better days paired with loose trousers, the flared and tattered hems billowing around her ankles. Lucetta's golden hair was pulled into a messy knot on top of her head, and a large streak of what seemed to be grease was smeared across her nose.

"If only your admirers could see you now," Harriet said with a grin, earning a grin from Lucetta in return.

"Perhaps I *should* allow some of them to see me like this," Lucetta said. "Maybe then I wouldn't be plagued with so many pesky gentlemen trying to attract my attention—most of whom insist on pronouncing my name *Loo-chet-a* instead of *Loo-set-a*."

"For most ladies, gentlemen trying to capture a woman's attention is a sought-after circumstance."

"As you very well know, Harriet, I'm not most ladies, but now is not the time to discuss me or the gentlemen who plague me far too often. Explain the pooch."

"That's going to have to wait until we get him off these stairs. It's starting to drizzle, and that's not going to help our plight."

Lucetta smiled. "Leave him to me." She crouched down and

rubbed Buford's head. "You poor little darling," she crooned. "There's no reason to be afraid."

Buford went from rigid to relaxed in a split second.

"That's amazing, Lucetta. Who knew you had the same effect on dogs as you have on gentlemen?"

"I'm not sure that's something I should be proud of," Lucetta said before she straightened. "You said his name's Buford?"

Harriet nodded.

"Come along, Buford." Lucetta began climbing, and to Harriet's amazement, Buford trailed willingly up the remaining two flights of stairs and disappeared from view.

"Aren't you coming?" Lucetta yelled.

Picking up the pot of beef, Harriet hurried up the stairs, walked through the door, and entered the cramped space she and her friends fondly referred to as their receiving room. She set down the pot on a table that was surprisingly free of clutter and glanced around. "Did you clean?"

Lucetta beamed back at her. "I know it's completely unlike me, but I thought it would be the perfect gift for your birthday."

A lovely feeling of warmth swirled through Harriet. "It *is* the perfect gift, but I feel horrible that you spent the one afternoon you have off cleaning."

Lucetta waved away the protest. "*Romeo and Juliet* wrapped up sooner than expected—due to a slight problem with an overly emotional director. My next venture doesn't open at Niblo's Garden for another six weeks, and rehearsals don't begin for two. Management there is bringing in a mad inventor to see if the place is suitable for him to experiment with some new form of electric lights, since everyone is concerned about fires from gas lights burning theaters to the ground these days." She blew a strand of hair out of her face that had come free from the messy knot atop her head. "But enough about that—where and why did you get the mutt?"

Harriet looked down and shook her head at the sight of Buford hovering by Lucetta's side. "You've made a new conquest."

Lucetta ruffled Buford's fur, which immediately set his tail to wagging. "He's a lovely conquest to be sure, and at least I know he won't send me any of those nauseating roses."

"Acquired more of your least favorite flower last night after your performance, did you?"

"I got bushels of them, and most of them sent by that horrid Mr. Silas Ruff." Lucetta shuddered. "I think he believes his persistence will eventually wear me down."

"He obviously doesn't realize you're a lady who can't be bought."

"Obviously, but again, we're getting off topic. Where did you get Buford? I know he's not a stray, because he's wearing a collar and looks remarkably well fed."

"He's Oliver Addleshaw's dog."

Lucetta's mouth made an O of surprise. "Are you talking about the Oliver Addleshaw who recently built one of the most extravagant houses on Fifth Avenue?"

"One and the same. I saw his house today, and it certainly seems to be extravagant, at least on the outside."

"And you have his dog because . . . you found him wandering around outside that house and . . . Oh dear, please tell me you're not considering holding Buford for ransom? Jail is not a place you'd care to visit."

"You've evidently been immersing yourself entirely too much in those Shakespearian plots, and . . . how would you know that jail is not a place I'd care to land?"

Lucetta gave an airy wave of her hand. "I spent a few hours in one when I needed to prepare for a particularly difficult part, and I did not enjoy the experience. However, that has nothing to do with what you're doing with Mr. Addleshaw's dog or what you were even doing on Fifth Avenue." She narrowed her eyes. "Your aunt doesn't have something to do with this, does she?"

"Considering Aunt Jane is extremely put out with me since I once again refused her lovely offer of joining her less-than-savory business operation, I haven't had the pleasure of speaking to or even seeing her since my last birthday." Harriet bit her lip. "Although, I do believe she's taken to having me followed again." She waved her hand. "But enough about that. I was at Oliver's house because Mrs. Fienman sent me there to make a delivery."

"Mrs. Fienman prefers you remain in the back room, and . . . did you just call Mr. Addleshaw by his given name?"

"He told me to use his name, and yes, Mrs. Fienman did prefer to keep me to the back room, but there were extenuating circumstances that required her to shove me out of that room today."

"And those circumstances culminated with you becoming so well acquainted with Mr. Addleshaw that you're now addressing him by his given name and taking care of his dog?"

"When you say it like that, it sounds a little . . . unseemly." She felt her shoulders sag. "And here I was trying so hard to convince myself that this was the "something wonderful" God sent me for my birthday."

"Oh . . . Harriet." Lucetta moved up next to her, Buford still attached to her side, and pulled Harriet into a clumsy hug. "Don't tell me you asked God for another gentleman this year, *and* that you believe He sent you Oliver Addleshaw as your something wonderful. From what little I know of the man, and believe me, that isn't much, he's ruthless, with only one ambition—that of amassing a fortune greater than Cornelius Vanderbilt's."

Harriet stepped out of Lucetta's embrace and wrinkled her nose. "While I certainly don't understand why anyone would feel the need to have more money than Cornelius Vanderbilt, I didn't ask for a gentleman this year, and I certainly don't consider Oliver my something wonderful. I was entertaining the idea that it's the money Oliver's giving me that's wonderful."

"What money?"

Reaching for her reticule, Harriet managed to get the clasp undone, but before she could show Lucetta the contents of her bag, the outside door burst open and Miss Millie Longfellow, her other roommate, stomped through it. Forgetting all about her reticule when she saw that Millie was covered from head to toe in something pink, Harriet stood there gawking, as Lucetta did the same.

"Well, as you can see," Millie said with a jerky motion of her hand, the action causing some of the pink to go flying, "I've been dismissed once again from my position. Dismissed all because of a baking lesson with the children that went horribly, horribly wrong, and . . ."

Whatever else Millie was going to say seemed to get stuck in her throat when Buford moved from Lucetta's side and charged directly at Millie, skidding across the floor and finally coming to a stop when he plowed into her skirt and promptly began to chew on it.

Millie's eyes went wide as she remained frozen on the spot. "Would it be too much of a bother to beg the two of you for some assistance before this creature gnaws off my leg?"

"He won't hurt you," Harriet reassured her, hurrying forward. "He just wants to sample whatever that is you have on your gown." She stopped by Millie's side, reached out her hand, swiped at the pink, and brought it up to her nose. "Is this strawberry icing?"

Millie grinned, the action causing a delightful dimple to pop out on her pixie-like face. "It is."

Harriet was tempted to lick her finger, decided it was probably less than sanitary, so settled for wiping it on one of the few icing-free spots on Millie's apron. "Should I ask why you're covered in icing?"

"I told you, I had an unfortunate baking incident. I'll be more than happy to share all the gory details, but only after you've called off the dog."

"That might be problematic since Buford seems to enjoy strawberry icing and he's not exactly good at listening to commands."

"Nonsense," Lucetta said as she snapped her fingers. "Buford, be a dear and leave Millie alone."

Buford gave Millie's skirt a last lick before he loped back to Lucetta's side and pressed against her legs. Sending Harriet a grin, Lucetta picked up the dented pot. "I'm going to take him into the kitchen and feed him some of . . . well, whatever this is. It has to be better for him than icing." Waltzing across the room with Buford sticking closely to her, Lucetta disappeared.

"I take it that beast is a boy?" Millie asked dryly.

"How could you tell?"

"It wasn't difficult, since he seems to be completely under Lucetta's spell, but . . . why is he here?"

"It's a thrilling tale, much like the one I'm sure you have to share, but perhaps tale sharing should wait until you've changed your gown. Lucetta cleaned today, and you're dripping all over the floor—as am I, now that I think about it."

Millie smiled right before her bottom lip began to tremble. "I can't believe I lost another position today. Mrs. Sheppard was so angry about the mishap that she's refusing to pay me the wages I'm due." Millie's eyes turned suspiciously bright. "I have no idea how I'm going to be able to make the rent this month, and I dread going back to the employment agency and admitting another failure. The last time I was dismissed from a position, they told me they were running out of households willing to hire me, and—"

A loud rapping on the door interrupted Millie's sad tale.

Harriet frowned. "I wonder who in the world that could be?" Stepping up to the window, she peeked through the curtain, feeling an immediate stab of dread run through her. Reaching for the doorknob, she opened it up ever so slowly and summoned up a smile. "Timothy, this is a surprise. What brings you here?"

Timothy hung his head. "I sure do hate to be here right now, Miss Peabody, but Mrs. Fienman ordered me to bring you this." He handed her an envelope.

The dread turned to resignation as Harriet stared at the heavy vellum clasped in her hand. "I take it Mrs. Birmingham didn't waste any time besmirching my character?"

"I'm not sure what *besmirching* means, but she sure did give Mrs. Fienman an earful about you, and none of it pleasant." He shook his head. "She insisted I take her to the hat shop after depositing her daughter at the hotel. Curiosity got the best of me and I admit I took to listening outside the office door. I'm sorry to have to tell you that Mrs. Birmingham demanded Mrs. Fienman pen you that letter immediately while she looked on so that she'd be sure it was to her liking. I have a feeling you're not going to find what's written on the paper very nice."

"You didn't say anything about having trouble with Mrs. Fienman," Lucetta said, hurrying back into the room with Buford trailing behind her.

"I haven't had time to say much," Harriet muttered before she slid her finger under the flap and opened the letter. It didn't take her long to read the contents. "My services are no longer required at Fanny's Millinery, and . . . Mrs. Fienman feels that because I've caused her undue distress, she does not feel obligated to pay me my wages owed."

"Oh no, not you as well," Millie moaned. "We're . . . doomed."

Harriet lifted her chin, thanked Timothy—who seemed as if he couldn't get out of there fast enough—and shut the door.

Turning to face her friends, she realized in that moment that she really had no other option but to go through with the madness Oliver had offered.

Millie had been let go from yet another position.

Lucetta, while earning somewhat substantial pay, had mysterious obligations she had to meet on a regular basis. While Harriet knew her friend would offer to pick up the rent for a few months until things got settled, Harriet couldn't allow that.

She moved past Millie, who seemed ready to burst into tears, patted Lucetta's arm, sidestepped Buford, and didn't stop walking until she reached their miniscule kitchen. Pulling off the reticule looped around her wrist, she dumped the contents over the scarred surface of their wobbly table.

"What is that?" Millie whispered from the doorway.

"It's money I've been given to purchase clothing, but I'll have three thousand dollars more after I complete my obligation to Oliver Addleshaw."

"But . . . Harriet," Lucetta began slowly, "what are you going to have to do to earn those three thousand dollars?"

"Not what you're obviously thinking, Lucetta. I've been hired to pose as Oliver's lady friend. And before you start arguing with me, you must realize that I have no other choice, since I've lost my position, as has Millie."

"But . . . what of your reputation?" Lucetta questioned.

"I'm a hat maker, Lucetta, or at least I was. My reputation is really not important to anyone but me, and I assure you, I have no intention of ruining it." She blew out a breath. "I know what I'm about to do sounds untoward, but it's really just a clever bit of acting, and . . ." Her words trailed away to nothing when she heard the sound of footsteps clunking down their hallway. Before she could even become concerned, Reverend Gilmore stepped into the room.

"Ah, wonderful," he said, pulling a dripping hat from his

head. "All of you are here, safe and sound—especially you, Harriet."

"What led you to believe I wouldn't be safe?" Harriet asked.

"It's more of a *whom* rather than a *what*," Reverend Gilmore said with a smile. "Mrs. Palmer just ran me down, and I'm not exaggerating when I say ran. The poor dear was completely out of breath when she reached the church, and she had a very outlandish tale to tell, one that I knew couldn't possibly be . . ." His words trailed off as his gaze settled on the kitchen table. "Goodness, my dear, where did all of that money come from?"

Harriet felt her cheeks heat again. "I got it from Mr. Addleshaw and . . . I'm praying that it's my 'something wonderful' God sent me for my birthday."

"My dear child, prayers should certainly commence immediately, especially since it's clear you might have gotten yourself embroiled in something . . . disturbing."

6

Slouching down in a chair made of the finest leather, Oliver took a sip of his drink, allowing himself the luxury of relaxing, something he hadn't been able to do since he'd returned to New York the day before.

Stretching his legs out in front of him, he gazed fondly around at his surroundings. Astor House wasn't nearly as plush as the Metropolitan Hotel or even the Fifth Avenue Hotel. In all honesty, most of his associates found the Astor House to be down-right old-fashioned. He, however, enjoyed it—especially the idea that gentlemen of business had sought refuge there for years, using the dark and quiet confines of the private rooms the hotel offered as a place to escape the hectic pace of their lives.

It was also a perfect place to enjoy a leisurely lunch and hide from lecturing housekeepers, opinionated butlers, and irate fathers who happened to believe their daughters deserved a second chance at becoming Oliver's bride. After all that had occurred in the last twenty-four hours, he felt he was entitled to a few hours of hiding, especially in a place where no one spoke above a whisper, at least as pertained to the well-trained staff Astor House employed.

He lifted his glass, took another sip, and then glanced to his right, his lips quirking at the sight of his best friend, Everett Mulberry, slouching in the chair next to him. The poor man had dark shadows staining the skin underneath eyes that were currently closed. Everett also had a decidedly grumpy look about him, clear evidence that the man was suffering the same type of week Oliver was.

"How are the brats?" Oliver asked, causing one of Everett's eyes to pop open, peer at him for a second, and then close again.

"They're bratty," Everett muttered. "They're always bratty."

"And the latest disaster would be . . . ?"

Everett rubbed his temple. "When was the last time we spoke?"

"I've been out of town six weeks, but I believe we had dinner the night before I left."

"Is that all the time that has passed since I last saw you? To tell you the truth, it felt like years, but that might be because my life drags on through one horrific incident after another these days." Everett opened his eyes. "Let me see, in the past six weeks I've gone through four governesses, two nannies, and had one driver and one kitchen maid tender their resignations due to an overabundance of stress."

"That has to be a new record."

"I'm sure you're probably right. To top matters off, the employment agency where I get my staff has recently informed me that if I don't get the children under control soon, they will not provide me with any additional help, whether they be governesses, maids, or drivers. I certainly don't know how to bring the children under control, and the agency is supposed to have professionals at their disposal. One would think, given all the money I've shelled out, that these professionals could easily manage three children."

"Have you reminded the agency that you've only recently inherited these children?"

Everett released a grunt. "They don't seem to care." He snatched up his glass, took a hefty gulp, and set the glass back on the table a little harder than was strictly necessary. "I still cannot fathom what Fred Burkhart was thinking, leaving his children to me. Why, I barely knew the man."

"You stood up for him at his wedding."

"Oh . . . right, but—"

"You're godparent to all three of his children."

"True, but honestly, Oliver, I thought that only meant I would be expected to watch them sing in the church choir, or send them outlandish presents at Christmas. I never thought I'd be expected to raise them if something dastardly happened to Fred and his wife. Besides, Miss Marybeth Thornridge is also godparent to the little monsters, and she's a woman. I really don't understand why she wasn't given guardianship."

"I would have to believe, since Miss Thornridge is off on a mission in the wilds of some backward country and has been off on that mission for at least two years, Fred thought you'd be easier to locate if something were to happen to him, which it did."

"Being the easiest godparent to locate does not make me the most viable candidate. I'm a single gentleman who spends his time immersed in business and society matters. I don't have time to raise three children, all of whom seem to have made it their goal in life to slowly drive me insane with their daily bouts of mischief."

Oliver thought it was a sign of true friendship that he didn't laugh. Everett looked so disconcerted that he'd hardly appreciate amusement, and Oliver really couldn't blame the man. It wasn't every day a person got saddled with someone else's children. "I imagine Fred really never thought he'd die, but it's a great testimony to how much he trusted you that he left you his children."

"I'd rather have been left a yacht." Everett shuddered. "Elizabeth, she's the oldest of the bunch, actually took down all the curtains in the receiving room, cut them up, and sewed them into dresses for herself and the twins."

"Isn't one of the twins a boy?"

"That was exactly my point. Poor Thaddeus looked ridiculous in the mauve-colored frock Elizabeth stuffed him into." Everett shook his head. "Unfortunately, when I made mention of that, Elizabeth burst into tears, Rosetta, the other twin, bit me, and Thaddeus now refuses to wear anything *other* than dresses." He blew out a breath. "How could I have possibly known that Elizabeth was not proficient with sewing and had tried to make Thaddeus a pair of trousers out of the drapes, but they didn't work, and because of that, she'd made him the only thing she was capable of making, a frock." He released a heavy sigh. "She didn't want her little brother to feel left out."

"I'm almost hesitant to bring this up, but that was rather sweet of Elizabeth."

Everett slouched down into the chair again. "I know, and quite frankly, it would be easier if they were horrible all the time. That way I could send them off to some boarding school, wash my hands of them, and not feel a sliver of guilt about it."

"Aren't the twins only around five years old?"

"They are, but Miss Dixon managed to find a school that *will* take them, even given their tender ages."

Oliver crossed his ankles. "Ah, the ever-resourceful Miss Dixon. May I assume your association with the lady is going according to plan?"

"I imagine it is, although nothing is official just yet." Everett swiped a hand through his hair, leaving it standing on end. "She's certainly an ideal candidate for the position of Mrs. Mulberry. She's friends with all the right people, and my parents approve of her."

"Do *you* approve of her?"

"What's not to approve? She's beautiful, fairly well-educated, has stellar manners, and we rub along quite nicely together."

"But she doesn't care for the children?"

Everett frowned. "Why would you say that?"

"She took it upon herself to search out a boarding school for them."

"Hmmm . . . I never thought of it in that light, but enough about the brats. They plague me all too often as it is." Everett smiled. "Tell me about you—is there anything new and exciting happening in your life?"

"You could say that."

Everett's eyes widened. "You've finally buckled under the pressure of your grandfather's badgering and gotten engaged, haven't you."

"No, I'm not engaged, although I must tell you, a Miss Birmingham seems to have spread it about town that she was soon going to become the new Mrs. Addleshaw. Luckily for me, I discovered her true nature before our association could progress. I'm hopeful she's even now on her way back to Chicago— even though she did end up costing me a pretty penny in the process."

"Pennies are worth the cost if you managed to dodge a nasty bullet."

"Miss Birmingham certainly did turn nasty, as did her father." Oliver grinned. "I shudder to think how he'll react if he learns about Miss Harriet Peabody."

Everett moved his chair closer to Oliver. "You'd better start at the beginning."

Fifteen minutes later, Oliver concluded his story, unable to help but notice that Everett was staring back at him with undisguised shock on his face. He was about to ring the bell to order a fresh drink when Everett released a grunt.

"And *you* had the audacity to tell poor Mr. Birmingham that *his daughter* was mentally unstable."

"I'm not insane, Everett. Hiring Harriet to accompany me as I proceed forward with the Duke of Westmoore is one of the most ingenious ideas I've ever come up with. I can't dine with the gentleman without having a lady around to add a touch of charm to the atmosphere. The duke will expect to be properly entertained, and I'm not willing to disappoint the man. I'm determined to finalize my deal with him and procure wool that's considered the finest in the world."

"It's only wool, Oliver. Don't you think you might be taking things too far?"

Oliver shrugged. "I've spent countless hours formulating this deal, and my time is money. Besides, hiring a lady to help me entertain business associates instead of counting on ladies with marriage on their minds will save me a huge amount of aggravation. I should have thought of it years ago."

"But it simply isn't done. I'm of the firm belief that the social classes shouldn't mingle—something I thought you believed as well. There are a million things that could go wrong with this plan of yours. She's a *hat* girl, Oliver."

"She's remarkably refined."

"You told me she slung Miss Birmingham over her shoulder and tossed her into a carriage. I wouldn't think it necessary to point this out—but refined young ladies don't normally spend their time tossing other people about."

"She was trying to conceal a nearly naked Miss Birmingham. If you ask me, that shows she has a great deal of compassion."

"You call it compassion, I call it self-preservation. Miss Birmingham was beating Miss Peabody with a parasol."

"True, but again, she merely tossed the woman into a carriage. She could have done something far worse, which proves she's a lady of great restraint and will be an asset on my arm."

"I think a bigger factor in your decision to hire her was that she turned you down at first."

"What does that have to do with anything?"

"Oliver, I've known you since we were children. You're competitive. You were shocked when Miss Peabody turned down your first proposal. That is what had you throwing caution to the wind and increasing the amount of your offer." Everett shook his head. "Why, I can't help but wonder what you'd have done if she'd turned down the three thousand dollars. Proposed to her, perhaps?"

"Now you're just being ridiculous. I may have no hesitation about bringing Harriet on to work for me, but I know perfectly well she's not remotely acceptable as a candidate for the future Mrs. Addleshaw."

Everett narrowed his eyes. "Society will make that assumption once she's seen by your side."

"No they won't. Society, it is my belief, has moved forward regarding such matters, given that it's the eighteen hundreds, not the Dark Ages. Just because a lady is seen on a gentleman's arm does not mean a wedding is imminent."

"I don't think we've progressed as far as you believe," Everett countered. "Tell me, though, what's to happen to this Miss Peabody after your association ends?"

"I assume she'll take the money she earns from me and go about doing whatever it is hat girls do when they come into possession of unexpected funds."

Everett shifted in his seat. "Out of curiosity, what exactly do you expect Miss Peabody to do in order to earn three thousand dollars?"

"Her most important responsibility will be to charm the duke."

"And you honestly believe that a hat girl will be capable of that daunting task?"

"She charmed me, and—"

"She charmed you?" Everett interrupted, looking more shocked than ever. "Good heavens, Oliver. This truly is madness, then. You're attracted to the woman, and you mark my words—disaster is right around the corner if you go through with this."

Oliver felt an unaccustomed rush of heat travel up his neck. "I'm not attracted to her. Well, she is lovely, but . . . what I meant to say is that she has an air about her that I'm sure the duke will find charming, and . . ." He lapsed into silence when Everett began muttering dire predictions under his breath. To Oliver's relief, he was spared further embarrassment when a quiet knock sounded on the door before it opened and a member of the Astor House staff stepped into the room.

"Begging your pardon, gentlemen, but Mr. Ruff is waiting outside to speak with you, Mr. Addleshaw. Shall I send him in?"

For a second, Oliver thought about saying no. Silas Ruff was one of his business associates, brought into Oliver's employ after Oliver invested in the man's ore mining venture. Silas had been exactly what Oliver needed—a ruthless, ambitious man who had no qualms about getting things done, no matter what means it took to turn a profit. Silas had been with Oliver for four years, and while his temperamental personality sometimes grated on Oliver's nerves, he kept Silas on because profitability had never been better.

However, Silas's habit of tracking Oliver down whenever he wanted to speak to him was beginning to become a problem. The fact they'd had plans to meet that morning, but Silas hadn't shown, made it all the more annoying.

"Since it appears Mr. Ruff knows I'm here, you might as well bring him in," Oliver finally said.

With a nod, the man withdrew from the room. A moment later, Silas strode through the doorway with the Astor House employee following a step behind him.

"Get me a whiskey, neat," Silas threw at the man. "And something to eat, a steak, I think, bloody, and make it quick. I'm starving."

It was a mark of how well Astor House trained their staff that the man Silas had just barked at didn't even flinch. "Very good, sir," he said before turning to Oliver and Everett. "May I bring you fresh drinks?"

Oliver nodded, as did Everett. The man bowed, turned, and quit the room, right as Silas grabbed a chair and pulled it over toward Oliver, the legs making a loud scraping noise against the floor. Silas eased his bulky frame down into it and folded his hands over his stomach.

"I've been looking for you for over two hours," he complained.

Oliver arched a brow. "I was under the impression you and I were supposed to meet early this morning, as in at seven."

"That must have slipped my mind, but I'm here now." Silas settled into the chair. "Some problems have cropped up."

"Oh?"

"Mr. Birmingham tracked me down this morning. He's not happy with you and is demanding more money for the purchase of his business. And he wants to retain full control of that business after we buy it from him."

Oliver frowned. "I spoke with him yesterday, and we agreed that our deal would proceed forward as planned. He made no mention to me that he was going to seek greater compensation, and . . . no, he can't retain control. His leadership is what sent that company plummeting toward ruin in the first place."

Silas nodded. "I know that, Oliver, but Mr. Birmingham isn't in a reasonable state of mind at the moment. He expected you to offer his daughter marriage, but now that his dream apparently isn't going to happen, he wants to see you pay."

"I only asked Miss Birmingham to accompany me to a few

social events. Forgive me if I don't believe taking a lady out for dinner demands a proposal afterward."

"He thinks you jilted his little precious."

"Miss Birmingham insisted she wasn't interested in marrying *me*." Oliver's lips curved up. "She believes I'm a tyrant and that I'm not considerate of her tender feelings."

"You are a tyrant," Silas retorted. "But tyranny aside, how is this parting of the ways with Miss Birmingham going to affect your dealings with the Duke of Westmoore?"

"I don't believe it'll affect it at all."

Sitting forward, Silas placed his hands on his knees, the action causing the buttons of his jacket to strain against the bulk of his stomach. "Are you going to be making the rounds this week to what few soirées might be held in the city to see if there are any suitable candidates who would be willing to help you entertain the duke?"

"I don't need to resort to that. I already have someone in mind."

"Who is she?"

"Since it would appear the Birminghams have yet to leave the city, I'm not comfortable divulging that information just yet."

Silas nodded. "Understandable, although I do hope you've chosen someone a little more high in the instep than Miss Birmingham. Her family, while respectable, is certainly not as desirable as someone of your status deserves. If you want to continue increasing your holdings as well as your standing within society, you'll need to have a lady of worth by your side."

"My family is one of the most powerful families in America."

"True, but it's not *the* most powerful, is it?" Silas returned. "Combining your power with that of an equally powerful family will only increase your appeal, which brings me back to this mysterious lady of yours. She is well connected, isn't she?"

Since Oliver had no idea what, if any, connections Harriet

had—although he doubted she knew or was related to anyone of importance—he decided it was time to change the subject. "You mentioned that a few problems have cropped up. May I assume there are other matters to discuss besides the ridiculous notion of Mr. Birmingham trying to squeeze more money out of me?"

"You shouldn't take Mr. Birmingham lightly," Silas said, easing back into his chair. "He's furious, and furious men can do dangerous things."

"True. Set up another meeting with him soon, and remind him that he's the one who sought out our assistance, not the other way around. And, he did so because he's desperate for money. Once his temper cools, I'm sure he'll remember that."

Silas shook his head. "I wouldn't count on that. He's been bragging amongst our contemporaries that you were soon to become his son-in-law. He'll suffer quite a bit of embarrassment once word gets out that isn't going to happen *and* that you've settled your attention on someone else. You'll need to watch your back."

"That's what I pay you to do." Oliver turned his head as the door opened and the Astor House server appeared, pushing a cart filled with food and fresh drinks.

No one spoke as the man served the drinks, set up a small table right in front of Silas, took off a silver domed lid from a large platter, slid it onto the table without making a sound, and then pushed the cart from the room, closing the door softly behind him.

"One thing you can say about this place is they give good service," Silas said as he scooted closer to the table and began to attack his food. The entire steak was devoured in mere minutes, and after a loud belch and a swig of his drink, Silas pushed the table aside and belched again.

"I should be going," he said before he stood up, tugged his

jacket over a stomach that seemed even larger, and smiled. "I have amusement on my mind for the rest of the afternoon."

"Not that I want to stifle your amusements, but don't you think you should have business matters on your mind?"

"I've done quite enough business today—thank you very much."

Oliver considered the man for a moment. "Planning another trip to the theater, are you?"

"Unfortunately, no. *Romeo and Juliet* ended its stint earlier than expected."

Oliver tilted his head. "I know I've mentioned this before, but I find your pursuit of the lovely Lucetta Plum somewhat disturbing."

Silas rubbed at what looked to be a gravy stain on his jacket. "I have no idea why you'd be disturbed about anything I choose to do, Oliver. Even though we're in business together, my personal life shouldn't affect you in the least. As for Lucetta, she's a delightful minx, even if she's playing coy at the moment." He smiled. "She and I both know she's only doing so to increase her value. I'm sure I'll be forced to spend an exorbitant amount of money on her once she agrees to become my mistress, but it'll be worth it."

He brushed some crumbs from his sleeve. "Just make certain you don't mention anything about Lucetta around Doreen or her family. I don't think my wife actually cares if I spend my time with a few light-skirts, but her father is a rather pious man and might have something to say about it. I absolutely loathe listening to his lectures."

"You wouldn't be forced to listen to any lectures if you'd simply pay attention to your wife and abandon your quest to keep company with Miss Plum," Oliver pointed out.

"But where's the fun in that?" Silas asked with a hearty laugh. He turned and walked to the door, pausing for a moment before he crossed back to the chair he'd just abandoned and looked down at Oliver. "I almost forgot to tell you—there's been an accident at the Fayette mine."

"And you're only getting around to mentioning it now?"

"I don't have much to report as of yet." Silas shrugged. "The telegram I received simply stated there'd been a fire, caused it seems by a faulty piece of machinery."

"I thought the Fayette mine was supposed to get all new machinery."

"We did put the costs for that into the budget, but the profit margins were steadily increasing at the mine without new machinery. I didn't see the need to replace it just yet. The money we would have used has been put into the market, where it's yielding a hefty return."

Rising to his feet, Oliver took a step closer to Silas. "I don't recall our discussing putting off the buying of that equipment."

"You didn't hire me to discuss every little situation. You hired me to make you money. That's what I'm doing, increasing *your* fortune."

"And yours as well," Oliver countered. "We won't see any profits if we have to rebuild the mine and replace the machinery that burned."

"The entire mine didn't collapse, only one shaft."

"Were there injuries?"

"It was a telegram, Oliver, not a news release. There weren't many details, except that a few men had gotten trapped, but I think they got them out because there was no mention of any deaths."

"Men were trapped?"

"It happens. Mining is a dangerous business. It's to be expected."

Oliver drew in a long breath and slowly released it. He'd always known that Silas was ruthless, crude, and lacking in normal emotions, but he'd never realized until just this moment how incredibly heartless the gentleman was. "We'll have to send someone down to West Virginia to handle this mess."

"It won't be me. I hate West Virginia. The people are ignorant, dirty, and there's absolutely nothing to do down there."

"I don't know who else I'd send *except* you, Silas. I'd go myself, but the duke is expected soon, and I wouldn't have enough time to make it back here to complete our deal. You'll have to go, and I want you to leave by tomorrow morning at the latest."

For a moment, Oliver thought Silas was going to refuse, but then the man rolled his eyes.

"Fine, I'll go, but don't think I'm happy about it—and we'll discuss the business of you ordering me around when I get back." He brushed at his sleeve again. "Since it appears my time in New York is limited, I'm going to take my leave. I'm debating whether or not to go to Mrs. Crawford's lovely establishment, since I've heard she's recently acquired some new girls, or travel to Canfield's to do a little gambling. Would either of you care to join me?"

Distaste flowed over Oliver at how easily Silas could announce a mining accident with one breath, and then blithely announce he was off to a brothel or a gambling establishment with another.

Unease suddenly replaced the distaste.

He'd hired Silas to help him achieve his goal of amassing extreme wealth, but he couldn't help thinking that might have been a mistake. He'd obviously brought onboard a man with little to no moral code, which until that moment hadn't really bothered him. His troubling thoughts were interrupted when Everett stepped forward.

"While a trip to Canfield's sounds *delightful*, I'm afraid I'm going to have to pass, old man. I've got a disastrous situation at home at the moment, so I can't be away long, and . . . I don't think Miss Dixon would approve of me jeopardizing the fortune she seems determined for me to increase."

"Ah, I'd forgotten you were making a play for Miss Dixon," Silas said. "She's another lovely minx. I've always enjoyed her deliciously caustic tongue."

Everett frowned. "Is she caustic?"

"My dear Everett, Miss Dixon causes grown gentlemen and ladies to tremble whenever she enters a room. You'll be fortunate indeed if you can convince her to meet you at the altar." Silas turned to Oliver. "What about you, care for a bit of feminine company or a roll of the dice?"

"Brothels have never appealed to me, Silas, and you know I don't gamble."

Instead of taking offense at Oliver's words, Silas chuckled. "I sometimes forget how prudish you can be, Oliver—but to each his own." Silas sent Oliver a wink, slapped Everett on the back, and strode from the room, closing the door loudly behind him.

Everett shook his head. "I realize Silas is brilliant at making money, Oliver, but I have to tell you, if you don't get rid of him, and soon, he just might end up ruining your life."

Oliver found he couldn't disagree.

7

A sense of unsettledness mixed with irritation continued to plague Oliver long after parting ways with Silas. He'd gone to Astor House in search of peace, but peace certainly was not what he'd received. Leaning his head against the cool glass of the carriage window, he permitted himself a long, drawn-out sigh.

Miners were suffering, and he was ultimately responsible—it was as simple as that.

For years he'd skirted around ethics in his quest for profitability, but never had that skirting caused physical injury to another person. Granted, he'd thought improvements were under way at the Fayette mine, but that didn't excuse his negligence in not making certain those improvements had actually started.

It was abundantly clear Silas had taken entirely too much liberty in the matter, but the question of the hour now was how to proceed.

A part of him believed he should cancel his meetings with the Duke of Westmoore and travel to West Virginia with Silas to assess the situation. The other part of him, however—the part that paid Silas an exorbitant salary—believed Silas had played a major part in creating the disaster, so it was up to him to set matters to rights. That would allow Oliver to continue on with the duke and secure a deal he'd been working on for months.

His contradictory thoughts came to an abrupt end when the carriage shuddered to a stop. Peering out the window, Oliver's gaze sharpened on the traffic clogging the street. He reached for the door and got out, feeling the distinct urge to immediately jump right back in when he realized he was standing in the midst of the Ladies' Mile. This particular stretch of New York was filled with department stores, exclusive dress and jewelry shops, and many fine places to dine, but it was also brimming with ladies, all out for an enjoyable day of shopping, many of them unmarried.

It was a distinct possibility he could be mobbed at any second.

"There's an overturned wagon up ahead, Mr. Addleshaw," Darren called. "We're going to be stuck here for a while."

"I think you may be right." Oliver sent Darren a nod and took a step toward the carriage, but before he had an opportunity to climb in, a burst of giggling sounded right behind him. Knowing it would be less than gentlemanly to ignore the women responsible for those giggles, he summoned up a smile and turned. To his dismay, he found five young ladies waving back at him—each and every one of them clutching delicate handkerchiefs in their hands, handkerchiefs that suddenly began fluttering to the ground. He bent over and began retrieving various bits of lace when from out of the corner of his eye he caught sight of another lady, one who immediately captured and held his attention.

What was so intriguing about her, he couldn't actually say. Perhaps it was the fact her face was almost completely obscured by a large, elaborately decorated hat, lending her a rather mysterious air. Or, perhaps it was simply that she wasn't paying him the least bit of attention, even though the crowd of ladies

gathered around him had grown substantially. The lady spared
him not a single glance as she breezed past, lifting the skirt of
her ice-blue gown to step around a lingering puddle. Her arm
suddenly swung into view, and looped around that arm was a
reticule that seemed oddly familiar.

His mouth dropped open when he realized the lady was none
other than Miss Harriet Peabody.

Straightening, he handed the beaming woman standing nearest to him the handkerchiefs he'd scooped off the ground, nodding at her rather absently when she let out a breathy word of
thanks. Looking over the heads of the crowd that surrounded
him, his attention finally settled on the very top of Harriet's
hat, the only thing he could still see of her.

"Miss Peabody," he called, causing each and every one of the
giggling ladies to immediately stop giggling. They turned as
one in the direction Harriet was disappearing, and for a brief
moment, Oliver swore they all resembled colorful birds of prey,
just waiting to devour a weaker bird—or in this case, Harriet.

He pushed aside that ridiculous notion when he realized Harriet was completely out of sight. Sending the gathering of now
disgruntled-looking ladies a muttered excuse over his shoulder,
he strode into the crowded sidewalk, craning his neck as he
tried to bring Harriet into view. He finally caught a glimpse of
an outlandish hat.

It was quickly becoming apparent the lady enjoyed wearing
unusual creations on her head.

"Miss Peabody," he called again, louder than before, and
couldn't believe his eyes when the tip of her hat began bobbing
faster than ever, leaving him with the distinct impression she'd
heard his call but was deliberately trying to get away from him.

Plowing forward, he edged around two servants in formal
livery burdened with excessive packages, and tipped his hat to
a lady gesturing his way. Temper began churning through him

when he saw Harriet duck into a narrow space that seemed to be some type of alleyway between two shops.

There was now no doubt left in his mind—she *was* trying to make a speedy escape.

Breaking into a run, something he couldn't remember being forced to do in quite some time, if ever, he reached the alley a moment later, and sure enough, Harriet was racing down the cobblestone path, holding her hat with one hand and her skirt with the other.

"Miss Peabody . . . Harriet!" he bellowed, "I insist you stop at once."

To his annoyance, she continued dashing away, but then she slowed, turned on her heel, and peered across the distance that separated them. He couldn't be absolutely certain, given the space between them, but he thought he detected a slight drooping of her shoulders before she suddenly squared them.

"Oliver, well, this is an unexpected surprise," she called before she began walking his way, although her feet seemed to be dragging. "What in the world are you doing here?"

Oliver drew in a breath of much-needed air and swiped a hand over his perspiring brow. "I might ask you the same question. Do you make it a common practice to dash off through derelict alleys?"

Harriet gave an airy flick of a hand. "Of course I don't normally spend my time in alleys, but . . . ah, I thought someone of a dastardly nature was following me, hence my decision to take the path less traveled, so to speak."

"I was the one following you, and I assure you, I don't possess a dastardly nature."

"Of course you don't," she returned with a nod. "However, I'm not overly familiar with your voice, which is why I wasn't taking any chances. My reticule is currently stuffed with the funds you so generously gave me, and I'm not willing to allow someone of a dastardly nature to abscond with those funds." She drew in a breath, seemed about ready to continue on with her speech, but then dropped her gaze and, strangely enough, smiled.

"Forgive me, but I find nothing amusing about this situation," he said when she continued perusing him even as her smile widened.

Harriet lifted her head. "I'm almost hesitant to point this out, given that you appear to be rather touchy regarding your wardrobe, but you're missing some buttons."

Oliver looked down, and sure enough, all but one of his buttons were gone. "My tailor obviously didn't realize I'd be forced to participate in strenuous activities, such as running after a lady through the Ladies' Mile, when he created this for me."

"If he were any type of tailor at all, he'd keep all activities in mind when making you a garment."

"While that is a remarkably valid point, I believe we have more important matters to discuss than my tailor's proficiency or lack thereof. Tell me, do you often find gentlemen of a dastardly sort trailing you about the city?"

"The streets are full of crackpots and are hazardous at the best of times, especially for a lady traveling alone."

He had the strangest feeling she was dodging the question. "Do you, by chance, have overzealous admirers who plague you?"

Harriet let out a snort. "I don't have time for admirers. I spend most of my hours working, or at least I used to, when I still retained a position."

"So you *have* been released from your millinery job?"

"Mrs. Fienman sent a note yesterday, informing me of my dismissal. From what I've been told, Mrs. Birmingham was most insistent regarding my termination."

"I am sorry to hear that, but on the bright side, at least now you should feel more comfortable regarding my offer."

Her eyes immediately turned stormy. "I wouldn't have been fired in the first place if you'd been more diligent in getting to know Miss Birmingham before she descended on this city."

Seeing no advantage whatsoever in agreeing with that piece of logic, he summoned up what he'd been told by numerous ladies was his most charming of smiles. "But then we would never have met."

Harriet muttered something that sounded very much like "Unbelievable" under her breath, and then began marching down the alley toward the main street, apparently not moved in the least by his charm.

It was rather unnerving, her lack of expected behavior.

Forcing his feet to motion, he began trailing after her, searching for something to say that wouldn't offend the lady. When nothing pertinent sprang to mind, he settled for falling into step beside her, where an uneasy silence descended over them.

Reaching the end of the alley, she came to an abrupt stop as a remarkably grumpy expression crossed her face. "Don't you have somewhere you need to be?"

"There was an accident on the street, so I'm stuck here until traffic gets moving again." He tried his charming smile again but felt it fade almost immediately when she looked even grumpier. Instead of bidding her good day—something she clearly wanted him to do—a perverse streak of stubbornness he hadn't realized he possessed took that moment to seize hold of him. "Since you are so concerned about that money in your reticule, I'll walk with you. I wouldn't want a genuinely dastardly gentleman to join you and make off with it."

Her only response was a single arch of a delicate brow.

Undaunted, he gestured to the shops lining the streets. "You are intending to shop, aren't you?"

For some odd reason, a wash of pink suddenly stained her cheeks. "I *was* intending to shop. However, I have not met with much success so far and was actually on my way home when you stopped me."

Oliver frowned. "Are you suggesting that none of these fine shops have anything in them that appeals to you?"

"Don't be ridiculous."

"Then why aren't you buried under packages?"

"I assure you, it's not for lack of trying," she grumbled even as she began edging down the sidewalk, as if she'd once again discovered an urge to dash off.

Not wanting to have to chase her down again, Oliver took a firm grip of her arm and held on tightly as they walked through the crowd. "Do you want to tell me what happened?"

"Not particularly."

"I'm afraid I must insist. Did I not provide you with enough money to purchase whatever fashions caught your eye?"

Harriet stopped walking, forcing him to stop as well. "You gave me more than enough money, which I hope was intentional."

"Of course it was intentional. I told you to get a few fashionable items, and I certainly didn't expect you to dip into your own money to pay for them."

"Thank goodness," Harriet said before she bit her lip. "Although, I do have to tell you, I used a small bit of that money to buy Buford a steak—well, three steaks, since your dog seems to have a voracious appetite. Oh, and I bought another two steaks for the yippers."

"I have no idea what 'yippers' could possibly be, but you're feeding Buford steak?"

"I told you I've never had a pet before, but I do know that dogs enjoy meat. Since it just so happens I was at Mort's last night, a dining establishment that grills a most excellent steak, with my friends, celebrating my, err . . ."

"Newfound fortune?" Oliver finished for her when she seemed reluctant to continue.

"Not exactly."

"Your dismissal from Mrs. Fienman's shop?"

"Losing one's position is never cause for celebration, no matter that you're giving me funds to see me through for quite some time." She let out a huff. "If you must know, yesterday was my birthday."

"You neglected to tell me yesterday was your birthday."

"There was much that was neglected to be said, given Mr. Birmingham's untimely appearance."

"Good point, but we have time to discuss matters now. May I inquire as to what birthday you celebrated?"

"It's hardly proper to ask a lady her age."

"Normally I would agree with you, but since you're going to be seen on my arm, it's most likely a question others are going to ask. It might bring up unwelcome speculation if I can't answer properly."

"I'm twenty-two."

"Are you really? I thought you were closer to my age, and I'm thirty-one, which just goes . . ."

The next thing Oliver knew, he was standing by himself, Harriet having shaken out of his hold and taken off down the sidewalk again.

Apparently the events of the past day or so were catching up with him, because it was completely unlike him to make such a huge faux pas.

No lady, be she society or of the working class, wanted to hear that a gentleman thought her to be older than her years. However, there was just something about Harriet—an air of confidence, he supposed—that made her seem older than twenty-two.

He shook himself out of his thoughts when he realized the exasperating lady was rapidly getting away from him and hurried to catch up with her. "Harriet, wait up. I didn't mean to insult you." He reached her side but didn't take her arm again when she sent him a glare.

"I don't believe, Mr. Addleshaw, it would be in either of our best interests to continue forward with this idiotic association we seem to have landed ourselves in. I don't have a desire to find myself in jail, but if I'm forced to continue spending time with you . . . I fear I might be compelled to do something to you that will certainly land me there."

"Have you forgotten you're currently without another position?"

Harriet stopped moving. "You're incredibly annoying. Has anyone ever told you that?"

Before he could reply to that piece of nonsense, she lifted her chin. "But, annoying or not, you do make a most excellent argument. I *am* without a position, which, I must add, is somewhat your fault, so I'm going to have to force myself to go through with this plan of yours. I'll reluctantly take your money for my cooperation, but don't think for a minute I'm going to be happy about it."

A surprising flash of relief stole over him, causing him to smile, something he quickly stopped doing when she crossed her arms over her chest and began looking grumpy again.

"Your smiling is definitely contributing to my lack of happiness," she muttered.

Swallowing a laugh, because he knew she certainly wouldn't appreciate that, he summoned up a look he hoped would pass for somber. "No smiling, I can do that, and I won't bring up age again, but . . . I do need to understand what difficulty you ran into while shopping. I've never met a young lady whose mood wasn't improved by visiting the shops."

"One would think shopping would, indeed, improve my spirits, but sadly enough, that hasn't been the case today."

"I'm afraid I don't understand."

"And I don't really feel like explaining my sad day to you."

"Why not?"

"Because . . . I'm embarrassed—which is one of several reasons why I pretended not to hear you when you first called out to me. I knew it was you, but . . ." She dropped her head and began scuffing her foot against the sidewalk.

She looked so dejected yet oddly adorable at the same time that Oliver suddenly found himself standing right before her, lifting her chin up with his finger. "What happened, Harriet?"

Her eyes turned a deep shade of violet. "Oh, very well, I'll tell you. But I'm afraid you're going to be very disappointed to learn how greatly I failed at the first task you gave me." She released a huff. "I decided to go to Madame Simone's shop, since Miss Birmingham had spoken so enthusiastically about the place. I will admit I wasn't exactly certain I'd be able to buy much there, given the very dear prices Madame Simone charges for her designs. But it was a place to start, and I never dreamed everything would go so horribly wrong."

"And . . . ?" Oliver prompted when Harriet stopped speaking and didn't look like she particularly wanted to continue with her tale.

"Madame Simone took issue with my gown."

Oliver looked her up and down. "Your gown is delightful, and you look no different from any of the other ladies strolling around the shops today. Quite honestly, I think you put most of them to shame."

A lovely shade of pink stole across Harriet's face. "Thank you, Oliver. That's very kind of you to say, and I do think this gown is delightful, but . . ." She bit her lip. "It turns out that this particular gown was once owned by one of Madame Simone's best customers, *the* Mrs. Astor. One of the snotty ladies working the front room of the salon recognized it straight away and called for Madame Simone. She breezed into the room, gave me a single glance, and then announced to everyone milling about that they were in the company of a thief. She immediately came to the conclusion that I was nothing more than a maid for the Astor family, and a maid who apparently had a propensity for being a bit light-fingered with her employer's belongings." Harriet shuddered. "I tried to protest, but she wouldn't listen to a word I said and instead summoned the authorities."

"Dare I ask what happened next?"

"Well, obviously I got away, but only because the doorman Madame Simone ordered to hold me clearly wasn't expecting me to stomp on his foot and dash out the door." She looked over her shoulder. "For all I know, there could be policemen searching the street for me as we speak."

"You have nothing to be worried about, Harriet. You're with me now."

Harriet turned skeptical eyes on him. "Madame Simone was really upset. She seems to be incredibly protective of her designs, even though the gown I'm wearing bears no resemblance whatsoever to the one she made. It was just poor luck that this material came from a single bolt of fabric, that fabric destined for Mrs. Astor and Mrs. Astor only."

"How *did* you come into possession of a gown that originally belonged to Caroline Astor?"

Frost clouded Harriet's eyes. "I didn't steal it."

"I never said you did."

"Your tone implies otherwise."

A sliver of chagrin took him by surprise. "I apologize, and you're right. I did consider the idea that you might have obtained the gown through dishonest means, but tell me, how did it come about that you're wearing a gown that once belonged to the leader of society?"

"Mrs. Astor abandoned this gown when she donated it to the castoff bin at my church. Reverend Gilmore has given me leave to take some of those castoffs because I have a need for them, whereas most of the poor don't have a use for such fancy pieces." She wrinkled her nose. "Speaking of Reverend Gilmore, I do feel I should warn you that he's intent on seeking you out in the not-so-distant future."

"While the idea that a reverend wants to seek me out is a little unsettling, I find I'm more curious about the cast-off clothing. Why do you take it?"

Harriet shrugged. "I salvage the material and remake the gowns into different styles."

"You do this for your personal use?"

"Well, no, except for this gown I'm wearing today and a few others I've been experimenting with." She lowered her voice. "I'm hoping to open up my own shop, you see. There are hundreds of working ladies who occasionally need a special dress but can't afford to visit the department stores or fancy designer shops. I can provide them with what they need at a reasonable cost."

"That's the real reason behind your agreement to our deal, isn't it."

"I must admit that it is. Your money will allow me to proceed with my plan without starving to death in the process."

Oliver's thoughts immediately turned to business. "What a fascinating idea, and . . . completely brilliant, I might add."

Harriet blinked. "Do you really think so?"

"Of course. Your costs are almost nonexistent, since you get your material for free. The most expensive part of your idea would be labor, which you do yourself. The money I've given you can be used to rent a storefront and . . . Yes, it's brilliant."

"You won't steal my idea, will you?"

"No, of course not, but I wouldn't be opposed to discussing it with you further at a later date. I know many gentlemen who own buildings in the city, and I'm sure I'd be able to help you negotiate a fair deal on rent."

Harriet regarded him a little warily. "Hmm . . . Well, that's very kind and . . . unexpected of you, but isn't anything we need to worry about right now. My most pressing problem is what I'm going to wear when I come to work for you, because I'm not going back to any of those shops."

"Madame Simone's behavior was beyond unacceptable. I just sent her an incredible amount of money to pay Miss Birmingham's bill, and finding out she and her staff treated you so shabbily today has annoyed me no small amount." He nodded. "We're going back there right this minute. You may rest assured that Madame Simone and her snooty helper will be extending you their most profuse apologies."

Clear horror settled in Harriet's eyes. "That's a dreadful idea. How about if I return the money you gave me—except what I used to pay for the steaks, of course—and then sew as fast as I can and try to pull together a few pieces that I think you'll find acceptable?"

"I don't expect you to work yourself to the bone in order to produce an acceptable wardrobe."

"Well, I'm not going back to Madame Simone's. There's only so much humiliation I'm willing to suffer in a single day."

Oliver watched her for a moment, unable to help but recognize that underneath her air of bravado was a hint of vulnerability. It affected him in a most peculiar way and had him stepping closer to her. He took her arm and tugged her into motion. "Fine, we won't visit Madame Simone's, or any of the other small shops, but we *will* secure you a new wardrobe."

"I don't need a new wardrobe, just a few pieces to see me through the short time we're going to spend out and about."

He tightened his fingers around her arm. "Would it be possible for you to just be quiet and go along with me? I assure you, your shopping experience will be quite different while you're in my company. I would think you'd try to relax that guard of yours and simply attempt to enjoy yourself. Most ladies I know love to shop."

"Most ladies you know aren't hat girls who get booted out into the street or threatened with arrest."

Seeing no advantage to addressing that disturbing bit of truth, he looked around and smiled. There it was, only a block away— a department store that was certain to have everything Harriet needed. He began walking faster.

"If you haven't noticed, you're beginning to drag me," Harriet complained. "And why are we walking? Isn't your carriage around here somewhere?"

"I almost forgot about my carriage." He turned them around and began heading the other way. "I'll tell Darren where we'll be, and *then* we'll begin our shopping adventure."

It took a good five minutes to reach his carriage because Harriet kept dragging her feet. He glanced up at Darren as he let go of Harriet's arm, having no choice in the matter because she'd begun to wrestle her way out of his hold. "Miss Peabody and I are going to visit Arnold Constable & Company, Darren. I expect it'll take a good few hours to get Miss Peabody all she needs, and I would hate for you to miss your lunch. Why don't you park the carriage in front of the store and go get yourself something to eat?"

Instead of nodding in agreement, Darren shook his head and grinned. "Forgive me, Mr. Addleshaw, but I don't think Miss Peabody is exactly keen about going to Arnold Constable & Company."

"Why would you say that?"

"She's dashing away in the opposite direction."

Oliver turned, and sure enough, Harriet was quickly disappearing into the crowd, her huge hat once again bobbing in the breeze.

She was exasperating, annoying, and continuously causing

him to move at a pace he was unaccustomed to moving as he kept having to dash after her.

"Just meet me at Arnold Constable's," he called to Darren as he began to jostle his way through the crowded sidewalk. He increased his pace but then smiled when a swish of an ice-blue skirt through a doorway captured his attention. Strolling a moment later into a small shop that sold unmentionables, he set his sights on Harriet, who was already at the very back of the shop, pretending an interest in what appeared to be bustles. He stalked over to join her.

"You're trying my patience."

"I could say the same of you," she retorted without lifting her gaze. "Did I mention that I'm attempting to create a new bustle, one that would fold up when a lady sits down and then spring back to position once she stands up?"

"No, you didn't, and that has nothing to do with . . . A collapsible bustle, did you say?"

"Indeed, but so far I haven't been able to develop a spring that will actually work."

Even though he was highly intrigued with the idea, he pushed it aside and sent her what he could only hope was a formidable glare. To his annoyance, it didn't have any effect on her whatsoever, probably because she still wasn't looking at him.

"Why did you run away?" he asked.

"I can't go to Arnold Constable & Company."

"Why not?"

"Because it's too . . . too . . . everything."

"It's one of the leading department stores in New York."

"Exactly. That store caters to the elite. Why, I've heard the Vanderbilt family shops there, and the Astor family, and the list goes on and on. Your mother probably shops there."

"She does, frequently at that, which is how I know they'll have everything you need, all under one roof. Quite frankly,

I'm a little confused as to why you didn't start at department stores in the first place."

"Because, again, they draw in elite crowds."

"Madame Simone is one of the leading designers in the city, and yet you went to her shop."

"I thought I would be less conspicuous there, since there wouldn't be as many ladies roaming around."

"You think entirely too much," he said before he took hold of her arm again, and with quite a bit of prodding on his part, finally got her out of the unmentionables shop and back on the sidewalk.

"I'll embarrass you," she finally whispered.

"You won't," he said softly. "You're now, for all intents and purposes, a lady I hold in deepest affection. Once you show up at Arnold Constable & Company on my arm, you'll be treated like a princess, but you need to trust me."

She stopped moving, but since he wasn't willing to stand for another hour on the sidewalk, he prodded her forward, not speaking until they reached the department store—where he found he couldn't actually make her walk up the steps.

For a wisp of a lady, she really was incredibly strong—and . . . stubborn.

"I can't do it."

"You *can* do it. Just think about that shop you want to open and know that this is just something you have to do to attain your goal."

Harriet opened her mouth, looked as if she wanted to argue, but then pressed her lips together right before she nodded. "Very well, but do remember that this was *your* idea." She tightened her fingers around his arm and, with her feet dragging only a little, allowed him to escort her through the front door.

8

*T*error seized hold of Harriet and wouldn't let go as Oliver escorted her across the marble floor. He led her deeper into the bowels of Arnold Constable & Company, and with every step they took, her terror increased. Her mouth felt incredibly dry, her heart was racing, and when she looked up and saw not one but several glass chandeliers swaying from the ceiling, her stomach immediately turned queasy.

A strange ringing sounded in her ears when she glanced around the room and discovered a well-dressed lady staring in her direction, the scarf the woman had evidently been considering for purchase dangling forgotten in her hand. The lady caught Harriet's eye and sent her a nod, right before she imperiously summoned a gentleman wearing a dark suit to her side with the deliberate movement of a gloved hand. Harriet watched as the gentleman hurried over to the woman and bent his head as she began to whisper furiously in his ear.

Her queasiness increased. This was it—the die was cast. She'd been found out. How, she couldn't really say, but she knew she was about to be ejected from yet another store, no matter that

Oliver was standing by her side, practically propping her up now that her legs seemed to be giving out on her.

"You need to calm down," he said, placing a hand against the small of her back to steady her.

"That lady is staring at me," Harriet whispered.

Oliver squinted in the direction Harriet was looking, smiled at the lady and gentleman, who both smiled back, and then returned his attention to her. "Of course she's staring at you. You're wearing a very fashionable dress, paired with an unusual hat—but one that, I imagine, will soon be the hat to have in New York City. You're also beautiful, and . . . you're with me."

The ringing in her ears disappeared. "Beautiful?"

Oliver arched a brow. "Fishing for a compliment?"

"For some unfathomable reason, I find myself in desperate need of one right about now."

"Well then, I'll have to see what I can do about getting you more than one."

Bracing herself for whatever outlandish thing would soon come out of Oliver's mouth, Harriet wrinkled her nose when he simply smiled. But then she was distracted by the disturbing sight of the man in the formal suit making his way directly for them. Fresh terror kept her rooted to the spot—the only movement she seemed capable of making was to peek at Oliver out of the corner of her eye.

To her annoyance, even though Oliver clearly saw the man approaching them, he certainly didn't seem to realize the gravity of their situation. He was standing there, calm as could be—for all appearances a gentleman who was simply out for a bit of shopping, not a gentleman who was inappropriately escorting a hat girl through one of the most elite department stores of the day.

"Mr. Addleshaw," the gentleman exclaimed, "this is a pleasant surprise. We haven't seen you here in months, nor have I seen your mother."

"Mr. Lamansky, always a pleasure to see you as well," Oliver returned. "I'm afraid I've been out of town of late, and my parents are visiting India at the moment." He turned and gestured to Harriet. "May I introduce to you Miss—"

"Ah, you must be Miss Birmingham," Mr. Lamansky interrupted before Oliver had a chance to finish the introduction. Mr. Lamansky's smile dimmed for a second before he hitched it back into place. "I've heard *wonderful* things about you since you've arrived in our city. Tell me, how do you find the shopping?"

Before Harriet could get so much as a single sputter past her lips, Oliver took a firm hold of her arm. "This lady," he began, "is *not* Miss Birmingham, but Miss Peabody."

Mr. Lamansky's eyes went wide. "Oh, forgive me. I assumed she was your fiancée. I must admit I imparted the wrong information to Mrs. Gould when she begged me to come ask you who designed Miss, ah, Peabody's dress." He sent her an expectant arch of a brow.

"Er . . . " was all Harriet could think to respond.

"This is one of Miss Peabody's own designs," Oliver said, coming to her rescue when she continued struggling for words.

The look Mr. Lamansky sent her had Harriet wishing a large hole would open up right in front of her feet, or better yet, that a train would suddenly go rushing through the store, at which time she'd fling herself in front of it and be done with this nonsense once and for all.

"Begging your pardon, Mr. Addleshaw," Mr. Lamansky said in a lowered voice as he stepped closer to Oliver. "Do you think it wise to bring Miss Peabody, a dress designer by the sound of things, into this particular store? Surely you must realize that my customers are bound to take note of her, and I'm certain they'll make mention of it to Miss Birmingham."

Oliver's hand tightened on her arm, and with that tightening, she felt him stiffen. His eyes turned hard, the vein began throbbing on his forehead, and he looked downright menacing, even with all but one of the buttons missing on his jacket and his hair untidy from chasing her through the streets.

Why hadn't she suggested he fix his hair?

A bubble of hysterical laughter caught in her throat, and she struggled to hold it in, but the urge to laugh disappeared completely when Oliver began to speak.

"I fear there are numerous misconceptions floating around the city," he drawled, the measured tone of his voice causing Mr. Lamansky's face to pale. "First of all, I'm not engaged to Miss Birmingham, no matter the rumors you might have heard."

"Not . . . engaged . . . ?"

"No, not to Miss Birmingham, but I am engaged." He turned to Harriet and sent her a smile that was so surprisingly sweet she felt the unusual urge to dissolve into a puddle of blubbering incoherency right at his feet—until she remembered the pesky little notion that Oliver seemed to have an entire arsenal of smiles at his disposal, which he apparently brought out as needed. "Allow me to start again." He inclined his head at Mr. Lamansky. "I would like to introduce you to my fiancée, Miss Peabody. Miss Peabody, this is Mr. Lamansky, one of the managers here. I'm quite certain he's going to do everything within his power to provide you with a shopping experience you'll never forget."

"Your . . . fiancée?" Mr. Lamansky whispered.

"Exactly right, Mr. Lamansky, and do feel free to tell Mrs. Gould that my fiancée designed her dress. In fact, tell her Miss Peabody is soon to open up her own design shop here in town. You may assure her we'll send her the shop's location once it's officially open."

"Your fiancée is going to run a shop?"

Oliver let out a chuckle. "My Harriet is quite the independent lady. Why, the only way I could convince her to marry me was to agree to allow her to continue on with her pursuit of becoming one of the most sought-after designers in New York."

Harriet's mouth dropped open. She had no intention of opening a shop that catered to the elite, so . . . why would he say that . . . *and* . . . why in the world would he have proclaimed to this gentleman that she was his fiancée? She was only supposed to be posing as his social companion, and now, well, this was certainly going to open up a whole can of worms.

Unfortunately, Oliver didn't seem to understand the ramifications of what he'd just so blithely announced. Instead of panic clouding his eyes, there was a strange gleam of intensity, but what that intensity meant . . .

"I'm going to be backing my fiancée's venture, and I must say, she's incredibly talented. I fully expect her shop to become a place where all the ladies go to seek out original designs."

In the blink of an eye, everything became crystal clear. Oliver was a businessman forever on the lookout for opportunities that might be profitable or pique his interest. He'd apparently, during the midst of the nonsense unfolding around them, decided he wanted to partner with her on her plan to open up a shop. The problem with that decision, however, was that she had no desire to wait on the wealthy. She wanted to help ladies who were much like herself—ladies who had limited funds but still possessed a keen sense of style.

"Now then," Oliver said briskly, "we're here today to secure a new wardrobe for my darling, and I'm hopeful she'll be able to find everything she desires under this one roof. She's been much too busy of late to design clothing for herself, which is why I suggested we come here to secure everything she needs." He sent Harriet a look she assumed was supposed to be one of indulgence, but she couldn't help but notice a distinct trace of amusement lurking in his eyes.

She blinked and then blinked again. She hadn't expected that Oliver Addleshaw might have a sense of humor.

Mr. Lamansky cleared his throat. "Did you say an entirely new wardrobe?"

"I'm not certain I used the word *entirely*, but I do believe that might be exactly what my fiancée needs."

Before Harriet had a moment to breathe, let alone think, she was ushered into one of Arnold Constable & Company's private rooms and helped into a cushy chair. Handing her tea in a bone china cup, Mr. Lamansky smiled a very satisfied smile.

"I'll send in ladies to assist you immediately," he said before extending her a short bow and quitting the room.

The second the door shut behind the man, Harriet set aside her tea and turned to Oliver, who was lowering himself into a chair right beside her. "What have you done?"

Oliver picked up his cup, took a sip, grimaced, and set it right back down. "Have I ever told you I loathe tea?"

"I don't believe that has ever come up in the few conversations we've had, but honestly, Oliver, what were you thinking telling Mr. Lamansky I'm your fiancée? That wasn't part of our deal."

"I didn't appreciate the man's attitude toward you."

His response took her by complete surprise and had tears stinging her eyes. There'd never been a time in her life when a gentleman had come to her defense, and she was suddenly thankful she was sitting down. Otherwise, she was fairly sure she'd be unable to stand, given that her entire body felt somewhat like jelly. She swiped a hand over her eyes and, when she was certain she wasn't about to turn into a watering pot, looked back at Oliver. "I do appreciate you putting that man in his place, but surely you realize this latest turn of insanity is going to cause both of us no small amount of difficulty."

Oliver shrugged. "Telling him we are engaged was a means

to an end, and you have to admit it was better than what I first thought about doing, which was pummeling the man."

"Pummeling might have been the lesser of the two evils. We'd surely have been shown the door, but we wouldn't now be engaged."

"Harriet," Oliver began slowly, "you do realize that we're not *truly* engaged, don't you?"

Rolling her eyes, Harriet picked up her tea and took a sip. "There's no need to get nervous, Oliver. Of course I know we're not truly engaged. What we are is worse—we're liars."

"Shall I assume you have a problem with that?"

"I don't like to lie, nor do I believe God approves of people who do, and this—our pretend engagement—feels pretty much like a spectacular lie to me."

Oliver frowned. "I find myself somewhat confused with your reasoning. How was it that agreeing to pose as my companion wasn't a lie, while posing as my fiancée is one?"

Harriet regarded Oliver over the rim of her cup. "It's funny you should bring that up, because I was actually discussing that very idea with my friends last night. It was bothering me somewhat dreadfully, but then Miss Longfellow, one of my roommates, pointed out that she has occasionally taken positions as a paid companion. She received compensation for that role, and even though those positions never worked out well for her, they were completely respectable positions for a lady to take. So, you see, there was absolutely nothing in the least shady about me agreeing to be your paid companion."

"Forgive me for bringing this up, but paid companions are normally hired by ladies in their dotage, something I'm clearly not."

"True, but it's the same principle. You've hired me to be a companion, even if not exactly in the same role as most paid companions take on. Now, however, with your declaration that

I'm your fiancée, you are asking me to live a lie, plain and simple, because we're not engaged."

Oliver tilted his head. "Would it make you feel better if I got down on bended knee and asked you to be my pretend fiancée?"

An image of Oliver on bended knee immediately sprang to mind. Something warm and mushy began to travel through her, until she staunchly pushed the mushiness aside. No good could possibly come from dwelling on fantasies, and it wasn't as if Oliver had offered to really propose to her, given the whole *pretend* business. Besides, she was quite certain she didn't even like the gentleman, so . . . what could possibly have brought about the whole mushy feeling?

"Harriet, is something the matter?"

Taking another sip of tea to allow herself time to collect her composure, Harriet swallowed and quirked a brow. "Of course nothing's the matter—except that you've just announced our engagement to a man I'm fairly sure is even now spreading the word."

"And you're still bothered by the idea we're perpetuating a lie?"

"We *are* perpetuating a lie."

"I disagree. As you mentioned before, I've hired you to play a part, whether companion or fiancée, and that's how you need to look at it. You should think of yourself as an actress, someone who assumes different roles with every new script. You don't believe actresses are perpetuating a lie every time they take to the stage, do you?"

"Of course not, and speaking of actresses, don't you think it would have made matters less complicated if you'd just hired one of them?"

"Actresses are hardly respectable."

"Neither are ladies who make hats for a living—at least not in your world."

119

"You no longer make hats for a living."

"As I think I mentioned before, you're very annoying."

"And you really should remember it's not advisable to insult your employer."

Harriet brightened. "That's exactly the reason we can use to dissolve this pretend engagement. You can tell Mr. Lamansky that you and I have had a terrible row, brought about because I have the unfortunate habit of insulting you."

"You're reaching now, Harriet, and no, I won't be doing any such thing. You and I have an agreement, one that will benefit both of us."

Throwing up her hands in defeat, Harriet blew out a breath. "Fine, you win. I suppose I'll just have to appease my conscience with the idea that I can now add actress to the list of positions I've held."

"You don't have to sound so sulky about it."

Waving the comment aside, Harriet frowned. "Why did you tell Mr. Lamansky that I'm opening up my own shop? *And* why did you tell him to tell that Mrs. Gould you were going to send her my direction once my shop was ready to do business?"

Oliver settled back in his chair and pulled the edges of his open jacket over his trim stomach. "Mrs. Gould is the wife of Mr. Jay Gould, and he's incredibly wealthy. He owns over ten thousand miles of railroad lines, and rumor has it he's recently started investing heavily in the El. If you can garner the attention of someone like Mrs. Gould, you'll have more orders than you'll be able to fill." His smile faded. "We might need to develop a plan for you to bring on other seamstresses and figure out how much you can pay them based on projected profits."

Harriet's head suddenly felt as if it might explode. "While that's an interesting idea, I have to tell you that I have no plans to . . ." A soft knock on the door interrupted Harriet's speech. She watched as the door opened and five ladies, all dressed in pristine white blouses with navy skirts, waltzed into the room, their arms filled with what looked to be magazines.

"Ah, perfect timing," Oliver said as he got to his feet. He sent the ladies a smile and walked to the other side of the room. Taking a seat in a chair situated under a window, he plucked a newspaper from a basket at his feet and snapped it open. "Do try and enjoy yourself, darling," he said right before he disappeared behind the paper.

"Don't you want a say in what I select?" she asked.

Oliver peered at her from over the top of the paper. "I'm sure you know exactly what you want, and . . . your sense of fashion is probably keener than mine."

Harriet watched him disappear again, feeling a touch off-balance. He was a very complicated man, one she didn't understand in the least. Dragging her attention away from him when the ladies began introducing themselves to her, Harriet soon found herself buried under fashion plates and fabric swatches. Before she knew it, clothing was being hauled into the room at a rapid rate, followed by shoes, gloves, hats, undergarments, and reticules.

To her amazement, once she began trying everything on, the ladies fawned over each outfit, extending her outrageous compliments with every change of clothing.

Oliver, it seemed, had known exactly what he was promising when he'd told her he would see about getting her more than one compliment.

"Ah, that is simply delightful on you," a lady she thought was named Edie gushed when Harriet stepped out from behind a silk curtain and shook out the folds of a lovely yellow gown. "Mr. Addleshaw, doesn't Miss Peabody look enchanting in this particular shade of yellow?"

Oliver lowered the paper, his gaze traveled over her, and then something rather warm flickered through his eyes. "She does indeed."

His perusal left her flustered. Harriet felt heat travel from her toes, up her torso, to finally settle on her face. She'd never been a lady who blushed much, but ever since she'd met Oliver, she was doing so quite regularly. "Thank you," she managed to mumble.

Oliver gestured to another gown. "I'd like to see that one on her next."

Harriet glanced at the gown he was gesturing to and frowned. "That one seems rather formal."

"Which means it'll be perfect for you to wear to the opera."

"I wasn't aware we were going to the opera."

Oliver smiled. "Well, we are, and that means you'll need something new and pretty to wear." He nodded to Edie. "I do so enjoy indulging my fiancée."

It took everything Harriet had in her to not roll her eyes. She was rapidly coming to the belief that Oliver was finding this situation vastly amusing, but she was beginning to think he was getting a touch carried away with the role he'd embraced. Before she could put her foot down once and for all, though, Edie smiled in obvious delight.

"How lovely to witness a gentleman so very fond of his fiancée and so eager to lavish presents on her," Edie exclaimed. "We here at Arnold Constable & Company are only too happy to oblige you with that lavishing." She clapped her hands. "Girls, we need to get Miss Peabody into this blue gown, and . . . yes, I think the gold one we have hanging in the designer salon that just arrived from Paris will be perfect with her hair." She nodded to Harriet. "I will get some of the garments that don't need alterations packaged up for you, if you are ready to decide on which ones you'd like to purchase?"

"We'll take all of them," Oliver said before Harriet could speak.

Apparently, Oliver had lost his mind, much like he'd lost his buttons, probably right along the Ladies' Mile somewhere when he'd been chasing her down.

Sending Oliver what she hoped would be construed by the sales ladies surrounding her as a loving smile, Harriet then turned to Edie. "Would it be possible for me to speak with my . . . er . . . fiancé . . . alone?"

"But of course, Miss Peabody," Edie said, nodding to the other ladies. "Girls, they need the room."

Just like that, the room emptied, and picking up her skirt, Harriet marched over to stand in front of Oliver. Leaning down, she lowered her voice, not wanting to be overheard but knowing perfectly well that Edie and the rest of the ladies were probably pressing their ears up against the door.

"You were more than generous with the allowance you gave me to purchase clothing, but I have to tell you, I don't think it was enough to cover all of this." She straightened and waved a hand to the shoes, hats, and gowns littering the room. "I think we should choose three or four items from the bunch and call it a day."

"Do you now?" Oliver sent her an odd smile before he rose from the chair and strode to the door. He reached for the knob, pulled the door open, and two of the sales ladies tumbled into the room, landing in a heap at his feet, while the rest of the ladies stood in the doorframe, attempting to look innocent.

Oliver didn't bat an eye as he helped the ladies up and then smiled at them, causing a few of them to sigh and flutter their lashes. "We'll take everything here, and I'll thank you to put it on my account." He turned to Harriet. "I'm off to wander around the store, but I'll be back to pick you up in an hour." With that, Oliver nodded to the ladies and left the room.

9

Two hours later, Harriet dipped a spoon into a rapidly melting mound of ice cream, plopped it into her mouth, and couldn't quite stifle the moan of delight that slipped past her lips. Allowing herself a moment to savor the treat on her tongue, she finally swallowed and moved her spoon toward the bowl to get another bite. She paused when she realized Oliver wasn't eating his ice cream, but was watching her instead.

"Do you like it?" he asked.

"It's the most delicious treat I've ever had."

Oliver frowned and leaned across the small table they were sharing at Davis and George's ice cream parlor. "Haven't you ever had ice cream?"

"Well, I have now."

Something that looked remarkably like pity flickered through his eyes. "I'm sorry, Harriet. No one should have to wait until they're over twenty to experience ice cream."

She lifted her chin. "There's no need to feel sorry for me, Oliver. Yes, I've lived a completely different life than you have, but I've never once bemoaned the fact I've missed out on ice cream. One cannot miss what one has never experienced."

He looked at her for a long moment. "Fair enough."

"That's it? You're not going to try and pull other unfortunate events from my past out of me?"

"Do you want to talk about unfortunate events?"

"Not particularly."

"Wonderful. We should talk about the opera instead and when you'd like to go. I'm of the belief that Monday is the night to see opera, since that's when the largest number of society members go, and then—if we were actually in the midst of the social season—we'd travel on to a ball, which I'm sure you'd enjoy tremendously."

"If I *were* actually a society member, I'm sure I *would* enjoy a ball. However, I'm not, so instead of talking opera and balls, we should talk about what you were thinking, buying me so many clothes."

He licked a drop of ice cream off his spoon. "I'd rather talk about the opera. Do you enjoy it?"

"Of course I enjoy opera, and yes, I have been fortunate enough to attend the opera numerous times. Miss Plum, one of the ladies who shares rooms with me, is often given tickets to different shows around the city."

Oliver set his spoon down. "I thought you lived with your grandmother."

"Why in the world . . . ? Ah . . . your driver."

"Darren told me that when he saw you home yesterday, your grandmother was waiting for you on the stoop."

"I didn't tell Darren Mrs. Palmer was my grandmother. He simply assumed that, probably to alleviate the guilt he seemed to feel over dropping me off at what he felt was a questionable location."

"So Mrs. Palmer isn't your grandmother?"

"No, she owns the boardinghouse, and I do believe she jumped to a few unpleasant conclusions when she got a look at your fancy carriage."

"Why do you believe that?"

"Because she literally ran over to the church I attend and told Reverend Gilmore. He arrived at my door soon after he spoke with her, and as I mentioned before, you may expect a visit from him sometime in the near future."

"Is this Reverend Gilmore a relative of yours?"

"No, he's simply a friend, but one who believes it's his job to watch out for my well-being and reputation." She trailed her spoon through the last remnants of her ice cream. "I'm not exactly certain how he plans on doing that, but you should be forewarned."

"That's a touch . . ." Oliver stopped talking and leaned forward until he was only inches away from her face. She could feel his breath tease her cheek, and that had her pulse hitching up a notch, but it slowed considerably when his brows drew together. "This Miss Plum you live with—she wouldn't happen to be Miss Lucetta Plum, would she?"

"She is."

His brows drew closer together. "You never told me you live with an actress."

"You never asked. But just so we're crystal clear, Lucetta is completely respectable."

"She's an actress, and I've heard otherwise."

Temper began to sizzle through her body. "You should know better than to listen to gossip."

"Has Miss Plum ever mentioned Mr. Silas Ruff?"

"Of course."

"And yet you have the audacity to tell me she's respectable?"

If anything, her temper boiled hotter. "I don't know what this Mr. Ruff has told you, but Lucetta can't abide the gentleman."

"Really?"

"Indeed," Harriet snapped before she went to take another bite of her ice cream and realized the bowl was empty. She looked at it longingly for a second and then folded her hands in her lap.

"Would you care for another?"

"Certainly not," she said, wincing when she detected a clear trace of snippiness in her tone. She cleared her throat. "Although I did enjoy that tremendously. It was very kind of you to provide me with such a treat."

"*Kind* is my middle name."

"I don't think I'd go that far."

To her surprise, Oliver laughed. "Yes, well, perhaps you're right. Since it appears we're not meant to agree about actresses and their respectability, tell me, did you have fun shopping today?"

Deciding it would be less than gracious to continue being annoyed with the man, Harriet smiled. "I really can't recall a day I've enjoyed more, although, I do feel horribly guilty about the money you spent on me."

Oliver shrugged. "There's no reason for you to feel guilty, especially since it was my idea in the first place." He set his napkin on the table and pushed back his chair. "If you're certain you don't want more ice cream, shall we get on our way?"

Harriet bit her lip. "Do forgive me, Oliver. I've been keeping you from your work, haven't I?" Struggling to get out of her chair, she found Oliver by her side a second later. He helped her up with one hand, while with the other he slid her chair effortlessly out of her way.

She refused to sigh as she got to her feet. There was something to be said about a fine-looking gentleman paying a lady special attention.

Her knees turned weak when Oliver took hold of her arm, until she realized how completely ridiculously she was behaving. They had a business arrangement, nothing more, and she needed to remember that.

"There's no reason for you to apologize for taking up my time," Oliver said as he began steering her around the many tables and toward the door. "It's been a lovely day, and I've enjoyed your company. It's not often I'm given a chance to speak with a pretty lady and not have to fear her father will come charging at me with a marriage proposal in mind."

"That's because we're already engaged," she said with a grin, earning a grin from him in return.

That grin sent trepidation cascading over her. He was far too attractive when he grinned, *and* when he casually mentioned how pretty she was and how he enjoyed her company. It was going to be next to impossible to keep her feet firmly settled on the ground if he continued in such a way, and . . . She stumbled as a realization struck her hard.

She'd made a huge mistake.

She'd agreed to be at Oliver's beck and call to earn the funds he'd offered, but not once had she considered that she just might become attracted to the man.

She needed to back out of their deal. She needed to . . . Her thoughts stopped midstream when she suddenly noticed that each and every patron in the parlor was looking at her. She sucked in a deep breath and didn't—or rather couldn't—release it until they walked out the door and reached the sidewalk.

"Is something wrong? You're beginning to turn blue."

Gulping in a breath of air, she knew that everything was wrong, but she certainly couldn't explain that to Oliver. What would he think if he learned she found him attractive? Would he take it in stride, or might he not like it at all and stop talking to her, or . . . She gulped in another huge breath of air, blew it out with one loud huff, and finally remembered he'd asked her a question. "Everyone was watching us leave, and it made me . . ."

"Stop breathing?"

"I always forget to breathe when I get nervous."

"I suppose you should be thankful then that you don't appear to be the type to get nervous often, but I must tell you—you'll have to get used to people watching you, because watch you they shall once they take note of you on my arm."

The panic came from out of nowhere as she finally fully realized what she'd signed up for. It was quite ridiculous to think she'd be able to mingle with Oliver's peers.

"I don't think that's going to be possible," she finally managed to say.

"Then you're going to have an uncomfortable few weeks, because people always watch me."

She slowed her steps. "Do they really?"

"I'm a very wealthy man, Harriet—with that comes attention."

"I loathe attention."

"I'm not exactly thrilled with it all the time, but it's the price demanded of a gentleman of my social and business status." He smiled. "But uncomfortable notions aside, would you care to take a short stroll before we return to the carriage, or do you need to get back to your home?"

"Don't *you* need to get back to business?"

"Strangely enough, I'm in no mood for business today."

"Why do I have the feeling that's a first for you?" Harriet asked before her attention was suddenly drawn to a small girl peddling flowers. "Good heavens, there's little Clarice, but . . . where's her mother?" Propelling Oliver into motion, she hurried over to Clarice. "Hello, darling."

Clarice's small face lit up, and she grinned at Harriet, showing a huge gap between her front teeth in the process. "Miss Peabody, what are you doing in such a fancy place and with . . ." Her nose wrinkled, and she stopped speaking as she gawked at Oliver.

"I had some shopping to do, but tell me, where is your mother?"

"She's home with my baby brother. Donnie isn't feeling well today, so Mama couldn't leave him with Mrs. Golhem, the lady that takes care of us." She puffed out her little chest. "I told her I was big enough to sell the flowers, and since we won't have milk if . . ." Her voice trailed off, and she began scuffing her battered shoe in the dirt.

"I was just telling Mr. Addleshaw how I adore flowers," she said, catching Oliver's eye. "Doesn't Clarice have some lovely flowers today?"

Oliver, to her extreme disappointment, looked at the basket of flowers Clarice was holding and frowned. "They look wilted, and I—"

She stomped on his foot.

"Ouch, you stomped on my foot."

"And I'll do the same to the other one if you don't . . ." She nodded at Clarice, who wasn't looking at either one of them but was staring at the puffs of dirt her scuffing was making.

Oliver blinked. "Oh, yes, quite right. You'd like me to buy you a flower." He reached into his pocket and pulled out his billfold. "How much."

Clarice held up five fingers.

"You expect me to pay five dollars for a wilted flower?"

Harriet stomped on his other foot and gave his arm a forceful squeeze for good measure. "It's *cents*, Oliver, five cents." She dropped her hold on him and squatted down next to Clarice, opening her reticule as she did so. She took out five dollars, pressed them into Clarice's little hand and gave the child a kiss on her forehead. "You take that back to your mama now, darling, and you can tell her you sold all of your lovely flowers."

"It's too much money," Clarice whispered.

"No, it's not," Harriet said firmly, rising to her feet and taking all the wilted flowers out of Clarice's basket. "Tell your mama I hope Donnie gets better soon." She narrowed her eyes at Oliver, turned on her heel, and began marching down the sidewalk, hoping the man wouldn't feel compelled to follow. Unfortunately, it quickly became clear he didn't take kindly to being dismissed, because he caught up with her a few seconds later.

"You're upset," he said as he fell into step beside her.

"And you're a genius."

"That wasn't well done of me, was it?"

Harriet stopped in her tracks. "No, it wasn't. Clarice is just a child, Oliver, with a sick baby brother at home, whom I know her mother can't take to a doctor because they can't afford it. I find it vastly disturbing to learn you don't have so much as an ounce of compassion for those less fortunate than you."

"I've never really taken notice of street vendors before or contemplated their plight in life," he admitted slowly.

Harriet gestured around. "Then open your eyes. Look at all of these people just trying to scrape by. See that woman over there selling apples? Her name's Martha and she once gave me an apple when I was practically starving to death right after I found myself on my own. She takes care of an elderly relative, and all the money she has in the world is earned by selling apples or whatever else she can manage to beg from the fine restaurants that are going to throw out the produce that's less than perfect." She pointed to a man pushing a cart. "That's Herman, and he sells sandwiches out of that cart—sandwiches, I might add, that are the best I've ever tasted."

Oliver stepped closer to her. "You think I'm a snob."

"You are a snob."

Watching Oliver's face darken, Harriet thought he was going to start yelling, but then, to her surprise, he took her by the arm and began to escort her from one street vendor to another.

Fifteen minutes later, with her arms filled with a variety of goods, from Martha's apples, to Herman's sandwiches, and even a few beaded bracelets a blind woman had been selling, Harriet was feeling a little more charitable toward the man. He'd obviously been very uncomfortable at first, interacting with the people hawking their wares, but then, once they'd reached Herman's cart, something had changed. Herman had whipped him up a special sandwich, and after the first bite and a very loud groan of appreciation, Oliver took to chatting with the man, asking him everything from where he got his ingredients to what type of traffic he saw on a daily basis. When Herman finally told them he needed to go find other customers, Oliver had given the man an outrageous tip and told him he'd be sure to tell all of his business associates, as well as family and friends, to come try Herman's food.

Harriet's opinion of Oliver had grown the longer she'd watched him with Herman, something that bothered her no small amount. She'd already come to the unwelcome realization that she was somewhat attracted to the man, but discovering he *did* have a compassionate side—even though that side had been buried deep within him—left her . . . bothered.

"You were right, Harriet. Herman does make a great sandwich," Oliver said, steering her over to an empty bench and sitting down beside her. "I wonder if he'd be interested in opening up a shop."

"Do you ever think of anything other than business?"

"Of course I do."

Taking a bite of the apple they'd gotten from Martha, she tilted her head. "Like what?"

"Ahh . . . well . . ."

"Do you have any hobbies?"

"Hobbies?"

"What do you like to do when you're not working—besides going to the opera, that is?"

"I like sailing. Does that count as a hobby?"

132

"Indeed it does, if you sail on a frequent basis."

"Define *frequent*."

"I don't know—a few times a month, I suppose, when the weather permits?"

Oliver shook his head. "It's not a hobby, then."

"But you enjoy being out on the water?"

"I do, in fact I was thinking about joining the Yacht Club, but I haven't had the time lately."

She suddenly felt a little light-headed. "Don't tell me you own your very own yacht?"

"Are you going to call me a snob again if I admit I do?"

"Probably."

"Fair enough, as long as you don't start stomping on my feet again, but yes, I do have my own yacht. She's a beauty."

"But you rarely get to go out on her, even though you enjoy it?"

"I enjoy making money."

"There are other things in life besides making money."

"Not from what I've seen."

She considered him for a moment. "No, I imagine you haven't noticed other things, but . . . speaking of money, I need to give you back the money you gave me yesterday since you put all those purchases on your account." She reached for her reticule.

"Keep it. You can consider it a bonus for having to deal with Miss Birmingham and all of her nastiness."

"I most certainly will not. You'll hardly manage to obtain your goal of collecting obscene wealth if you continue handing out money in such a cavalier fashion."

"Are you trying to lecture me?"

"Someone has to be the voice of reason here."

Oliver leaned closer and stared at her as if he didn't quite know what to make of her. For one of the first times since she'd met him, Harriet felt completely in accord with the gentleman, because she didn't know what to make of him either.

He was a snob, but there was something more to him . . . something she didn't think even he'd figured out.

Time seemed to stop as the crowd around them faded away and the only thing in the world for Harriet at that moment was Oliver's face.

It was an interesting face, one she knew full well could turn intimidating in a split second, but it wasn't intimidating right now, it was . . . confused and compelling all at the same time, and . . . He was one of the most sought-after gentlemen in the country, and yet he was nothing like what she'd expected.

He was kind, in a blustery and peculiar way, and he was overly generous—something that seemed to take *him* by surprise—and he was all too attractive, even in an ill-fitting jacket with almost all the buttons missing, and . . .

"Harriet, yoo-hoo. Harriet Peabody, over here."

Switching her attention from Oliver to the two women waving madly at her from the other side of the street, Harriet smiled as she lifted a hand and waved back. "It's Ginger and Tawny. Why I haven't—" Her words came to an abrupt end when Oliver suddenly stood up, took her by the arm, and began pulling her down the sidewalk in the opposite direction of the women who were calling out to her.

She shook out of his hold. "Have you lost your mind? Those are friends of mine, and I certainly don't like being handled in such a way."

"You have no business having friends like that, and since they're now running our way, we need to get to the carriage immediately."

Ignoring him, Harriet turned and discovered that Ginger and Tawny were, indeed, running toward her, their speed causing the feathery scarfs wrapped around their throats to flutter behind them.

"Do not even *think* about talking to them again," Oliver growled.

Stiffening, she lifted her chin and spun around, knowing full well as she headed toward Ginger and Tawny that her time with Oliver was about to come to a rapid end.

10

*L*urching to the left when the carriage jostled over a
rut, Oliver pushed himself upright and resumed the
business of watching Harriet.

She was sitting on the seat opposite him, looking out the
window, her usually expressive face devoid of emotion. She
hadn't spoken a single word since she'd parted ways with the
two ladies, not even when he'd practically dragged her back to
his waiting carriage and hustled her inside it. They were now
heading for Harriet's home, and disappointment warred with
anger the longer Oliver contemplated the situation he'd recently
witnessed in the middle of the street.

What could she have been thinking?

People had been told she was his fiancée, and those people,
as in the staff at Arnold Constable & Company, were probably
even now spreading the word. Because of that, Harriet should
have been aware that there was expected behavior she needed to
display in public at all times. She certainly should have known
it was beyond unacceptable to acknowledge undesirable women
who called to her in the middle of the Ladies' Mile.

It was obvious the ladies were of the demimonde—which

begged the question of how Harriet had come to be acquainted with them.

Seeing her chat so easily with the ladies had shaken him to his very core. It had also caused him to realize that he'd made one of the biggest mistakes of his life, greater even than that of forming an alliance with Miss Birmingham.

It wasn't like him in the least to behave so irresponsibly, and now . . . well, he was going to have to rectify the problem once and for all—before his reputation suffered irreparable harm.

His family was known throughout the city as Knickerbockers, or *Old New York* as they preferred to consider themselves, even though Oliver found the Knickerbocker title somewhat amusing. They were the elite of the elite, their ancestors having gained great social status through birth, accumulated wealth and land, and from being some of the first people to colonize New York, back when it had been called New Amsterdam. He and his family were included as members of the New York Four Hundred, a mysterious list Mr. Ward McAllister, one of the social arbiters of the day, had come up with, even though that particular list had never been formally published. But, published or not, he certainly wasn't anxious to be the one in his family to get them kicked off that illustrious list.

Clearing his throat, he felt his head begin to throb when Harriet refused to look his way.

"We need to discuss what happened," he began, frowning when Harriet, instead of turning her head to face him, lifted a gloved hand and began drawing a circle through the film of mist that coated the window.

"You could have caused me all sorts of unpleasant embarrassment if any of my friends had gotten a glimpse of you speaking with those women and then seen you with me."

Harriet's finger stilled for just a second, but then she continued with her tracing, adding a half circle inside the larger circle.

"You do realize you should have ignored them, don't you?"

She leaned toward the glass and breathed against it, right before she resumed her tracing, this time adding what appeared to be two eyes.

"Those ladies were, at best, members of the demimonde."

Her tracing stopped, but she remained stubbornly silent.

Irritation began to trickle through him. "Exactly how did you come to be acquainted, let alone friends, with ladies of ill-repute?"

Harriet turned her head ever so slowly and pinned him with a stare bright with fury. "I'd like to get out of the carriage now."

"We haven't finished our discussion."

"I'm fairly sure we have." Harriet reached for the door handle, and then, before he had the presence of mind to stop her, jumped out and disappeared from sight.

"Harriet!" he bellowed as he launched himself after her, grunting when he slipped and hit the hard stone street with his shoulder and then rolled to the right, narrowly missing the wheel of his own carriage. His hand slid through something squishy before he pushed himself to his feet. Panic seized him as he tried to locate Harriet, expecting to discover her lifeless body under one of the many wheels trundling around him. To his relief—and concern—there was no sign of the lady, mangled or whole.

"She went that way, Mr. Addleshaw," Darren called, gesturing up ahead before he pulled on the reins and steered the horses to the side of the street.

Oliver nodded and dodged a carriage that was heading his way, waving an apologetic hand at the driver, who was screaming at him. He took off for the sidewalk and darted through the crowd, disgruntlement replacing the panic as he ran.

How had Harriet, a lady—and one wearing a dress, no less— managed to land on her feet, while he, a gentleman in fine form, had barely managed to escape his plunge from the carriage with nothing more than a ruined jacket and bruised shoulder and backside?

She truly was a confounding sort, but . . . No, he couldn't allow himself to start thinking about things like that, especially since he knew the prudent step to take, once he caught up with the exasperating lady, was to end matters quickly, before disaster had a chance to fall. But . . . why was he even bothering to chase her? She'd made it clear by leaping out of his carriage that she wanted nothing further to do with him, and yet, here he was, sweat beginning to dribble into his eyes, charging after a lady who was doing her very best to escape him.

It was enough to boggle a gentleman's mind and did have his feet slowing, until he glanced around and noticed he was in a less than respectable part of the city. The very idea of Harriet left to her own devices in such a derelict atmosphere had him picking up his pace. Angling around a gathering of elderly gentlemen, he raised his hand to tip his hat at some careworn-looking ladies staring at him with open mouths, but realized that somewhere along the way he'd lost his hat, most likely when he'd jumped from the carriage.

His head began throbbing harder than ever.

He'd liked that hat—it'd been one of his favorites—and now, because of Harriet and her impetuous nature, he'd have to buy another.

A burst of bright color captured his attention, and he realized the color came from Harriet's hat, a hat she'd been able to retain in her mad leap from the carriage. He broke into a run but then slowed to a mere stalk when Harriet stopped in her tracks and stood on the edge of the sidewalk while people jostled around her, her attention fixed on something he couldn't see. She spun on her heel and headed back in his direction, stopping yet again when she caught sight of him.

She muttered something he couldn't hear because of the distance that separated them and then plowed forward, waving a dainty hand in his direction as she sailed past him.

"Go away."

He caught up with her easily. "I promised to see you home, so see you home I shall."

"I wouldn't want you to get embarrassed if someone you know happens to see you in my company."

"I never said I was embarrassed to be seen with *you*."

An unladylike snort escaped her even as her pace increased.

"Harriet, please, we need to speak frankly."

She began walking faster, causing Oliver to break into a near run.

"Well, go on, then," she said with a slight pant lacing her words. "I'm listening."

"Can't you slow down?"

Harriet looked up and, to his surprise, stopped rather abruptly. Her eyes widened, and she spun around yet again and began heading back in the direction they'd just come.

He paused for just a moment, his gaze traveling over two large gentlemen striding his way, their attention seemingly on Harriet's rapidly retreating back. Oliver took off after Harriet and grabbed hold of her arm. "Are you in some type of trouble?"

"Why would you assume that?"

"What do those men want with you?"

"What men?"

"If I'm going to be able to help you, you have to tell me what's wrong."

"Who said anything's wrong?"

Oliver ran his hand through hair he knew had to be standing on end. What he really needed to do, instead of dealing with the madness of his life, was plan a nice, long holiday, well away from ladies and well away from drama.

"Do you remember when you told me you don't care for lies?" he finally asked.

"It wasn't that long ago, Oliver. Of course I remember."

"And you want me to believe you're telling the truth about not noticing those men following you?"

Harriet stumbled, righted herself, and continued forward. "Fine, maybe you're right. Maybe since I've made your acquaintance I've taken to lying on a regular basis, because agreeing to this ridiculous plan of yours is nothing *but* a lie, even though I keep trying to convince myself otherwise. It's become clear that we've made a huge mistake, and I, for one, believe God is surely punishing me, given the fact that . . ." Her voice trailed off as she came to another sudden stop, her attention riveted on a fancy carriage parked in front of a shabby four-storied building.

"I was hoping that would be gone by now," she muttered. She glanced over her shoulder, bit her lip, glanced to the fancy carriage, and then edged to the right—leaving Oliver no choice but to believe she was about to take off running down a rubbish-strewn alley.

"Harriet, you're going to have to tell me . . ."

"Miss Peabody, ah, there you are at last."

Harriet froze as a well-dressed and rather formidable-looking older lady suddenly appeared from behind the carriage and began marching their way.

Recognition set in, followed immediately by confusion.

"How do you know Mrs. Hart, and what do you think she's doing here?" he asked.

"I've never seen that lady before in my life."

"Then why is she calling you by name and heading our way?"

"I'm sure I have no idea."

Mrs. Charles Hart, one of the wealthiest yet most reclusive society matrons in all of New York, came to a stop directly in front of Harriet. Then, without a by your leave, she snatched

Harriet into her arms, gave her a good hard squeeze, and then released her, stepping back with a huge smile on her wrinkled face. "It is so fortunate you returned home at such an opportune time, my dear. Why, I'd almost given up hope of seeing you today. I fear I kept those delightful young ladies, Miss Longfellow and Miss Plum, at my mercy for quite some time as they were forced to entertain me while I awaited your return."

"I beg your pardon?" Harriet asked.

"Well, there's no need for that, my dear. It was hardly as if you were aware I planned to visit you today, so there's no reason to beg my pardon. I assure you, your friends kept me well amused, and the conversations we shared were downright riveting."

She patted Harriet's cheek, which had Harriet looking more confused than ever, but Mrs. Hart didn't appear to notice as she turned her attention to him. "Mr. Addleshaw, this is an un-expected, yet fortuitous, surprise. I was not aware you were to escort Harriet about today—which, I must add, was completely inappropriate—but . . . good heavens, what has happened to you? You have the smell of the barns about you, and the look as well, if I might be so bold to add, and . . ." Her gaze traveled down his length. "Are you aware you're missing almost all of your buttons?"

"I fear they fell off when I was, er, running."

"Ah, I see, well, not really, but I'm not surprised your buttons popped off. That jacket is ill-fitted. Do remind me before I take my leave to give you the direction of my late-husband's tailor. That man fits a gentleman's clothing to perfection, and I don't ever recall a time when my darling Charles ever lost his buttons."

Oliver blinked, his mind churning to come up with an ap-propriate response to that declaration, but he was spared any response at all when Mrs. Hart let out a *tsk* and shook her head. "Could it be possible you've done something to incur the displeasure of your tailor?"

"I don't believe so . . . but . . ."

"You might want to ask him, dear. A gentleman of your status certainly shouldn't traverse the city in anything less than the finest of clothing. That jacket you're currently sporting, even without the muck attached to it, does nothing to assure people you're a leader of the business world."

Mrs. Hart suddenly craned her neck and peered over his shoulder. "Oh look, I think that young man is bringing you back your hat."

Oliver turned and discovered Darren running up to join them, the remains of what used to be Oliver's favorite hat held somewhat gingerly between two of Darren's fingers.

"I'm not sure you're still going to want this, Mr. Addleshaw, but I rescued it from a puddle on the street, just in case you did," Darren said, holding out the hat. Oliver reluctantly took it, swallowing a sigh as its dismal state became apparent and another glob of slime oozed through his fingers.

"Thank you, Darren. Your thoughtfulness is much appreciated."

"Miss Peabody," another voice called, causing Oliver to switch his attention from Darren and settle it on an older lady who was scurrying off the stoop of the peeling brown house and hurrying toward them.

He wasn't certain, but he thought he heard Harriet release a groan right before a rather forced-looking smile tugged her lips. "Hello, Mrs. Palmer."

"My goodness but this is exciting!" Mrs. Palmer exclaimed, coming to a stop right in front of Harriet and looking everyone over with a sharp and speculative eye. "Why, here's the young man who brought you home just yesterday, and would you look at that? Not one but two fine carriages parked in front of my house." She raised expectant eyes to Harriet, whose smile dimmed ever so slightly.

"Yes, it is exciting, isn't it, and somewhat unexpected." Harriet drew in a breath and gestured to Darren, who stepped forward and presented Mrs. Palmer with a short bow. "Allow me to present to you Darren . . . ?"

"Thompson, Miss Peabody. I'm Darren Thompson."

"Thank you, Mr. Thompson," Harriet said, turning back to Mrs. Palmer. "This is Mr. Thompson, Mrs. Palmer, the young man who did indeed see me home yesterday."

Mrs. Palmer narrowed her eyes. "But you told me that he was not your suitor."

"Well, no, he's not, but he is standing nearest to you, so I thought I'd start the introductions with him first."

"In the future, dear," Mrs. Hart whispered in a voice that still carried, "it is best if you introduce the person who holds the highest social standing, which, in this case, would be me."

Harriet's pale cheeks flushed with color, and Oliver was about to intercede, knowing all too well that Mrs. Hart could be somewhat daunting, but Harriet lifted her chin and sent a surprisingly cool glance to Mrs. Hart. "Of course, how silly of me, and I'll be happy to introduce you just as soon as I figure out exactly *who* you are and *what* you want with me."

To Oliver's surprise, Mrs. Hart let out a booming laugh, patted Harriet's cheek again, and turned to Mrs. Palmer. "Doesn't she have just the keenest sense of humor? I'm Mrs. Hart, by the way, but you may call me Abigail. All of my friends do, and that gentleman over there is Mr. Oliver Addleshaw, but you should probably call him Mr. Addleshaw." She winked. "These important men of business like to hold on to their dignity."

Mrs. Palmer seemed to struggle for a reply, but then Mrs. Hart continued on, acting as if it were a common occurrence for her to converse in the middle of a tenement slum with a lady who was wearing a shapeless gown and sported a smudge of flour on her cheek.

"I must thank you, Mrs. Palmer, for all you've done for my dear Harriet. Why, Reverend Gilmore has frequently declared how helpful you've been in keeping a sharp eye on her and making certain she doesn't get into mischief."

Harriet's nose wrinkled. "You're acquainted with Reverend Gilmore?"

"Indeed," Mrs. Hart said, sending a fond smile Harriet's way. "I'm a patroness of the church, albeit a silent one. Reverend Gilmore and I have known each other for years. He immediately sought me out this morning and delivered the news about you and Mr. Addleshaw, which . . . is why I'm here."

"What news?" Mrs. Palmer asked, her tone rising ever so slightly, probably in the hopes of being heard over Harriet, who'd begun to sputter.

"Why, that Miss Peabody and Mr. Addleshaw have formed an . . . attachment," Mrs. Hart said with another one of her beaming smiles. She turned to Oliver. "I took the liberty of sending a telegram to your grandfather. He's already responded—which I'm not surprised about in the least—and you'll be delighted to learn he's coming to town, immediately from the sound of things."

Oliver felt the distinct urge to begin sputtering exactly as Harriet was still doing. "My grandfather is coming to town?"

"Of course, dear. You know how Archibald enjoys being in the thick of things, and you really can't expect him to ignore something as thrilling as your involvement with Miss Peabody. Why, I bet he'll be absolutely tickled to death to participate in the upcoming festivities."

Harriet turned to him with eyes that had grown huge. "What upcoming festivities?"

"How would I know? This is the first I'm hearing about Grandfather coming to town, or any festivities, for that matter. And, I have yet to understand how and why Mrs. Hart is involved in our private matters."

"Oh, did I forget to mention that?" Mrs. Hart exclaimed as she batted innocent lashes his way. "I'm here to assume the position of chaperone."

Oliver narrowed his eyes. "Forgive me, Mrs. Hart, but I was under the impression you'd chosen to withdraw from society."

"Choices are made to change, my boy."

"And you've, for some unfathomable reason, *chosen* to involve yourself in my affairs?" he asked slowly.

"I owe Reverend Gilmore a favor, so I certainly couldn't refuse his request of seeing after Harriet."

It was too late—his decision to end matters with Harriet was not going to be a feasible option, and his well-organized life, something he cherished, was rapidly going by the wayside. And strangely enough, it was all due to the machinations of some gentleman by the name of Reverend Gilmore and a society matron no one had seen out and about for years.

"I don't need, or want, a chaperone," Harriet said firmly.

"Of course you do," Mrs. Hart countered before she turned to Mrs. Palmer. "Now then, from what I've learned, you're the owner of this charming house where Harriet and her friends reside, and as such, you and I should probably have a little chat regarding future rent. I've convinced Miss Longfellow and Miss Plum to come stay with me while I go about the business of chaperoning Harriet, but I would like to take it upon myself to pay their rent in advance for the next couple of months."

She smiled even as she shook her head. "Why, between the three ladies, their rooms are filled to bursting with various items, items I believe should stay here until I get the ladies' lives . . . Well, no need to get into that." Mrs. Hart slid a sideways glance at Harriet, who seemed to be swelling on the spot, and grabbed hold of Mrs. Palmer's arm and hustled her over to the brown house.

"You have to go after that crazy lady and tell her our association has come to an end."

Oliver pulled his gaze from the retreating back of Mrs. Hart and frowned at Harriet, who was glaring at him. "I don't believe that's an option, Harriet. Mrs. Hart is one of those formidable ladies you don't want to tangle with if at all possible, and I fear she's decided to take you in hand."

"You can simply tell her that I don't need anyone to take me in hand, and you can tell her that I've broken things off with you."

Before Oliver could utter a single protest, Harriet sent a smile to Darren, who was still standing beside him, and then marched off in the direction of the peeling brown house, disappearing a moment later around the corner of the building. No more than a second passed before her head popped back into view. She scanned the surrounding area, seemed to blow out a breath of relief, and then disappeared again.

He'd forgotten all about the two gentlemen he'd thought were following Harriet. He scanned the assorted people walking on the sidewalk, but the gentlemen he'd seen before were nowhere in sight.

She'd conveniently neglected to explain the men, but he couldn't really blame her for that, not when Mrs. Hart and her overabundance of personality had descended on them.

How was he going to tell Mrs. Hart there was no longer any need for her help in chaperoning, or more worrisome, how was he going to explain this mess to his grandfather?

"Should I take the boxes from Arnold Constable & Company up to Miss Peabody?" Darren asked, breaking through Oliver's thoughts.

In all the chaos of the past hour, he'd neglected to remember that Arnold Constable & Company had efficiently gathered together some of Harriet's selections and delivered them to the carriage for Harriet's immediate use. He certainly had no issue with allowing her to keep the items purchased today, but what concerned him more at the moment was what Darren had just said. "What do you mean, *up* to her?"

"I assume she lives on one of the upper floors since she went around the corner of the house. Boardinghouses usually have outside stairs leading up to the tenants' rooms."

All the air disappeared from Oliver's lungs as his gaze traveled over the peeling paint, lingered on the sagging shutters, and he finally came to the realization that he was standing in front of the place Harriet called home.

How had he neglected to realize that the lovely, vivacious, and yes, annoying, Miss Harriet Peabody lived in one of the meanest slums he'd ever seen?

Had he been so distracted by the appearance of Mrs. Hart that he hadn't taken the time to figure it out, or could it be possible that some unconscious part of him had simply not wanted to delve into this alarming bit of reality?

Drawing in a deep breath, he caught sight of what could only be a rat foraging around in some rubbish strewn against the side of the sad-looking house. The rat scurried into a large hole leading to the basement in the house where Harriet resided.

Did rats know how to climb, and if so, did Harriet ever have to fend them off as she tried to sleep?

The mere idea of that caused his temper to stir, replaced quickly with dismay.

"Mr. Addleshaw, are you feeling all right?"

Oliver drew in another breath, that action having the unfortunate result of a rather pungent odor sweeping up his nose. He began breathing through his mouth before he managed to nod in Darren's direction. "I wasn't aware that Miss Peabody lived in such a deplorable part of the city, but now that I do, I'll need to rectify that situation."

"Begging your pardon, sir, but I got the distinct impression, given that Miss Peabody flung herself from your carriage, that the two of you are not in accord at the moment."

"I should probably go straighten that little misunderstanding out." Oliver extracted the pistol he always carried with him from the waistband of his trousers. "Best keep this with you, Darren, to guard the carriage."

Accepting the pistol, Darren frowned. "Are you certain you wouldn't rather keep the pistol, sir? If you ask me, you're in more danger from Miss Peabody than I am out here on the street."

A grin caught Oliver by surprise even as he shook his head. He watched his driver walk away and climb up on the carriage before he turned and headed toward the boardinghouse, wondering what he should say to Harriet when they came face-to-face.

They would have to go through with the plan—there was no other option, especially now that he'd seen her home.

Harriet would have no reason to live with Mrs. Hart unless she played the role of his fiancée, and he knew her well enough, even in the short time they'd been acquainted, to realize she wouldn't let him just give her money without doing anything to earn it.

She was too proud, too conscientious, and had too much appreciation for the value of a dollar, but he could not allow her to remain living in squalor. Somehow, he was going to have to convince her to continue on as his fiancée. How he was going to do that, he had no idea, but he needed to move quickly.

He strode to the side of the house, grunted in disgust at what someone apparently thought passed for stairs, grabbed hold of the rickety railing, and began to climb, having no idea what floor Harriet lived on or if she'd even answer the door once he figured that out.

11

arriet, I think your Mr. Addleshaw is climbing up our stairs," Millie announced as Harriet was reaching a hand underneath the kitchen table in an attempt to pull a trembling Buford out from under it.

Snatching back her hand when Buford growled at her, Harriet glanced at Millie who was standing in the doorway of their tiny kitchen. "He's not my Mr. Addleshaw, and I'd appreciate it if you'd inform him that I'm unavailable to speak with him . . . now or anytime in the future."

"Oh dear, something happened, didn't it?"

"You could say that."

"And . . . ?"

"There's no time to explain, especially if he's on his way up, but I'll tell you all about it after you get rid of him."

Millie bit her lip. "I don't think Mr. Addleshaw is going to appreciate me trying to get rid of him."

"You're probably right, but just be firm and I'm sure you'll persevere."

"I have no idea what *persevere* means, and you, of all people, should remember that I'm hardly good at dealing with the socially elite. Besides, I thought you'd decided it was in your best interest to accept his offer."

"I've changed my mind."

"Well, that's unfortunate, especially since Mrs. Hart seems quite excited to step in and chaperone you around town." Millie's brow furrowed. "She's also excited about bringing you 'up to snuff'—whatever that means. I couldn't find a credible definition of that particular expression in any of my dictionaries, but now, since I'm going to have to look up what *persevere* means, I'll once again look for the meaning of *up to snuff*."

Harriet grinned. Millie was a lady who was determined to improve herself, and at the moment, she was doing said improvement by memorizing the dictionary. The words that frequently poured out of Millie's mouth were always a surprise, especially when Millie didn't have their meanings exactly right. "*Up to snuff* means that Mrs. Hart wants to pretty me up and hone my manners so that I'll be acceptable to society."

"How delightful."

"I'd rather be boiled in oil."

"Hmm. . . ."

"Exactly. So, you'll need to think of something to say to get Oliver to leave. And . . . tell him I'm returning all of his money to him, except for the amount I spent on Buford's meal."

"You do realize that if you're determined to end your association with Mr. Addleshaw, you're going to have to give him back his dog, don't you? That might prove a little tricky since Buford doesn't seem to want to come out from under the table."

Looking back at Buford, Harriet saw that the poor pooch was trembling harder than ever. "Any thoughts as to what's wrong with him?"

"When Lucetta and I got back from paying a visit to Reverend Gilmore about an hour ago, the door was wide open, and we were afraid Buford had run off, but then we found him hiding underneath the table. It's rather strange." Millie frowned. "Do you think he somehow opened the door and then remembered he's afraid of heights and that's what sent him into hiding?"

"I think a more pertinent question would be how he could have opened the door in the first place."

"Maybe he used his teeth," Millie suggested right as someone began knocking on the door in question. "I think Mr. Addleshaw's found you."

Harriet blew out a breath. "I was hoping he'd give up after knocking on Lulu's door down on the third floor. She's a darling lady—don't get me wrong—but she is a little . . ."

"Scary?" Millie finished for her.

"I think it's the different colored eyes and the hair that almost reaches the floor." Harriet scooted down on her stomach and began edging toward Buford, even as he started edging farther away from her. "If you'll just come out, darling, I'll give you to your master."

"Mr. Addleshaw might have to come in and fetch his dog," Millie said, her voice muffled since Harriet was now completely under the table. "Buford wouldn't even come out for Lucetta, and you know how much he adores her."

The knocking suddenly intensified, the sound making Harriet's teeth grind together. "The sooner you cooperate, Buford, the sooner you'll be reunited with Oliver."

A pitiful whimper was Buford's only response.

"Does no one but me hear that someone is trying to pound down our door?" Lucetta called from the receiving room.

"Don't—" Harriet began as she shot up, the impact from her head hitting the underside of the table, cutting off the rest of her warning. Stars began dancing behind her eyes, and she could only drop back to the floor in a daze while the sound of Lucetta's bare feet padding down the small hallway mingled with Oliver's determined knocks.

The creak of the door came next, and then Oliver's voice rang out. "I do beg your pardon, but I'm looking for Miss Harriet Peabody. Does she happen to live here?"

"You're Mr. Addleshaw."

"Indeed, and . . . you're Miss Lucetta Plum . . . the . . . actress . . . but what have you done to your hair? It's . . ."

Whatever else Oliver was saying got lost when the door slammed right before Lucetta's stomps echoed down the hallway and then her feet came into view.

"What an unpleasant, hideous man," Lucetta said with a huff. "Did you hear how he said *actress* in that snotty tone of voice?" She let out another huff. "I'm afraid I might have been completely off the mark, Harriet, regarding my support of the alliance you've formed with that man."

Pushing herself up from the floor, Harriet rubbed her head. "Oliver can certainly be unpleasant, but . . ." Her eyes widened as the stars disappeared and she got a good look at Lucetta. "What *have* you done to your hair?"

Lucetta raised a hand and touched one of the many braids sticking out on her head. "Oh, I forgot about this. I was reading over my lines for that new play, and, well, you know how I get bored when I do that."

"One braid wasn't enough to push away the boredom?" Millie asked with a grin.

Lucetta waved the question away. "It's not like anyone's around to see me, except for that horrid man on our landing, and I don't really care what he thinks of me, which obviously isn't much." She plopped her hands on her hips. "You must realize you can't continue forward with this, Harriet. He's a nightmare."

"You'll be pleased to learn I've already come to that very same conclusion, Lucetta, but I do have to say that Oliver isn't unpleasant all the time, and really, he's far from hideous, and . . ."

Harriet pressed her lips together when Lucetta and Millie suddenly gawked at her with wide eyes. "What?"

"Good heavens, Harriet, this is a disaster," Lucetta whispered.

"What's a disaster?"

"You're . . . attracted to him."

"No. I'm. . . . well . . . perhaps a bit, but it's just because he's not always grumpy, and I think, deep down inside, *very* deep down inside, he's . . . slightly . . . nice."

She pointed to Buford still under the table, ignoring the looks of shock Millie and Lucetta were sending her way. "Take Buford, for instance. While I was having ice cream with Oliver, we got to talking about his dog, and I learned he didn't *buy* Buford. He found the poor thing starving in an alley, and instead of leaving Buford there to die, he brought him home."

"He rescued a dog and bought you ice cream?" Lucetta asked slowly.

Harriet nodded. "He did, and when he discovered I'd been treated shabbily by Madame Simone when I was trying to buy some dresses, he took me to Arnold Constable & Company and practically bought out the store for me."

Lucetta took a step closer. "This is worse than I thought. You *like* the man."

"No, I don't," Harriet argued. "Or, maybe I did, until he tried to take me to task for speaking to Ginger and Tawny. Honestly, he was appalled to learn I'm acquainted with two women he was so certain were from the demimonde." She shrugged. "Granted, Ginger and Tawny *used* to work in that profession, but they've abandoned their old ways and now earn their living by taking in laundry. Since they don't make much in the way of a wage, it's hardly their fault they still dress in the clothing they used to be required to wear in their other profession."

The sound of pounding started again.

"He's not going to just go away," Millie yelled. "Besides, we still have his dog."

"Oh, very well, I'll deal with him," Harriet said, struggling to her feet and heading out of the kitchen. She stalked down the short hallway, reached the door, pushed aside the bolt that secured it, twisted the lock, and then wrenched it open, her temper steadily rising when she looked at Oliver and found him smiling back at her, although his eyes held a distinct trace of temper.

"What?"

"Is that any way to greet your fiancé?"

"You're not my fiancé, you've only ever been my pretend fiancé, or maybe temporary fiancé would be a better way to put it. But since I've decided I can't be trusted not to harm you if I have to spend any additional time in your company, you need to go away and leave me alone."

"Don't you think you're being a little overly dramatic? I mean—"

Not allowing the annoying man to finish his sentence, Harriet shut the door in his face, locked it, brushed her hands together, turned, and pretended not to hear his demands for her to open up as she headed back toward the kitchen. She knew full well she'd have to open the door again to give him Buford, but . . .

Her steps slowed when a letter, sitting directly on top of a clumsily wrapped package and positioned on a side table, caught her eye. Dread was immediate when she picked up the letter and found her name scrawled in an untidy hand across the front— that particular scrawl far too familiar.

It was from Aunt Jane, but . . . how had it gotten on the table?

She picked up the package and hurried to the kitchen, finding Millie and Lucetta both on their knees, trying to coerce Buford from under the table. She had to clear her throat twice to get them to look at her. She held up the letter and package. "Were these waiting outside the front door when the two of you came home today?"

Lucetta frowned. "No, they were on the table."

"Are you sure?"

Lucetta's frown deepened. "Didn't you leave them there because you were avoiding dealing with your aunt?"

"Perhaps she's sent you a birthday present," Millie said, eyeing the package. "You should open it."

"My aunt never sends me presents."

"She gave you that dress of your mother's last year on your birthday," Millie argued.

"Only because she wrongly believed if she buttered me up with that offering, I'd be more inclined to join her little confidence-swindling thing she has going on in the city."

"But at least she didn't try to take the dress back after you refused her offer," Millie said weakly.

"There's no need for you to try so hard to bring out positive aspects about my aunt, Millie. She has nothing whatsoever positive about her, and just because she's likely related to me, doesn't mean I have to like her." Harriet tore off the brown wrapping and considered the box for a second before she finally opened it up. What was nestled inside had alarm flowing freely through her. She plucked out the diamond necklace and held it up.

"That's . . . hmm . . . really nice," Millie said as she nodded to Lucetta. "Isn't it nice?"

"Stunning, but . . . " She turned to Harriet. "Do you suppose that used to belong to your mother?"

"Highly doubtful, since Aunt Jane has never given any indication she or my mother came from wealth, and . . ." Her words died in her throat as something more concerning than receiving what was most likely a stolen necklace hit her. "I'll be right back." She dropped the necklace into the box, spun around, marched her way back to the door, and pulled it open, barely flinching at the glare Oliver sent her.

"Why didn't you mention that Buford can open doors?" she demanded.

Oliver's brows scrunched together. "Buford can't open doors."

"Are you quite certain about that?"

"Well, yes, seeing as how he's a dog, and"—he lifted his hands and turned them from side to side—"he has paws. Why do you ask?"

"Never mind." She shut the door in his face again and willed her breathing to slow, knowing this was not the appropriate time to descend into a fit of the vapors.

Her aunt, or the men her aunt employed who'd been following her around town of late, had been in her home.

She'd been left an expensive piece of jewelry, which meant her aunt was up to something and wanted to get Harriet's attention, but what could that something possibly be?

"She's going to frame me for theft, or blackmail me, or . . ." Horror was swift as Harriet realized that not only could *she* be harmed by an accusation of theft—her friends could be as well. Her breath caught in her throat when the idea sprang to mind that authorities could even now be getting a tip from Jane. They would be led to this very apartment, where they'd discover a glittering diamond necklace that, clearly, none of the ladies living on the Lower East Side could afford.

They'd be hauled away to rot in jail, probably Jane's plans all along, and then she'd come to the rescue and bail them out . . . leaving Harriet, Lucetta, and Millie in the woman's debt.

That idea was completely unacceptable, although . . . She might be completely off the mark, but . . . what if she wasn't? What could she possible do to avoid suffering the consequences of whatever duplicity her aunt intended?

The solution was clear, and although it left a sour taste in

Harriet's mouth, she marched back to the door, pulled it open, ignored the complaints that poured out of Oliver's mouth, grabbed hold of his arm, and ushered him into her home.

"Just let me stuff this dictionary into my trunk, since it won't fit in Millie's, and then you and Darren can cart it down to the carriage."

Oliver simply stared at Harriet as she threw a remarkably large dictionary into her battered trunk and slammed the lid shut. She brushed her hands together before sending him a look that had expectation written all over it. He didn't exactly appreciate the look, nor did he appreciate the fact he was more confused than he'd ever been in his life, but no one seemed inclined to alleviate his confusion by explaining exactly what was going on.

"And *why* is it that you've decided to take Mrs. Hart up on her offer *and* continue on as my pretend fiancée?" he finally asked.

"Don't you want me to complete the deal with the duke so that you can get your hands on that wool you seem so keen to acquire?" she countered.

"Well, certainly, but I have to tell you, Harriet, you're acting a little peculiar. Does the reasoning behind the peculiarity have something to do with thinking Buford knows how to open doors?"

"It's really not very gentlemanly of you to point out I'm peculiar," Harriet said before she turned away from him when Darren stepped into the room. "Ah, Darren, thank you so much for agreeing to help us. This trunk is ready for you and Mr. Addleshaw to take out to the carriage now."

"She says that as if we don't have to negotiate down four very steep flights of wobbly stairs, but simply stroll outside and toss the thing into a carriage," Oliver said to Darren, who grinned as he took hold of one end of the trunk while Oliver took hold of the other.

It took a bit of maneuvering to get the trunk down the stairs, but they managed to do it unscathed, even if both he and Darren were perspiring rather profusely by the time they reached the bottom step. Miss Plum's trunk was next, and except for the unwelcomed suggestions Harriet, Miss Longfellow, and Miss Plum called to them as he and Darren struggled their way down the steps yet again, their trip was uneventful. However, when they took hold of Miss Longfellow's trunk, the situation immediately turned difficult.

"What do you have in here?" Oliver asked Miss Longfellow, pausing right in the middle of the front door because Mrs. Hart seemed determined to take that precise moment to try to squeeze her way past him.

"One should never question what essentials a lady needs to take with her, Mr. Addleshaw," Mrs. Hart said with a sniff. "Why, I'm sure you've just embarrassed Miss Longfellow quite dreadfully since she's most certainly stuffed that trunk to the gills with her unmentionables."

"It's actually filled with all my dictionaries, along with a thesaurus and my recently acquired collection of Jane Austen novels," Millie said with a grin.

"Essentials to be sure," Oliver said dryly before lugging his end of the trunk the rest of the way through the door right as Mrs. Hart managed to scoot around him, giving him an unexpected jolt forward when she bumped into him. He was propelled out the door a little faster than he'd been anticipating, which caused Darren, who'd evidently not been prepared to be thrust forward so rapidly, to slip on the wet steps. That unfortunate circumstance resulted in Darren jerking the trunk forward, making Oliver drop it in the process. Oliver could only stand there, frozen in horror, as Darren careened wildly down the stairs with Miss Longfellow's trunk chasing after him.

"This is no time to dither—help him!" Harriet yelled, reminding him of a not-so-distant admonishment she'd sent him when Miss Birmingham had gotten on the bad side of Buford.

Oliver began running down the steps, but they were slicker than ever, and he slid, tumbling down a good few steps before he finally landed on the third-floor landing. Before he could so much as shake the stars from his eyes, he found himself trampled underneath the dainty feet of the ladies, including Mrs. Hart, as they dashed past him. Pushing up to a sitting position, he peered through the railing, finding all the ladies hovering around his driver, who'd stopped on the second-floor landing. Miss Plum, he noticed, was tearing off a piece of her petticoat, which she immediately began wrapping around Darren's head—a head that seemed to be bleeding.

"Are you all right?" he called to his driver before he rose to his feet and began making his way cautiously down the steps on legs that were less than steady.

Though there was a dazed expression in Darren's eyes—not an expression Oliver believed was a result of the fall but from the fact Miss Plum was crooning to Darren in that amazing voice of hers—Oliver came to the rapid conclusion his driver was going to be just fine. When he made the mistake of mentioning that, though, he earned himself a scowl from each and every one of the ladies, right before they sent him back up the stairs to collect a few remaining items.

By the time he'd retrieved those items, which turned out to be more than a few, and they had started off for Mrs. Hart's home, Oliver was thin on patience. Wincing as a dress form conked him in the head when his carriage made a rather abrupt turn, he shoved the form aside. Looking to Harriet, who was frowning at him from her squashed position on the opposite seat, he arched a brow. "Are you sure it was wise to allow Miss Plum to take Darren's place and drive the carriage?"

"Lucetta is perfectly competent with the reins, as you can see," Harriet said even as the carriage jolted over what had to be a huge rut in the street that a competent driver would have surely missed.

"I was more than willing to drive us to Mrs. Hart's," he insisted.

"Yes, I know, you told me, several times, but that wouldn't have allowed Darren, the man who suffered a troubling accident because of you, the opportunity to spend time with Lucetta." She smiled. "I must say, it's wonderful to see he's already on the mend, probably because he's been given the extreme treat of having Lucetta's undivided attention."

"Miss Plum should be giving all her attention to the road, not to Darren, and if I were at the reins, we would have arrived by now."

Harriet batted long lashes his way, an action that was completely out of character for her. "Lucetta's apparently decided to take a more scenic route to Mrs. Hart's."

Edging forward, Oliver peered past Buford and looked out the miniscule patch of window that wasn't blocked by the ladies' possessions. "I hardly believe this back alley we seem to be trundling down is even close to being scenic. Although"—he leaned back—"it would be a perfect route to take if someone was, perhaps, trying to make certain no one is following us."

"Who would want to follow us to Mrs. Hart's?"

"I'm sure I have no idea, other than the two men you were obviously trying to avoid earlier."

"I never said I was trying to avoid two men."

Oliver blew out a breath. "You didn't have to. Your suspicious behavior spoke for itself."

"I must say, all these compliments you keep sending my way

are bound to go to my head soon. Why, I don't recall the last time I was deemed *peculiar* and *suspicious* in the same day."

"You can hardly fault me for being a little suspicious, especially when you had Miss Plum drive you to that church instead of following Mrs. Hart's carriage."

"I needed to let Reverend Gilmore know where we were going so he wouldn't worry about us."

"What was in that box you took into the church?"

Harriet eyed him for a moment, and then, strangely enough, she smiled. "Honestly, Oliver, we're hardly going to enjoy a pleasant ride in your carriage if you continue questioning me in such a concerning fashion."

"Our ride was doomed to be less than pleasant from the start, considering we barely have enough room to sit, let alone comfortably, and you've been glaring at me for most of our journey."

"I wouldn't continue glaring at you if you'd simply extend me the apology I so richly deserve."

"The agreement you and I struck does not require me to apologize to you for anything."

"Then I suppose you'll just have to become accustomed to me glaring at you."

"You agreed to be charming."

"And I shall be, when we're out in public—unless, of course, you try to take me to task for speaking to people I consider friends."

"It's beyond inappropriate for you to count women of Tawny and Ginger's ilk as friends."

"It truly is a lucky circumstance I can't reach the door at the moment, Oliver. Otherwise, I'd feel a distinct urge to throw myself out of it again."

Oliver frowned. "While I know this has nothing to do with the conversation at hand—and we will return to that conversation—tell me, how was it possible that when you threw yourself out of this carriage the first time you were able to land on your feet?"

"I spent time in a circus."

He couldn't help himself, he laughed. "You have quite the imagination, don't you?"

Harriet opened her mouth, but before she could say a single word, the carriage lurched to the right and began traveling at an even faster rate of speed. He struggled to reach the handle to roll down the window. "I think I should take over driving."

"Don't be silly. Lucetta's doing a fine job, and . . . Good heavens, you've just squished my bustle."

Wincing as he realized something that felt remarkably like metal was piercing his stomach, Oliver cautiously leaned back right as Harriet snatched the bundled package of wrapped linen straight off his lap. She set it on her knees, parted the linen and then scowled at him. "You broke my collapsible bustle."

Oliver eyed the contraption. "It doesn't look broken to me."

"It certainly is. It won't spring back into place."

"Forgive me, Harriet, but if women are going to be sitting down with that bustle on their backsides, I would have to imagine there's going to be more force used than what I exerted by merely leaning on it for a second."

Harriet began muttering under her breath, but her mutters came to an abrupt end when the carriage began to slow. Craning her neck, she peered out the window. "Is this Washington Square?"

Struggling to see past Buford, who was trying to crawl into Oliver's lap, he finally caught a glimpse out the carriage window. His gaze traveled over rows of brownstones, all looking remarkably the same.

"From what little I can see, yes, I do think we're on Washington Square."

"The houses are very different from those on Fifth Avenue, aren't they?"

"That's because Washington Square is home to many old New Yorkers, Harriet. These families were some of the first to live in New York, back in the day when it was New Amsterdam. They're very set in their ways and prefer brownstones to the more progressive houses being built on Fifth Avenue. But, brownstones aside, this is a very respectable area, and you and your friends will be safe here." He tilted his head. "Although, given that you've yet to explain what trouble you're in, and I don't see you doing that in the near future, given your stubborn nature, I'm going to have Buford stay with you for a little longer."

Buford let out a loud snore as he sprawled across Oliver's lap.

"I don't believe that's . . . " Harriet's words faded to nothing when the carriage suddenly made a sharp turn and jostled both Oliver and Harriet around before it pulled to a stop behind one of the brownstones.

Oliver shoved aside the dress form yet again and pressed closer to the window. A typical three-story brownstone met his gaze, but upon further inspection he noticed the dwelling had a somewhat neglected air about it. The windows appeared to be dirty, and cats seemed to be lounging in each and every one of those windows. For a moment, he thought they'd stopped at the wrong house, but then Mrs. Hart's voice rang out.

"Miss Plum, my goodness, have you been driving the carriage? I can see the two of us are going to have to have a long chat about what is appropriate and what is not."

Miss Plum simply laughed and then the carriage shook just a bit as someone jumped to the ground. A second later, the door opened and Miss Plum stuck her head in. "You have a very fine set of horses, Mr. Addleshaw, although the one with the black star on his nose does tend to shy a little when other carriages approach."

"When other carriages approach, or when you're driving on the wrong side of the street?" he countered.

Miss Plum sent him a sniff and turned to Harriet. "I think our extended journey through the city did the trick."

"Wonderful," Harriet exclaimed, handing Miss Plum the rewrapped bustle before she began scooting for the door.

"What trick?" Oliver asked.

Miss Plum didn't so much as blink. "Why, that poor Darren seems to be doing much better now that he was given an opportunity to enjoy all of that lovely fresh air."

Before he could argue with that bit of nonsense, Miss Plum grabbed a bag filled with odds and ends and disappeared, leaving him to watch Harriet struggle out of the carriage.

"Aren't you coming?" she asked when she finally managed to reach the ground.

"I don't seem capable of moving just yet, given that Buford is still lying over me. Do you think you can get him out of the carriage?"

Harriet looked over her shoulder before she turned back to him. "I think we should leave Buford here, especially since Mrs. Hart seems to have a fondness for cats. It would be horrible if Buford decided to eat some of them."

"Buford won't eat the cats. He's . . ." Oliver's voice trailed off when Buford suddenly lifted his head and licked his lips. "On second thought, maybe I should take him home with me."

"That might be for the best."

Unfortunately, Buford seemed to have other ideas. He wiggled his way off Oliver's lap and slipped out of his collar when Oliver grabbed it. Before Oliver could get a hold on him, the dog leapt out of the carriage and took off for the house. Less than a minute later, the sound of outraged cats split the air, followed quickly by the yells of an outraged Mrs. Hart.

12

*A*h, Harriet, I thought I'd find you in here." Millie breezed into Mrs. Hart's formal dining room, a ratty old dictionary clutched in her hand. "How goes the cutlery lesson?"

Harriet gestured to the massive place setting spread in front of her, one she'd been spending countless hours with during the three days she'd been living under Abigail Hart's roof. "It's confusing, and every time the sun streams through the windows, I'm in danger of going blind from the reflections bouncing off the silver and crystal." She grinned and held up a strange-looking spoon. "I'm making progress, though, since I've recently discovered, according to the notes Oliver's grandfather made up for me, that this spoon is specifically used for pudding."

"Archibald Addleshaw is such a dear gentleman for taking the time to assemble those notes for you, Harriet," Abigail said, walking into the room with Buford and a slew of cats trailing after her. "Why, we're fortunate indeed that he traveled straight-away to the city after he received my telegram, *and* that he's decided to throw himself wholeheartedly into this daunting business of polishing up your manners."

"I do have a few manners at my disposal, Mrs. Hart, so I'm not certain your claim of it being a *daunting business* is exactly accurate."

Abigail waved Harriet's protest aside before she smiled and nodded at Buford, who was now lounging in a spot of sun with the cats curled around him. "Isn't he simply adorable?"

"You didn't find Buford adorable when you thought he was about to eat your cats."

Pulling out a chair upholstered in gold damask trimmed with black, Mrs. Hart took a seat. "All water under the bridge, my dear, and no one can blame me for thinking Buford was about to eat Fluffy, considering he had her in his mouth."

"I certainly was amazed when he spit her out, but that might have been because he didn't enjoy the taste of her," Millie said before she plopped the dictionary on top of her head and began walking. She made it all the way across the room before the book tumbled to the ground. Picking it up, she set it back on her head and stood stock-still for a moment. "I'm definitely making headway with this whole posture business, although I'm a little confused about why I need to improve mine in the first place. It's not like anyone is going to be watching me as I go about being your lady's maid, Harriet."

"I wasn't aware you were *going* to pose as my maid."

"That's why I was looking for you, to discuss matters, but you don't need to look so alarmed. I *have* been a maid before." Millie edged forward a few inches and stopped when the dictionary began teetering. "Abigail thought it would be a wonderful way for me to earn a few dollars while I wait for the employment agency to contact me with another position. She's footing the bill for my services." With that, Millie began walking slowly across the room and straight out the door.

Harriet quirked a brow in Abigail's direction after the last of Millie's skirt disappeared.

Abigail barely batted an eye. "I assure you I have more than enough money at my disposal to pay Millie, and I also have no problem with any of you calling me Abigail."

"You know addressing you by your given name isn't what's bothering me, nor is the state of your bank account."

"I think you and I can both agree that what's truly bothering you at the moment has nothing to do with Millie and everything to do with Oliver. You're conflicted about him."

Harriet opened her mouth to refute that nonsense but then snapped it shut when she realized that Abigail was exactly right. She was conflicted about Oliver. What bothered her most of all was that even though he'd yet to apologize about the whole Tawny and Ginger fiasco, she continuously got a little weak in the knees every time he stopped by to check on her.

It was ridiculous—that's what it was, her traitorous body's reaction to him—but she seemed to have no control over it. It certainly wasn't helping matters much that Oliver had taken to being very solicitous toward Millie and Lucetta, something that warmed Harriet's heart to no small end, even if it did appear Oliver's liking for her friends took even him by surprise at times.

"Tell me, dear," Abigail suddenly said. "What do you believe is the most pressing issue you have with Oliver?"

Since she could hardly tell Abigail her most pressing issue was that she found the man all too attractive and her knees kept wobbling whenever he showed up, Harriet took a minute to sort through all the things about Oliver that really annoyed her.

"He's very high-handed," she finally said. "Do you know that yesterday he had the audacity to ask me to practice adoring looks while peering into a mirror because he felt I was glaring at him too often?"

"You can hardly fault the man for that, Harriet, considering you have been glaring at him on a frequent basis. Why, you must know that society will find it difficult to accept your alliance if you don't gaze adoringly at him every now and again."

"You're taking his side?"

"Of course not," Abigail said with a sniff. "My job is to see you kept safe, which also extends to your health."

"My . . . health?"

"Indeed. You've been in a perpetual state of annoyance practically from the moment you stepped foot in my house. I must tell you, such a state is not conducive to good health, especially in regard to digestion. Stomach issues, my girl, are hardly in vogue at the moment."

"I wasn't aware health issues were ever in vogue."

"Fainting has always been popular amongst the more dramatic set. Not that I recommend it, of course. Why, I shudder to think how many dinners have been disrupted when ladies have slumped to the ground at the slightest provocation."

"Yes, well, fascinating fainting tidbits aside, perhaps it would be for the best if we'd return to the subject of Millie and . . ."

A clearing of a throat had Harriet stopping midsentence as Abigail's butler, Mr. Kenton, stepped into the room. "Mr. Addleshaw has come to call, Mrs. Hart. May I tell him you're receiving?"

For a second, Harriet's heart began galloping in her chest, until she reminded herself that her heart had no business galloping, or even mildly picking up its beats, just because Oliver had come to call.

"Of course I'm receiving today, Mr. Kenton. Show Mr. Addleshaw right in."

"Very good, Mrs. Hart." Mr. Kenton bowed and exited the room.

"I must say, I'm delighted to be receiving guests again," Abigail said right before footsteps sounded in the hallway.

Ignoring the fact her breath seemed to have gotten stuck in

her throat, Harriet craned her neck as she watched the door. Air came whooshing back to her, though, when Archibald, not Oliver, Addleshaw walked into the room.

That Oliver was his grandson, there could be no doubt. Both gentlemen possessed impressive height, and even though Archibald was somewhat advanced in years, his features were still strong—his hair, although silver, still thick, and his shoulders broad, without even the slightest droop to them.

"I hope I'm not interrupting," Archibald said.

"Archibald, how lovely you've decided to pay us a call," Abigail exclaimed. "I wasn't expecting you until this evening."

"Oliver's left me to my own devices today, so I thought I'd come early and see if young Harriet could use my help with anything."

He moved to Abigail's side, kissed her knuckles, which had her turning pink, and smiled. "You're looking absolutely charming today, Abigail. Have you done something different with your hair?"

Abigail patted the white locks in question. "I've hired a new maid, one who is incredibly talented with hot tongs and a handful of pins."

Harriet sat forward. "Perhaps you could lend me your new maid for a few weeks and *you* could use Millie."

"I wouldn't want to deprive you of your friend's company, dear."

"Yes, well, I don't particularly want to be deprived of my hair, and allowing Millie anywhere near hot tongs puts my health—something you recently claimed you were determined to keep safe—in immediate danger."

Abigail shook her head at Archibald. "Young people are so dramatic these days. Don't you agree?"

Archibald, evidently a true diplomat, spoke not a word of agreement to that assessment but moved to Harriet's side, took her hand, kissed it, and then smiled down at her. "Table lesson going well?"

Harriet returned his smile. "Your notes have proven invaluable, Mr. Addleshaw, but I'm still not certain how I'm going to do around real food."

"Then you'll be pleased to learn we're going to sit down to a formal dinner tonight, with real food no less, and Abigail and I are going to do our very best to make you feel completely competent at the table." He smiled. "We didn't tell you before because I wasn't certain I was going to be able to steal Oliver's chef away, but since I'm pleased to announce I have been able to abscond with the chef, we'll dine in fine form tonight."

"Aren't you worried Oliver might be a little upset that you've absconded with his chef?"

Archibald pulled out a chair and sat down next to her. "Since he stole this particular chef away from me a year ago, I don't think he'll protest too strenuously."

"I also absconded with quite a few members of his staff," Abigail added. "But since that was done because I was anxious to get my house set to rights, especially with having three delightful young ladies here for a visit, I'm sure he understood. Do make certain to tell him, Archibald, if you see him before me, that the employment agency will have me fully staffed by the end of the week, at which time I'll send Oliver's staff back to him."

Archibald regarded Abigail for a long moment. "You and I have yet to discuss the reason behind your formerly reclusive behavior, my dear. I cannot adequately express the sorrow I feel over not being privy to the fact you've been spending years with only cats for company."

"Regrets can cause a person to do odd things, Archibald," Abigail said. "But I have no desire to speak further about me and my peculiar ways of late. I've made a promise to Reverend Gilmore to prepare Harriet for the task awaiting her, and we don't have a second to spare, considering we need to shove years of etiquette into a span of days. We also need to devise a credible story regarding her past, so . . ." She settled her attention on Harriet. "Tell us a little about your family."

Harriet's stomach immediately turned into one large knot. "There isn't much to tell."

"Nonsense, dear. We'll start with your birth. Where were you born?"

"I was once told I was born in Boston, but since my aunt Jane is the one who told me that, I'm not certain it's the truth."

Archibald frowned and leaned closer to her. "Why would you think your aunt Jane lied to you?"

"She's not what anyone would consider trustworthy, Mr. Addleshaw. Why, when I was about nine, she told me she was related to aristocrats, as in people living in England, and she did that while affecting a British accent. Granted, she was on her second bottle of wine when she told me that outlandish tale, but it just goes to prove she's predisposed to lie."

"But . . . what about your parents?" Abigail asked softly.

"Harriet doesn't have any parents," Millie said, edging back into the room with the dictionary still firmly in place on her head. "She's an orphan, just like me, and she had an unconstitutional upbringing." Millie nodded to Archibald, which sent the book tumbling to the ground. "Lovely to see you, Mr. Addleshaw," she said before she bent to fetch her book.

"You might want to check your book while you have it handy, Millie," Harriet said. "I'm fairly sure I didn't have an *unconstitutional* upbringing."

"Did she mean *unconventional*?" Abigail asked.

"Don't tell me," Millie grumbled, opening the dictionary and immediately beginning to flip through the pages. "How am I to learn these words if I don't look them up and see their proper spelling and definition?"

Harriet felt something squeeze her hand and realized it was Archibald.

"I am sorry, my dear, that you weren't able to enjoy the benefits of having a loving family surrounding you."

For a second, tears stung her eyes, but then Harriet blinked and summoned up a smile. "There's no need for you to feel sorry for me, Mr. Addleshaw. As I told your grandson when he expressed concern regarding the idea I'd never tasted ice cream before, one can't truly miss what one has never experienced."

"Please, call me Archibald, and I must say, it's very refreshing to meet a young lady who looks at life so practically." His eyes suddenly began to gleam with something Harriet found a little concerning. "It was a very fortunate day indeed when Oliver made your acquaintance. You are exactly what my grandson needs in his life."

Harriet's feeling of concern increased. "Forgive me, Archibald, but you do remember Oliver and I aren't actually engaged, don't you?"

"But of course." He gave her hand another squeeze right before he exchanged an all-too-significant look with Abigail.

Harriet's mouth dropped open. "Good heavens . . . the two of you are . . . plotting."

"You're only figuring that out now?" Millie asked, raising her head from her dictionary. "I knew minutes after making Abigail's acquaintance that she was up to something, and . . . I found *unconventional* and it exactly explains your upbringing." Millie's lips curved into a grin. "*Unconstitutional* doesn't explain you at all, unless you've been participating in something that goes against our country's constitution."

Harriet returned the grin, but before she could question Abigail and Archibald further about the whole plotting business, Lucetta glided into the room, dangling what appeared to be a script from her hand.

"I'm finished, and . . . Oh, hello, Mr. Addleshaw. Delightful to see you again." Lucetta beamed as Archibald rose from his chair and presented her with a charming bow.

"Miss Plum, delightful to see you as well, and . . . my . . . you're looking . . . lovely today."

Harriet's grin widened as she got a good look at her friend. Once again, Lucetta's head was sporting a variety of braids, she was wearing a pair of trousers that had seen better days, and her feet were bare. "Got bored going over your lines again?"

"Why would you assume that?" Lucetta asked.

"Your hair is braided on one side, but the other . . . Are those beads woven into the strands?"

"Never mind about her hair," Abigail said, pushing herself out of her chair before she proceeded to glare Lucetta's way. "You're wearing trousers, a circumstance that is not remotely acceptable when entertaining guests."

"I always wear trousers when I'm learning my lines. As for entertaining guests, I had no idea Mr. Addleshaw would be visiting, but I'm sure he'll forgive my lack of suitable apparel, given that he seems to be such an understanding sort." She sent Archibald a smile, which he immediately returned before he settled that smile on Abigail.

"I think it might be for the best if I went to check on how dinner preparations are going." He looked at Lucetta again, grinned, shook his head, and quickly left the room, something that sounded suspiciously like laughter trailing after him.

"You've run off poor Archibald," Abigail said as she wagged a finger at Lucetta. "And here I was coming to the belief that you, out of all three ladies, weren't going to need as much work, but now . . ."

Lucetta arched a perfect brow. "I, being one of the most re-nowned actresses of the day, don't need fixing, Mrs. Hart. But since my clothing of choice seems to offend you, I'll go change."

"You being a renowned actress is exactly why you need some work, but we won't discuss that quite yet." Abigail smiled at Harriet. "Harriet deserves all of my attention at the moment, and since I'm sure you and Millie want to help her, both of you will join us tonight at this very table. We're going to use this dinner as a way to teach all three of you how to eat a proper eight-course meal."

Lucetta began backing away. "While that certainly sounds fun . . . I do believe I haven't quite learned all of my lines just yet, so you'll have to forgive me and excuse my absence tonight. Besides, no one expects an actress, even a renowned one, to know what an oyster fork looks like."

Harriet looked at the place setting in front of her. "Which one *is* the oyster fork?"

"It's the one sitting on top of the spoon," Lucetta said before she snapped her mouth shut and began fiddling with one of her braids.

"And why does it have to be placed on top of this large spoon instead of just sitting on the table like the rest of the cutlery?" Harriet asked slowly.

"I'm . . . sure I have no idea," Lucetta muttered.

"The only reason the oyster fork has to be placed on top of that spoon is because some society lady decided it would be a clever way to separate the snobs from the masses."

Looking up, Harriet caught sight of Oliver, in the company of a distinguished-looking gentleman with brown hair, stepping into the dining room. Annoyance was swift, but it wasn't his appearance that annoyed her—more that her pulse had begun racing the moment she laid eyes on him.

They had a business arrangement, nothing more, and Harriet knew her attraction to the man would not serve her well in the end. The last thing she wanted to endure was a broken heart, which meant she was going to have to push her attraction aside and strive to maintain a strictly business relationship with him. Rising to her feet, her annoyance increased when she discovered her traitorous knees had gone all wobbly. "Oliver, this is a surprise. What are you doing here?"

Oliver's long legs ate up the distance that separated them, and before she knew it, he was standing right next to her. "I thought I'd stop by and see how my fiancée was fairing. Any luck with that charming look I asked you to perfect?"

The wobbling immediately stopped. "You asked me to practice an *adoring* look, not a *charming* one."

"By the scowl you're currently directing my way, I'm assuming you haven't been practicing very diligently."

"Is this really something we should be discussing while in the presence of that gentleman standing by the door?" she muttered.

Oliver blinked and turned, gesturing to the man to join them. "I do beg your pardon, Everett. I fear Harriet's scowls have caused me to misplace my manners." He waited until the gentleman reached his side and then began a round of introductions. "Harriet, this is Mr. Everett Mulberry, a friend of mine since childhood. Everett, this is Miss Harriet Peabody. And to relieve your anxiety, Harriet, he knows everything about our situation."

Mr. Everett Mulberry presented Harriet with a bow before he straightened and turned to Lucetta and Millie, who were watching him warily. His eyes widened as his gaze settled on Lucetta. "You're Miss Lucetta Plum, but . . . oh my, don't you look . . . delightful?"

Lucetta nodded rather regally, an impressive feat considering her hair looked as if it'd had an unfortunate experience with a meat grinder. "Thank you, Mr. Mulberry, and as you can see, I wasn't expecting to receive guests, which is why I'm now going to excuse myself and go hide in my room." She turned and disappeared through the door.

Everett watched her leave. "That certainly wasn't a sight I ever expected to see."

"Just make sure you don't mention it at any of your clubs," Abigail ordered. "I've heard tell Miss Plum attracts admirers, and I don't want those admirers tracking her down here."

To Harriet's surprise, Everett laughed. "Honestly, Mrs. Hart, who would I tell? It's not like anyone would believe me if I told them I'd seen Lucetta Plum, dressed in trousers, no shoes, and hair that was . . . Well, what can one really say about that hair?"

"Excellent," Abigail proclaimed before she gestured to Millie. "Now then, moving on to my other ward, allow me to present to you, Mr. Mulberry, Miss Millie Longfellow."

To Harriet's concern, Millie didn't so much as move a muscle, although that might have been because she'd stuck the dictionary back on her head. When her friend remained mute as well as motionless, Harriet realized the sight of the very handsome and debonair Mr. Mulberry had apparently affected Millie in a very unusual way. Harriet hurried to stand beside Abigail, who was watching Millie with a considering look on her face.

"Your other *ward*? Don't you think Lucetta, Millie, and I might be a little old to be called your wards?" was all Harriet could think to ask to break the strained silence now settled over the room.

Abigail switched her attention to Harriet. "Nonsense, it's the perfect solution to the dilemma of how I should best present you. And"—she smiled at Everett—"I have you to thank for my clever idea of making the ladies my wards, although I didn't think of it until you strolled into the room. Tell me, how are the brats?"

Everett blinked. "How in the world did you learn about my brats?"

"Just because I've not ventured forth much in the past few years doesn't mean I don't still have ears in the most influential of places." Abigail tilted her head. "Although, a word of advice, it might be for the best to choose a different form of endearment for the children now in your care. You'll have a difficult time of it making matches for the girls in the future if society takes to calling them brats."

"I never thought about that," Everett muttered.

"Then I'm thrilled I was able to lend you some of my expert advice, as I've been lending it to my wards. Why, with my support, I wouldn't be surprised in the least if these ladies soon find themselves in high demand."

"I don't want to be in high demand," Millie proclaimed, suddenly finding her voice as she took a step forward, which immediately sent the dictionary tumbling to the ground. She didn't bother to pick it up as she set her sights on Abigail. "The only thing I want to be is a nanny to a family who really needs me."

Before Harriet could so much as blink, Everett had joined Millie and was gazing at her as if he found her to be the most delightful woman in the world. "You're a nanny?"

Millie took a step back. "Ah, yes, I am, well, not at the moment you see, because . . ."

"Absolutely not!" Abigail barked, causing everyone to jump and stare her way. "Honestly, Everett, do not even think about coercing Millie into working for you. You've gone through at least a dozen nannies since you took charge of those children, and sweet little Millie wouldn't stand a chance against them. Besides, she's agreed to stand in as a lady's maid for Harriet."

"I don't actually need a lady's maid," Harriet pointed out.

Millie crossed her arms over her chest. "I would make a perfectly credulous maid."

Silence met Millie's remark. Oliver's brow wrinkled, Everett looked confused, and Abigail simply appeared resigned.

"What?" Millie demanded.

"You might want to check your dictionary again," Harriet said, causing Millie to release a snort even as she picked up her dictionary and began to flip through the pages, finally stopping as she ran a finger down the page. Her lips moved, but no sound escaped before she finally lifted her head.

"I meant *credible* maid, and I would be credible because I've been a maid before, right after I was released from the orphanage."

"You really were a lady's maid?" Harriet asked.

"Well, not exactly, but I did work upstairs tending to Mrs. Templeton's rooms, so I was around all that feminine nonsense, before . . . "

Harriet felt an immediate urge to groan. "May I ask how long you were employed by Mrs. Templeton?"

"There's no need for that tone of voice, Harriet. I held on to that position for quite some time. But because I know this will be your next question, I was let go after an unfortunate incident with a warming pan. Although, as to that particular incident, it really could have happened to anyone. Those pans have hot coals in them, and it has to be a frequent occurrence for beds to catch fire."

"Perhaps it would be for the best if we simply forget I have any children in my care," Everett said firmly.

Millie narrowed her eyes, looking incredibly fierce for a lady who normally resembled a character straight out of a fairy tale. "I have never caused any of the children in my care to be harmed. I mean, yes, there was that almost-drowning incident, but that was caused because of a small misunderstanding on my part. I'd always been told that swimming was a natural thing, that one really didn't need to be taught how to do it." She shook her head. "Turns out I was wrong."

Everett's face turned pale. "You almost drowned a child?"

"Good heavens, no. I threw little Billy into the water, and he popped right back up and paddled to shore, but immediately after I released him I had second thoughts and went in after him." She shuddered. "I sank like a rock and Billy's father was forced to rescue me. I was dismissed from my position and not given the funds owed me. Something to do with me causing the family undue fright." Millie began swinging her arms back and forth as she rocked on her heels. "It was quite distressing."

Everett began slowly edging away from Millie. "Forgive me, Miss Longfellow, but I've just remembered a pressing engagement that I really shouldn't ignore." Turning he walked back to Oliver. "I'll just wait for you in the carriage."

Everett vanished out the door a second later and silence settled around the dining room, until Abigail let out a huff. "It really is amazing how quickly you ladies are able to clear a room. First Archibald and now poor Mr. Mulberry."

"My grandfather was here?" Oliver asked.

"He still is here, dear, although he's made himself scarce due to Miss Plum's unfortunate choice of garments today." Abigail moved closer to Oliver. "Which reminds me, your grandfather has been kind enough to provide us with the use of your chef. I'll need you—along with Mr. Mulberry, if you can get him to return—to come back here around seven."

"My grandfather brought my chef over here?"

Abigail smiled. "Archibald's been such a dear, helping me get Harriet ready. Why, it was ingenious, his idea to serve an actual formal meal. I'm hopeful our lesson tonight will go far in preparing everyone for the dinner Archibald and I have decided to hold for the duke."

"What dinner?" Harriet asked—apprehension stealing through her when Abigail didn't bother to answer but simply sent her a smile before she turned back to Oliver.

"There is no need to dress formally, dear. Reverend Gilmore has also agreed to attend our little meal, and I wouldn't want that lovely gentleman to feel out of place. Since he's so dedicated to helping the poor, he spends his money on those in need, which means he doesn't have funds, or any desire, I might add, for formal clothes. And that is why I intend to keep our attire simple tonight." She eyed him for a moment. "Why . . . surprisingly enough, that jacket you have on is very nice and will be quite suitable for you to wear this evening."

Harriet took a second to look Oliver over. Since she'd come to the recent conclusion she needed to keep matters strictly businesslike between them, she'd been avoiding looking at him, but now that she did, she found her mouth turning a little dry.

His broad shoulders were currently encased in a jacket made of fine wool, that wool cut to perfection and tapered expertly to showcase his trim waist. His trousers were creased with a smart line and cut in a manner that allowed him ease of movement, yet highlighted the strength of his legs.

"I made a visit to my tailor before I came here," Oliver said, pulling her abruptly from her perusal.

Her face began to warm when she caught his eye and realized he'd caught her in the act of gawking at him. Clearing her throat, she struggled to come up with something to say. "May I assume you and your tailor came to some type of agreement regarding the fit of your clothing?"

"I don't know if we came to any type of agreement," Oliver said before he sent a nod to Abigail. "But, you were right, Mrs. Hart, in regard to my tailor being upset with me. When I confronted Mr. Clay, my tailor, today about my ill-fitting clothes, he barely blinked an eye before he owned up to tailoring them poorly on purpose."

"And the reasoning behind that bit of skullduggery would be?" Abigail asked.

Oliver's lips thinned. "It turns out Mr. Clay has a son, Mr. Franklin Clay, who works at a factory I secured about a year ago. His father, my tailor, Mr. Henry Clay, holds it against me that his son was not promoted into management once I became involved. Quite honestly, I never agreed to push the promotion through. I might have nodded my head once when Mr. Clay brought up the topic while he was taking some measurements to fit me for a new jacket, but I certainly didn't promise the man anything."

All thoughts of perfectly tailored jackets showing off Oliver's fit form disappeared in a split second, replaced with the strange ringing noise she'd experienced at Arnold Constable & Company. "You didn't make certain Mr. Franklin Clay received a promotion?"

"I rarely concern myself with the day-to-day operations of the many businesses I invest in," Oliver said. "If memory serves me correctly, Mr. Ruff was responsible for sorting things out with that particular factory. I believe he brought in some of his men to assume management positions there."

"That was hardly fair," Harriet said, moving closer to him as her finger, seemingly on its own accord, poked Oliver in the chest. She drew back her hand after she'd poked him and plunked it on her hip so that she wouldn't be tempted to poke him again. "There were probably men who'd worked at that factory for years, and yet you allowed men who most likely didn't have the same amount of experience take over the coveted positions."

"It's business, Harriet, which I'm quite certain you wouldn't understand."

"It's *bad* business, and I assure you, I understand more than you think. Did it never occur to you that if you promoted men who'd been loyal to the factory, morale would increase, as would your profits?"

"My profits are just fine."

"Are you so consumed with making money that you truly believe it was fine for you to slight the son of a man you've known for years?"

"Mr. Clay is just my tailor, or I should say, *was* my tailor.

After learning he purposefully dressed me in clothing that was less than perfect, I've severed all ties with him. I'm now using Everett's tailor, who whipped this jacket out from storage and fit and altered it as I waited."

"You've discontinued using your old tailor?"

"Do you honestly believe I should have continued giving him my business?"

"You disrespected his son."

"He should have simply told me he was angry with me instead of charging me for clothing that was ill-fitting and convincing me that I was roaming around town dressed in the latest styles."

"It's hardly Mr. Clay's fault you're an idiot. Any normal person would have realized from the lack of the ability to breathe, or even move comfortably, that something was the matter ages ago."

"He was perpetuating a fraud."

Harriet saw red. "So are we, in case you've forgotten. Is it your belief that only those of high society are permitted to engage in fraud, while those poor souls who are simply trying to right an obvious wrong are punished for them?"

"I did not come here to argue with you," Oliver practically shouted.

"Oh, why did you come?"

"To inform you that I'm taking you to Delmonico's tomorrow night. We're dining with Everett and his Miss Dixon."

"Why in the world would we do that?" Harriet railed. "I've barely learned half of this table setting, and you told me you wouldn't need me to be at your beck and call until later next week, when the duke is expected, and . . . I have nothing suitable to wear to dinner. I've yet to get a delivery from Arnold Constable & Company and was only able to take home a few day dresses they had available for me."

"I thought you might like Delmonico's because they serve an excellent steak and you told me you enjoy steak. I've already stopped at Arnold Constable & Company, and one of the dinner dresses you ordered is being completed as we speak and will be delivered to you tomorrow morning."

Some of her anger seeped away.

Oliver was clearly a ruthless and unlikeable businessman, and yet, at times, he could be completely sweet, charming, and far too considerate.

He'd remembered she liked steak, and remembered she'd have nothing suitable to wear. It was more than likely he'd applied a bit of pressure to get her dress finished so quickly, but . . . he'd done so because he apparently wanted to give her a nice evening out.

It was enough to make her head spin.

" . . . and besides wanting to tell you about dinner," Oliver continued, causing Harriet to realize she'd missed a portion of his rant, "I've also secured premises for your shop and thought you might like to learn the address." He reached into his pocket, pulled out a small card, tossed it on the table, and turned and stormed toward the door. Pausing for just a second, he looked over his shoulder at Abigail. "I'm afraid I won't be available for your dinner tonight, Mrs. Hart, but do give my regards to my grandfather." With that, he stalked out of the room, leaving an uncomfortable silence in his wake.

"Oh dear, this is unfortunate," Abigail muttered right before she began moving out of the room. "If you'll excuse me, I find I have a distinct need to confer with Archibald."

Millie caught Harriet's eye. "Why do I have a sneaking suspicion more plotting is about to commence?"

Even though anger was still pulsing through her, Harriet felt her lips twitch. "That was an excellent use of the word *commence*, Millie, but I must admit that I do believe you're right about the plotting, which means my life is certain to become more complicated than it already is."

13

It was now Oliver's staunch belief that ladies—more specifically, Miss Harriet Peabody—had been put on the earth in order to create havoc with his well-organized life.

She'd had the audacity to reprimand him the day before at Mrs. Hart's house—something he found somewhat confusing, especially since he was doing *her* a service.

Didn't she realize that?

Shoving aside a stack of business papers he'd brought home from his city office that, oddly enough, couldn't hold his attention, Oliver leaned back in his chair and looked out the window.

It was all Harriet's fault, this inability to concentrate on work and his suffering from an almost constant feeling of disgruntlement. Quite honestly, he was coming to the rapid conclusion that the wool he would acquire from the duke, if all went according to plan, wasn't looking nearly as appealing anymore. If it weren't for the fact he couldn't abide the thought of Harriet returning to that miserable little place she called home, he'd call the whole thing off immediately.

She'd actually lectured him about Mr. Clay, and if he wasn't much mistaken, she thought he should apologize to the man and offer his son a position in management.

She didn't understand business at all—which was unfortunate considering she wanted to open up a shop of her own.

He would be forced to continue checking in on her if only to offer her his invaluable business savvy.

Strangely enough, that idea was somewhat appealing instead of daunting, but why . . .

A knock on the door disrupted his thoughts before Mr. Blodgett stepped into the room.

"Mr. Ruff is here, Mr. Addleshaw. Shall I tell him you're at home or should I have him make an appointment to see you later?"

"There's no need for me to make an appointment, Mr. Blodgett," Silas said, brushing past the butler. "I can clearly see Oliver's here." He strode across the room, but paused and turned back to Mr. Blodgett. "I wouldn't be opposed to accepting a meal if that temperamental chef of Oliver's can be bothered to rustle something up."

"Mr. Addleshaw's chef is not here at the moment, Mr. Ruff," Mr. Blodgett said coolly. "But, I'm sure Mrs. Rollins, our *temperamental* housekeeper, will be able to *rustle* you up something at least edible."

"Where's your chef?" Silas asked, lowering himself into a chair that faced Oliver's desk as Mr. Blodgett disappeared with what sounded like a sniff trailing after him.

Not particularly caring to share the explanation that his chef was currently cooking away over at Abigail's, Oliver shrugged. "He's apparently not here, but, what are *you* doing here? I wasn't expecting you back from West Virginia for at least a week."

Silas leaned forward, flicked open Oliver's humidor box, helped himself to a cigar, and a moment later disappeared behind a thick cloud of smoke. A full minute of silence settled over Oliver's office as Silas puffed away, until the man suddenly leaned through the smoke, the expression on his face hardly reassuring. "I'm afraid events took an unexpected turn in West Virginia. Disturbingly enough, I got run out of town."

"What?"

"The miners didn't like the compensation I offered." Silas took a draw on the cigar, blew out the smoke, and shuddered. "There was a riot."

"A . . . riot?"

"Indeed."

"What, pray tell, prompted a riot?"

"Like I said, the miners weren't agreeable to what I was offering and they turned a little nasty." Silas shook his head. "The only reason I'm here to tell the tale is because I jumped on someone's horse and hightailed it back to the train station."

"You stole a horse?"

"'Course I did, but just so you know, I left the horse at the train station, so if anyone sends you a bill, don't pay it."

"What type of compensation did you offer the miners?" Oliver asked slowly.

"Five extra dollars in every miner's pay and expenses covered for the men who were injured. I even went so far as to find the name of a reputable orphanage when I learned one of the injured men, a widower, wasn't going to be capable of caring for his children for the foreseeable future."

Oliver rubbed his temple where a dull throbbing seemed to be settling in for a long stay. "And you're surprised that your all-too-generous offer was met with a riot?"

"There's no need to be snide."

"Did it never occur to you that this injured man, the one who is currently unable to take care of his children, might take issue with the idea of giving them up?"

"They're just children, Oliver. The man should have been

happy to learn he was going to be given the chance to be rid of them for a while."

A knot of something foul began to form in Oliver's stomach.

This was his fault. He'd sent Silas to West Virginia to deal with the mining situation, knowing perfectly well Silas was ill-suited for the art of the negotiation. While he'd expected there'd be friction between Silas and the miners, he'd never, not in a million years, dreamed Silas would offer up the address of an orphanage as compensation for children who were without anyone to care for them because of his company's neglect.

"I've been thinking we should just close down the mine," Silas said, dragging Oliver back to the conversation at hand.

"You do realize that if we were to close down the mine the town would die, don't you?"

Silas smiled. "'Course it would, and it would be fitting justice, if you ask me. Those lunatics chased after me with shovels, which was hardly a respectful thing for them to do."

"I've always been of the belief that gentlemen need to earn respect."

Silas frowned. "Are you feeling all right?"

"I must admit I've begun to feel a little queasy."

"I know exactly what you mean," Silas said with a nod. "I was served an unfortunate dinner on the train yesterday, some dish that had meat drenched in a cream sauce. It was not good for my digestion in the least." He smiled. "I was vastly relieved to get off that train last night and find my way to Canfield's. I enjoyed a lovely bottle of port there that immediately set my stomach to rights."

"If you returned to the city last night, why is it that you're only now seeking me out to tell me about the riot? It's almost noon."

"I would hope you'd understand the necessity of me delving into a bit of amusement after my near brush with death," Silas returned. "Quite frankly, I'm of the belief that my distress is firmly your fault, and I'll thank you to remember that once you get around to compensating me for my troubles." Pushing himself up and out of the chair, he ambled over to a small table and picked up a crystal decanter. Splashing a generous amount of the contents into a glass, he turned and held it up to Oliver. "Care for a drink?"

"No, thank you, and getting back to the whole compensation idea, you do realize that you've made this situation with the mine worse, don't you? I'm not exactly certain why you feel you should be compensated for your less-than-stellar performance."

Making his way back across the room, Silas retook his seat, gulped down half the liquid in the glass, and let out a belch. "There was nothing wrong with how I chose to handle the matter, Oliver. Those men were unreasonable, that condition brought about no doubt by their lack of education. That's why I've come to the belief we should shut the mine down and move on to another venture, one that wouldn't have either of us dealing with such undesirable workers."

"Surprising as this may seem to you, Silas, I'm not comfortable with taking away the livelihood of thousands of men."

"The men aren't actually earning a livelihood, since they're refusing to step back into the mine until we buckle to their demands. They want raises and new machinery, but I made it clear they won't get paid while waiting to hear our answer about their demands unless they get back into the mines."

"You forgot to tell me that the miners aren't currently working."

"Well, now you know."

"Yes, I do, but you should have come to see me right after getting off the train last night. We could have sent someone to West Virginia right away, but instead, you chose amusement over your responsibilities."

"I don't appreciate lectures, Oliver, especially from a business partner."

"We've never been partners, Silas."

"I suppose you have a point, since nothing has ever been made official, but I've helped you increase your fortunes exponentially. Since you brought the matter up, though, I do believe as we move forward, we'll need to do so as equal partners. I'll need that in writing, along with a substantial raise that will suit my new title."

Temper began to curl through Oliver. "I think we're about to suffer a difference of opinion on a variety of issues, Silas. I don't need or want a partner, and given that you and I seem to have opposing ideas on how my businesses should operate . . . I think our only option at this point is to consider a parting of the ways."

Silas tilted his head. "I must have something in my ear, because I thought I just heard you suggest we dissolve our business alliance."

"That's exactly what I suggested, or perhaps a better way to put it would be that I'm *telling* you we're going to dissolve our alliance."

"It wouldn't be in your best interest to tell me something so absurd."

"And it isn't in your best interest to threaten me," Oliver countered as he rose to his feet.

Silas's face turned ruddy. "You can't dismiss me as if I'm some lackey in your organization. As I said, I've made you a fortune."

"You helped *increase* my fortune, and you also increased your own very nicely in the process. I'm sure the money you've earned while in my employ will go far in soothing your indignation over us parting ways."

Silas pushed himself out of his chair before he took a moment to grind his still-smoldering cigar into the priceless Oriental carpet. "You'll regret this."

"I'm fairly sure I'd regret it more if I continued doing business with you."

Silas let out a laugh that held more than a touch of malice. "In case you've forgotten, Oliver, I'm privy to information that can ruin you. All I have to do is let your competitors know about the underhanded methods we've used to gain inside information. Once those juicy tidbits get out, your reputation will be in shreds."

Drawing in a deep breath in order to calm the temper that was swirling through him, Oliver took a step closer to Silas. "Clearly I've allowed you far too many liberties in regard to my business ventures, but by all means, let the truth come out. I'm willing to accept full responsibility for actions that have been taken on my behalf, even if I had no direct knowledge of those actions."

"You and I had an unspoken agreement that I was to do whatever it took to close a deal."

Oliver shrugged. "Perhaps we did, but I now have a problem with doing business that way."

"How noble of you, but tell me this—you may not be concerned how the business world will view you after the truth comes out, but how do you think society will react? More specifically, how do you think that new ladylove you seem so reluctant to talk about will view you after she becomes privy to your shady dealings?"

Oliver knew exactly how Harriet would react. Her eyes would turn a dark shade of violet, her lips would definitely thin, and then . . . she'd launch into yet another lecture, taking him to task for transgressions he was evidently guilty of perpetuating. After she was done, she'd no doubt expect him to correct those transgressions, and . . .

"Is something amusing you?"

Blinking, Oliver realized his lips had taken to twitching as he'd been picturing Harriet and her indignation, but now was hardly the moment to become distracted, not with Silas threatening to ruin him. Taking a second to get his amusement firmly under control, he gestured to the door. "Perhaps it would be best if you were to take your leave."

"I'm not leaving until we get matters settled between us once and for all."

"We've settled everything we need to settle."

"Forgive me, gentlemen," Mr. Blodgett interrupted in a very loud voice from the doorway, causing Silas, who'd been approaching Oliver in a somewhat aggressive manner to stop in his tracks and glare at the butler. To Mr. Blodgett's credit, he didn't so much as bat an eye. "A Reverend Gilmore has come to call, Mr. Addleshaw. He's waiting for you in the drawing room."

Silas stopped glaring at Mr. Blodgett and swung his attention back to Oliver. "A reverend has come to call, Oliver?" Not bothering to allow Oliver a response, Silas laughed and shook his head. "It certainly explains your new position on ethics. I find the idea of you entertaining a man of God rather disturbing, but . . . to each his own." He made a point of grinding the cigar even farther into the rug, then strode to the door. Looking over his shoulder, he sent Oliver a sneer. "Do make sure to have that reverend say some extra prayers for you—you're going to need them." With that, he vanished from sight.

"Good heavens, sir, is everything all right?" Mr. Blodgett asked.

"Mr. Ruff and I have dissolved our business relationship, and I'm afraid he's not happy with me at the moment, but now is not the time for us to discuss the matter further. Reverend Gilmore is here, you said?"

Mr. Blodgett nodded. "He's in the drawing room, but I'll be happy to tell him you're unavailable if you'd like some time to yourself after your unfortunate encounter with Mr. Ruff."

Oliver smiled. "Thank you for that, Mr. Blodgett, but I'm not exactly comfortable turning away a man of the cloth."

He headed for the door and then walked down the long hallway, entering the drawing room a moment later. His attention settled on an older gentleman who was studying one of the many paintings hanging on the walls.

"It's by Delacroix," he said, walking to join the man who turned and smiled back at him.

"It's beautiful, and I have to imagine it's quite priceless," the man replied as he held out his hand. "I'm Reverend Thomas Gilmore, Mr. Addleshaw, Harriet's guardian, if you will."

Oliver shook the offered hand. "Harriet told me to expect you, although she wasn't exactly clear on when you'd be paying me a visit." He gestured to a settee done up in a blue watered silk. "Would you care to take a seat?"

Reverend Gilmore moved to sit down, his gaze settling on another painting, this one by Bonheur, hanging a few feet away from the Delacroix. "You have quite the collection of fine paintings here, Mr. Addleshaw. May I assume this is a room you seek out often to enjoy a bit of peace?"

Oliver lowered himself into a chair beside the settee. "I rarely spend much time in this room, Reverend Gilmore. I have an art dealer in my employ who travels around Europe, searching for paintings that are supposed to 'speak to me.' I've never quite had the heart to tell the man I've never heard or felt anything from a painting, but that I look at my acquisitions as more of an investment opportunity."

"How . . . sad," Reverend Gilmore began before he nodded, just once. "While I would love nothing more than to discuss your reasoning behind purchasing breathless works of art but not appreciating or sharing them, that's not why I've come to call. I'm here to discuss Harriet."

"You know, I think I've just found a new appreciation for these paintings, and I'd be more than happy to show you my entire collection, including the *really* nice ones that are hanging in my art gallery on the third floor."

Reverend Gilmore smiled. "And I'll be delighted to view those paintings, Mr. Addleshaw, but *after* we complete our discussion pertaining to Harriet. Tell me—and I'd appreciate the complete truth, if you please—how do matters stand between the two of you?"

Immediately swallowing the "We're fine," he'd been about to say, Oliver blew out a breath. "We're not exactly in accord with each other."

"Ah, well, that explains why you were absent from Mrs. Hart's delightful dinner last night, but if you're not in accord with her, have you decided to abandon your plans?"

"Certainly not."

"May I inquire as to why you're not abandoning your plans? Is this deal with the duke truly that important to you?"

Knowing the reverend expected more than a blithe reply, Oliver took a second to collect his thoughts. "The deal with the Duke of Westmoore is important to me since I've spent countless hours on it, however . . . it is more than that. If I abandon the plan, Harriet won't accept any money from me. She'll be forced back to that hovel she calls home, and I find that completely unacceptable."

Reverend Gilmore considered him for a long moment, and then, to Oliver's surprise, rose to his feet. "I don't believe I need to take up any more of your time, young man."

Oliver got to his feet as well. "That's all you needed to talk to me about?"

"I came here today to make certain you have Harriet's best interests at heart, and since you seem to have that well in hand, there's nothing left for me to say. Although, if I could make one tiny request? Please keep her safe, Mr. Addleshaw."

Oliver tilted his head. "Forgive me, Reverend Gilmore, but that request almost suggests Harriet's facing some manner of trouble."

Reverend Gilmore patted Oliver's arm. "Harriet's troubles are hers, and hers alone, to share with you, if she so chooses, Mr. Addleshaw. However, it would relieve this old man's mind to know someone other than myself and Mrs. Hart is watching out for Harriet."

"I'm fairly sure my grandfather has been keeping an eye on Harriet, and her friends as well, Reverend Gilmore. He seems to have become quite fond of the ladies, and you may rest assured he'll do everything in his power to keep them safe, as will I."

"Wonderful, and . . . " Reverend Gilmore looked past Oliver and smiled. "Speaking of your grandfather . . . Mr. Addleshaw, we were just discussing you."

Turning, Oliver watched as Archibald strode into the room, followed by none other than Everett. "Grandfather, this is a surprise."

Archibald lifted a brow. "I don't know why you'd be surprised to see me, since I'm actually staying in your home at the moment."

"True, but I wasn't aware you've taken to keeping company with Everett, as well as Harriet and her friends, unless . . ." He turned to Everett. "You haven't changed your mind about hiring Miss Longfellow as a nanny for the brats, have you?"

"I'm not quite that desperate yet, and Archibald and I didn't arrive together. We simply ran into each other outside the house," Everett said before Archibald gestured him forward and introduced him to Reverend Gilmore. Pleasantries were exchanged, and then Reverend Gilmore stepped closer to Everett.

"Tell me, Mr. Mulberry, why are you so reluctant to hire Miss Longfellow? After sharing dinner with her last night at Mrs. Hart's, I must tell you, I got the distinct impression she's incredibly put out with you—something to do with you refusing to even entertain the thought of her watching over your wards."

"I wasn't trying to insult her by refusing to consider her as a nanny," Everett said quickly. "I was simply trying to protect the children I've been plagued . . . or rather blessed with, or at the very least, keep them alive."

"Your wards might benefit from a nanny with Miss Long-fellow's qualifications, but it's not my place to try to convince you of that," Reverend Gilmore replied before he turned back to Oliver. "Since you have new guests to entertain, I'll take my leave, but I'm sure we'll meet again soon for another delightful chat, or at least to give you an opportunity to show me all of those paintings you have hanging about your house."

"No need to leave on my account," Archibald said. "I'm not staying long. Abigail sent me over to give Oliver some new details regarding the dinner party we're intending to hold once the duke arrives in town. After that, I'm back to her house to give Harriet one last lesson in cutlery placement before she goes off to Delmonico's tonight." He nodded to Oliver. "You are still intending to take her there, aren't you?"

"I am, although I will admit it temporarily slipped my mind." He narrowed his eyes. "Delmonico's aside, though, what was that about a dinner party you and Abigail are going to host for the duke?"

"Oh, nothing for you to worry about. We thought it would be easier for Harriet to help you entertain the duke in familiar surroundings, but Abigail did want you to know she's started writing out a few invitations, so . . ."

"I'll have to go along with it whether I'm willing or not?" Oliver finished for him.

"Exactly." Archibald smiled. "Tell me though, what was so distracting that you forgot about your plans with Harriet? She's certainly not a lady many gentlemen forget."

Alarm bells began going off in Oliver's head. "Grandfather, forgive me, but . . . you and Abigail haven't taken to . . . plotting, have you?"

"Didn't I promise after the disastrous results of bringing you into contact with that lovely, or so I thought, young lady from Georgia, that I was giving up my plotting days?" Archibald countered.

Oliver narrowed his eyes. "Miss Savannah, or whatever her name truly is, was three plots ago."

"Really?" Archibald asked. "Well, getting back to the dinner party . . ."

"We weren't talking about the dinner party, we were talking about plotting."

"Oh look, Mr. Blodgett's bringing us a feast from the looks of that laden tray he's pushing," Archibald exclaimed, turning from Oliver as Reverend Gilmore moved to help Mr. Blodgett negotiate the heavy cart over to a low table surrounded by settees and wing-back chairs.

"This was very kind of you, Mr. Blodgett," Archibald said, "but I have to ask, since Abigail has Oliver's chef, who put together such a delightful spread?"

"Mrs. Rollins," Mr. Blodgett replied. "It was originally meant for Mr. Ruff, but since he stormed out of here in a huff before the meal he demanded could be served, I figured we shouldn't let Mrs. Rollins's efforts go to waste."

"Mr. Ruff left in a huff?" Everett asked as Mr. Blodgett set about the business of serving up food.

Oliver nodded. "He made a huge mess of things down in West Virginia, and because of that mess, I told him we needed to part ways."

Archibald sat down on the settee, placing his plate of food on a nearby table. "How did he take that?"

"As one would expect. He threatened me and told me he'd see me ruined."

Reverend Gilmore moved to take a seat beside Archibald, balancing the plate of food Mr. Blodgett had insisted he take on his lap. "Forgive me, but this Mr. Ruff wouldn't happen to be Mr. Silas Ruff, would he?"

"One and the same," Archibald admitted. "Are you familiar with him, Reverend Gilmore?"

"I am." Reverend Gilmore looked to Oliver. "I have to say that this puts a whole different twist on your situation, Mr. Addleshaw. From what I know of Silas Ruff, he's a ruthless and vindictive gentleman. He won't take his dismissal lightly, which means he's a distinct threat to you, and that means he's a threat to Harriet."

"Silas might be ruthless, Reverend Gilmore, but I don't think he'd stoop so low as to hurt a lady."

"I'm more afraid he'll use her to hurt you," Reverend Gilmore said softly. "He'll strike where he thinks you'll be most vulnerable. Harriet, given her current situation, is very vulnerable indeed, and if Mr. Ruff takes the time to find out about her and then delves into her history, I'm afraid what he might uncover could hurt you both."

"Are you suggesting Harriet may have some skeletons rattling around her closet that would be best left not rattled?"

"Harriet's skeletons are not mine to share, Mr. Addleshaw. She, along with everyone else in the world, has crosses she's been given to bear, but she certainly doesn't need more crosses given to her at this particular time." He released a breath. "I'm afraid, in the interest of keeping her truly safe, it might be for the best if you and she parted ways before any damage can be done."

"But then she'll have no choice but to go back to the slums," Oliver pointed out.

"I think we can trust Mrs. Hart to make certain that doesn't happen," Archibald said, although his tone held a distinct trace of disappointment.

"Harriet won't accept charity," Oliver argued. "And what everyone seems to be forgetting is that I'm one of the most powerful gentlemen in the country. Yes, Silas is ruthless, and he's angry, but I'm angry as well, and I certainly can't see how abandoning my plan is going to keep Harriet safe."

"Besides, since so many people know about her now, there's really nothing left to do *but* go forward with things," Everett added.

Oliver frowned. "What do you mean, 'so many people know about her now'?"

"Ah, well, as to that," Everett began, "that's actually why I'm here."

Oliver's head immediately began to throb again. "Go on."

Everett blew out a breath. "Miss Dixon and I went shopping today, at Arnold Constable & Company, and the manager there just couldn't tell Miss Dixon fast enough all about your Harriet and how the two of you are engaged."

Oliver frowned. "Miss Dixon was already aware of Harriet, since the four of us are supposed to go out to dinner tonight."

Everett nodded. "True, but I never told her about the whole engagement business, mostly because I had no idea what to say, but . . . after the manager told Miss Dixon about the engagement, we just happened to encounter about twenty people she knew at the store, and of course she told all of them about your engagement, and then . . ." Everett's voice trailed off, and he began to study the cut of his sleeve.

"And then what?"

Everett looked up. "This is going to come as a bit of a shock, but we ran into none other than the Duke of Westmoore, who just happened to arrive in the city earlier than expected."

"The duke's in town?"

"I'm afraid he is, and . . . Miss Dixon told the duke we were planning on going to Delmonico's tonight, along with you and Harriet." Everett's expression turned a little pained. "You'll be happy to learn that Miss Dixon then extended the duke and his family an invitation to join us this evening and he was only too happy to accept. So you see, it's hardly advisable now to discontinue your plan with Harriet, but we can always hope that you're right and keeping her by your side will, indeed, keep her safe."

14

Squinting against the bright afternoon sun, Harriet considered the address painted across the awning of the shop she was standing in front of. Looking down at the card in her hand, she frowned and turned to Lucetta. "Oliver must have written down the wrong address, since it's clear this location is currently occupied."

"We should have known something was wrong when we ended up on the Ladies' Mile," Lucetta said before she adjusted the huge hat she'd placed over a wig of dowdy brown. "It's a truly enviable space, but . . . why are you looking at me like that?"

Harriet grinned. "I still don't understand why you insisted on traveling out and about in disguise, especially since you had to raid Abigail's attic to find something to wear. That dress you chose has to be at least thirty years out of date, and I'm quite certain you're drawing more attention wearing it than if you'd simply come out as yourself."

"I'm on holiday from the theater at the moment, which means I have no desire for anyone to recognize me." Lucetta smiled. "Besides, Millie's wearing a costume, and I certainly didn't want her to feel odd about that circumstance."

Harriet looked to the left and settled her attention on Millie, who was dressed as the perfect lady's maid in a skirt of navy, white shirt, and pristine apron. She was trying to tug an obviously reluctant Buford, who didn't seem too keen to be on the end of a brightly colored piece of rope. By the time Millie finally dragged him up beside Harriet, she had a decidedly grumpy look about her.

"I don't think Buford likes this fancy collar and leash you made for him," Millie said with a huff. "The pink and purple is obviously embarrassing him, which is causing him to be a touch capitalistic."

"He's an advocate of capitalism?" Lucetta asked slowly.

Millie let out another huff. "I knew I shouldn't have tried a big word when I don't have my dictionary handy. Now it's going to drive me mad trying to figure out what I meant to say."

"*Cantankerous*, perhaps?" Lucetta suggested.

"What does that mean?"

"Grouchy," Harriet supplied before giving Buford a good scratch, earning a tail wag in the process. "And I told you I'd take care of Buford, but you, being annoyingly stubborn, refused my offer."

"Society ladies don't walk their own dogs unless they're in Newport," Millie said. "Since I'm your maid, it's my job, but . . . why did you and Lucetta stop in front of this shop?"

"According to the directions Oliver gave me, this is supposed to be my new space, but he clearly wrote down the wrong address." Harriet shrugged. "It's probably for the best this space is occupied, given that I'm sure the rent is outrageous. I will need to pinch pennies for the first couple of years, even given the money Oliver's paying me."

"Speaking of Oliver," Lucetta began, "I have to admit, unwillingly of course, that he's really not what I expected."

"You didn't expect him to be a seriously flawed gentleman with a propensity for arrogance?"

"Of course I did," Lucetta said with a snort. "All society gentlemen are arrogant, but most of them aren't . . . thoughtful."

"You think Oliver's thoughtful?"

"Occasionally, yes. He didn't have to search out premises for your shop."

"He gave us the wrong address for that shop."

"True, but there is shop space out there somewhere that he has found for you, and that's rather sweet, don't you think?"

"I'd prefer not to think of Oliver at all."

"Now *you're* being cantankerous."

"Since we seem to be at the wrong place, and since Buford is certain to take my arm off soon with his tugs, shall we go back to Abigail's house?" Millie asked.

Harriet shook her head. "We can't go back just yet because I told Abigail we'd be gone a few hours. Truth be told, she seemed downright tickled to have us out of the house for a bit."

Millie bit her lip. "But aren't you a little concerned that Jane might find us out here in the open?"

"The main threat we were facing from Jane stemmed from that necklace she sent me," Harriet said. "Since I gave the necklace to Reverend Gilmore, and he has discreetly handed it over to the police on the chance someone has reported it missing, Jane currently has no hold over us."

"She might not have a hold on you, Harriet," Millie argued, "but you have to know she's figured out we've moved, and that she's probably learned where we're living now."

"True, but she also knows, being as cunning as she is, that it wouldn't be in her best interest to try anything while we're under the protection of members of high society," Harriet argued right back. "She certainly wouldn't dare try anything while we're in the midst of the Ladies' Mile. Since I did assure Abigail we'd be gone for a few hours, and again, she seemed tickled about that, I'm going to suggest we stroll around and enjoy ourselves."

"Abigail was only tickled to get us out of the house because she and Archibald had their heads together all morning but kept getting interrupted when one of us would enter whatever room they'd taken to skulking in," Lucetta said. "Without us underfoot, they'll have plenty of time to plot."

"That certainly explains why she didn't insist on accompanying us." Harriet grinned. "If you ask me, she and Archibald are beginning to enjoy each other's company quite a bit."

Lucetta returned the grin. "Now that you mention it, you're right. And . . . we should do our own plotting and come up with a plan that just might see them embracing a touch of romance, especially since they're currently trying to figure out how to get you and Oliver together for . . ." Lucetta snapped her mouth shut and batted far-too-innocent lashes Harriet's way.

"What do you mean, getting Oliver and I together?"

The batting stopped in a flash. "Oh, very well, but I have to tell you that I didn't mean to eavesdrop, which is how I managed to come across the information I'm about to impart. Abigail and Archibald didn't know I'd fallen asleep on the chaise in front of the fireplace when they snuck into the library in order to have a private chat." Lucetta's lips curled. "They were certainly surprised to discover me there, and *after* they'd divulged quite a bit of their scheme."

"Why didn't you let them know you were there from the beginning?" Millie asked.

"Well, ah . . . I was just waking up, you see, and—" Her eyes widened and she looked around. "Did either of you just hear someone scream?"

For a second, Harriet thought Lucetta was simply trying to distract Millie, but then a woman's scream really did sound from the very shop they were standing in front of. Turning, she watched as the door sprang open and three ladies rushed out, the sound of additional screams following them out to the sidewalk.

"My gracious," one of the ladies said as she hurried past. "Poor Mrs. Henderson."

"Perhaps we should have stayed to help her," another one of the ladies said.

"That's Mr. Bambini in there," the third lady exclaimed. "He owns most of this street, and my husband rents from him. I can't get involved in that nasty business."

The ladies' retreating backs soon disappeared, but then the door opened again and the sound of a dog barking drifted out to the sidewalk. Buford evidently heard it, and before Harriet could catch him, he lunged forward, ripping the leash out of Millie's hand. He raced through the open door, knocking over the lady who'd frozen right in front of that door the moment she caught sight of the huge dog barreling her way. Harriet rushed to her aid, and after getting the woman back on her feet, muttered a quick apology before taking off after Buford. She made it all of five feet into the store before she skidded to a halt when the tinkles of breaking glass sounded around her.

She stood stock-still for a moment when she realized Buford was loose in a china shop but found the incentive to move when additional shrieking began, more glass shattered, and Buford began to howl. Harriet hitched up her skirts and darted down the aisle, wincing when shards of something that had probably been expensive crunched under her feet. She hurried around a display of delicate-looking plates, caught a teacup tipping precariously close to the edge, set it back a safe distance, and continued forward, slowing to a stop and releasing a groan at the sight that met her eyes.

A lady wearing a white shirtwaist paired with a dark skirt, and who had puffy, red-rimmed eyes, was standing next to an intimidating-looking gentleman with brown hair, huge shoulders, and a curled mustache that took up a good deal of space on his face. They were staring off to the right, neither one of them speaking, and when Harriet turned her attention to where they were staring, she understood why they seemed incapable of uttering any sounds.

Buford was under a small table, the only parts of him visible being his nose peeking out from one side and his tail from the other. A tiny wisp of a dog was positioned right in front of Buford's nose. The little beast was growling deep in its throat, which seemed to be causing Buford to tremble, because everything on top of the dainty table he was under was shaking.

"Don't just stand there," the lady snapped. "Get your dog."

"He's not exactly mine," Harriet muttered before she stepped forward, crouched down, and then blinked when the tiny pooch switched its attention to her and began making cute little doggy noises. "How adorable are you?" she asked before she looked under the table and met Buford's terrified gaze. "It's not going to hurt you, Buford. It's friendly. You need to come out from under there right this minute."

If anything, Buford's shaking increased. Harriet scooped up the tiny dog, got to her feet, and held the dog out to the lady. "If you could just hold this for a moment, it might help me get Buford out from under the table."

The lady took the dog, leaving Harriet to crouch in front of Buford again. "Oliver's going to have to have a heart-to-heart with you, Buford, about this whole cowardly giant business. You're a fierce beast—at least you look like one—and it's past time you remember that."

The gentleman with the large mustache stepped up next to her and leaned over. "Excuse me, but did you mention a gentleman by the name of Oliver?"

"I did."

"You're not speaking about Mr. Oliver Addleshaw, are you?"

"I am, and that large bit of trouble hiding under the table is his dog. I'm watching over him at the moment, although, given that he's just destroyed a good portion of this store, I'm not doing a very good job of watching."

Buford let out a whine.

"You have no reason to whine," Harriet admonished, looking Buford in the eye. "You've been a very bad boy, and Oliver's not going to be happy with you once I hand him over a bill for all this damage."

Buford seemed to realize he was in a smidgen of trouble, because he closed his eyes and refused to look at her. Unable to come up with a suitable way to get him out from under the table, Harriet straightened and looked to the woman with the red eyes. "I really must apologize for all of this, Mrs. or Miss . . . ?"

"I'm Mrs. Henderson, proprietress of this shop—at least I was until Mr. Bambini informed me I'm being evicted." With that Mrs. Henderson dissolved into great, heaving sobs.

Before Harriet could offer a single word of comfort to the distraught lady, Mr. Bambini suddenly beamed at her.

"You must be Miss Peabody."

"How in the world do you know my name?"

"Mr. Addleshaw told me all about you, and I offer you my congratulations." He winked. "You are the reason many a young lady is going to be despondent once word officially gets out about the engagement. But enough about that—what do you think of this wonderful space? I should have realized you'd want to look it over once Mr. Addleshaw told you about it, but he neglected to tell me you were planning on stopping by today." Mr. Bambini sent a pointed look toward Mrs. Henderson. "If I'd have known, I would have made certain there was nothing of a distressing nature to greet you."

Harriet barely had time to duck as a piece of china, hurled by none other than Mrs. Henderson, sailed her way. She felt it graze the top of her head, heard a resounding crash and then dropped to the ground and rolled to the right when Mrs. Henderson grabbed a beautiful crystal vase and chucked that in her direction. Shards of glass stung her cheek and she knew she was bleeding, but the ramifications of what Mr. Bambini had stated finally settled in, and she didn't have the heart to fight back.

"Have you lost your mind?" Mr. Bambini yelled as he grabbed a plate from Mrs. Henderson and took hold of both her arms, effectively restraining her even as the tiny dog the lady had dropped to the ground began to scamper around their feet. "That is Miss Peabody you're assaulting, fiancée of Mr. Oliver Addleshaw."

Mrs. Henderson began to struggle against the arms that bound her, causing Harriet's heart to ache as she pushed herself up from the floor. She wiped her hands on her gown, winced when a shard of glass sliced her, plucked it out of her palm, and drew in a steadying breath. She felt something dribble down her face but ignored it as she stepped closer to Mrs. Henderson and Mr. Bambini. "I'm afraid there's been a grave misunderstanding."

Mrs. Henderson stilled as Mr. Bambini sent her a frown. "A misunderstanding? I assure you, there has not. Mr. Addleshaw sought out my services yesterday, telling me of his desire to find his fiancée a most desirable location, and this is the location he decided he wanted to obtain." Mr. Bambini's frown turned to a smile. "I must say, he certainly seems to adore indulging you, my dear. Why, for a gentleman of society to actually encourage his future wife to dabble in . . . trade . . . Well, it's not something I've ever seen before."

For a second, something warm traveled through her veins, but then reality pushed the feeling away as temper replaced it. "While my fiancé certainly does seem to enjoy indulging me, tell me, Mr. Bambini, was Mr. Addleshaw aware of the fact this particular space was occupied by Mrs. Henderson?"

"He bought a vase from me," Mrs. Henderson said. "I was thrilled, thinking he would tell others of his social set about my place, but now . . . I think he only did so to ease his conscience

because he knew in order to give you this shop, I'd have to go."
She dissolved once again into a fit of weeping.

Every pleasant thought and every unlikely dream Harriet
had begun to dream died a rapid death. Disappointment, mixed
with a healthy dollop of temper, settled over her, and she found
she had to take in quite a few deep breaths before she was even
able to speak. She looked up and found Lucetta standing a few
feet away from her, Millie hovering right behind her. "It seems
to me, ladies, that Abigail and Archibald's plotting is all for
naught." She drew in another breath. "Would you be so kind,
Lucetta, to fetch Buford? I'm sure he'll come out from under
the table for you."

"Of course I'll fetch him." Lucetta moved forward, but paused
midstep when Mr. Bambini moved to block her progress.

"Good heavens, you're Miss Lucetta Plum—in disguise, of
course, but I'd recognize your voice anywhere."

"I'd appreciate it if you wouldn't draw attention to me, sir,
especially since I am, as you pointed out, in disguise, and there
is a reason for that."

Mr. Bambini tilted his head. "But . . . what are you doing
here, and from the looks of things, with Miss Peabody?"

"She's my friend," Harriet said, her temper going from sim-
mering to boiling when Mr. Bambini's eyes widened.

"I'm her maid," Millie added when he turned his attention
to her.

"Maids don't normally speak unless spoken to," he pointed
out.

Millie grinned. "That's helpful to know." With that, she turned
on her heel and hustled as fast as she could over the broken glass
and out of the shop.

"This is all very unusual," Mr. Bambini muttered.

"And it's about to get more unusual," Harriet muttered right
back. She watched as Lucetta coaxed Buford out from under

the table and then winced when the tiny little dog charged from behind Mrs. Henderson and directly at him, causing Buford to stick his nose into the folds of Lucetta's skirt and shake uncontrollably. Harriet stepped forward and scooped the tiny scrap of fearsomeness off the floor, nodded to Lucetta, who then began to pull Buford away, taking him down an aisle that wasn't littered with glass. There was another sound of something breaking, but Harriet ignored it as she turned her attention back to Mrs. Henderson.

"I cannot apologize enough, Mrs. Henderson, for the distress you've been made to suffer over something I had a part in. Allow me to make it up to you."

Mrs. Henderson frowned, reached out and took the dog from Harriet, and then reached with her free hand to a table, snagged a lacey doily that was resting on it, and thrust it into Harriet's hand. "Your face is bleeding."

Harriet dabbed at her face, grimaced when she saw the blood staining the lace, then lowered her hand and turned to Mr. Bambini. "You will not be evicting Mrs. Henderson."

"Mr. Addleshaw has already paid the rent on this space for the next year, and Mrs. Henderson is behind on her rent by an entire week."

"I told you I'd have the money by the end of the day," Mrs. Henderson said. "It's just that with Mr. Henderson unable to find work and our two children being so sick lately, well, I haven't been able to keep everything straight."

Harriet closed her eyes and fought to suppress the rage that had begun to course through her veins.

What type of man was Oliver?

Could he truly believe there was nothing wrong with casting out a hardworking woman from her business—the Henderson family's only source of income from the sound of it—because he'd wanted to present her with this prime location?

Was he really so ruthless?

The answer immediately flung to mind. Yes, he was, and here she'd been thinking all sorts of ridiculous thoughts, the most ridiculous being that he was actually a kind man underneath all of that arrogance, and that she was developing a small amount of affection for him.

Dabbing at her face again, she squared her shoulders. "Mrs. Henderson, as I just said, there will be no evicting of you done today or for the next year for that matter. You'll be happy to learn that I've decided I don't care for this spot in the least. It's much too fancy for what I have in mind. But . . . since my *darling* Mr. Addleshaw, inadvertently, I'm sure, caused you a considerable amount of distress and pain, the money he gave to Mr. Bambini will be used for your rent this year. I'll also need you to prepare a bill that I'll give to my fiancé for all the damage his dog did in your shop." She forced a smile. "You have my word he'll pay it promptly."

"I'm afraid I can't allow you to make such a completely ludicrous offer," Mr. Bambini said, going from an indulgent-looking gentleman to an intimidating one in a split second.

"You can't *allow* me?"

"This is business, Miss Peabody, and business is done between men. I'm sure that you're a lady possessed of deep emotional feelings, which are currently getting in the way of what, for me, is a lucrative business alliance. I won't have you coming between me and Mr. Addleshaw, so you'll need to simply go along with this deal he and I brokered and be happy about it."

"I don't take well to gentlemen trying to order me around, Mr. Bambini."

"The deal's done."

"Yes, it is, and you won't be losing a dime since I just promised Mrs. Henderson the use of that lovely money Oliver gave you toward rent." She lifted her chin. "Now, if you'll excuse me, I need to go find my darling fiancé and have a little chat with him."

She sent Mrs. Henderson what she hoped was a reassuring smile, sent Mr. Bambini a glare, picked up her skirts, and tried to sail dramatically from the shop, her sailing hampered by the pesky fact she had to dodge numerous broken items that littered the floor. She finally made it to the door, pushed it open, and stepped onto the sidewalk, squinting as the sun hit her eyes. Shielding them with her hand, she felt her temper burn even hotter as she caught sight of Lucetta and Millie. They were standing on the sidewalk in the company of a well-dressed lady—that lady being none other than Harriet's aunt Jane.

Blowing out a breath, Harriet tilted her head and scanned the sky. "You're obviously a little annoyed with me at the moment, Lord, given the numerous dastardly situations I keep finding myself in. But if I promise to walk the straight and narrow from this point forward, would you consider making Jane go away?"

When her aunt didn't immediately disappear into thin air, Harriet's lips twitched just a touch as she realized how absurd her request had been. Lifting her chin, she began stomping forward, praying that her aunt didn't have something of a diabolical nature on her mind.

15

*H*arriet, there you are my darling," Jane purred when Harriet came to a stop beside her. "You look simply delightful today. Is that a new dress?"

Ignoring the question, Harriet narrowed her eyes on her aunt. "What are you doing here, Jane?"

Jane's green eyes narrowed right back at her. "It's *Aunt Jane*, and . . . honestly dear, given the amount of money I spent on deportment lessons for you, surely you're aware that when someone extends you a compliment, the proper response should be *Thank you*." She twirled her parasol around. "And then good manners dictate you respond in kind. What do you think of *my* dress?"

Taking a moment to consider her aunt, Harriet came to the immediate conclusion that Jane was looking very well indeed as she preened in the middle of the sidewalk. The muted green of Jane's gown lent itself well to her pale complexion, and the ornate hat on her head was perched exactly right, showcasing Jane's expertly styled red hair underneath. The perfection of Jane's hair gave clear proof that she'd somehow secured the means to hire on a lady's maid. Overall, she presented a most respectable picture, even if Harriet knew there was next to nothing respectable about her aunt. "Your dress is beautiful and certainly proves that thievery is allowing you to live in style."

The parasol twirling came to an immediate halt. "Don't be snide, Harriet. And for your information, I've put that particular business aside, at least for the most part." She fingered a diamond brooch pinned to her dress before she tilted her head. "You're not wearing the necklace I sent you for your birthday."

Since Harriet had no intention of telling her aunt the necklace was currently residing with the police, she decided her best, and perhaps only option, was distraction. "Surely you, being an expert on deportment, must know that diamonds aren't to be worn during the day."

Jane's hand dropped from the brooch as her expression turned sulky. She turned from Harriet and gave a wave of her hand, that action summoning a well-equipped carriage. The coachman pulled on the reins, the carriage came to a smart stop, and two familiar-looking brutes hopped off the back and immediately took to looking intimidating as they crossed beefy arms over their chests.

Suppressing a shudder, Harriet turned back to her aunt. "Dare I hope you've had enough of my *delightful* company and are now going to get on your way?"

"Don't be ridiculous. I came out specifically to speak with you."

Dread was immediate. "So this isn't just an unfortunate happenstance, meeting up with you today?"

"Good heavens, no. This *fortunate* happenstance is a direct result of me having you watched around the clock ever since you moved into that house on Washington Square." She smiled. "I've been taxing my mind no small amount to come up with an explanation as to how that came about."

"How long have you been having me followed?"

"Oh, a few years." Jane turned to Lucetta, who was wobbling a little on her feet, probably because Buford had stuck his nose into the folds of her skirt and was trembling like mad. "I must say, Miss Plum, you certainly gave my handsome Martin over there an unpleasant time of it when you took the reins of that carriage the other day." She nodded to one of the brutes, who smiled a most gruesome-looking smile back at her, his face anything but handsome. "Your reckless manner of driving caused him quite a bit of aggravation, but because he's a determined sort, he kept after you and discovered your final destination. Someone could have knocked me over with a feather when I did a bit of snooping and discovered the three of you were living under the roof of one of society's most respected matrons."

Harriet's sense of dread immediately increased. "May I assume there's a reason behind all of your subterfuge?"

"Would you believe I've simply been longing to have a lovely chat with my most cherished of nieces?"

"I'm your only niece, and you've never cherished anything except money."

Jane's lips thinned. "Very well, since you obviously don't care to exchange the expected pleasantries, we'll get right down to business." She closed the parasol and used it to point at the carriage. "Shall we make ourselves comfortable and take a few turns about the city while we have ourselves a little chat?"

"I think I'd prefer chatting out here on the sidewalk," Harriet countered. "I find carriages a little . . . secluded."

"What I have to say is not something I care for anyone to overhear, and besides, I'm beginning to perspire out here in this dreadful heat." Jane glanced to Lucetta. "Your friends may join us, but you'll need to leave that beast behind. I'm certainly not going to make myself uncomfortable by having all of us squeeze together so that the dog can ride about the city in style."

Harriet's teeth clinked together. "Since, given your tenacious nature, you won't leave me alone until you've had your say, I will join you, but Lucetta and Millie will not."

"And you, Harriet," Lucetta said through teeth that seemed to be as gritted as Harriet's were, "will only be taking a ride around town with Jane over my dead body."

Jane wagged a finger in Lucetta's direction. "Famous actress or not, my pet, that can be arranged." She nodded to one of her men, who immediately pushed aside his jacket, revealing the handle of a pistol.

"Enough of your threats, Jane," Harriet said before she caught Lucetta's eye. "You and Millie need to take Buford back to Mrs. Hart's house, and no, I don't want to hear any arguments about that," she added when Lucetta began muttering. "I'll be fine."

"We'll never see you again if you go off with Jane," Millie said, speaking up in a voice that had taken to quivering.

Harriet smiled. "Jane's not going to hurt me, Millie. She needs me for something, and I won't be able to fulfill that need if I'm dead." She looked at the watch pinned to the underside of her sleeve. "However, to be on the safe side, I'm going to limit our little chat to one hour, so if I'm not back at Mrs. Hart's within that hour, feel free to contact the police."

That pronouncement earned her a rapid hustle over to the carriage as Jane took a death grip on her arm and certainly didn't seem as if she intended to let go anytime soon. Looking over her shoulder at her friends—both of whom were now almost completely blocked from view by the two thugs—she opened her mouth to assure them she'd be fine one more time, but Jane suddenly shoved her, leaving Harriet no choice but to stumble into the carriage in order to avoid a nasty fall. Landing hard on the seat, she rubbed her elbow and watched while Jane, after speaking in a hushed tone to her driver, settled herself on the opposite side right before the carriage lurched into motion. A heavy thud sounded behind Harriet, leaving her little doubt that Jane's men had rejoined them, making the idea of a quick escape, if Jane turned unusually nasty, infeasible.

"Now see, isn't this much cozier than lingering on the street?" Jane asked, smoothing a gloved hand against the red crushed-velvet upholstery.

"Most people don't consider abduction to be cozy."

"It's rather irksome to discover you still possess such a flair for the dramatic," Jane said with a roll of her eyes before she leaned down and pulled a very large, very black cat out from under the seat. She settled it on her lap and began stroking it, although the cat didn't seem to be enjoying it much, since it kept letting out little hissing noises every other stroke.

Harriet frowned. "I thought you loathed cats."

"I wouldn't go so far as to say I loathe them, but Precious—that's truly her name—isn't mine. She belongs to a Mrs. Fish, and that lady's growing quite distraught over the idea her cat has yet to be found. Why, I expect if I maintain possession of Precious for another couple of days, the reward Mrs. Fish keeps increasing for its safe return will be up to at least five hundred dollars."

"You stole Precious in order to claim a reward?"

"Hmm . . . would you believe I just happened to discover this cat in my carriage, *and* that I didn't have the slightest idea Mrs. Fish was so attached to the creature?"

"I thought you said you'd put your thieving ways behind you?"

"I said *for the most part*, but if you must know, Precious here was just a little too tempting for me to resist."

"Give me the cat."

"I most certainly will not. I have bills to pay, and this little darling is an easy way to pay them."

Reaching over, Harriet plucked Precious away from Jane and settled the now purring cat on her lap. "She obviously likes me more, but enough about the cat. What is so important that you felt it necessary to go through such extreme measures to get my attention?"

"I wouldn't have had to resort to such trying means if you'd only had the courtesy to acknowledge that letter I left for you."

"I didn't read your letter."

"Then you really can't complain about your current situation, can you? Since you didn't bother to read what I wrote—which was quite rude of you, by the way—I'll tell you what the letter said. I want you to come and work for me."

"Didn't we have this exact same conversation last year on my birthday, and . . . didn't I make myself perfectly clear when I said I wasn't interested in joining forces with you because I'm not really keen on illegal activities?"

"Oh, you made yourself clear, Harriet, but the last time we spoke, you were mostly uncomfortable with the idea of stealing for me. You'll be happy to know I've moved on to a more lucrative business, one where I'm rarely dealing in tangible goods." She leaned forward. "However, now that you've somehow managed to get yourself involved with high society, I've come up with the most wonderful of plans, one that will finally allow you to pay me back for everything I've done for you over the years."

Harriet's mouth dropped open. "Pardon me?"

"You've evidently put aside those pesky moral convictions you always stood behind, and I couldn't be more delighted about that. But you really should have sought out my counsel when you decided to try your hand at scheming. You don't have the experience to pull off a scheme effortlessly, and I would hate to see you land yourself in jail."

"We are obviously having two different conversations here, Jane. What, pray tell, are you talking about?"

"You . . . following in my footsteps, of course. As I mentioned before, I was flabbergasted to learn you'd gone to live with Mrs.

Charles Hart. But when Martin discovered the gentleman you were riding with in that carriage Miss Plum was driving was none other than Mr. Oliver Addleshaw, well . . . it almost brought me to tears."

A hiss of protest from the cat had Harriet relaxing the death grip she'd taken on it. "You've heard about Mr. Addleshaw?"

Jane's lips thinned. "Not much, other than he's been seen coming and going from Mrs. Hart's house, and that the two of you were seen shopping together at Arnold Constable & Company. I don't currently have informants in houses owned by members of the true quality, but I do believe, given Mr. Addleshaw's obvious interest in you, that may be about to change."

"Did you ever consider that he may simply be a good friend of Mrs. Hart?"

"You really shouldn't doubt my intelligence, Harriet. Gentlemen don't escort ladies shopping unless there's a very good reason behind it. At first I thought you may have agreed to become the man's mistress, but then . . . that didn't make any sense, because Mr. Addleshaw certainly wouldn't take his mistress to the leading department store in the city. It's driving me mad, trying to figure out what confidence scheme you're actually perpetuating, which is why I felt compelled to track you down today. Quite honestly, if you hadn't been so kind as to leave the safety of Mrs. Hart's house, I was actually considering marching up to the door and demanding to speak with you."

"I'm sure that would have provided everyone with a bit of amusement—you trying to take on Mrs. Hart—but back to this confidence scheme idea. Don't you remember me telling you last year that I'm of the firm belief God wants me to live a good life? I highly doubt He'd consider my participating in a confidence scheme to be an acceptable way of living honorably."

Releasing a snort, Jane waved a hand in the air. "Yes, yes, I remember that nonsense about your God and what He wants for you, but tell me . . . if you're not scheming, what exactly are you doing with Mr. Addleshaw?"

"It's really none of your concern."

"Oh, but that's where you're wrong, my pet. My business of choice these days is collecting information, and if you now find yourself in the midst of society, I can use that to my advantage. And again, you owe me."

Harriet frowned. "You're blackmailing people now?"

"Exactly, and I wanted you to join me while you were working in that hat shop, because you must have been privy to juicy gossip overheard from customers. But . . . since you're apparently no longer employed there, there's no reason to discuss that particular plan."

"There's no reason to talk blackmail at all, since I'm not going to help you with whatever mad scenario you've come up with."

Jane waved Harriet's words away with a single flick of her wrist. "Tell me, do you happen to know where Mrs. Hart keeps her safe?"

"Why would I want to know where Mrs. Hart's safe is located?"

"Don't be coy, Harriet. It doesn't become you."

"I'm not intending to steal from Mrs. Hart."

"How very noble, but again, do you know the location of her safe?"

"I'd like to get out of the carriage now."

"We're not done talking."

"I have nothing left to say to you."

Jane leaned forward. "I'll let you out as soon as you explain to my satisfaction what you're doing with Mr. Addleshaw."

"He's my fiancé."

As soon as the words left her mouth, Harriet knew she'd made a dreadful mistake.

Jane's face was beginning to mottle, her freckles were standing out in high relief, and her eyes had turned to green shards of ice. "You're lying."

"I assure you, I'm not."

For a second, Harriet thought Jane was going to launch herself at her, but then her aunt gripped the seat with both hands, drew in a deep breath, slowly released it, drew in another, and then began to speak, far too calmly. "May I assume he's taken with your beauty?"

"I'm fairly certain he's more taken with my wit."

"You're beginning to wear on my patience."

"As you are on mine," Harriet retorted. "I've now told you the truth about Mr. Addleshaw and would like to get out of this carriage. Obviously, I'm *not* following in your footsteps, which means you, my *dear* aunt, need to leave me alone from this point forward."

"Not until I'm given some type of compensation for raising you." Jane tapped a gloved finger against her chin. "Since blackmail seems to be beneath you, as does stealing, I'll make this easy on you. You're going to introduce me into society."

"How would you expect me to do that?"

"If what you claim is true, that you're really engaged to Mr. Oliver Addleshaw, it won't be difficult for you to introduce your *loving* aunt to the New York Four Hundred. I've never been given an opportunity such as this before, or at least not in quite some time, and since, again, you owe me, I'm sure you can grant me this one tiny favor."

"Absolutely not."

Jane narrowed her eyes. "That's unfortunate, especially since I now have no choice but to blackmail *you.*"

"What could you possibly blackmail me with?"

"I'm sure you won't want your darling Mr. Addleshaw to learn anything about your mother."

"We'll leave my mother out of this, thank you very much."

221

"Oh, I'm sure you'd love to, but a man of Mr. Addleshaw's social position will clearly not want to discover that his fiancée is illegitimate and . . . that her mother was actually nothing more than some man's mistress."

"You will watch your tongue in regard to my mother."

"I'm only speaking the truth," Jane said. "Your mother used her good looks to snag the attention of a wealthy gentleman— or *gentlemen,* I should say—although, unlike you, she never managed to procure a proposal. Unfortunately, she very rudely up and died after giving birth to you, and since I had no idea who your father was, I got stuck raising you. For that, I deserve compensation."

Pain tore through Harriet as her aunt's hateful words settled in. Jane had mentioned once before that her mother had a bit of a shady past, but she'd neglected to mention anything about numerous men.

A snap of Jane's fingers in front of her face had Harriet pushing aside her troubling thoughts.

"So what's it going to be? Me blackmailing you, or you choosing to introduce me into society as your loving aunt?"

Unexpected tears stung her eyes, and Harriet turned to look out the window as she tried to hold them at bay. Fresh pain settled in her heart, the reasoning behind that pain suddenly becoming crystal clear.

Her aunt was a despicable woman—of that there was no denying—and yet she was the only mother figure Harriet had ever known. A piece of Harriet, a piece she'd never once acknowledged, had apparently been holding out a small smidgen of hope that her aunt actually cared about her, loved her in some small way. She knew that was a foolish thought, especially since it couldn't be true, not with her aunt threatening her with blackmail, but . . .

Blinking away the last of her tears, Harriet pulled her gaze from the window and settled it on Jane. "Have you ever cared about me?"

"What a ridiculous question."

"It's not so ridiculous, considering you're my only living relative."

"You're being very annoying, and . . ." Jane's words trailed off right as her eyes began to gleam in a rather disturbing manner. She stared at Harriet for a good second, then pushed up from the seat, sat down again right beside Harriet, and ignoring the hiss the cat sent her way, proceeded to take Harriet's hand in hers.

Jane gave the hand a rather tight squeeze before she smiled. "Is that what's truly bothering you, my pet? You don't think I care about your well-being?"

Jane's touch sent a shiver of what felt remarkably like revulsion through Harriet, and she resisted the urge to scoot closer to the window. "Threatening me with blackmail can hardly be taken as a sign of affection."

"I know it must seem to you that I don't always care, but I've never been an overly demonstrative person, and being given the responsibility of your care did place a large burden on me. I can clearly tell my lack of expressing to you my . . . er . . . love . . . has hurt you no small amount, but do know that I hold you in deepest affection and really want only the best for you."

Although Jane's words were something Harriet had evidently been longing to hear for a long time, the malice the woman couldn't conceal in her eyes gave Harriet the unvarnished truth.

Jane hated her, had probably always hated her, but instead of causing another ache in her heart, Harriet felt only relief.

Perhaps God wasn't put out with her after all. Maybe He had allowed her the opportunity of this daunting meeting with Jane to help Harriet discover the true measure of the woman who'd raised her. Perhaps He'd done so to finally set her free from any childish hopes she'd been harboring, and . . .

"Feeling better now, my pet, since we've squared away my feelings for you?" Jane asked.

"Strangely enough, I am."

Squeezing Harriet's hand one last time, Jane released it and moved back to the opposite seat. "Wonderful . . . and you'll agree to introduce me to society?"

Swallowing the immediate "no" that had been on the tip of her tongue, Harriet forced a smile instead before she dropped her head and gave her attention to the cat, stalling in order to collect her thoughts.

Her aunt was dangerous—of that there could be no doubt—and Jane wasn't likely to put her latest desire to be introduced to society aside easily. The one thing Harriet knew with absolute certainty was that she was going to have to come clean with Oliver the moment she got away from Jane. He needed to be warned about her aunt, needed to warn others in society about Jane as well, but . . . she needed more time to come up with a way to thwart her aunt once and for all, so that her friends would be safe and she could go about living a respectable life.

Lifting her chin, she nodded, earning a blink of the eyes from Jane in the process. "Because you have taken *very* good care of me over the years, *and* you hold me in great affection, I'll do it."

"You'll introduce me to society?" Jane asked slowly.

"I'll introduce you to everyone in society I'm fortune enough to become friends with, but . . . you're going to have to wait for me to get a foothold in the door so to speak before I make any introductions." She leaned back against the seat. "I'll need a good month to do that, two at the most."

Silence settled over them as Jane stared back at Harriet—and then she nodded. "Very well, I'll give you a month to charm your way into the highest circles, but I expect you to be paving the way for me as you charm. Little mentions of your doting aunt will go far in preparing society for my entrance. However, if you get invited to any of those delicious society balls, you're to contact me immediately, because that would be the perfect opportunity for me to . . . Well, I'm sure you can figure out where I plan to go from there."

"It's June, Jane. Society has slowed to a stop here in the city, with most people currently in Europe or having their houses closed down while they go off to Newport or Saratoga Springs for the summer. There won't be many balls in my immediate future."

"But . . . if there are . . . you'll get me invited?"

"I'll get you invited to all the balls I'm invited to once the social season starts up in the fall."

"You're being a little evasive, my pet, which I find somewhat troubling." Jane's eyes narrowed. "Do know that I'll make your life miserable if you're lying to me."

Since Harriet knew she'd be far removed from society in a month and would be able to call exactly zero society members friends after she and Oliver parted ways—except for Mrs. Hart, who was probably more than capable of taking on Jane—she was completely at ease with what she'd offered her aunt. Leaning forward over the cat, she smiled. "That hardly sounded very affectionate, *Aunt* Jane."

Jane didn't bother to respond but instead thumped the tip of her parasol against the roof of the carriage. "I think this little meeting between us has been rather productive, so now I'm going to allow you an opportunity to put our plan into action."

"I told you, I need a month and you agreed to that."

"Of course I agreed, darling, but I'd like you to at least tell Mr. Addleshaw about me, because that would put . . ." Jane continued speaking, her words traveling in one of Harriet's ears and directly out the other as she went on and on about what lovely things Harriet could tell Oliver about her.

When the carriage began to slow, Harriet peered out the

window, irritation running over her when she noticed they were stopping, not in front of Abigail's house, but Oliver's. "I think your driver delivered me to the wrong house."

Craning her neck, Jane glanced out the window as well. "Oh no, this is where I told him to end up." She smiled. "I thought I was going to have to be more forceful getting your cooperation, so I intended to . . . Well, no need to explain that since it's ancient history now. Do use some of those suggestions I just gave you to explain me to your Mr. Addleshaw, and I'll check in on your progress soon."

"I can't go up and knock on Mr. Addleshaw's door. It's hardly proper behavior."

"If he's truly infatuated with you, he'll be delighted you've come to call, and I want to ascertain that you're really engaged. Engaged ladies often pay visits to their future husbands."

"No they don't."

Jane arched a brow right as the door opened and Martin thrust a beefy hand Harriet's way. Ignoring his hand, she clutched the cat closer to her and moved to get out of the carriage.

"I will need the cat back."

Brushing past Martin, who seemingly only stepped aside because Precious had started hissing, Harriet turned after her feet were firmly on the sidewalk. "The cat is coming with me."

"But what about my reward?"

Pretending not to hear her, Harriet swiveled on her heel and began walking for the front door. When she traveled out of earshot of her aunt, she leaned closer to Precious. "I can only hope, Precious, that Jane will, someday, get the reward she so richly deserves."

16

*C*losing the desk drawer on business papers Oliver knew he wouldn't have a chance to look over again in the foreseeable future, he leaned back in his chair. Impatience spread through him as he regarded Mr. Bambini, who'd arrived unannounced a short time before, the man proclaiming he had a matter of utmost importance to discuss. Considering the gentleman was currently twirling his large mustache over his finger, but had yet to state the reason for the visit, Oliver wasn't exactly certain the matter was of an urgent nature. "May I assume there's a problem with the deal we closed yesterday?" he finally asked when Mr. Bambini remained irritatingly mute.

The twirling stopped. "I wouldn't say there's exactly a problem, more of a complication, if you will. I simply wanted to take this opportunity to explain my side of the story before your . . ."

A knock at the door had Mr. Bambini's explanation coming to a rapid end when Mr. Blodgett stepped into the room. "Begging your pardon, Mr. Addleshaw, but another caller has just arrived, one I believe you're going to want to . . . Good heavens." Mr. Blodgett jumped back right before one of the largest, ugliest cats Oliver had ever seen darted into the room, hisses of displeasure emitting from it, which certainly explained his butler's unusual action of actually jumping.

"Don't let it escape."

For a second, Oliver remained stuck in his chair when the door flung fully open and Harriet barged into the room.

"She's heading for the window," Harriet yelled, the clear panic in her voice finally registering, which had Oliver up and on his feet a second later. He snatched the cat as it leapt for the open window, immediately regretting that particular decision when the monster dug its sharp claws into his arm. Prying himself free of the claws, he breathed a silent sigh of relief when Harriet plucked the cat away from him.

She cuddled the ball of ugliness against herself before she sent him a smile. He couldn't help notice that even though she was smiling, it seemed somewhat strained, and there was a distinct touch of redness to her nose, giving him the impression she was either coming down with a cold or . . . she'd been crying.

"Good thing Precious didn't make it out the window," she began in a voice that didn't sound as if she were coming down with a cold. Which meant . . .

"I'm pretty sure poor Mrs. Fish would have been beside herself if her cat went missing for good," she finished, giving the cat a quick hug before she caught his eye.

"Who is Mrs. Fish?" he heard himself ask, even though he was more interested in learning why her nose was red and what she was doing at his house.

"No idea, but I'll tell you all about that later. I do apologize for bursting in on you, but I couldn't let Precious make her escape. I'll go back to the drawing room and allow you to continue on with your meeting." Turning, she nodded toward Mr. Bambini, but then she stiffened, her smile slid right off her face, and the next thing he knew, he was once again holding the squirming and hissing cat as Harriet advanced on Mr. Bambini.

"I thought I told you I'd deal with Mr. Addleshaw," she said, standing in front of Mr. Bambini, who'd risen to his feet and was seemingly bristling with indignation.

"And I thought I told you this was gentlemen's business and I'd deal with it," Mr. Bambini countered.

Shifting the cat in his arms, another decision he immediately regretted when the cat left a long rip in his sleeve, Oliver moved closer to Harriet. "You know Mr. Bambini?"

Harriet nodded. "We met today and had a most illuminating discussion."

Mr. Bambini let out a grunt. "There was nothing *illuminating* about what we discussed, Miss Peabody, and I have to imagine Mr. Addleshaw is going to be most displeased when he learns the particulars of what transpired."

"He can't be nearly as displeased as I am," Harriet said, but even though she was standing her ground against a gentleman who was looming over her, and not giving an inch while she stood that ground, Oliver detected the faintest trace of a quiver in her tone, that quiver causing his temper to rise even as a strange feeling settled in the vicinity of his heart.

The cat took that moment to let out a howl of protest, which had him unclenching the fingers he'd dug into it before he walked over to his butler and held out the now spitting cat. "Would you be so kind as to take this little darling to the kitchen? I'm sure it'll settle right down if it's given some milk."

Mr. Blodgett looked downright alarmed at that idea. "You want me to put my life at risk by trying to get that beast to drink some milk?"

"Precious won't hurt you," Harriet said as she took the cat from Oliver and moved closer to Mr. Blodgett. "She's simply had a tough time of it of late, but I imagine if you add some fish to that milk, she'll be your newest best friend."

Mr. Blodgett reached out and took the cat, although he did

so remarkably reluctantly, and holding it as far away from his person as he could, began heading for the door. "If you ask me, it wouldn't hurt this cat in the least to miss a few meals."

Harriet smiled at the butler. "I'm fairly sure Precious is a bit spoiled, which goes far in explaining her girth and cantankerous nature, but . . . Oh, speaking of cantankerous, if it wouldn't be too much trouble, could you send a note around to Mrs. Hart, telling her I'm here and that I'm . . . fine?"

Oliver exchanged a glance with Mr. Blodgett, whose eyes had widened. But, given that the butler was the consummate professional, he sent Harriet a nod and walked out the door, still holding the now squirming cat at arm's length.

"While this is a delightful surprise, Harriet," Oliver said, lowering his voice. "What are you doing here?"

"That thrilling tale will need to wait until after I'm done with Mr. Bambini," she returned before she marched her way back to Mr. Bambini, who didn't appear delighted she was once again giving him her undivided attention. "There's no reason for you to linger, sir. I'm here now, and I'll tell Mr. Addleshaw what happened today on the Ladies' Mile."

"You're going to tell him how Mrs. Henderson assaulted you?"

Oliver was by Harriet's side before she had an opportunity to respond. "You were assaulted?" He reached out and turned her face toward him, taking a finger to gently touch a scratch marring her delicate skin. "Did Mrs. Henderson do this to you, or was it the cat?"

He felt Harriet shiver ever so slightly as she leaned closer into him, but then she froze, released a breath, and immediately took a step back, leaving him no choice but to withdraw his hand.

"Precious adores me, and Mr. Bambini is exaggerating. Mrs. Henderson didn't exactly assault me."

"I beg to differ, Miss Peabody," Mr. Bambini began, nodding

to Oliver. "I'll have you know that Mrs. Henderson was pitching porcelain left and right, mostly in the direction of your fiancée, and that is what marked Miss Peabody's face. And yet, even though she suffered blatant abuse at Mrs. Henderson's hand, Miss Peabody allowed the woman to believe that she did not need to remove herself from the shop space you've rented. *And* your fiancée informed the woman that the rent you've generously paid me in advance will be put toward that woman's rent for the next year."

Oliver turned to Harriet, noticing as he did so that her eyes had turned a deep shade of purple, a circumstance that clearly showed she was about to let loose that temper of hers. "Is that true?"

"It is, and I expect you to honor what I offered, given that it was completely unacceptable for you to have that woman displaced simply because you wanted to give me the storefront she currently occupies."

Oliver blinked. "What are you talking about . . . displaced the woman?"

Harriet poked him hard in the chest with her finger. "What could you have been thinking . . . agreeing to evict a woman who has a husband unable to find work and sick children?"

Stepping around Harriet, Oliver arched a brow in Mr. Bambini's direction. "You told me Mrs. Henderson was behind on rent and that you'd already begun the process of evicting her."

"She *was* behind on rent."

"Only a week," Harriet argued, leaning around Oliver. "And she told you she'd have the money today."

Mr. Bambini shrugged. "I'm not in business to extend favors, Miss Peabody, and late is late, be it a week or a month. Mr. Addleshaw and I have done business before. I'd much rather lease that space to him for your use than to continue having Mrs. Henderson deliver her rent late whenever that shiftless husband of hers loses another job."

Oliver grabbed hold of Harriet's arm when she began edging forward, his lips curling ever so slightly when she sent him a glare. "I'll deal with this, Harriet."

"Because you're a gentleman and I'm just a delicate little lady?"

"You and I both know that, other than your appearance, there's nothing delicate about you." He frowned and glanced back to Mr. Bambini. "I'm afraid you and I are suffering from a bit of a misunderstanding. I certainly never intended for you to evict a woman in order to rent me that space. I feel distinctly misled, and I must tell you, I'm beyond annoyed over the idea you didn't do anything to ensure my fiancée didn't come to harm when Mrs. Henderson went on a rampage."

Mr. Bambini let out a nervous laugh. "I could hardly have known Mrs. Henderson was going to begin flinging dishes. Why, that right there proves the woman doesn't have a mind for business. She destroyed her own merchandise and can no longer receive a profit from it."

Harriet tugged on Oliver's arm. "Speaking of Mrs. Henderson's merchandise, she'll be sending you a bill for the damage Buford did in her shop."

"You took Buford into a china shop?"

"Not intentionally," she muttered.

"You have had a tough time of it today, haven't you?"

"Wait until you hear what happened next."

"There's more?"

She bit her lip and nodded. "But I can't tell you about it right now."

Oliver found it incredibly difficult to pull his attention away from her lip. She'd taken to nibbling on it, and for some reason, he found the nibbling fascinating. He'd never noticed before how full her bottom lip was compared to the top, but now that he had, it was . . .

"So, you'll let Mrs. Henderson retain the use of the shop *and* allow her to use the money you gave Mr. Bambini for my rent for the next year?"

The peculiar thought struck from out of nowhere—that if Harriet happened to ask him for the moon at this particular moment, given that she looked far too vulnerable, that vulnerability playing havoc with every one of his senses, he'd do his very best to give it to her. It was completely ridiculous, and quite unlike him, but . . .

"You're *not* going to let Mrs. Henderson keep her shop?" Harriet asked in a small voice, right as her slim shoulders drooped.

Blinking rapidly out of his odd musings, he couldn't resist reaching out a hand to smooth it over the drooping shoulder. "Forgive me. I fear my mind was wandering, but of course I'll let her keep the shop."

"And you'll pay for the damaged merchandise as well?"

"Since Buford seems to be the culprit behind that madness, of course."

"And you really *didn't* know Mrs. Henderson was getting evicted because you wanted to rent her place?"

Harriet's words had come out in a mere whisper, and it took everything he possessed to not pull her into his arms and soothe away whatever else was bothering her. "I *didn't* know, which is why I bought a vase from her. I thought it would ease her mind about closing up shop if she made a few last sales."

"You're making this very difficult for me," she said softly, but before he could ask her to explain what she meant by that, Harriet looked back at Mr. Bambini. "I think we've settled everything to satisfaction now."

"I'm hardly satisfied," Mr. Bambini returned, surprising Oliver when he actually sent him a wink. "I certainly understand that you're in a difficult position at the moment, given that your fiancée is standing right here, batting those pretty eyes at you, but—"

Oliver held up his hand, cutting Mr. Bambini off. "You'll leave my fiancée's pretty eyes out of this, Mr. Bambini, and everything *has* been settled, at least in my mind. Mrs. Henderson will retain possession of her shop, and you will use the money I gave you to put toward her rent. And, if the woman happens to fall behind on rent next year, you'll agree to let me know."

Harriet lifted her chin as the most beautiful smile he'd ever seen spread over her face. "Thank you."

His "You're welcome" got lodged in his throat as he found himself lost in the violet pools of her eyes, until Mr. Bambini let out a very large grunt, shook his head at Oliver in obvious disgust, and without a single word, strode out of the room.

"He's a very unpleasant man," Harriet said.

"He's not any more unpleasant than most of the men I deal with on a regular basis, but enough about Mr. Bambini. I think you had a distinct reason for coming here today, and I'm dying of curiosity to learn more about that cat."

"Curiosity can kill a cat."

Oliver smiled. "Yes, I've heard, but . . . you wouldn't happen to be trying to distract me now, would you?"

"It would have been much easier to say what I have to say if you'd deliberately evicted Mrs. Henderson and not agreed to pay her rent for a year."

Taking her arm, Oliver steered her over to a chair in front of the fireplace and helped her into it, before sitting down in the one right next to her. "It troubles me that you would think so poorly of me."

Harriet leaned forward, surprising him when she placed her hand on his arm, her action causing any thought of troubles to immediately disappear, replaced with something of a more disturbing nature.

"I do apologize, Oliver, and you're quite right, it was very unkind of me to immediately think the worst about you, but again, it would have made what has to be said so much easier to say." Her eyes turned suspiciously bright. "My aunt wants me to introduce you to her."

Oliver frowned. "That's what's gotten you so upset? Your aunt? Are you afraid I won't be receptive to meeting her and that her tender sensibilities will be hurt?"

"Good heavens, no. Jane doesn't have tender sensibilities, and the last thing in the world I'd want to do is put you into direct contact with her. She's dangerous."

"Perhaps you should start from the beginning."

Twenty minutes later, Harriet finished the sad story of her life with " . . . and then I told her I'd introduce her to society, but not for a month, since that was the only thing I could come up with spur of the moment." She bit her lip again. "I know it wasn't exactly a stellar plan, but in a month's time, I won't be traveling in society, so there won't be anyone for me to introduce her to."

Pulling his attention away from the bottom lip he still found fascinating, Oliver felt his lips twitch. "You really were in a circus?"

"With everything I've just disclosed to you, you're most interested in the idea I was once in a circus?"

"Well, that explains how you were able to throw yourself from my carriage and not suffer any harm, whereas I almost killed myself in the process."

Harriet rolled her eyes. "You're somewhat deranged, but yes, I was in the circus, excelled at tumbling, and would have been magnificent on the wire if my aunt hadn't pulled me out of bed in the middle of the night to abandon our circus adventure." She blew out a breath. "She'd gotten a little too greedy sticking her fingers in the owner's ticket money."

Oliver smiled. "I imagine you were adorable back then, dressed in a circus outfit and performing for the crowds."

"I don't know how adorable I was, given that I was at that

somewhat awkward stage. However, I truly adored the circus and loved performing because it gave me a feeling of freedom, but . . . that was a long time ago. As most people discover, real life doesn't allow much freedom."

He had the means to live a life of freedom, but he'd never thought about his wealth that way. It was an intriguing idea, though. He could enjoy sailing around in his yacht, showing Harriet different places, and . . .

Shaking himself, he forced aside those disturbing thoughts and tried to concentrate on what Harriet had imparted about her past. Strangely enough, her past didn't bother him at all, although the thought of her aunt hurting her was enough to set—

"Now that I've had time to think about matters, I do believe, in the interest of keeping your reputation safe and my aunt away from you, we're going to have to part ways and abandon our original plan."

"That's a ridiculous idea," was all he could think to respond.

A spark of temper clouded her eyes. "It's not ridiculous at all, and it is the only way I can think of to keep you safe from my aunt."

He suddenly felt as if he'd been walloped over the head with a heavy object. "Are you saying that—although your aunt has threatened to blackmail you, spewed hateful things about your mother, taken to calling you 'my pet,' and sent you a necklace you're fairly certain she was planning to use to frame you—your biggest concern at the moment is *my* safety?"

"She's a very disturbed woman, Oliver. It wouldn't be fair for me to continue on with you. Jane has information about me that she won't hesitate to use against you if she comes to the realization I'm not going to be giving in to her demands in the end."

The sheen of tears now present in Harriet's eyes almost undid him. Taking her hand in his, he brought it to his lips, a flash of satisfaction flowing over him when the tears immediately disappeared as her eyes widened and he heard her take a swift intake of breath.

"I think you're forgetting one very important fact," he said quietly.

An arch of her delicate brow was her only response.

Lowering her hand, even though he longed to kiss it again, he smiled. "I, my dear—and you'll notice I didn't call you 'my pet'—am Oliver Addleshaw. I can guarantee you I'm far more dangerous than your aunt, and I am your best chance of getting away from her. I promise you, here and now, that I will protect you, along with your friends, and if Jane so much as looks at you in a threatening manner, I'll see to it that she never looks at you again."

"What's wrong with you? Why wouldn't you get yourself as far away from me as possible?"

Before Oliver had a chance to answer, the sound of someone shouting reached them, someone who sounded exactly like Mr. Blodgett.

"Oh no, he's lost the cat," Harriet exclaimed, snatching her hand from his before she jumped to her feet and raced out of the room.

It took Oliver only a few seconds to catch up with her, and when he did, the sight that met his eyes had him grinning. Mr. Blodgett was standing inside the private elevator Oliver's architect had convinced him was not a luxury but a necessity in a house so large, his wrinkled face pressed against the closed metal gate. The cat was sitting directly in front of the gate, licking its paw in what appeared to be a very satisfied manner, as if she'd personally been responsible for the troubling situation at hand.

"Good heavens, Oliver," Harriet exclaimed, scooping up Precious and earning a purr in the process, "I didn't know you had an elevator."

237

"It wasn't my idea." He grabbed hold of the lever that opened and closed the gate and gave it a good shove, but after the gate opened, Mr. Blodgett refused to get out.

"There's something wrong with that cat, and I'm not getting out of here until it's gone from this house," Mr. Blodgett said, backing slowly away until he came to a stop against the elevator wall. "In fact, perhaps it would be for the best if you sent me up to the fourth floor until that vindictive creature is gone." He held out a hand. "It tried to bite me when I was feeding it fish, and then it chased me here when I stopped feeding it."

Harriet hugged Precious to her. "She probably just smelled the scent from the fish on your gloves and thought you had more to give her, but if either of you knows who Mrs. Fish is, I'll take Precious back to the woman right this minute." She smiled. "That's why I thought it would be a good idea to feed her fish since her human mother is named Fish."

"You have a very unusual mind, Harriet," Oliver said.

"Yes, yes, Miss Peabody is extraordinary," Mr. Blodgett said, "and Mrs. Fish lives over by Mrs. Hart on Washington Square. So you can just drop the little darling off on your way home." The butler pressed more tightly against the back elevator wall. "Now, if someone would be so kind as to close the gate, I'd like to put a bit of distance between myself and Precious."

Oliver grinned and closed the gate, but before Mr. Blodgett pulled up the lever, he took a step closer to the door. "I almost forgot. Silas was watching the house earlier, sitting on his horse across the street. I was going to summon the authorities to run him off, but then Miss Peabody arrived. When I went back out to check on him, he was gone."

"Was the carriage I came in gone as well?" Harriet asked, a distinct note of hope in her tone.

"It was," Mr. Blodgett replied. "And while I'd love to know

what's going on at the moment, I fear my nerves aren't what they used to be, so I'll bid both of you good day." With that, he shoved up the lever and the elevator began slowly ascending.

"Was Mr. Blodgett talking about Silas Ruff?" Harriet asked after Mr. Blodgett disappeared from sight.

"I'm afraid he was, but Silas isn't anyone for you to worry about. He and I had words this morning and decided to discontinue our association. Since he's watching the house, it's clear he's still bearing ill-feelings toward me, but . . ." Oliver shrugged. "You and I were discussing our association, and I'm hopeful you'll come to the realization that you'll be safest with me, and that I truly will make certain your aunt can't hurt you."

"I'm not worried about her hurting me," she muttered.

"And that right there is why I'll do everything in my power to keep you safe."

Hugging Precious closer, Harriet looked at him for a long moment, and then, to his relief, she nodded.

"Wonderful." He moved to take her arm but stopped when Precious let out a hiss. "Shall we get you back to Mrs. Hart's house so you can begin getting ready for our night out at Delmonico's?"

"I forgot all about that."

"I'm not surprised. You've had a very trying day. I do hate to add more to that, but . . . I probably should tell you something."

Harriet edged an inch away from him. "They serve more than eight courses at Delmonico's?"

"No, or they might, but . . . are you worried about that?"

"I only know the proper cutlery use for eight courses, and even that might be a stretch."

Oliver smiled. "I'll make certain that eight and only eight courses are served."

"That would be appreciated and makes me feel a little better."

"How would you feel if I told you the duke arrived early in town and he and his family will be joining us tonight?"

Harriet's eyes widened and she turned a little pale, but then she lifted her chin. "I suppose I'd feel grateful that Abigail's put me through my paces in regard to table manners, because apparently, we'll be dining with a duke tonight."

17

*T*here, all done," Millie said, draping a borrowed strand of Abigail's pearls around Harriet's neck before she stepped back and looked Harriet over with a critical eye. "I must say, even though you look very well indeed, I'm of the belief that the gold gown would have been far nicer than this blue one you've chosen."

Harriet tilted her head. "Weren't you listening to that lesson Abigail gave us, the one concerning what was appropriate to wear to a place like Delmonico's compared with having dinner at a private home?"

"Honestly, Harriet, it's a little difficult to keep up with all the lessons Abigail keeps throwing our way. Why, my poor mind can barely take in half of it, so no, I wasn't listening. But it would have been more challenging for me, as your personal maid, to have laced you into a gown with an even smaller waistline than the one you're currently wearing, and . . . well . . . I have to admit I'm curious now as to whether or not I'd be able to get your waist to eighteen inches instead of twenty."

"And since I'm expected to eat eight courses tonight, I'm perfectly fine wearing a gown where you've only had to squeeze, instead of smash, my inner organs together." Harriet grinned. "But, squeezing aside, considering I'm supposed to be blending in with society tonight, I shudder to think what the reaction would be if I arrived at Delmonico's in a gown that bared my shoulders."

Millie returned the grin. "I bet it would create a huge fresco."

"I think the word you meant was *fiasco*," Lucetta said, as she waltzed into the room. "And yes, if Harriet were to go against the social expectations of dressing for dinner at a restaurant, it would create a fiasco, and would most likely end up with her being marched out the door."

Lucetta smiled at Harriet. "I'm sure you'll be relieved to know you look absolutely lovely and will have no reason to fear you'll be escorted out of Delmonico's by any of their always handsome doormen."

"Their doormen are always handsome?" Harriet asked.

"I think it's a requirement to get hired there," Lucetta said. "But speaking of handsome, I came to tell you that Oliver's just arrived."

"If I remember correctly, only a few days ago you made the claim that Oliver was a hideous and disagreeable sort."

Lucetta laughed and sat down on a dainty chair covered in pink upholstery, crossing her ankles, which brought immediate attention to the fact she was missing her shoes again. "No man who has such a delightful grandfather can be completely disagreeable. And, since Oliver also takes after Archibald in regard to his appearance, it would be silly of me to continue to proclaim that he's hideous, when clearly, that isn't the case."

Not particularly caring to dwell on Oliver's handsomeness, Harriet decided a change of subject was needed. "Speaking of Archibald, have you heard any further mentions of plotting?"

Rolling her eyes, Lucetta shook her head. "Abigail and Archibald are being annoyingly stealthy at the moment, but I do believe they're most likely still hatching plans. Although, I have recently gotten the distinct impression you're not the only one in their beady sights, Harriet."

"What an overactive imagination you have, Lucetta," Abigail said, breezing through the door before she hurried over to Millie, who'd picked up an atomizer and was aiming it at Harriet. "My dear girl, don't even consider spraying Harriet again with that perfume. A lady must never smell as if she's doused herself with scent."

Setting the atomizer aside, Millie plopped her hands on her hips. "I was just telling Harriet that you're throwing too many rules my way, but . . . if you'd allowed me to style Harriet's hair tonight, instead of bringing in that hairdresser, well, I wouldn't be trying to spritz her with anything because I'd still be arranging her hair."

"And since Oliver and Archibald have arrived to escort us to dinner, it's fortunate I did bring in a hairdresser—otherwise we'd be late." Abigail smiled. "You did a very nice job getting Harriet dressed, Millie, but I don't want you to become accustomed to being a lady's maid, since I have other plans for you."

Millie's mouth made an O of surprise. "Goodness, you've turned your beady eye on me now, haven't you."

"I do not have a beady eye, and there's no time to discuss your situation further, given that the Addleshaw gentlemen are waiting."

Harriet's palms immediately turned moist underneath the silk gloves that covered her hands. "Are you certain this is a good idea, going through with everything, given that my aunt is lurking out there somewhere?"

Abigail stepped to Harriet's side and surprised her when she pulled her into a firm embrace and gave her a good squeeze. "My dear, I willingly admit I was appalled by the story you told me regarding your life with your aunt, but know that Jane Peabody is no match for me. I will not turn you, Millie, or Lucetta out of my house simply because some confidence artist is threatening to worm her way into my life, and . . . my safe." Abigail stepped back. "I, my dear Harriet, have been told I'm a force to be reckoned with, so don't you worry about me."

"You shouldn't take Jane lightly, Abigail. She's a distinct threat, and I wouldn't put anything past her."

"And you should believe me when I tell you I'm more of a threat to Jane than she is to me, especially when people I've come to care about are put in harm's way." She took hold of Harriet's arm, and with Millie and Lucetta walking beside them, they left Harriet's bedroom, descended the stairs, and made their way to the drawing room.

" . . . and I still don't understand why you and Abigail feel it's necessary to come with us tonight, Grandfather," Oliver was saying as Harriet lingered in the doorway, unable to get a good look at him since his back was turned.

Archibald, wearing a formal jacket paired with an intricately tied cravat, crossed his arms over his chest. "Abigail is her chaperone, Oliver, so of course she has to go tonight. As for me, you're tossing the poor girl to the wolves, my boy, and you're going to need some help. Why, Miss Dixon, Everett's dear friend, is known to be an absolute nightmare, and don't forget, you're also sitting down with a duke. I met the man once, granted it was years ago over in London, but I still recall he had a somewhat intimidating presence."

"That certainly is going to calm those nerves our darling Harriet must be experiencing at the moment," Abigail said, walking into the room. Oliver turned at her words, and the sight of him in his dark evening clothes left Harriet at a loss for words.

His black hair was combed away from his face, for once not rumpled in the least, and his eyes were twinkling at Abigail as she presented him her hand, which he immediately brought to his lips and kissed. He released his hold on Abigail, lifted his head, and then . . . his mouth dropped open and he simply stared at Harriet.

She felt heat settle over her face, but she couldn't seem to tear her gaze away from Oliver, nor could she seem to find her voice.

"This is certainly an encouraging turn of events," Abigail said smugly, her smugness breaking through the fog that had settled over Harriet.

Knowing she was blushing from the top of her head to the tips of toes encased in a lovely pair of shoes that exactly matched her dress, Harriet's breath hitched when Oliver began heading her way. He stopped directly in front of her and took her hand, placing a kiss on it as he studied her face.

"You look exquisite this evening, but what happened to your scratch?" he asked even as he lowered her hand but, strangely enough, kept possession of it.

"Thank you," she managed to get out of a mouth that had turned dry. "And Lucetta fixed my face for me, since she's incredibly competent with a touch of theatrical paint."

"I must say, my wards have turned out to be very talented indeed," Abigail said, with a satisfied nod in Archibald's direction. "I haven't been so impressed with young ladies for years. It's been an absolute delight having them come into my life. I must admit that after my Charles died, and my issues with my daughter and grandchildren remained unresolved, I do believe I took to wallowing. I spent too many days buried in this dreary home simply waiting for the end to find me." She lifted her chin. "That changed the second these delightful young ladies entered my life and gave me a purpose."

"She and Archibald really *are* including us in their mad plotting attempts," Lucetta said, stepping into the room with Millie by her side, although by the grin on her face, it was clear she wasn't exactly worried about the plotting. "Heed me well, Millie, if we're not careful, we'll find ourselves embroiled in something concerning, just like Harriet."

"I'm not exactly certain what *embroiled* means, Lucetta, but I've misplaced my dictionary in all the hectic business of getting Harriet ready."

Oliver released Harriet's hand and walked over to her friends, kissing first Lucetta's hand, then Millie's. "I must say, Miss Long-fellow, if you were responsible for Harriet's hair, you deserve everyone's apology for doubting your competence."

Millie's face turned pink. "Although I have been practicing with the hot tongs, I wasn't allowed near Harriet's hair."

"Only because you burned off one side of your own hair while you were doing that practicing," Harriet said with a shudder. "That's why you're wearing a cap."

"Honestly, my darlings," Abigail said with a wag of her finger in Harriet and Millie's direction. "Surely you're aware that it's hardly proper to discuss disasters that occurred in the middle of your toilettes in the company of gentlemen."

"On the contrary," Oliver argued with a grin. "I find it completely charming that Miss Longfellow was so diligent in regard to her new position as lady's maid that she actually tried out the hot tongs on her own head before attempting anything on Harriet's."

"Don't encourage her," Abigail said with a sniff, even as Millie sent Oliver a cheeky wink.

Oliver returned the wink, and right there and then, Harriet's knees turned weak. He was so agreeable at the moment, so very different from what she'd first thought about him, that she couldn't help her knees going weak, or her mouth turning dry, or her heart . . .

"Well, since I didn't have my maid stuff me into this dress for no reason at all," Abigail proclaimed, pulling Harriet rapidly from thoughts of weak knees and dry mouths. "We should be off, and let us hope for the best."

"That's an encouraging thought," Lucetta said before she padded up to Harriet on feet that were still bare and gave her a kiss on the cheek. "Now, don't worry too much. I'm sure you'll be fine."

"Of course she will," Millie exclaimed as she joined them, although given that her nose had taken to wrinkling, Harriet wasn't exactly reassured. "Just remember to use all the lessons Abigail and Archibald have taught you, don't insult Miss Dixon, and I'm pretty sure you'll need to curtsy when you're introduced to the duke."

Biting her lip, Harriet looked at Oliver. "Are you certain you really want to go through with this, because there'll be no turning back in the midst of dinner . . . and . . . *am* I supposed to curtsy when I'm introduced to the duke?"

Instead of answering her, Oliver was staring at her lips, his staring having the immediate effect of additional heat traveling up her neck to settle once again on her cheeks. "Do I have something on my face?" she finally asked when he continued staring.

Blinking, Oliver seemed to shake himself before he smiled. "Forgive me, I was . . . What was the question again?"

"I asked if you really wanted to go through with this."

"Since all of *this* was my idea in the first place, of course, and besides, what could go wrong?"

"I don't think I should answer that," Harriet muttered before she took his offered arm, said a last farewell to her friends, and followed Abigail and Archibald out of the room.

As the carriage trundled down the street, Harriet smoothed her gloved hand against the seat, this one done up in blue velvet, before she caught Oliver's eye. "How many carriages do you have?"

"I'm not exactly certain, a good dozen or so, but I had this one brought out tonight because it can seat six comfortably, and requires two footmen on the back." He smiled. "I thought you'd feel more at ease if you knew I'd already taken steps to keep you well protected. And to relieve your mind about Millie and Lucetta, I've hired men to watch Mrs. Hart's house."

Feeling an immediate urge to hurl herself once again from his carriage, if only to escape from his far-too-considerate nature, Harriet resisted the urge and summoned up the only thought left in her mind. "I couldn't help but notice that your footmen were wearing livery and had powdered their hair."

Oliver frowned. "Have they really powdered their hair?"

"They have, and I'm fairly certain, given that Gladys, one of the ladies I used to work with, kept company with a footman, you pay them extra for using powder."

Oliver looked over at Archibald. "Do you remember if I asked to have the footmen powder their hair when I hired on additional staff after my house was completed last year?"

"The agency probably suggested that idea to you, given your position within society," Archibald said. "But, if you ask me, having your staff powder their hair is a little . . . ostentatious."

"From what I've heard," Harriet added, "it's quite the bother for the men, but . . . if you really think it's necessary, you might at least notice the effort they've gone to on your behalf."

Oliver smiled. "I think I'll just inform Mr. Blodgett that hair powdering is no longer in the job description."

Harriet realized her hand was actually inching for the door after Oliver's surprisingly considerate conclusion, but knew if she leapt out of the carriage, Abigail would be beyond annoyed with her. Settling for looking out the window instead, she tried to get her pesky emotions in check but found that next to impossible when thoughts of how charming Oliver was being toward everyone, including her friends, kept tingles running up and down her spine.

"Are you looking at Mrs. Fish?" Oliver suddenly asked, joining her at the window, his closeness bringing with him the scent of sandalwood.

Not turning her head a single inch, because that would have her face almost pressed up against his, Harriet peered into the darkness and smiled. Mrs. Fish was standing underneath a gas lamp in front of her house, the one Harriet and Oliver had visited only a few hours before, cradling Precious in her arms.

"I think she's taking her cat for an evening stroll," Oliver said before he leaned back and Harriet did the same.

"It was very touching how delighted she was to get her cat back," she said.

Oliver patted her arm. "I found it very touching that you refused to take the reward she so very determinedly tried to give you."

"Given that my aunt was responsible for abducting the cat in the first place, I actually felt as if I should pay Mrs. Fish for her distress."

Alarm replaced every single one of Harriet's tingles when she caught Archibald exchanging a very significant look with Abigail before both of them directed their attention to her. "What?" was all she could think to ask, earning herself another lesson from Abigail regarding the proper way to pose a question.

By the time Abigail finished, the carriage was pulling to a stop. Terror was immediate and only increased as one of the footmen helped Harriet down to the sidewalk. She found herself standing before an imposing building, one that had not one but four covered awnings guarding the doors leading into Delmonico's. Perfectly groomed and, as Lucetta had mentioned, handsome doormen manned each door, and fashionably dressed customers were breezing through those doors as if they had every right in the world to be there.

Her terror kept her rooted to the spot.

She didn't have that right. She was a hat maker, or at least she'd been one before she'd been dismissed from her position. Now she was simply a lady intent on becoming a seamstress, but not a seamstress for high society, a . . .

"You're thinking entirely too much," Oliver whispered in her ear, the feel of his breath against her skin causing her knees to begin wobbling all over again.

"I'm not thinking—well, not anything of worth," she returned, wincing when she heard the clear panic in her voice. "I don't think I'm ready for this yet."

"The only way you'll ever be ready is to just move forward." Oliver grinned. "At least you know which fork is the oyster fork."

"Yes, but I never bothered to actually eat any of those oysters your fancy French chef served, and . . . what if they make me gag?" She shuddered. "They're . . . slimy."

"True, but they taste exactly like steak, and you love steak— you told me so."

Before she could protest further, Oliver took her by the arm, and she suddenly found herself standing in the entranceway of the most elaborate restaurant she'd ever seen. Each and every table she saw through the doorway was draped in fine linen, with candles fluttering everywhere, the light from them causing the crystal glasses on the tables to sparkle. Servers moved on silent feet around them and a delicious aroma of well-prepared food filled the air. She drew in a deep breath, slowly released it, but was still feeling a distinct desire to bolt when Mr. Everett Mulberry suddenly appeared right in front of her and sent her a wink.

The wink had her feeling a little better until the lady walking a step behind him came into view and Harriet felt her stomach lurch. Given that the lady was keeping remarkably close to Everett, Harriet knew she had to be none other than Miss Dixon—*the Nightmare*, as Archibald had called her. She was dressed in an exquisite gown of beaded silk, one that had most likely come from Paris, and she was beautiful. Her light brown hair was styled to perfection, but . . . the closer she came, the better Harriet could see her, and the hardness residing in the lady's eyes diminished her beauty ever so slightly.

"That's Miss Dixon," Oliver told her.

"She's . . . lovely."

"Not as lovely as you are, and she's not nearly as interesting."

It was fortunate Oliver had a firm grip on her arm, because Harriet was fairly certain if he didn't, she would have swooned right to the ground for the first time in her life, right at the man's feet.

"Mr. Addleshaw," Miss Dixon drawled as she came to a stop in front of them. "I hear congratulations are in order."

"Miss Dixon," Everett said, before he gestured to Harriet. "Allow me to present Miss Harriet Peabody. Miss Peabody, this is Miss Caroline Dixon."

Miss Dixon barely spared her a glance and didn't wait for a response from Harriet before turning her attention back to Oliver, handing him her hand, and then batting her lashes when he took it.

Irritation was immediate, but before Harriet could dwell on the reasoning behind it, Everett leaned closer to her.

"You're doing fine."

"What was that?" Miss Dixon snapped.

"I was telling Miss Peabody that she looks very fine this evening."

"You didn't tell me I look fine."

"I believe I mentioned that you look stunning, which I believe is a fair deal better than fine," Everett said calmly. "Now then, Oliver, I'm sure we should inquire whether or not the duke has arrived, but . . . never mind, I see him over there with your grandfather and Mrs. Hart."

Harriet looked up, and sure enough, Archibald and Abigail

were in the midst of a conversation with a gentleman who certainly appeared duke-like, not that Harriet had ever seen a real live duke before.

"Shall we join them?" Oliver asked.

"I wouldn't want to interrupt what seems to be a lovely conversation," Harriet said weakly.

"Since we are here to dine with the duke," Miss Dixon said coolly, "I'm sure he's expecting us to go greet him, even if that means interrupting Mrs. Hart." She lifted her chin. "Everett, take my arm and—"

"Oliver, come meet the duke," Archibald called, his request cutting Miss Dixon off midsentence.

Oliver took hold of Harriet's arm. "Ready?"

Knowing she really had no choice in the matter, and she *had* promised Oliver from the very beginning that she'd help him entertain his duke, she squared her shoulders. "As ready as I'll ever be."

Oliver lowered his head even as he did the same with his voice. "You're looking a little terrified, so it might be a good idea to pull out one of those adoring looks I know you've been practicing, per my request, which will go far in allowing the duke to believe we're truly attached."

Harriet's lips twitched. "I never got around to practicing that look again."

Oliver grinned. "You really don't enjoy taking orders, do you."

Before she could respond to that bit of nonsense, he led her forward, bringing her to a stop directly in front of the tall and distinguished-looking gentleman standing by Archibald's side.

Archibald smiled at her and then turned back to the gentleman. "Your Grace, allow me to introduce you to my grandson, Mr. Oliver Addleshaw and his lovely fiancée, Miss Harriet Peabody. This is the Duke of Westmoore."

"How delightful, you're engaged," the duke said, his blue eyes twinkling as he nodded to Oliver and then stepped forward and took Harriet's hand. He placed a dramatic kiss on it, released it and smiled. "Mr. Addleshaw is a very lucky gentleman."

Right there and then, Harriet fell in love—not the romantic kind of love, but the adoring love one would have given to a favorite uncle or father, two things she'd never had. There was something that just seemed so normal about the duke, even though he possessed a lofty title. "Thank you," she managed to mumble.

"You're very welcome," the duke replied before he nodded to Oliver. "We've corresponded, of course, but it's a pleasure to finally meet you in person. I met your grandfather years ago when he was visiting London."

"He's spoken quite highly of you," Oliver said as he shook the duke's hand and gestured Everett and Miss Dixon forward. Introductions were made and then Harriet looked up and found herself staring at a young lady with deep blue eyes who was dressed in the first state of fashion, and who was also looking Oliver over as if he were a tasty treat she longed to sample.

"This tardy lady," the duke said fondly, "is my daughter, Lady Victoria Grenville, but I'm afraid I must extend to everyone an apology from my wife, the Duchess of Westmoore. She was forced to remain back at the hotel due to the fact she isn't feeling well."

Lady Victoria pulled her attention away from Oliver, although she seemed to do so rather reluctantly, before she stepped to her father's side and smiled. "And I must apologize for being inexcusably late in greeting everyone, but the manager offered to give me a tour of Delmonico's, and I simply couldn't resist going up to the third floor to view the ballroom. It's quite impressive, although I found myself wishing the season was in full force so I'd be able to dance the night away in that room."

"You'll have to come back during the season, then, Lady Victoria," Oliver said with a smile. "Our famous Patriarch Balls are held here upon occasion, and they always provide wonderful opportunities for dancing."

Lady Victoria looked Oliver up and down, and then up and down again, even as her smile widened and her lashes began to flutter. A knot began forming in Harriet's stomach the longer the lady fluttered, but then the duke stepped forward and began performing introductions. "Darling, may I present to you—Mr. Archibald Addleshaw, Mr. Oliver Addleshaw, Mrs. Hart, Mr. Mulberry, Miss Dixon, and Mr. Oliver Addleshaw's fiancée, Miss Harriet Peabody."

Lady Victoria's fluttering came to an immediate halt as her gaze traveled over Harriet, then back to Oliver, and then . . . she released a sigh.

It was the sigh that had Harriet's stomach unknotting as dismay flowed through her. The ramifications from Archibald announcing her and Oliver's engagement were immediate, and she opened her mouth, intent on saying what, she really had no idea, but then Archibald gestured to a server dressed in a white shirt paired with black pants, and the opportunity to speak was gone.

"We've prepared the best table for your party," the server said before he began leading them through the front entrance and into the dining room, where guests immediately turned their attention to them, their stares a little disconcerting.

Wanting to get to her seat as quickly as possible, Harriet increased her stride, allowing her to overhear Lady Victoria's furious whispers to her father.

"You never mentioned he was engaged, and . . ."

Whatever else she was whispering got lost when Oliver pulled her to a more sedate pace.

"We're not in a race, Harriet, and I'm fairly sure the table isn't going anywhere, although . . . I do hope you're not too upset over the idea we've been given a table that'll be in clear view of all the other patrons."

Stopping, Harriet waved his comment away. "While I certainly find the idea of everyone watching us as we eat a little daunting, that's not what has me upset at the moment."

"Honestly, Miss Peabody, it's not quite the thing to stop with no warning. You almost caused me to run straight into you," Miss Dixon snapped before she stepped around Harriet and pulled Everett forward, almost dragging the poor man in her obvious haste to get back to the duke.

"What has you so upset, then?" Oliver asked.

"We're going to have to let it be known that our engagement isn't exactly official and that we're not truly attached."

Frowning, Oliver leaned closer to her. "Why in the world would we do something like that? You're doing marvelously at the moment, well, not standing here in the middle of the room, but I do believe you've already charmed the duke, and we haven't even gotten to the first course yet."

"Lady Victoria is interested in you. I have to say, given that she's beautiful, wealthy, and holds a title, that the two of you would make a perfect match. That'll never happen, though, if she continues believing your interest resides with me."

"What?"

"Good thing Abigail isn't close enough to hear your less-than-adequate posing of a question, but since you don't seem to be comprehending what I'm telling you, I'll keep this as simple as possible. Lady Victoria is attracted to you, and she also was under the impression you were eligible." She drew in a breath and quickly released it. "Quite frankly, I wouldn't be surprised to discover the duke brought his daughter to New York in order for the two of you to form an attachment to each other."

Oliver, for some annoying reason, laughed. "You're imagining things. No duke is going to try to wed his daughter to a man who has made his fortune through trade and finance."

"You're handsome and wealthy, so of course he's going to try. Really, Oliver, since you and the duke are considering forming a business alliance, I hardly believe he's opposed to gentlemen who earn their money through trade."

"You find me handsome?"

"What are the two of you doing?" Abigail demanded, allowing Harriet the luxury of not answering Oliver's question. "Archibald and the duke are waiting to take their seats, but they can't do that until you take yours, Harriet. And I wouldn't think it necessary for me to point out the obvious, but I don't believe conversing in the middle of Delmonico's—and in whispered tones, at that—is exactly what the two of you want to be doing. You're now the objects of everyone's speculation because it appears as if the two of you are arguing."

"But . . . that's perfect," Harriet exclaimed, "and will go far in allowing Lady Victoria to realize Oliver and I aren't in accord."

"She's lost her mind," Oliver said to Abigail as he took a firm grip of Harriet's arm. Before she knew it, she was sitting at a linen-draped table covered with crystal and gold-gilded china, staring at a menu that seemed to be in French.

She'd never had much exposure to French, and the little exposure she'd had certainly hadn't prepared her for understanding what appeared to be exotic dishes.

Oliver leaned close to her. "Would you care for me to order for you?"

"Don't you read French?" Miss Dixon demanded as she leaned over Everett and arched a brow at Harriet.

Harriet arched a brow of her own but was spared responding anything at all when the duke set aside his menu and sighed.

"I have no idea why menus must be written in French. Why, I've never taken to that language and am always forced to simply make an uneducated guess, never knowing what dishes are going to show up in front of me." He looked directly at Harriet and then, to her amazement, he winked.

"Allow me to order for you as well," Oliver offered, amusement lacing his tone.

"I too have trouble with French," Lady Victoria proclaimed, batting her lashes again at Oliver, which he didn't appear to notice as he disappeared behind his menu.

Why wasn't he noticing?

Lady Victoria was perfect for him, and yet, he was barely paying the woman any mind at all. Even she knew that marrying an aristocrat was extremely sought-after amongst the elite of America and . . .

Four men in black jackets took that moment to appear at the table, reminding Harriet that she was supposed to be engaged in dinner conversation, not lost in confusing thoughts. She almost jumped out of her seat, though, when one of the men snapped an expensive-looking napkin right beside her and then placed it over her lap. She forced aside the instinct to slap the man's hand away and summoned up a smile. "Thank you," she said, which earned her a nod from the server and a grin from Oliver, as if he'd been perfectly aware of the fact she'd almost just assaulted a member of the staff.

Wine flowed into the crystal glasses as Oliver began to place their orders, pausing when Miss Dixon cleared her throat. Oliver set his menu aside when Miss Dixon tossed him a charming smile and placed her own order in a somewhat questionable French accent. Everett, Harriet noticed, looked slightly appalled and more than a touch disgruntled.

Hiding a smile behind her wine glass, Harriet took a sip and immediately wished she hadn't. The wine tasted bitter, and it took everything she had not to spit it out but swallow it instead.

"Do you not care for the wine?" the duke asked. He sat directly across the table from her, with Lady Victoria on one side of him and Abigail on the other.

"It's . . . ah . . . hmmm," was all she could manage to get out, her taste buds still reeling from the unpleasantness she'd forced on them.

"I've always believed that wine is an acquired taste," Miss Dixon said, taking up her own wine glass before she sniffed it, smiled, and took a sip. "Delicious."

Harriet looked away from Miss Dixon, noticed that the duke was still watching her, and decided there and then that she wasn't going to spend the evening pretending to care for things she didn't like in the least. "Wine is not my favorite choice of beverage, Your Grace. If you must know, I really prefer milk, or tea or . . . Apollinaris water." She shot a glance to Abigail, and since Abigail was beaming back at her, she released a silent sigh of relief that she'd remembered the name of the mineral water that was apparently becoming all the rage within society.

The duke's eyes crinkled at the corners. "I always enjoy a cold glass of milk as well, Miss Peabody, although Apollinaris water certainly does quench a thirst." He snapped his fingers, a server immediately appeared by his side, and to Harriet's amazement, not only did he order her a milk, but himself one as well.

He was a true gentleman, something she'd rarely seen in her life.

She looked to Lady Victoria and found the young lady smiling at her father and couldn't quite hold back the wistfulness that settled into her very soul.

What would it have been like to have grown up with a father such as the duke—a gentleman who was kind and clearly adored his daughter, and a man who went out of his way to ease a young lady's discomfort?

Abigail leaned forward. "I don't know if Archibald has mentioned this to you or not, Your Grace, but he and I have been planning a dinner party for you and your family to welcome you to our fair city. We're going to hold it at my home, which I hope you'll find to your satisfaction."

The duke frowned. "I must beg your pardon, Mrs. Hart, because while I was intending to spend a few weeks here in the city, my plans have changed, given that we've been invited to a wedding being held in Scotland. It's a distant relation, but it would be unacceptable to miss it. I fear we'll be leaving New York in only a few days—after Mr. Oliver Addleshaw and I have an opportunity to discuss and, hopefully, close our business deal."

"But Father," Lady Victoria said, "surely we could stay just a little longer, can't we? We've been traveling around the world for months, and I do so miss sitting down with civilized people in order to enjoy a good meal."

"You're sitting down to enjoy a meal right now, and with very civilized people," the duke pointed out.

Lady Victoria's eyes narrowed, but before she could speak, Abigail cleared her throat.

"If Lady Victoria is truly desirous of a dinner party, Your Grace, then I'm only too happy to accommodate her." She tapped her finger against her chin. "I should be able to work out all the particulars and host it . . . two days from now?"

"I would not want to cause you such a great amount of work, Mrs. Hart, and since the duchess is currently battling a bad cold, I'm not certain she'd even be up for attending," the duke said.

"Mother will be fine staying at the hotel if she's still feeling under the weather," Lady Victoria said, earning a frown from her father, which she blatantly ignored as she looked to Oliver and sent him a lovely smile.

The duke frowned at his daughter, but then cleared his throat and nodded to Abigail. "My family and I would be honored if you would host a dinner for us, Mrs. Hart, but again, I wouldn't want you to feel obligated to do so, especially since it's incredibly short notice."

"It would be no obligation at all," Abigail said as her gaze traveled from Lady Victoria, to Oliver, to Harriet, and then back to Lady Victoria again, who suddenly sat forward, pulled her attention from Oliver, and then set her sights directly on Harriet.

"Tell me, Miss Peabody, however did you meet Mr. Addleshaw, and how long have you been engaged?"

All conversation stopped at the table as everyone swung their attention Harriet's way. Taking a deep breath, she realized this was her opportunity to allow Lady Victoria to know that she and Oliver weren't truly engaged, and hopefully that would open the way for Oliver to pursue a woman who was perfect for him. "Mr. Addleshaw and I aren't . . ."

"Comfortable sharing how we met," Oliver interrupted, ignoring the kick she sent him under the table. He smiled one of his most charming of smiles at Lady Victoria. "I fear I made something of a spectacle of myself, trying to attract Miss Peabody's attention, and because of that, I've made her promise not to tell anyone the tale, and . . . Oh, here comes our first course. What a perfectly timed distraction."

Any further attempt on Harriet's part to argue was put on hold when she suddenly found herself staring at a plate that sported not oysters but a dish Harriet could not identify, much less know what fork to use on it.

"Do you not care for terrapin either?" Miss Dixon suddenly asked.

Since Harriet had not the slightest idea what terrapin was, she settled for an "Ah . . . ?"

"Turtle," Oliver whispered.

"I once found a turtle when I was little and brought it home with me. I even went so far as to name him Sam," she said weakly, as her stomach turned queasy. "My aunt made me release him back into the wild a few days later, but I never thought I'd be eating him someday."

The duke set down his fork and gestured to the server. "Miss Peabody and I would prefer a different option, perhaps a soup?"

"Or maybe just some oysters," Harriet suggested since she knew what fork to use for that.

"Is the entire dinner going to be like this?" Miss Dixon demanded. "I could barely enjoy my wine since Miss Peabody kept grimacing through hers and now . . . am I going to be forced to hear stories about Sam the turtle as I try to devour what I've always thought of as a delicious dish? I must say . . ."

Miss Dixon continued speaking, but Harriet didn't hear the words pouring out of the lady's mouth. She was instead caught under the glare of none other than Miss Birmingham, who was standing a few tables away, clutching her mother's arm with one hand and pointing directly at her with the other.

Harriet's only thought was to escape. She pushed her chair back, tossed her napkin onto the table, and dropped to the ground, where she immediately crawled under the table.

Unfortunately, she'd forgotten all about the numerous candles that were lit on that very table, and a second later, shrieks erupted, the loudest coming from Miss Dixon, and then the smell of smoke permeated the air.

18

*H*aving no idea what would have possessed Harriet to duck out of sight, but knowing now was hardly the time to worry about that, given that all the linens were going up in flames, Oliver dropped to his knees and poked his head under the table. His gaze immediately met that of Harriet's horrified one. Holding out a hand, he motioned her forward, irritation humming through him when she shook her head and began inching away from him.

"I can't come out because Miss Birmingham and her mother are out there."

"While that certainly explains a lot, if you've neglected to notice, the table is on fire, which means I need to get you to safety, and quickly, before the whole restaurant burns down."

Harriet's eyes turned impossibly wide. "You think the whole restaurant is going to burn down?"

The sound of splashing water, then sizzling, followed by water dripping through the cracks in the table and dripping on him and Harriet in the process delayed his response. The smell of smoke grew noticeably stronger, and his eyes began stinging before he began coughing. "*Please,* Harriet," he finally managed to rasp, but to his extreme annoyance, she refused to budge.

"I just heard someone say the fire's out, so feel free to leave me here," she said.

He coughed again and narrowed eyes that were now watering on Harriet. "I'm not leaving you here, and you can't stay under the table all night."

"As I mentioned before, Miss Birmingham and her mother are out there, probably waiting to scream at me as soon as they catch sight of me, and that's going to cause you no small amount of difficulty with the duke."

"There's no one left in the restaurant, save the staff, because the moment the table linens burst into flames, the guests made a mass exodus for the doors."

Harriet looked more horrified than ever. "Management is going to be furious with me because I doubt any of those guests bothered to stop and pay their bill before they fled the fire."

Before Oliver could respond, Harriet scooted backward and disappeared. By the time he managed to crawl out from under the table, she was in the midst of apologizing profusely to servers covered in soot standing around the charred remains of what had recently been a delicious dinner.

"I cannot put into words how sorry I am," she said, her expressive eyes filled with what seemed to be tears, although given the amount of smoke still in the air, he wasn't exactly certain about that. "Throwing my napkin down so carelessly was beyond irresponsible, and do know that I'll personally take responsibility for the damage I've caused."

A man wearing a suit, one that suggested he was the manager, stepped closer to Harriet and smiled.

"My dear lady, you must not dwell on this another minute. Fires happen here all the time, and I don't hold you responsible."

To Oliver's surprise, Harriet immediately took to arguing

with the man, her arguments only ending when he stepped up, introduced himself to the manager, and then promised the man he'd take responsibility for the damage, including all the bills that were not paid. With a very relieved manager left behind, one whom had been very gracious toward Harriet but hadn't exactly hesitated to have them shown the door, Oliver tugged Harriet out of Delmonico's.

"You'll have to deduct the amount for the damage from the fee you're paying me," she said when they reached the sidewalk and she suddenly refused to take another step.

Rolling his eyes, Oliver let out a grunt. "Don't be ridiculous. I'll do no such thing, and as the manager kept telling you, situations such as setting the restaurant on fire happen all the time, so I'm sure the bill I'm going to receive won't be that extensive."

"You and I both know it's not a common occurrence for a lady to set the table to flames."

His lips began to curl but then thinned when he caught a glimpse of Mr. Birmingham glaring his way as Mrs. and Miss Birmingham pointed in his direction. For a second, Oliver thought the man was going to approach him, but then Mr. Birmingham took hold of Mrs. Birmingham's arm, said something to his daughter, and with one last glare sent to Oliver, spun around and disappeared through the crowd lingering in front of Delmonico's.

"Oliver, we're over here."

Pulling Harriet back into motion, even though she was dragging her feet, Oliver finally reached his grandfather's side. Before he could do more than assure everyone gathered in a circle that he and Harriet were fine, Lady Victoria stepped close to him, began coughing uncontrollably, and then, to his great concern, began wobbling on her feet.

Dropping his hold on Harriet's arm, he managed to catch Lady Victoria before she hit the hard sidewalk, and the second he lifted her up into his arms, her arms snaked around his neck. Tucking her face into his shoulder, she began sobbing . . . dramatically.

"I . . . need you . . . to take me . . . back to the hotel," she managed to get out between sobs.

Just when Oliver was about to hand the young lady off to her father, who'd stepped up to them, Lady Victoria tightened her grip around his neck and wouldn't let go.

"You should escort Lady Victoria and His Grace back to their hotel," Harriet said firmly.

The last thing Oliver wanted to do was leave Harriet, given that she'd just set a restaurant on fire and had to be experiencing at least a little bit of emotional distress. Not that she was showing that distress, but . . .

Lady Victoria began coughing again, rather violently at that, and realizing she probably should be taken back to the hotel sooner than later, he sent Harriet a frown, which she ignored, and then followed the duke to a carriage that had just pulled up next to the curb. He suddenly found it a little difficult to breathe, and not because of the smoke he'd recently sucked in, but rather because Lady Victoria had a death grip around his neck and was efficiently choking him. He helped her get settled on the seat, but as soon as the carriage jolted into motion she dissolved into sobbing once again, and didn't stop until they reached the Fifth Avenue Hotel.

Helping Lady Victoria out of the carriage, Oliver took hold of her arm and managed to get her up to her suite of rooms with the duke leading the way. He had no idea what was expected of him after he got Lady Victoria into a chair but took a seat in the chair she was pointing to in the hopes of sparing everyone another bout of weeping.

"Would you stay with her while I go have management summon a physician?" the duke asked.

265

Alarm was immediate. "Are you sure that's wise?"

The duke actually smiled. "I trust you, Mr. Addleshaw, and Victoria's mother is sleeping in a connecting room. I assure you, it's completely proper." With that, the duke disappeared, leaving Oliver alone with Lady Victoria.

Unfortunately, Lady Victoria didn't seem to have propriety on her mind. She waited just until her father vanished from sight before she . . . pounced.

He suddenly found himself knocked out of his chair and on the ground, before Lady Victoria plopped down right on top of him.

"What in the world are you doing?" was all he could think to ask.

"I've come all this way, under the misimpression that you were eligible, but since your fiancée behaved so poorly this evening by ruining our dinner, I have to believe you've had a change of heart in regard to her, so . . ."

Before Oliver could utter a single protest, Lady Victoria leaned forward and tried to kiss him, even though he turned his head to avoid her lips. Evidently being a somewhat determined sort, she tried again, right as her father reentered the room.

The next day, Oliver jumped off his horse and handed the reins to a waiting groom, enjoying the feel of the sun on his face as he walked to the front of Abigail's brownstone. His stride lengthened as his desire to see Harriet increased, and he reached the front door quickly, blinking in surprise when Abigail opened it.

"I was expecting you hours ago."

Oliver took Abigail's hand, kissed it, and frowned. "It's not quite eleven in the morning, and in case you've forgotten, I do have a business to run. I've spent the morning with an earnest young gentleman by the name of Mr. Harrison Simmons who has agreed to go to West Virginia for me and settle the disturbing situation that's transpiring there due to the inadequacies of Mr. Ruff."

When Abigail looked as if she were about to begin arguing, he continued, "I was here last night, trying to see Harriet, but your butler informed me you weren't accepting callers and wouldn't allow me to step through the door." He smiled. "So there's absolutely no reason for you to lecture me, Abigail, and again, it's still morning."

Abigail muttered something under her breath before she pulled him into the house and began striding down a long hallway.

"Where are we going?" he asked, breaking into a trot in order to keep up with her.

"I need to speak with you privately." Abigail made an abrupt turn to the right and plowed forward through a dreary-looking parlor filled with dark furniture. She looked somewhat stealthily over her shoulder before she pulled a book from a floor-to-ceiling bookshelf, which caused the bookshelf to open up to reveal a door. Placing her finger over her lips, she ushered him forward into a cheerful room decorated with green silk on the walls and furniture upholstered in yellow.

"This is my personal parlor," she explained, gesturing him toward a chair by the window that was now so clean it sparkled. "When my daughter was young, we used to spend hours here, reading and chatting, and . . ." A flash of what looked to be regret flickered through Abigail's eyes, but then she blinked, and it disappeared right as she took a seat. "So . . . do you have much to discuss with me regarding the duke and his daughter?"

Oliver lowered himself into the chair. "I do have much to discuss, not that it centers around the duke and Lady Victoria, though. I was hoping to talk to Harriet last night, but as I mentioned before, your butler wouldn't let me."

"He's always been rather diligent regarding following orders."

"You told him to keep me from the house?"

Abigail shrugged. "I didn't want you to cause Harriet more distress, at least not last night, considering all the embarrassment she suffered at dinner."

"My intention was not to distress Harriet. Surely you didn't think I would take her to task for setting the table on fire, did you?"

Abigail waved his question away. "Of course not. I was concerned about what you would tell her regarding Lady Victoria."

"I have no idea what you're talking about."

"Come now, Oliver, it was clear to everyone that Lady Victoria only had eyes for you last night. She's remarkably beautiful, comes from the aristocracy, and would make you a more-than-suitable spouse."

Leaning back in the chair, Oliver considered Abigail's words. Marrying a woman like Lady Victoria would definitely raise his status in society's eyes, but . . . he'd not been the slightest bit attracted to her and had truly only wanted to get back to Harriet as soon as possible, which . . . His eyes widened as the ramifications of that thought suddenly struck him.

He was attracted to Harriet—there was no escaping from that troubling bit of truth any longer.

But . . . what to do about it?

"Did Lady Victoria allow you to know of her interest?" Abigail asked.

"She knocked me to the floor and tried to kiss me."

"Oh . . . dear."

"Then her father walked in and . . . he was less than pleased to discover his daughter sitting on top of me." Oliver raked a hand through his hair. "It's questionable at the moment whether or not the duke and I will be proceeding with our business deal.

I distinctly heard him tell his daughter, as I beat a hasty retreat, he wanted to leave New York immediately."

"But . . . what about Harriet, and . . . what about the ball I've just sent out invitations for?"

"I thought you were going to host a small, intimate dinner party."

"I couldn't very well have an honest-to-goodness duke going back to England and telling everyone we over here in America are still provincial now, could I?"

"Abigail, forgive me, but I was under the impression that balls take at least a good month to plan and that society expects their three-week notice to such an event."

"The spontaneous nature of this ball is what's making everyone so frantic to accept my invitation," Abigail said with a satisfied smile. "Why, I've already heard back from almost one-hundred invitees—all of them coming, of course—and it's the off season."

"As I just mentioned, I'm not sure the duke will still be in New York, let alone want to come to your ball—not given what happened last night with his daughter."

"You'll have to do your very best to convince him he needs to come."

"Are you forgetting the little part about where he walked in on his daughter trying to maul me?"

Abigail waved his comment aside. "He's probably used to her antics. She seemed to be a rather high-strung young lady, which means she most likely gets into mischief on a regular basis."

"I'm not actually sure I want to spend another evening in her company. She knocked me to the floor and then jumped on top of me."

"I doubt she'll try the same thing again."

"And that's supposed to reassure me?"

Abigail opened her mouth, but then closed it when two maids

hurried into the room, both carrying feather dusters and rags that gave off a distinct smell of lemon.

Oliver smiled at them and then frowned when they bobbed curtsies and disappeared the way they'd come. "Don't those maids work for me?"

"Of course they do. I've absconded with most of your staff in order to get ready for the ball, including Mr. Blodgett and Mrs. Rollins. I must warn you now, dear, your butler and housekeeper are entirely too capable, and I'm quite certain I'm going to try to lure them away from you."

"Mrs. Astor has already tried, at least in regard to Mr. Blodgett, but he, thankfully, is quite loyal to me."

"He's fallen in love with our dear Lucetta, and if she agrees to stay on with me, that might change Mr. Blodgett's mind."

"What do you mean, stay on with you?"

"The ladies certainly can't return to that hovel they called home, can they? Since the duke has declared his intentions to leave town earlier than expected, your business deal, if it's still a possibility, will have to conclude within the next day or so, and then your alliance with Harriet will be over, unless . . ."

"Unless what?"

Abigail shrugged. "That's up for you and Harriet to decide. But, I must warn you now, the reason I was concerned about your tardiness was because I'm afraid she's devising some type of plan that will graciously allow your supposed engagement to her to be broken with relative ease. Evidently, in Harriet's mind, that will leave you free to pursue Lady Victoria."

Oliver rose to his feet. "You really should have allowed me to see her last night."

Abigail rose as well. "How could I have possibly known that you would have no interest in Lady Victoria? From what Archibald told me, you're incredibly focused on improving your fortune *and* your social status. Lady Victoria could do both for you with one tiny crook of her finger." Abigail lifted her chin. "Her father, from what I've been told, is an incredibly wealthy man."

"I need to find Harriet," Oliver said, seeing little use in responding to Abigail's statement. Everything she'd said was indeed the truth, but . . . for some reason he found himself relatively unconcerned with his social status at the moment.

"She's up in the attic, sorting through my old clothes for some peculiar reason. But, don't linger too long up there. I'm still short a few footmen and there is some large furniture that needs to be moved around in the third-floor ballroom."

"You want me to help move furniture?"

"How else will I be able to fit in the orchestra?"

He felt his lips twitch. "You do realize that your ball might not actually have a guest of honor, don't you?"

"We'll worry about that when the time comes," Abigail said before she reached up and patted his cheek. "Now, off you go, but remember . . . third floor . . . furniture."

"You're incorrigible," he returned before he sent her a grin and made his way for the door, pausing to ask a maid dusting the bannister where he could find the stairs leading up to the attic. She told him, and smiling his thanks, he took off up a narrow flight of steps, feeling perspiration dribble down his neck by the time he reached the attic. He walked into a spacious room filled to the brim with abandoned belongings, pleasure mixed with amusement flowing through him when he caught sight of Harriet.

She was sitting on the floor in the middle of the attic, bouncing up and down, which was rather strange, but then she jumped to her feet, looked at a concoction made of metal she'd been sitting on and let out an ear-piercing shriek.

"It worked, would you look at that . . . it sprang back into shape."

271

"Is that your bustle?" he asked, stepping farther into the room.

"It *is* my bustle," she exclaimed as she practically hopped to his side and grinned. "I made a coil and . . . it doesn't stay collapsed now."

Her enthusiasm was contagious, and before he actually thought about what he was doing, he moved closer to her, pulled her into a tight hug, and then lifted her off her feet. For a second it seemed as if she hugged him back, but then she stiffened, he immediately set her down, and both of them turned to Lucetta, who was making a *tsk*ing sound under her breath.

"It's a good thing Abigail, being Harriet's chaperone, didn't see you doing that, Oliver."

"She really makes an abhorrent chaperone," Millie said, speaking up as she walked around what appeared to be an old freestanding wardrobe with a gown in her hands. She stopped walking and let out a sigh when no one said anything. "Wrong word again?"

Lucetta laughed. "Not at all, that was an excellent use of the word *abhorrent*, Millie. I do believe your hard work with your dictionary is finally paying off."

Looking completely delighted, Millie moved to an old dress form that was standing off to the side and threw the gown over it, stepping back a moment later as she eyed the dress. "I don't know, it's rather . . ."

"Frumpy?" Oliver supplied before he walked over to stand beside Millie. "What's that for anyway?"

"Harriet's trying to decide what to wear to Abigail's ball," Lucetta explained.

"Isn't that dress a little . . . dated, and what happened to the gowns from Arnold Constable & Company?"

Lucetta and Millie exchanged rather significant looks before they abruptly walked out of the room.

"What was that about?" he asked.

"Maybe you should take a seat," Harriet said, moving over to what turned out to be a slightly worn chaise. She dumped a pile of gowns to the floor and gestured for him to sit down next to her.

Taking a seat, he waited while Harriet rearranged the folds of her skirt and then braced himself when she lifted her head and turned rather determined looking.

"I've come up with a plan to end our engagement that will allow us to part amicably, but also allow you to pursue Lady Victoria before she leaves to return home."

Abigail had been right—Harriet *had* been plotting.

"I don't recall stating that I have an interest in Lady Victoria."

"Well, when could you have stated much of anything to me, given the fact I set a restaurant on fire and embarrassed you beyond belief?" She blew out a breath, surprising him when she took his hand in hers. "I cannot express to you enough how truly sorry I am for causing such a ruckus."

"There's no need to apologize, Harriet. It could have happened to anyone."

"That's what everyone keeps trying to tell me, but I know perfectly well that ladies of society rarely set the table linens to flames, nor do they make outlandish comments about turtle dishes that cause everyone to lose their appetite for it."

Oliver grinned. "I must admit that the mere thought of eating your Sam did put me off terrapin for good, I think."

Harriet patted his hand and then withdrew hers. "For that, I must apologize. Everyone seems to enjoy that particular luxury and now I've ruined it for you forever."

"I'm fairly certain I'll survive."

"Yes, well, moving on to my idea."

"Must we?"

Harriet frowned. "I know you're probably concerned about my ability to plan, considering what happened last night, but I

assure you, this plan I've come up with will not end in disaster."
She leaned toward him. "What I believe we should do is this—I'm
going to dress in a rather dowdy manner, which will draw even
more attention to Lady Victoria's beauty. Then, you and I are
going to get in a slight disagreement regarding my . . . bustles
or perhaps my dress designing. Then, I'll dramatically release
you from our engagement, saying something to the effect that
you stifle my muse and I simply cannot move forward with a
gentleman who doesn't share my vision."

"Did you get Lucetta to help you with that?"

"How did you know?"

"It smacks of the theatrical."

"She suggested I throw myself at your feet and beg you to
release me from our engagement, but I thought that might be
a bit much."

"Just a bit."

Harriet arched a brow. "So . . . what do you think?"

Oliver drew her hand back into his and pressed it. "No."

"What do you mean, no?" Harriet asked as she tried to pull
her hand out of his, giving up a moment later when he refused
to relinquish his hold.

"I'm not interested in Lady Victoria."

"How could you not be interested in her? She's lovely, wealthy,
and won't embarrass you."

"She embarrassed me quite a bit last night when she tried
to kiss me."

Harriet's eyes went wide. "She tried to kiss you?"

Oliver felt a wave of satisfaction roll over him when he detected what he thought was a slight trace of disgruntlement in
her tone. "And knocked me to the floor in the process where
she immediately jumped on top of me."

"Well, she is young."

"She's a spoiled brat, is what she is, and we'll speak no further regarding any plan you might have for me to spend time in her company."

Harriet tapped a finger against her chin. "We can still move forward, though, with the argument part. Word has gotten out around town regarding our engagement, and since our time together is rapidly coming to an end, we might as well use Abigail's ball to allow society to learn that we've decided we won't suit. That will leave an opening for other young ladies to draw your attention."

"What if I've decided I'm not interested in other young ladies?"

For a second, something almost wistful settled in her eyes, but then they hardened and her lips thinned. She pulled her hand from his right before she got to her feet and began to pace back and forth across the room. Stopping directly in front of him, she blew out a breath. "What are you thinking?"

He reached out and pulled her down beside him, even as his pulse began to quicken. "We don't have to stop spending time together."

The moment the words were out of his mouth, he knew they were exactly what he'd wanted to say.

She intrigued him, fascinated him, and made him feel more alive than he'd ever felt in his life.

"You're talking complete nonsense," Harriet said.

"Why would you say that?"

"Because you and I live in the real world—me more than you, I think—and . . . your world will never accept me. You have to realize that, Oliver, somewhere deep down inside. Look what happened last night with Miss Dixon. She was vile and nasty in her remarks to me, as if she somehow instinctively knew I didn't belong in her company."

"We wouldn't have to associate with Miss Dixon."

"Would you be so willing to sever ties with everyone, then,

because if you continue spending time with me, that's exactly what you would have to do."

"My grandmother was not from society, but she was eventually accepted."

"I highly doubt your grandmother was illegitimate or had an aunt who earns a living through nefarious means." Harriet patted his hand. "You know that it wouldn't work for you to even remain friends with me, because society would eventually come to the conclusion I'm your mistress, and that's something I'm not willing to allow them to do."

"I wasn't suggesting you become my mistress."

"I know, Oliver, but again, there's no relationship that would work between us." Harriet drew in a deep breath and slowly released it. "It's best if we simply continue on with our original plan. I'll be on your arm at the ball, if there's still going to be one, but after that, we need to part ways and get on with the rest of our lives."

"What if that's not what I want?"

"I don't believe you truly know what you want, Oliver, but I know what I want." Harriet's lips curved ever so slightly at the corners. "I want the fairy tale, complete with a prince on a white charger who'll carry me away into the sunset."

"I'm not your idea of a prince on a white charger?" Oliver asked slowly.

"Of course you are, but you're not the right prince for me." She smiled. "You need to find yourself a princess much like Lady Victoria, someone who'll fit into your world and help you achieve your goals."

Oliver wanted to argue, but deep in his heart, he knew she made perfect sense. "You're sure about parting ways the night of the ball?"

"I think that would be for the best, as long as you've completed your business with the duke by then."

"I'm really not certain the duke still intends to come to Abigail's event."

Harriet's eyes widened. "But . . . Abigail's been working like mad and . . . what would we tell all the guests if the guest of honor doesn't show up?"

"He'll be there."

Oliver swung his attention to the doorway and found none other than Lady Victoria standing there, biting her lip and looking completely miserable.

"How long have you been listening to us?" Harriet asked as she got to her feet.

"Long enough to realize that the two of you are considering putting an end to your engagement and . . . it's all my fault."

With that, Lady Victoria dissolved into a fit of weeping, crossed the room in a flash, and much to Oliver's surprise, flung herself, not into his arms, but into Harriet's.

19

day and a half later, Harriet's nerves were stretched to the breaking point, quite like the laces Millie was currently torturing her with.

"I'm not going to be able to breathe, let alone eat, if you pull those any tighter," Harriet managed to get out in a voice that was barely more than a whisper, given that Millie seemed to have pushed all the air out of her lungs with her last tug of the corset.

"You're the one who insisted on wearing this refashioned gown of your mother's. As you remarked more than once while you altered it, your mother had a very small waist. Since you claimed it would ruin the line of the gown if you added additional fabric to the waistline, well, lacing you as tightly as possible is the only way we'll fit you into it. But at least now I know I can squish your waist to that desirable eighteen inches." Millie gave one last tug of the laces, tied them in a competent knot, and moved to stand in front of Harriet. "There, how do you feel?"

"Stuffed."

"Well, your waist looks absolutely tiny now," Lucetta exclaimed as she walked around Harriet and eyed her for a second, "and your bosom . . . hmmm . . . that might be a cause for concern." She turned to consider the gown that hung on a nearby dress form. "Perhaps we could add some lace to the bodice."

"I don't think we have time for that," Harriet said. "Maybe I should just wear the gold gown from Arnold Constable & Company. The sales lady assured me it was a design straight from Paris, so it would be completely acceptable—and I might even be able to breathe in it."

"Absolutely not," Millie argued. "You've been dying to have someplace to wear your mother's gown ever since you managed to get it away from Jane last year on your birthday. This ball is the perfect opportunity for that. Besides, since it was your mother's, I imagine it'll give you a little piece of comfort as you take on society tonight."

"And," Lucetta continued with a nod, "you told me bright and early this morning that you dreamed you wore your mother's gown to the ball. Honestly, Harriet, you must realize that could have very well been a little push from God, sending you that piece of comfort Millie just mentioned."

Harriet grinned. "With reasoning like that, I'd be foolish *not* to wear my mother's gown. And since Oliver and I will be parting ways after tonight, this might be my one and only chance to wear a ball gown."

"I noticed Abigail very considerately forgot all about her chaperoning duties when you had Oliver escort you over to the boardinghouse to pick up the gown," Lucetta said with a curve of her lips.

"She's still trying her very best to plot, but I'm afraid her efforts are for naught. Oliver and I agreed that after tonight we'll part ways. Even though I realize Abigail wishes things were different, they're not. Oliver is, and will always be, one of the wealthiest gentlemen in the country. I'll always be a woman with questionable parentage who makes her living as a seamstress. It would never work."

"But Oliver insinuated he might like to try to make it work," Lucetta argued.

"Oliver didn't know what he was insinuating," Harriet argued right back. "He certainly didn't mention a word about love."

Lucetta blew out a breath. "He didn't mention love because he's a gentleman, and they're rarely proficient with expressing their feelings. You also have to take into account that the two of you haven't exactly known each other for very long."

"Which is why it won't be all that difficult to continue on without him."

Lucetta's expression turned decidedly grouchy. "I wonder what more would have been said between the two of you if Lady Victoria hadn't interrupted."

"I was thankful she interrupted because, quite frankly, there really was nothing else to be said." Harriet shook her head. "I felt simply horrible for the girl. It couldn't have been easy for her to come and apologize to me for trying to abscond with my fiancé."

"I have a hard time sympathizing with a lady who was born to wealth and coddled her whole life—that coddling leaving her to believe that whatever she wants, she's entitled to get," Lucetta said.

Harriet drew in a breath, stopping midway when she realized her chest had no more room to expand. "It's not her fault she's been coddled, Lucetta. Why, after she finished apologizing to me, profusely at that, we ending up meeting with her father who was waiting in Abigail's drawing room. The poor man was completely appalled by what his daughter had done to Oliver, but he did hint that there's a reason behind Lady Victoria's sense of entitlement. Something to do with indulging her far too much throughout her youth because of . . . well, he never really explained properly, except to mention he was beginning to see there were going to be definite repercussions from that indulgence."

"Lady Victoria admitted to you she knocked Oliver down and then tried to kiss him." Lucetta let out a snort. "Honestly, if someone ever tries to kiss my fiancé, if I ever get around to even entertaining the thought of finding one, well, I'm certainly not going to pat that someone on the back and try to soothe away their guilt with kind words."

"If Oliver truly was my fiancé, I doubt I would have been as forgiving, but again, he's not."

"You hold him in affection," Lucetta countered.

"Perhaps, but there's no possible future for us. I'm simply going to take any affection I hold for the man and wrap it away much like I did with my mother's gown. Maybe, when I'm feeling sentimental, I'll pull out my memories of Oliver and sigh over them before I pack them away again."

"That's a bit of a maudlin thought," Lucetta mumbled.

Harriet laughed. "I don't intend on sighing over the gentleman very often, Lucetta. Starting up my own business is going to occupy most of my time."

"True," Millie said, "but enough about business and the relationship with Oliver that was destined to be doomed from the start. You have a ball to attend, and you need to keep your wits about you. You know you don't have all the uses for that silverware down, and you certainly didn't get much practice at Delmonico's since you almost burned the place to the ground. And don't even get me started on all the dance steps you're going to have to remember from clear back in the day when your aunt made you take lessons. How long ago was that anyway?"

"Far too long, and thank you for reminding me," Harriet muttered. "I forgot all about the dancing."

"Which is somewhat odd, considering you're going to a ball," Lucetta said before she whipped the gown off the dress form, gave it a good shake and smiled. "You've done wonders in the small amount of time you had to redesign this."

"I could hardly wear a gown tonight that was originally equipped to handle hoops—although, looking at it now, I probably should have used some of the excess fabric to shore up that bodice."

"No sense worrying about it now," Millie said, taking the dress from Lucetta and moving to Harriet's side. "We're losing track of time, and revealing bodice or not, we need to get you into this."

Two hours later, Harriet stared at the reflection in the mirror, hardly able to believe the elegant and well-coifed lady staring back at her had recently worked as a milliner.

Her black hair had been swept to the top of her head and anchored in place with pins covered in tiny pearls. Soft tendrils of curls teased her cheek, and her face was slightly flushed, the color highlighting the fact her eyes had taken to twinkling.

She raised her hand and tugged up her neckline the best she could, the diamond bracelet Abigail had lent her sparkling in the reflection of the mirror. Abigail had also lent her the use of the matching necklace, and while the diamonds glittering back at her gave her a very regal appearance, Harriet knew it was simply an illusion.

She wouldn't belong tonight—of that she was quite certain—but honor demanded she see the deal she'd struck with Oliver through to the end. Wearing the gown of her long-dead mother would also honor that mother, if only in Harriet's mind. Perhaps, in the process, she could finally lay to rest all the resentment she'd unconsciously been holding against her mother, that resentment stemming from leaving Harriet all alone—except for Jane, a poor excuse for an aunt.

Maybe it was as Lucetta had suggested and God had sent her that odd dream where she saw herself wearing her mother's gown. Perhaps He'd known she'd been harboring a hurt for most of her life, and by having her wear her mother's gown, had given her a means to heal that hurt.

She took a moment to consider her reflection again, her hands smoothing down the fine silk. Her eyes misted with tears as she gazed at her mother's gown, wondering how her mother must have looked wearing the dress, and wondering if her father had been the one to give the gown to her mother, perhaps as a token of his affection.

Brushing that ridiculous thought aside, given the reality of her mother's situation, she nodded, just once.

"I hope I'll make you proud tonight, Mother."

Closing her eyes, she took a moment to pray, asking God to give her strength to see the night through to the very end.

"Ready?"

Harriet opened her eyes, felt the all-too-familiar feeling of terror seize hold of her, and turned from the mirror, finding Abigail marching determinedly into the room. Abigail stopped dead in her tracks, right as her mouth gaped open.

"Good heavens, child, you're stunning."

Harriet grinned. "Thank you, but I must admit I feel a bit like a fraud."

"No fraud could look as beautiful as you do. Where in the world did you get such an original gown? Why, I haven't seen that particular shade of purple for decades, but I must say, it suits you to perfection."

Harriet ran a hand over the delicate silk. "It was my mother's."

"Your . . . mother's?" Abigail repeated slowly, moving to her side and reaching out a hand to touch the fabric. "It's very fine."

"It is, and I'm fortunate that my aunt kept it so well-preserved all these years."

"Forgive me, but from what I've learned about your aunt Jane, she really doesn't seem like the type to be overly sentimental."

Harriet frowned. "Now that you mention it, it is somewhat odd she'd save my mother's dress because Jane told me herself that she's been very annoyed with my mother for up and dying and leaving me in her care."

"What a completely horrid woman your aunt is, dear, but let us put such unpleasant thoughts aside. You look lovely, and I'm delighted you actually have something of your mother's to wear this evening." Abigail reached out and snagged hold of Harriet's hand, sliding a ring over Harriet's gloved finger.

Looking down, Harriet found a huge diamond ring glittering back at her. "Oh, I can't wear this," she muttered, trying to pull her hand back, but to no avail when Abigail refused to let go of it.

"It'll be expected that Oliver's fiancée has a ring, and . . . I would be tickled if you'd agree to wear this particular ring tonight. It's a family heirloom and I always intended to give it to my daughter, but . . . well, no need to get into the drama that happened there." Abigail blinked away tears that had sprung to her eyes before she let out a sniff, dropped Harriet's hand, and then patted Harriet on the cheek. "You, Lucetta, and Millie have, in a relatively short period of time, become like daughters to me, or granddaughters considering our age differences. I would be truly honored if you would wear the ring, if only for this evening."

Harriet's throat constricted, but she managed a nod right as Victoria burst into the room, Oliver by her side.

Any air she'd been able to keep in her chest left her the second her gaze settled on Oliver. He was looking more handsome than ever in his formal coat and cravat, the cut of the coat expertly fitting his broad shoulders and tapering all too attractively down to his slim waist. His hair was combed back from his face without a single lock falling out of place, and his eyes were . . . wide and staring in a somewhat dazed fashion back at her.

For the first time in her entire life, Harriet truly did feel beautiful.

"I do hope you won't be upset with me for coming early," Lady Victoria exclaimed, drawing Harriet's attention. "Father told me I was being inexcusably rude, but after your kindness of yesterday, Harriet, I've just felt this pull to be around you. I thought it might be lovely if we greeted guests together."

Harriet's lips curved into a smile as Victoria pulled her into an enthusiastic hug and then stepped back. There was something refreshing about the young lady, even though she was certainly spoiled and a bit strong-willed. Harriet took Victoria's hand in her own and gave it a good squeeze. "I would be honored to stand by you and greet the guests, but where is your father?"

"He's still back at the hotel, because Mother's running a little behind schedule. She began feeling better only a few hours ago, which is why she's coming tonight. But it takes her forever to get ready, so they'll be late."

Victoria grinned. "Oliver's delightful grandfather seems to believe that's a fortuitous circumstance, since my parents will then be able to make a grand entrance—something he thought you, Mrs. Hart, would appreciate."

"Indeed I do," Abigail agreed. "It's quite the feather in my cap to be fortunate enough to introduce your family to New York, Lady Victoria. I'm delighted your mother is feeling up to coming this evening, but we really must get to the ballroom. Our guests will be arriving shortly, and it wouldn't do to not be there to greet them."

She took hold of Victoria's arm, pulled her away from Harriet, and lowered her voice. "We should give Harriet and Oliver a moment alone." She sent Harriet a wink. "I'm leaving the door open and I expect both of you in the ballroom within the next five minutes." With that, Abigail strolled arm in arm with Victoria out of the room.

Harriet's nerves immediately made themselves known, increasing steadily when Oliver didn't say a single word but simply stood there, watching her. "Is something the matter?" she finally asked.

Oliver frowned. "Why would you ask that?"

"You're not speaking, and it's been my experience that you're never at a loss for something to say."

Laughing, Oliver took one step forward. "If you must know, the only thing the matter at the moment is that you look enchanting this evening, quite like a princess, and your beauty is what stole the words straight from my lips and fogged up my mind."

Harriet suddenly found *she* was at a loss for words.

Oliver grinned and moved across the room, stopping directly in front of her. He drew her hand up and placed a kiss on the knuckles, his gaze and the merest touch of his lips against her gloved hand sending shivers down her spine.

"Is something wrong, Miss Peabody?" he asked and continued before she could reply, not that she was certain she would actually have been able to do that. "Why, since I've become known to you, it's been my observation that you're never without words, and yet, here you are . . . speechless."

He was far too attractive when he was being charming, and charming he certainly was this evening.

He needed to stop it, before she threw aside all the decisions she'd recently made and told him she wanted to continue being his pretend fiancée, if only for another month, or two, or perhaps six, or . . .

"Where did you get this ring?"

Harriet pushed her less-than-helpful thoughts aside. "Abigail lent it to me. She thought people will expect me to be wearing an engagement ring."

"I do beg your pardon, Harriet. I never once thought about getting you a ring."

"Again, we're not really engaged, and besides, you've had quite a bit on your mind of late, so it's perfectly understandable why you didn't think of it."

"But . . . still . . . you deserved a ring."

"And now I have one, if only for tonight."

Oliver smiled. "You really are an extraordinary lady, Miss Harriet Peabody. Now, would you do me the supreme honor of joining me in the receiving line where ladies are certain to remark on that lovely dress of yours, and gentlemen are certain to drive me mad by lingering over your hand for an inappropriately long period of time?"

He really was going to have to turn down the charm or else . . .

Drawing in a deep breath, Harriet slowly released it and then took the arm he was offering her. Tears blinded her for just a moment as he escorted her down the hall, the knowledge that this was going to be the last night she spent in Oliver's company causing her heart to break just a touch. Blinking the tears away, she squared her shoulders and made a promise to herself as they drew closer to the ballroom. She was going to enjoy this night with the gentleman by her side because, quite honestly, she would probably never experience another night like this for the rest of her life.

20

*G*entlemen *were* lingering far too long over Harriet's hand.

Oliver had known the moment he'd seen her tonight that it would be a strong possibility the gentlemen of New York would take an immediate interest in her, but he hadn't been expecting their interest to cause him quite so much irritation.

That troubling business was probably what was behind him proclaiming to each and every guest they'd greeted so far the fact that Harriet was his *fiancée* in what sounded like a remarkably possessive tone of voice. That circumstance had caused Harriet to send him more than one disbelieving look, while Abigail, on the other hand, kept sending him smiles of pure delight.

He had no idea when he'd turned into a possessive sort, but he had the sneaking suspicion it might have occurred when the first guest, a Mr. Matthew Prescott, walked into the room, took one look at Harriet, and had almost begun to froth at the mouth.

Unfortunately, Mr. Prescott had not been the exception with that troubling reaction. Oliver had been forced to stand by and watch as gentleman after gentleman barely took the time to acknowledge him before moving on to Harriet, where each and every one of them had proceeded to ogle her.

Did they not remember that it was hardly appropriate to meet a lady for the first time, and be told said lady was firmly off the market, and yet still direct their attention to the lady's all-too-obvious charms? Quite frankly, he'd been considering covering up those charms with his handkerchief, or better yet, hiding them underneath his coat, which he certainly wouldn't mind shucking off to give her.

"You're glowering again," Abigail whispered, stepping to his side and giving him a sharp rap with the fan she was clutching.

"Can you blame me?"

Abigail shot a look to Harriet who was having her hand accosted by an earnest young gentleman by the name of Mr. Richmond Sprout. "Not in the least, dear, but you really should try to control that temper of yours. The last thing we need this evening is for you to punch someone."

"That thought never entered my head."

"Of course it did, but I find it rather sweet." Abigail sent him a wink, turned, and smiled. "Ah, there you are, Mr. Mulberry, and I see you've brought the always delightful Miss Dixon with you." She craned her neck and looked past them. "May I hope you're the last to arrive?"

Everett stepped forward and kissed Abigail's gloved hand. "I do beg your pardon, Mrs. Hart, for being somewhat tardy. Miss Dixon couldn't quite decide what to wear tonight, and I fear that has made us a trifle late."

"We're hardly late," Miss Dixon snapped. "And it's hardly appropriate for you to disclose such personal information about me." She nodded to Abigail. "I'm impressed by how quickly you pulled this together, Mrs. Hart. Why, I was worried no one would respond to your invitation, given that there was not even a week's notice, let alone the customary three.

It would seem I was mistaken, and I could not be more delighted."

Oliver was fairly sure Miss Dixon was more disappointed not to witness Abigail's failure than delighted by her success, but since she *was* the lady Everett seemed determined to continue on with, he kept his thoughts to himself and glanced to Harriet for a distraction.

Temper began to simmer when he realized that Mr. Sprout was still dawdling over Harriet's hand, bending forward as his lips lingered on her glove, his gaze focused on the front of her low-cut bodice.

Reaching out, he snagged Harriet by the shoulder and pulled her close to him, leaving Mr. Sprout with no option but to release the hand he'd been clutching, his lips still puckered but now finding nothing more than thin air to touch. Oliver narrowed his eyes at the gentleman, satisfaction flowing over him when Mr. Sprout blinked, straightened, and hurried in the opposite direction.

"Darling, look who finally arrived," he said, wincing ever so slightly when Harriet stepped on his foot.

"Mr. Mulberry, Miss Dixon," she began, "it's lovely to see you both again."

Miss Dixon edged closer, her gaze running over Harriet's gown. "What an interesting gown you've chosen this evening, Miss Peabody. I wasn't aware that violet was suddenly all the rage."

"It's the perfect color for you," Everett said, stepping ever so casually between Harriet and Miss Dixon before he took Harriet's hand in his and placed the now expected kiss on her glove. "I'm not surprised in the least you chose violet," Everett continued, still holding Harriet's hand, even though Miss Dixon had begun to turn a shade remarkably similar to Harriet's gown. "The color suits you and, if I may say, makes your eyes appear somewhat mysterious."

For a second, Oliver felt the distinct urge to throttle his best friend, but then he caught the gleam in Everett's eyes and realized that, for whatever reason, his friend was deliberately baiting him.

Refusing to rise to that bait, he summoned up a smile right as Miss Dixon began to rail at Everett.

"My goodness, Miss Dixon, it's hardly the thing to screech at Mr. Mulberry in such a common fashion," Abigail said as she bustled over to join them. Ignoring Miss Dixon's protests regarding the screeching, Abigail nodded to Oliver. "It seems all the guests have arrived—except for the duke and duchess, of course—which means we can repair to the ballroom."

"My father said to expect them around eleven, and it's only ten thirty now," Victoria said as she joined them, holding Archibald's arm.

"The perfect time for them to make a grand entrance," Abigail said. "But, I don't want our guests to get bored, so we'll open the ball. I've instructed Oliver's chef to hold dinner until midnight, which is such a delightful time to dine."

"I knew I should have eaten something before coming here," Miss Dixon muttered.

"Ah, Miss Dixon, I was hoping you'd attend this evening," Victoria exclaimed, stepping forward and taking what seemed to be a rather firm grip of Miss Dixon's arm. "Why, we barely had any time at all to get acquainted at Delmonico's."

"Because Miss Peabody set the place on fire."

"And wasn't that just so exciting?" Victoria chirped before she tugged Miss Dixon forward. "Mrs. Hart has very kindly set out numerous tables with scrumptious little treats. Would you care to join me as I go find some to sample?"

Miss Dixon, without so much as a single glance to Everett, fell into step beside Victoria and quickly disappeared into the crowd assembled in Abigail's ballroom. Oliver looked to his friend, but before he could say a single word, Everett held up his hand.

"I know. She's being exceedingly difficult."

"Which begs the question of why you continue spending time with her."

"The brats need a mother, Oliver, and she's everything my parents want for me in a spouse."

"Yes, but your parents won't have to wake up next to her every morning, will they?"

Everett shrugged and then smiled. "I must say, Lady Victoria is not what I expected."

"She's charming," Harriet said, speaking up. "I think what everyone has forgotten is that she's a relatively young lady and young ladies are known to make a few mistakes here and there."

Oliver gestured to the crowd. "She certainly was quick to haul Miss Dixon away from you."

Harriet smiled. "She's attempting to make up for the fact she tried to maul you."

Everett's eyes widened. "Lady Victoria mauled you? You never told me that."

"We've hardly had much time to talk of late, what with Abigail deciding to host a ball, Harriet's aunt on the loose, Silas threatening to ruin me, and all the issues I'm dealing with over that mining accident."

"Have there been any new developments in regard to the mine?"

"I've just sent a gentleman known for his negotiation strategies down to West Virginia, and I'm hopeful he'll have good news to report soon." Oliver blew out a breath. "I'm going to have to spend a fortune in new machinery, but . . ."

"It's the right thing to do," Harriet finished for him.

"It is."

"And you're feeling much better now because you're doing the right thing, aren't you?" she pressed.

"I'd feel even better if my profits began to move forward, but . . . yes, I do feel better."

"I'm delighted to learn there's hope for you yet, Mr. Addleshaw."

Oliver turned as an older lady who'd just made that declaration slipped out from what appeared to be a broom closet and marched their way, her grin surprisingly youthful.

"I should have known you'd find a way to attend the ball," Harriet said.

"You didn't think I'd leave you all alone to deal with this, did you?" Lucetta asked with a wave of her hand, before she patted her silver curls. "What do you think?"

Oliver took in the elaborately curled wig perched on top of Lucetta's head, the wrinkles she'd somehow managed to create on her face, and the very thick spectacles she'd perched on her nose. "Can you see out of those?"

Lucetta grinned. "Not really, but the fact my vision is a little skewed is helping me get into character. I've decided I'm a dotty old thing who is slightly related to Abigail. I'm one of those relatives who *has* to be invited but one whom no one actually acknowledges." She smoothed a hand down the skirt of her hideous floral gown. "I found this gem in Abigail's attic, along with the lovely wig I'm wearing."

"But I'm the one who was given the daunting task of picking old moth carcasses out of that wig and getting it to fit Lucetta's head," Millie said as she stepped out of the broom closet dressed as a proper maid. "And, just to be clear, she didn't suffer any ill effects from my efforts."

A smile teased Harriet's mouth. "I see you're still miffed over the fact Abigail brought in another hairdresser to do my hair tonight."

"I've been practicing hair styling with hot tongs for two days," Millie grumbled.

"Why don't you show everyone what that practice did," Abigail said, moving up to rejoin them.

"I don't think there's any need for that."

Everett grinned at Millie. "You burned your hair off, didn't you."

Millie lifted her nose in the air. "I don't believe you and I are familiar enough with each other, Mr. Mulberry, for you to ask me such a question. If you'll excuse me, I need to go check on the refreshments. Abigail has trusted me with making certain the punch bowl never runs dry."

With that, Millie bobbed a perfect curtsy, turned on her heel, and marched into the ballroom. Partway across the room, she apparently realized that maids normally didn't boldly walk through the middle of the dance floor, because she turned once again and practically ran to the side.

"She's an unusual lady," Everett said as he watched Millie's retreating back.

"That she is," Abigail agreed, taking his offered arm before she nodded to Oliver. "Are you ready to open the ball?"

Apprehension was immediate. "What do you mean . . . open the ball?"

"She means that you and Harriet," Archibald began, stepping forward, "being the newly engaged couple, will be expected to open the ball with the first dance." He looked at Abigail. "Did you forget to mention that to them?"

Abigail smiled. "I have been rather busy of late, pulling off this daunting feat of preparing a ball in two days, so, yes, I might have forgotten."

Oliver felt Harriet's fingers dig into his arm. Looking down at her, he frowned. "I probably should have asked this before, but do you know how to dance?"

"Of course, although I might be a bit rusty."

It hit him then, how little he really knew about the lady standing beside him. But . . . he wanted to know more . . . everything about her—not just how she came to know how to dance but what she thought about every second of the day. Who'd taught her how to sew, and how was she able to imagine and assemble a bustle that could collapse and then recover? And . . . did she regret not ever being able to perform on a wire because her aunt had hustled her out of the circus?

Unfortunately, the reality was that he wasn't going to get to learn more about her. Their time was almost over, and that realization caused something that felt remarkably like regret to settle deep in his soul.

"But . . . when did you learn?" he heard himself ask.

"Does it matter?" Harriet countered before she prodded him forward. The next thing he knew, he was standing with Harriet in the middle of Abigail's ballroom. The room went silent as Abigail took up a position in front of the thirty-piece orchestra she'd somehow managed to procure on remarkably short notice.

"I would like to take a moment to welcome all of you to my, shall we say, spontaneous ball," Abigail said as laughter filled the room. "The guests of honor will be arriving shortly, but their lovely daughter, Lady Victoria, is already here, as most of you know, since she was in the receiving line." Abigail waved a hand in the direction of Victoria, who was stuffing what appeared to be a piece of cake into her mouth. Undaunted, Victoria swallowed and grinned, executing a beautiful curtsy before she waved to the guests and then gestured back to Abigail.

"Now then," Abigail continued, "as most of you were made aware, Mr. Addleshaw has recently become engaged to the lovely Miss Peabody, and it is my wish that the couple open the ball with the first dance."

Oliver saw the members of the orchestra pick up their instruments, and he turned to Harriet, who instead of looking nervous was beaming up at him.

"See, I did finally practice that adoring look you demanded, and I'm now going to suggest you try your hand at looking adoringly back at me," she muttered out of the side of her mouth even as she kept her smile firmly in place. "The guests will get suspicious if I'm the only one doing the whole adoring business."

His lips curved into a returning smile. She was so beautiful and so different from anyone he'd ever known that he decided there and then that, although this was to be the last night they were together, he was going to make the most of it.

"Ready?" he whispered as he pulled her into his arms.

"I don't know if I'd go that far, but . . ."

The music began and he pulled her closer, breathing in the scent of her that smelled exactly like violets. He swept her across the floor, delighted when she matched his every step.

All of the worries that had been plaguing him of late simply disappeared as he waltzed Harriet around the room, enjoying the feel of her in his arms until it seemed as if they were the only two people at the ball.

He looked down at her face and felt more alive than he'd ever felt in his life. Her unusual eyes were sparkling with pleasure, and her face glowed from their exertions, but not once did she stumble. When she tilted her head back and laughed, he was hard-pressed to not give in to the urge he immediately felt to lower his head and claim the lips that were only inches away from his own.

He couldn't give her up—it was as simple as that, but . . .

He pushed the thought away, not wanting anything to intrude on the unexpected happiness that had descended over him. Disappointment was immediate when the music slowly came to a stop. He pulled her close for just a second, blinking as the sound of enthusiastic clapping drew him back to reality. He sent Harriet a smile, pleased to notice she looked somewhat dazed, and dropped his arms from around her. He was about to take hold of her hand, when a voice that sent anger coursing through him sounded throughout the ballroom.

"Bravo, my friend, bravo," Silas Ruff drawled as he continued to clap even though all of the other guests had stopped. "What a delightful couple you make."

Casually placing himself in front of Harriet, Oliver struggled to tamp down the temper that threatened to overtake him. "This is certainly a surprise, my *old* friend, finding you here at the ball since I wasn't aware you'd been extended an invitation."

Silas laughed, although it sounded anything but amused. "Given the—how did Mrs. Hart phrase it?—oh yes, *spontaneous* nature of this event, I assumed my lack of an invitation was a simple oversight. But—" he laughed again—"it was hardly difficult getting into the house, given that I brought with me a very special surprise for your lovely Miss Peabody."

Before Oliver could take so much as a single step, Silas turned and then stepped forward with a lady dressed in an elaborate gown of ivory, draped in diamonds and smiling back at him. Dread was immediate, and only increased when Silas smiled a nasty smile Oliver's way before he opened his mouth.

"It is my extreme pleasure to introduce to you, Oliver, Miss Jane Peabody, aunt to your lovely little Miss Harriet Peabody." Silas's eyes suddenly narrowed. "You'll be delighted to learn that Miss *Jane* Peabody is one of the most charming confidence artists I've ever had the fortune of meeting."

21

*F*orcing feet that wanted to remain stuck to the floor into motion, Harriet stepped around Oliver and set her sights on her aunt. Jane was still standing beside Silas, and she was smiling, although her smile appeared to be incredibly forced and she'd begun to turn a very ugly shade of red.

"Act as if you didn't know about my aunt," she said softly before she began forward—and then was tugged to an immediate stop when Oliver grabbed hold of her hand. Irritation was immediate. "Don't be ridiculous," she whispered. "You have much to lose here, while I have nothing. I'll handle Jane."

"Not likely," he said pleasantly before he tucked her hand into the crook of his arm. "We'll do this together, shall we?"

Before she could protest, he began strolling ever so casually across the ballroom floor, bringing her to a stop directly in front of Mr. Silas Ruff. "Shall we repair to a more private setting?"

Silas laughed even as his eyes narrowed. "You'd like that, wouldn't you, *old* friend?" He stepped closer to Oliver and lowered his voice. "I told you that you'd regret firing me, and this is me showing you what regret looks like."

He gestured to the silent crowd watching them closely. "I'm

of the firm belief, that you, as members of New York's highest society, deserve to know what our dear Oliver here, *unintentionally* I'm sure, almost unleashed on you—that being Jane and Harriet Peabody."

"This was not what we agreed on," Jane whispered furiously, stepping closer to Silas, her face now mottled with rage. "You promised to introduce me to society as Harriet's doting aunt because of information I gave you about my niece. However, you never mentioned anything at all about setting me up for embarrassment in the process."

Silas shrugged. "My dear woman, are you really so naïve that you actually believed I followed you that day from Oliver's house because I had anything other than a personal agenda on my mind?" He released a laugh. "I expected better of someone with your diabolical nature, but . . . as you can see, you, my dear, were only a means to an end for me."

He gestured to the crowd again. "When I learned that Jane Peabody's crime of choice these days is blackmail, I realized that her niece—lovely Harriet here—was obviously perpetuating a fraud against our very own Mr. Oliver Addleshaw. I immediately knew it would be less than responsible, being one of his *old* friends, to not point out to him that his fiancée is nothing less than a confidence artist following in her aunt's footsteps. You'll be surprised to discover that Harriet, until very recently, worked in a hat shop of all things, and . . . lovely Jane told me that her niece had readily agreed to bring her into society after Harriet got introduced around a bit. The purpose of that agreement, my friends, was undoubtedly to increase Jane's bank account since she wanted to use her introduction into society to collect juicy tidbits about each and every one of you. It doesn't take much deduction to realize she would then use those tidbits to divest you of your hard-earned funds."

"That's not true . . . . Well, the part about my aunt does hold quite a bit of truth, but"—Harriet ignored Oliver's warning squeeze—"I was not planning any confidence scheme with my aunt or on my own."

"Are you going to claim next that you were never a hat girl, because . . ." Silas raised a hand and waved someone forward.

A moment later, Harriet found herself facing Miss, Mrs., and Mr. Birmingham, all three of them looking exceedingly pleased with themselves, and all of them sending smug looks her way.

"Is this the woman who delivered your hats, Miss Birmingham?" Silas asked.

"Indeed she is," Miss Birmingham said with a sniff. "And . . . I know for a fact that, other than perpetuating a fraud against Mr. Addleshaw, she's also possessed of a most violent nature, given that she assaulted me. I'm sure I still have the bruises to prove it."

The whispers were immediate, but Harriet ignored them because Oliver had drawn himself up to his full height and was moving closer to the Birmingham family. "None of you have any business being here, and considering your less-than-acceptable behavior that day, Miss Birmingham, it's confusing to me why you'd throw nasty accusations Harriet's way. I'm too much of a gentleman to disclose the extent of your bad behavior in front of this gathering, but if you malign Harriet again, I might be forced to forget I'm a gentleman."

Mr. Birmingham clenched his fists. "No true gentleman would take up with a hat girl."

Silas rubbed his hands together. "I must admit I'm beyond curious as to how you became engaged to Miss Peabody, given that you only recently met her, and it also seems that you met her when she was still a . . . hat girl." He smiled. "Could it be possible that you were so taken in by her obvious beauty that you never bothered to investigate her past?"

"I know all about her past, Silas, including everything regarding her aunt. Why, I even know that Jane sent Harriet a diamond necklace on her birthday, probably to force her niece into doing her bidding, but . . . instead of keeping the necklace, or giving in to Jane's demands, Harriet had it delivered to the police." Oliver ignored Jane's hiss of rage. "Harriet's response shows you the true measure of her character. She might have suffered an unfortunate upbringing, but instead of becoming a lady possessed of questionable morals, she's honorable, charming, and I'm fortunate to have her in my life."

Right there and then, Harriet fell in love.

It would have been so easy for Oliver to have done what she'd asked, to let her take responsibility for everything, but that clearly wasn't in his nature. He was chivalrous, kind, surly upon occasion, and far too attractive for his own good, but he was a just and honorable man, and she could no longer deny that she held him in great esteem.

Jane stepped forward. "Did she tell you that she's illegitimate and that her mother was nothing more than a conniving . . ."

"You will not speak about Harriet's mother," Oliver interrupted in a lethal voice. "Nor will you ever contact Harriet again after you leave this ball."

Jane lifted her chin. "You dare to threaten me, boy? She's my niece, and I'll contact her whenever I please. You should be thankful you're being given the truth about her, although why you keep trying to defend her is a little confusing to me."

"I find I'm confused as well."

Harriet resisted a sigh when she looked over at the double doors leading into the ballroom and discovered none other than the Duke of Westmoore standing there.

Jane sucked in a sharp breath before edging behind Silas, but before Harriet could dwell on the reason behind that, Victoria materialized out of the crowd and hurried to her father's side. The young lady didn't seem bothered at all by the silence in the ballroom but simply took hold of her father's arm and immediately began trying to tug him out of the room.

"You're supposed to wait to make a grand entrance, Father, but . . . given that the conversation has turned a little disturbing, I think it might be for the best if you take me back to the hotel."

"You may wait for me outside this room, Victoria," the duke said. "I'll join you directly, but I need some answers before I take my leave, especially since I've agreed to enter into a business alliance with Mr. Addleshaw." He settled his attention on Oliver, quirking a brow.

Harriet started forward, wanting to get to the duke before Oliver got to him and took all the blame. Unfortunately, Oliver seemed to know exactly what she was about, because he wouldn't allow her to shake out of his hold. He pulled her to his side and began walking slowly in the duke's direction, speaking to her under his breath as they walked. "We're in this together, Harriet, so don't even think you're going to tell him this was all your idea."

"The truth will harm you and will certainly see the end of your deal with the duke."

"Perhaps, but you once told me that you're not fond of lies. I'm suddenly of the belief that this—" he stopped walking and looked back at Silas and Jane—"is Someone's way, if you will, of telling us we need to make this right."

"I'm not saying I don't agree," she said as they began walking again, "but you'll suffer more from what we've done than I will, which hardly seems fair."

"I'm not actually that worried about it," he said, slowing his steps to a stop when they reached the duke and Victoria, who clearly hadn't gone to wait for her father in the hallway.

Drawing in a breath, Harriet lifted her head to meet the duke's gaze, but found him looking not at her face but . . .

"Miss Peabody, where in the world did you get that gown?" he demanded.

Of all the words she'd been expecting to come out of the duke's mouth, those hadn't come close. "My . . . ah . . . aunt gave it to me."

"How did she come by it?"

Confusion, mixed with a hefty dose of alarm, swirled over Harriet. By the distinct edge in the duke's voice, she knew something was dreadfully amiss, but rather than speculate on what that could be, she decided on the spot that her best, and perhaps only option, was to direct the conversation to the one person who might have some answers. "Excuse me for a moment, Your Grace," she said.

Sending Oliver what she hoped was a reassuring smile as she withdrew her hand from his arm, she began marching across the eerily silent ballroom, determined to reach her aunt as quickly as possible. Unfortunately, Jane was no longer hiding behind Silas but was winding her way through the crowd, her goal apparently being that of making a hasty escape. Harriet took off after her, breaking into a run when Jane looked over her shoulder and then picked up her skirt and dashed forward. Snagging hold of Jane's arm right as her aunt reached a door leading to the servant stairs, Harriet pulled her to a stop.

"Since you obviously came to the ball this evening for the purpose of being introduced to society, you should be thrilled beyond measure that I, being your dutiful niece, am now going to fulfill your every dream by introducing you to a real live duke," Harriet said.

"I've changed my mind," Jane snapped, trying to tug out of Harriet's hold. When Harriet wouldn't let go, Jane resorted to kicking her, hard.

Digging her fingers into Jane's arm, Harriet began hauling her forward. "I'm not letting you slip out of whatever this is, Jane, so you might as well stop struggling. Tell me, before we reach the duke, why is he so interested in my dress?" she asked as Jane tried to kick her again.

"Let go of me, or I swear, you're going to regret it."

"I'm fairly sure I don't have much left to regret, thanks to you and Silas," Harriet said, pulling her aunt forward another few feet before a lady's voice suddenly rang out, stopping Harriet in her tracks.

"Good heavens! Is that you, Jane?"

Keeping a hand on Jane's arm, even though her aunt had stopped struggling, Harriet lifted her head and settled her attention on a beautiful lady who was framed in the doorway leading into the ballroom. She was dressed in an exquisite gown that could have been made by no other designer but Worth, and a tiara nestled in her dark, elaborately styled curls. When the duke moved to join the lady, Harriet realized she was looking at the duchess.

But . . . how in the world did the Duchess of Westmoore know her aunt, and . . . why did the duchess's face seem so familiar . . . and . . . why was a distinct feeling of queasiness beginning to settle in the pit of her stomach?

The room began to swim out of focus, but then Jane shrugged away from Harriet and walked not for the back door but directly across the ballroom and toward the duchess, spreading out her arms in a gesture of welcome.

"Margaret, my goodness but this is an absolute delight. Why, I haven't seen you for an age," Jane gushed in an accent that was distinctly British. "I had no idea you were expected in town."

Silas suddenly stepped out of the crowd, moved to stand in front of the duchess, bowed and then turned to Jane. "My, my, Miss Peabody, you have been busy over the years, haven't you, but tell me . . . how are you acquainted with the Duchess of Westmoore? Old friends, are you?"

The duchess lifted her chin. "Forgive me, sir, but did you just call Jane . . . Miss Peabody?"

Silas laughed. "Should I assume that's not her name?"

Before she could answer him, Oliver took Silas by the arm and hauled him out of the way, leaving Jane standing by herself, facing the duchess.

"When did you change your name from Waldburger to Peabody?" Margaret asked.

Jane let out an honest-to-goodness giggle. "You must remember that I never cared for the name Waldburger, and I always thought Peabody had a certain charm."

"It was the name of one of my dogs."

"So it was." Jane giggled again. "Now then, dear Margaret, while I'd love to catch up with you on everything that's been happening in your life over the past twenty or so years, I just recalled a most pressing appointment that I simply must keep. I'm afraid my niece and I must take our immediate leave."

"I wasn't aware you had a niece, Jane. Since you're going by the title of Miss, I would have to imagine you never married, and since you're an only child . . . ?"

"Harriet's more of an honorary niece," Jane said in a rush, "and although I'd welcome the chance to introduce the two of you . . . she's a shy sort and would die of embarrassment to be introduced to a duchess. But again, I do have that pressing engagement, so I really must get on my way." Jane spun around, trotted across the ballroom floor, snagged hold of Harriet's arm when she reached her, and proceeded to try to drag Harriet out of the room.

"Have you lost your mind?" Harriet asked, trying to free herself from Jane.

"Stop fighting me," Jane snapped. "I'm trying to keep both of us from being arrested."

"Is that young lady wearing my old dress?"

Jane froze, loosened her grip on Harriet, but then shoved Harriet behind her before she faced Margaret once again. "Fine, now you know why I didn't want you to meet my niece. I nicked your dress before I left England, and Harriet, unfortunately, took tonight of all nights to wear it."

Harriet tried to step around Jane, but Jane abruptly turned, and the sight of her eyes burning with what looked like insanity froze Harriet on the spot.

"Stay hidden," Jane hissed before she turned and positioned herself so that Harriet was hidden from the duchess's view. "I do hope you realize, my dear, dear Margaret, that I only took your dress so that I'd have a little piece of you to remind me of our friendship after we parted ways."

Standing on tiptoe, Harriet discovered the duchess walking slowly across the room, her beautiful face marred by a frown.

"If memory serves me correctly, Jane, you willingly left your position as my paid companion. Forgive me, but I thought the last time we saw each other, as you said your good-byes, you looked remarkably relieved to be parting ways with me."

Jane released an exaggerated sigh. "Don't be silly, Margaret, of course I wasn't relieved to be parting ways with you. If you must know, your sorrow was enough to break anyone's heart at that time, and I couldn't bear to witness you so distraught, which is why I resigned as your paid companion."

An elbow to her ribs had Harriet dropping from her toes, but then she leaned to the side and managed to catch sight of the duchess again. She was standing stock-still, her head tilted, and she was biting her lip, something Harriet did often when she was trying to figure something out.

"You mentioned your niece's name is Harriet?"

"Did I?" Jane countered in a voice that had turned shrill.

"Besides having a dog named Peabody, I used to have a dog named Harriet," Margaret said slowly. "It's odd that you'd take the last name of Peabody, and have a niece who just happens to have the name of Harriet."

"A peculiar coincidence to be sure," Jane said. "But surely you know that's all it is, Margaret."

Margaret's face suddenly paled as she raised a shaking hand to her lips. "What . . . have . . . you done?"

"I haven't done anything."

"Don't . . . lie. You were behind the ransom, weren't you . . . Which means . . . you are not only a thief—you're a murderer as well. You murdered my daughter, and then . . . your twisted sense of humor had you giving my dogs' names to your niece—whatever the relation."

"I've never stooped to murder, Margaret, and I can prove that, given that your daughter is standing right behind me."

A collective gasp rose from the crowd right as Harriet felt the room begin to spin. She feared she was going to faint, but then Jane grabbed her arm and pulled her forward, giving Harriet a clear view of the duchess, who just happened to be . . .

Harriet's thoughts came to an abrupt end, and the room stopped spinning when Jane let out a burst of maniacal laughter before she released a grunt, dropped her hold on Harriet, and . . . from her reticule pulled a pistol, which she began waving wildly around.

The room fell completely silent once again.

"Fine, so now you know."

The duchess stared at Harriet for a moment, but then turned back to Jane. "Why?"

"You know the answer to that."

"Humor me."

"I despised you, had always despised you. You had everything I ever wanted—loving parents, money, a beautiful estate in the country, and a townhouse in Mayfair. You were the darling of the London season the year you debuted, while I was forced to lurk on the sidelines as your companion. It wasn't fair. I hated you because you had everything, while I had nothing but a gambler for a father and a weak mother who pushed me out of the house and forced me to accept that companion position with you."

"I considered you more than my companion, Jane. I considered you my friend."

Jane stopped waving the pistol. "You were never my friend, Margaret. You had to have known that I wanted Richard for myself, pictured myself a duchess quite often, but then . . . you snagged his attention away from me the moment he caught sight of you, and he never bothered to look my way again." She gestured with the pistol to the duke, who was inching his way closer to the duchess. "Stop right there, darling, or I swear to you, I'll shoot your precious duchess and be done with this for good."

The duke held up his hands and stopped moving. "There's no need for more violence, Jane. You've caused Margaret and myself no end of suffering, but if you'll lower your weapon, I swear to you that I'll do my very best to—"

"To protect me from prosecution if I spare Margaret?" Jane finished for him before she turned the pistol directly on Margaret and smiled. "You and Richard underestimated me once, my dear. I suggest you don't attempt that again."

"When did you decide to ransom my daughter?" Margaret asked.

Jane pursed her lips. "I do believe, since we're being honest here, that I came up with my plan right about the time you announced to everyone you were expecting. The happiness surrounding your news made me downright nauseated, as did the adoring looks Richard kept throwing your way. I decided I had to leave because it was unbearable for me to witness your love. I had no love, no happiness, and no hope for a prosperous future, given that gentlemen had no interest in courting me since I was nothing more than your companion."

She smiled. "Obviously I was going to need money, and a lot

of it, so . . . once your daughter was born, I decided holding her for ransom was the only way to get the money I desired."

"But you never returned her after we paid the ransom . . . and who was that baby girl we buried in the family vault?" Margaret demanded.

Jane waved the pistol around. "Oh, I have no idea who that brat was, but you can console yourself in knowing that you gave a poor little soul—abandoned at the morgue, no less—a fitting burial." She lifted her chin. "If you must know, after I volunteered to deliver the ransom—a quick bit of thinking on my part since I was delivering the money to myself—I had every intention to return your daughter to you, but . . . then I got to thinking. I'd been made to suffer so much while I was in your employ that I wanted you to suffer as well. What better way could there have been to achieve that than for you to believe your daughter was dead?"

"You're insane," Margaret whispered.

"I wouldn't go so far as to claim I'm mad, more just a lady suffering from unrequited love who decided to get back at her tormentors." Jane smiled. "I didn't want to take over the care of Harriet, but I thought it would be poetic justice indeed if I were able to turn your aristocratic daughter into nothing more than a common thief."

Finally finding her voice, Harriet whispered, "No wonder you were so upset when I refused to go along with your plans."

"Shut up," Jane snarled before turning back to wave her gun at Margaret. "So, there you have it, the truth at long last. The only thing that would have given me greater satisfaction would have been to learn you were unable to have other children. Given that the young lady hovering on the edge of the ballroom bears a remarkable resemblance to the duke, well . . . I suppose all of my wishes didn't come true."

Margaret drew herself up and took a step forward but stopped when Jane turned the gun on Harriet. "Don't hurt her, Jane."

"I don't really have a choice, do I? Harriet has always been an extreme disappointment to me, always refusing to join in with my confidence schemes. Because of that disappointment, I find myself reluctant to see her happy, or to watch all of you have a joyful reunion."

The truth began to burrow into Harriet's head, but before she could truly grasp everything that had been said, the sound of a pistol being cocked drew her attention. Jane was pointing the pistol directly at her, her eyes burning with hatred, and in that moment—likely her last moment on earth—she threw out a prayer to God, asking for forgiveness and—

A hair-raising howl suddenly filled the ballroom, and she watched Buford bound across the room and leap for Jane right as the sound of the gun going off reverberated around the room.

Pain sliced through her, and the sight of what she now knew was her mother's face flashed in front of her, right before she collapsed to the ground and darkness slid over her.

22

Voices, spoken in a hushed tone, broke through the dark and silent place Harriet found herself in, but for the life of her, she couldn't seem to open her eyes. Straining to identify the voices, she tried to make sense of the words being spoken.

"What I find amazing about this whole situation is that neither you nor Victoria recognized Harriet straightaway."

"Honestly, Margaret, it's not as if that thought would have sprung to mind. Even though now, upon closer inspection, it's clear Harriet bears a distinct resemblance to you. I, along with everyone else, believed our daughter to be dead."

"I felt an immediate connection with her, even though it never entered my mind she was my sister."

"You tried to steal me away from her, Victoria, even though you were told I was her fiancé."

Harriet felt her lips twitch as the conversation taking place around her drifted through her mind. She tried to open her eyes again, but they wouldn't cooperate, and then another, more soothing, voice sounded, and she drew in a breath, wanting to hear what Reverend Gilmore had to say.

What if he was there to administer a last prayer?

What if the reason she couldn't open her eyes was because she was at death's door?

She didn't feel as if death was knocking at her door, but then again, she'd never actually been close to death, so perhaps this was normal. How long had it been since the ball and . . . what had happened to her?

Had she been shot?

Had Jane gotten away, or . . .

"I must agree with your husband, Margaret, in regard to not recognizing Harriet straightaway," Reverend Gilmore was saying, pulling Harriet back to the conversation swirling around her. "When a person is believed to be dead, another person really can't be expected to be looking for that person, even if that person is sitting right across a table from him at Delmonico's."

"Besides, Father didn't really get to inspect Harriet closely at Delmonico's, considering she set the place on fire," Victoria added. "I have come to realize my sister is a very unusual lady—one I'm looking forward to spending a great deal of time with in the future."

Relief was immediate, because mention of the future certainly sounded more promising than imminent death.

"Can you ever forgive me for convincing Harriet to go along with my plan to pose as my fiancée in order to secure the deal with you, Your Grace?"

Ah, that was Oliver's voice—such a wonderful voice, masculine but with just a touch of ruefulness mixed . . .

"Call me Richard, and yes, of course I forgive you. If you hadn't convinced my daughter to go along with your plan, Margaret and I would have never found her again."

"Harriet wasn't comfortable with what we were doing, but I can be quite persuasive when I set my mind to something, and . . . well, my original plan seemed to snowball into something neither of us expected—that being complete and utter madness."

"I've recently come to the belief that you and Harriet were brought together because God was setting matters to rights," Reverend Gilmore said softly.

"You believe God wants me to be with Harriet?" Oliver asked.

"As to that, I can't say. I do believe the two of you came together so that Harriet could finally experience the love of a true family, and that her mother, father, and sister, could finally meet the lovely young lady they'd been denied for so very, very long."

She wasn't certain, but she thought Oliver released a huff.

What could that mean?

Had he wanted Reverend Gilmore to confirm that they were meant to be together, because . . . It turned out she wasn't just a hat girl, in fact . . . she was a lady, an honest-to-goodness lady who had a duke and a duchess for parents.

Surely that would make it perfectly acceptable for her to be with Oliver, but . . . what if he didn't want to be with her, what if . . .

"Is she awake yet? It's been hours and hours."

Was that Millie or Lucetta?"

"No, but we've seen her twitching every once in a while, and the doctor did say, given that she took a blow to the head, that it might be more than a few hours before she comes to," Oliver said.

"She won't like it if she wakes up and finds all of us staring at her."

Ah, *that* was Lucetta—the first one was Millie.

"I'm not leaving."

Warmth flowed through her.

That was her mother's voice, a mother she'd thought was long dead, but a mother who'd never stopped loving her, even though *she'd* thought Harriet was dead.

"Her original name was Julia?"

Harriet's ears perked up again.

"It was, but I barely spent any time at all with her before Jane snatched her away," Margaret said. "I still cannot believe the woman stole my child from me. She then decided I hadn't suffered enough, so arranged for a dead infant, swaddled in my baby's clothing, to be delivered to our country estate. Then, after waiting what she apparently felt was a sufficient amount of time—holding my hand and crying with me over my loss, no less—she then went off, took Harriet from the miserable person she'd paid to watch over my baby, and spirited her straight out of the country."

"I'm still not exactly clear why she arranged for a dead infant to be delivered to you," Victoria said.

"Because she knew that if your mother and I had any hope she was alive we would never rest until we found our little girl," Richard said.

Someone let out a small sob, the owner of that sob becoming clear when Margaret started speaking again. "Jane caused me more pain than I can even express, but the mere thought of all my darling girl must have suffered because of Jane's evilness breaks my heart."

The pain in her mother's voice had Harriet concentrating as hard as she could to open her eyes. Light blinded her for a moment, but then, a face swam into view, the face of her mother.

Harriet licked dry lips, swallowed, and tried to smile, knowing she failed miserably when her mother released another sob.

"I don't want your heart to be broken . . . Mother," she finally said, stumbling just a bit on the word *Mother*. "I never knew what I was missing, which makes this business of finding you all so much more delightful."

With tears pouring down her cheeks, her mother moved closer, and the next thing Harriet knew, she was lifted up and cradled in her mother's arms, the scent of violets tickling her nose.

How long she stayed there, Harriet couldn't really say. She heard people leaving the room, most of them crying, but she couldn't raise her head to offer them reassurances—she could only cling to the woman she'd never known, even as she sent a prayer to God, giving thanks for the gift He'd bestowed on her.

This was what He'd given her for her birthday wish—her family.

Her mother let out a muffled laugh before she eased Harriet out of her embrace and gazed into her face. "You look so much like I did twenty years ago." She wiped tears that were still leaking out of Harriet's eyes with her fingers. "I cannot believe you've been returned to me."

"I can't believe it either," her father said, looking at her over her mother's shoulder.

Her mother edged away from her, and then her father, a real live duke, took her place and strong arms wrapped around Harriet, something she'd longed to feel her entire life.

It was little wonder she'd been drawn to the man when she first met him—he was her father, and somehow she'd known he was special before she even knew exactly who he was.

She buried her head into his broad shoulder and allowed more tears to flow, tears she'd been holding back for years, but tears of joy this time, each tear healing the bit of her heart that had been damaged over her youth.

After a few minutes or perhaps it was a few hours, her father eased back from her and smiled. "I'm going to buy you a pony."

"I might be a bit old for a pony."

"They bought me a pony when I was ten, even though I tried to convince them when I was six that I was old enough to ride."

Harriet looked up and the next thing she knew, her father had moved out of the way, which was probably fortunate since

Victoria flung herself across the bed and grabbed Harriet in a hug that stole the very breath from her. "I'm so glad you're not dead."

"You might want to loosen your hold, Tori, or she might go that way," her mother said with a laugh.

"Sorry," Victoria muttered before she scooted off the bed and grinned. "We're sisters. No wonder I adored you from the start."

"You loathed me on sight because you wanted Oliver."

"That was just a girlish infatuation. I've grown up since then."

Harriet returned the grin and then looked at her father. "I was the reason behind your overprotectiveness with Victoria, wasn't I?"

"When people suffer the loss of a child, it does tend to make them cling a little too tightly to the children, or in our case, child, who follows."

"But you can relax that attitude since you now have two children," Victoria proclaimed with a nod. "And since it seems that Harriet has a propensity for getting into dramatic situations, well, she'll need more looking after than I ever would."

"I'm twenty-two years old, Victoria. Believe me, I don't need looking after."

As soon as the words left her mouth, she immediately regretted them. Her father was looking upset and her mother downright distressed.

"Don't listen to a word Harriet says," Oliver exclaimed as he strode back into the room and smiled at her. "She, more than anyone I know, needs to be watched with an eagle eye." He crossed the room and sat down in a chair next to the bed. "How are you feeling?"

It took her a second to realize he'd spoken, being a bit distracted by the way his hair was oh so attractively rumpled and his jacket stretched across his broad shoulders. She couldn't remember what he'd asked, but since he was looking at her expectantly she blurted out the first thing that came to mind.

"Do you remember when I first met you and your jacket was so poorly fitted?"

"It wasn't that long ago, Harriet, so yes, I clearly recall that incident."

Harriet glanced at her mother. "He'd annoyed his tailor by not promoting the tailor's son at one of his factories, so his tailor decided to get back at him by creating garments for Oliver that barely fit him."

Margaret looked at Oliver, then back at Harriet, and frowned. "I . . . see."

"You'll be happy to know, Harriet, that Mr. Clay tailored this jacket and his son is now manager of that particular factory."

Warmth was immediate. "That's wonderful, and . . . the mining situation?"

"Is being handled capably by that brilliant gentleman I sent to West Virginia."

"You must be so relieved, but . . . tell me . . . what happened at the ball? Is society furious with you, and what happened to me? Was I shot and how long have I been lying here in bed . . . and am I still at Abigail's house?"

Oliver smiled. "That's quite a few questions, Harriet, but let me see if I can answer them. Yes, you're currently still at Abigail's, and you've been lying in bed for about twelve hours. No, you weren't shot, thank God, but you did get hit in the head with Jane's pistol. To make matters worse, you hit your head *again* when you fell to the ground because no one was close enough to catch you."

Harriet lifted a hand to her head. "It doesn't hurt."

Oliver smiled at her, his smile so filled with tenderness that she lost the ability to breathe. "I'm glad."

Margaret cleared her throat, drawing Harriet's attention. She couldn't help but notice that her mother seemed somewhat worried, and had no idea what was causing that worry.

"And of course society isn't angry with you," Margaret said, smiling back at Harriet, although the smile didn't quite reach her eyes. "No one heard the story Oliver told us later, about how you were only posing as his fiancée to secure the deal with your father, which I must admit I still don't truly understand, but—" she drew in a deep breath—"for all New York society knows, you and Oliver were the victims of a most dastardly lady, and strangely enough, poor Abigail has been besieged with calling cards. All of the ladies delivering those cards have been extremely reluctant to leave the house until they get Abigail's promise that she'll tell you they desire your company."

It was very peculiar, her life at the moment, but it almost seemed to her as if she'd truly become acceptable, but . . . would that change matters between her and Oliver? Would he look at her differently now, and did she want him to look at her differently?

She was still Harriet Peabody, had made hats for a living for years, but . . . did he see her in an improved light?

She wasn't quite certain she wanted that.

She wanted him to love her, just as she'd realized she loved him. She certainly wasn't comfortable with the idea that he might be more inclined to spend time with her now that her true parentage had been revealed.

"What happened with Jane?" she heard herself ask when a strained silence settled over the room.

Margaret's eyes turned stormy. "She's in jail, where she'll linger for a very long time."

"And Silas Ruff?"

Oliver released a sound of disgust. "He's gone off to take the waters somewhere out west, and he's, of course, completely unrepentant regarding what he did."

"What happened to Buford?"

318

Oliver reached out and took her hand in his. "He took that bullet meant for you."

Tears immediately blinded her. "He died?"

Squeezing her hand, Oliver leaned closer. "Good heavens, Harriet. No, he didn't die. Buford's entirely too tough to do something like that. He got nicked in the shoulder—the bullet didn't even lodge in his body—and he's been spending all of his time in Lucetta's room, basking in the sound of her voice." He grinned. "She's taken to singing to him, and I must say, your friend could make a fortune if she ever gives up acting for the opera."

"She's making a respectable living now—not that anyone would know it," Harriet returned with a smile.

"You'll also be happy to know that Miss Birmingham, along with her dreadful parents, have returned to Chicago. I'm sure they'll continue to be unpleasant, but at least we'll never have to suffer their company again, especially since I informed Mr. Birmingham in no uncertain terms that our business association was definitely at an end. I couldn't continue on with a person who'd deliberately caused you pain."

It was fortunate she was lying in bed, otherwise she would have been in serious danger of melting into a puddle on the floor.

"That's perfectly understandable," she managed to mutter.

"Forgive me for interrupting, but I must ask what your intentions are toward my daughter, Mr. Addleshaw." Her mother's words clarified the earlier worry Harriet had seen on her face.

Her mother had believed her dead for far too many years, and Margaret was obviously afraid that, just when they'd found each other, Harriet was going to be lost to her once again.

She deserved Harriet's attention for the foreseeable future, and Harriet knew she needed to create a bond with the woman who'd given birth to her, no matter that she'd come to care for Oliver, had fallen in love with him, in fact.

But . . . the reality was she barely knew the gentleman, and his life was in New York, while her family and their lives were firmly entrenched in England.

She gave Oliver's hand a squeeze before releasing it and then looked to her mother, a woman Harriet longed to know better and already loved more than she'd ever loved anyone in her life, including Oliver.

"As I assume you've been told, Mother, Oliver and I were never truly engaged. We formed an alliance to suit our different needs, but I will admit that, strangely enough, we came to care for each other, or at least I came to care for him during the time we spent together."

"That's so romantic," Victoria said with a sigh.

She was going to have to have long talks with this sister of hers, but now was hardly the time. She sent Victoria a rolling of the eyes and returned her attention to Margaret. "Oliver's businesses, at least most of them, are here in America, and while I have developed a great deal of affection for him, my life, for the foreseeable future, is no longer in this country but in yours."

She felt Oliver stiffen beside her but couldn't look him in the eye, instead keeping her gaze settled on her mother's face, a face that was now looking hopeful.

She summoned up a smile and felt her heart break just a bit. "I'm coming back to England with you, Mother. It's past time I returned home."

23

*H*arriet was leaving—and soon from what he'd been told.

Throwing down the pen he'd been using to try and total up a stack of figures, Oliver realized that in the mood he was currently in, he'd get no business done. Rising from the chair, he whistled for Buford and waited as his dog got up somewhat gingerly from the patch of sun he'd been lounging in and moseyed over to Oliver's side. Leaning down, he gave Buford a pat on the head before he straightened and walked out of his office, Buford dogging his every step.

"Would you like me to call for the carriage?" Mr. Blodgett asked, materializing in the hallway on silent feet.

Oliver shrugged. "I really have no place to go."

Mr. Blodgett cocked a brow. "Oh? You can't think of any place your company might be appreciated?"

"She's made her decision, Mr. Blodgett, and I know why she made that decision. Her mother needs her just as Harriet needs her mother. I won't step between them."

Mr. Blodgett opened his mouth, but then shut it when Archibald came strolling toward them. His grandfather stopped and smiled at Mr. Blodgett. "So is he going to see her? Have you called for the carriage?"

"He's going to let her go."

Archibald's smile slid off his face. "You won't find another like her, my boy."

"I'm perfectly aware of that."

"Then why are you letting her go?"

"She needs to be with her family. They live in England; I live here."

"That's just geography, easily overcome."

"It's geography that's separated by an entire ocean."

Archibald eyed him for a moment. "Is making more money truly that important to you?"

Oliver blinked, and instead of giving his grandfather the answer that immediately came to mind, he thought about it instead. "I don't know."

"Come with me," Archibald said before he headed for the door, paused, and looked over his shoulder. "Well?"

"Where are we going?"

"You'll see, and bring the mutt. He likes riding in the carriage."

For the first time in what felt like forever, Oliver felt a sense of peace. Perhaps it was because he was sitting smack in the middle of an old church, the pews empty except for Buford. Or, perhaps it was because his grandfather had spent the ride over to Reverend Gilmore's church in relative silence, something that was unusual, but something that had given Oliver a feeling of hope, as if his grandfather had figured out all the answers and was simply biding his time to reveal them.

Whatever the reason, Oliver wasn't feeling quite as despondent as he'd been ever since Harriet had proclaimed a few days before she was going home, and not the home she'd lived in when he'd first made her acquaintance.

"Ah, Oliver, I was hoping you'd pay me a visit soon."

Getting to his feet, Oliver walked over to greet Reverend Gilmore, who was entering the sanctuary with Archibald by his side. Holding out his hand, Oliver found himself smiling when, instead of taking his offered hand, the reverend pulled him into a strong hug.

"Your grandfather tells me you've got a bit of a dilemma on your hands, son," Reverend Gilmore said, stepping back.

"I do, but I'm not exactly certain how my grandfather expects you to help."

Reverend Gilmore gestured to the pew. "Why don't we sit down and discuss what's on your mind."

Making his way back to the pew where he'd left Buford, Oliver took a seat, Reverend Gilmore and Archibald joining him a second later.

"He's quite the hero," Reverend Gilmore said with a nod in Buford's direction.

Oliver gave Buford a scratch on the head, earning a whine of delight in the process. "That he is. I'm afraid he's missed the ladies dreadfully since he's returned to my house."

"And you? Do you miss the ladies—or more specifically, Harriet—dreadfully?"

The truth of the matter was yes, he did miss Harriet dreadfully, which was odd considering he and Harriet had not known each other long.

"It doesn't really matter if I miss her," he finally settled on saying. "Harriet's made up her mind, and I can't say I question her decision. She belongs with her family, but my many business ventures are mostly located here in the States, which means we really have no choice but to part ways."

"Would you be willing to give up your businesses for her?"

"Surely you're not suggesting I abandon my multi-million dollar enterprises in order to continue on with Harriet, are you?"

"I don't make it a point to suggest much of anything to people, Oliver. You should live your life in a manner that makes you happy, or more importantly, a manner in which you believe will please God." Reverend Gilmore leaned forward and placed his hand on Oliver's knee. "From what I understand, you've managed to amass quite the fortune at a relatively young age. Is that fortune enough for you, or do you still feel compelled to increase it?"

"I have more money than I could probably spend in a lifetime, but since I was a young boy my goal has been to secure a larger fortune than Cornelius Vanderbilt's. He left behind an estate worth more than one hundred million dollars."

"And do you believe Cornelius Vanderbilt has any need of his fortune now?"

Oliver frowned. "Probably not, considering he's dead."

"And do you think Mr. Vanderbilt embraced and enjoyed his life while he was on this earth, giving more than he received, or do you think he might have spent most of his time collecting money?"

Oliver sat there for a moment, his thoughts whirling as a sense of something odd and quite disturbing flowed over him.

It was true that he had more money than he could ever use, but it was also true that he'd rarely used that money in a manner that would be pleasing to God. Before he'd met Harriet, he hadn't even bothered to see the poverty that surrounded him, which God could hardly find acceptable, but . . . it certainly wasn't too late to give to those in need, especially if he had Harriet by his side, pointing him in the right direction.

She'd made her choice, that choice putting an entire ocean between them, but . . . he wasn't completely tied to America, except for the fact his businesses were there, and yet those businesses didn't provide him with lovely eyes, a beautiful face, or an intriguing attitude.

They also didn't keep him warm at night, whereas Harriet . . .

He released a breath. "You're a very wise man, Reverend Gilmore."

"My wisdom only goes so far, Oliver. What happens next is completely up to you, but I do hope that you'll place your trust in God and ask Him for guidance before you proceed with whatever you decide to do."

As Oliver looked around the small church, he knew in that moment that Reverend Gilmore was right. He'd never embraced God fully, but ever since Harriet had stormed into his life, God seemed to be making it clear that it was past time Oliver set aside his materialistic, and somewhat unfulfilling, life and begin down a path that would draw him closer to God. He needed to begin helping other people with the fortune he'd been blessed to make, instead of centering his every thought on matters that weren't important in the end.

Closing his eyes, he prayed—not just saying the prayers he repeated in church every time he went but truly opening himself up for the first time in his life. He first gave thanks for the many, many blessings he had, but then he asked for forgiveness for his many trespasses, and then . . . he asked for guidance and God's help in allowing him to know what to do in regard to Harriet.

How much time passed, Oliver really couldn't say, but he remained in prayer until a sense of happiness mixed with peace settled deep in his soul. Opening his eyes, he found his grandfather and Reverend Gilmore sitting with their eyes closed, so he waited for them to finish their own prayers before he smiled at them. "Gentlemen, I do believe I've just been granted the supreme gift of seeing the error of my ways, but it might take a miracle to convince Harriet I'm a changed man. Would either of you have any suggestions on how I should go about convincing her she's more important to me than the sum total of all my money, without having her come to the immediate conclusion I've lost my mind?"

"I cannot believe how many gowns you managed to stash away here," Lucetta said as she dumped another armload of gowns onto the receiving room floor of the apartment Harriet and her friends had once called home. "And I didn't even know we had an attic."

Harriet paused in her task of sorting and grinned. "I discovered that last year when Reverend Gilmore received all of those gowns from some elderly lady's estate and didn't know what to do with them. Mrs. Palmer saw me carting them up the steps, and she very kindly followed me and showed me the attic." She shook her head. "She also charged me five dollars to use the space for a year, even though both of us knew perfectly well that sum was outrageous since the attic was sitting there unused."

"I'll miss Mrs. Palmer, in a strange sort of way," Millie said. "She's always so nosy, but I must admit I found that somewhat endearing."

Lucetta plopped down on top of a pile of dresses. "Abigail is far nosier than Mrs. Palmer, so I don't believe you're going to have to worry about *not* having someone watching your every move."

"You and Millie have decided to take Abigail up on her offer of permanently moving in with her?"

Lucetta nodded. "She has that big old house all to herself, except for the servants, of course. I couldn't refuse her offer, especially when she got a little teary-eyed. She's been alone for far too long. Millie and I have been without any type of motherly figure for what seems like forever. Well, in Millie's case it was forever, so . . . our living with Abigail will benefit all of us. Although, I will admit I'm a little wary of Abigail and her plotting."

"It'll be interesting to see who she tries to get settled next," Millie added. "But, I don't think Lucetta and I are going to be nearly as exciting as you've been, Harriet. Honestly, finding out you're a lady . . . It's very odd." She sent Harriet a cheeky grin. "I keep wondering if I should curtsy to you every time you enter a room."

"I would have to hurt you if you did."

Lucetta hauled herself up from the stack of dresses and moved over to Harriet, sinking down beside her on the floor. "Are you sure this is what you want to do—move to England?"

"I need to spend time with my family."

"What about all this?" Lucetta asked with a gesture to the stacks and stacks of gowns.

Millie tossed aside the hat she was perusing and came to join them, plopping down with a poof of her skirt. "Harriet doesn't need to earn a living anymore. She's rich."

A twinge of something peculiar swept over Harriet. She still hadn't grasped the reality of what came with suddenly finding out she was a member of the aristocracy, and the daughter of a duke. Victoria had explained in some detail what being a lady entailed, but quite frankly, the more Victoria had explained, the queasier Harriet had begun to feel.

She would be presented to the queen, which meant she was looking at months of preparations. Then she'd be brought out at a special ball her parents would host for her and . . . Victoria had been completely delighted to inform her that gentlemen from across England would flock to make her acquaintance.

She didn't want to make any gentleman's acquaintance, because . . .

No, she was not going to think about Oliver.

She'd made her decision, and it was the right decision, but . . .

even though God had blessed her with one of the greatest blessings of all—a family to call her own—her heart was a little heavy.

"Speaking of riches," she said in an effort to drive away her pesky thoughts, "I've got something for the two of you." She struggled to her feet and hurried down the short hallway, entering the kitchen a second later. Walking over to the battered kitchen table, she rummaged through the hats and ribbons stacked on it until she finally found her reticule. Taking out the bills Oliver had given her to buy clothing, she rejoined her friends. "I'd like the two of you to have this money I got from Oliver. He refused to take it back from me, but it would ease my mind knowing you two have a bit of a cushion in case anything of a dastardly nature occurs to either of you while I'm all the way across the ocean."

"Harriet . . ." Lucetta began.

"I'll just leave it under your pillow if you don't take it now."

Millie let out a sniff. "You worked hard to earn that money."

"No, I didn't. All I did was shop, practice table manners, set a restaurant on fire, and danced one dance with Oliver at a ball before chaos descended."

Millie got to her feet and reluctantly took the money. "You also fell in love with Oliver."

"Perhaps."

"You're willing to simply sail away from him?" Millie pressed.

"Although I do think he cares for me, he never claimed to be in love with me." Harriet blew out a breath. "But in order for both of you to truly understand why I'm leaving, I'm going to tell you a little story about me. It's one I've shared with Oliver, and it'll explain why I have to leave—in addition to the fact that I need to spend time with my family."

Moving to a chair piled high with gowns, Harriet brushed them to the floor and took a seat. "Most people don't know this about me, but . . . I'm a hopeless romantic at heart."

Releasing a snort, Lucetta shook her head. "No, you're not."

Harriet narrowed her eyes. "Do you want to hear the story or not?"

"Sorry. Continue."

"Where was I?"

"You're a romantic at heart," Millie supplied.

"Yes, quite right. Thank you, Millie." Harriet settled back into the chair. "Well, you see, while I was in the circus, I got to be friends with the bearded lady, and she, being a truly delightful woman, began sharing her books with me, books that had more than one fairy tale residing within the pages."

Millie's eyes widened. "You read fairy tales with a bearded lady?"

Harriet nodded. "Strange, I know, but as I said, she was a delightful sort, and I've come to believe, given that her face truly was covered with a real beard, that she needed those fairy tales just as desperately as I did. She and I were prone to sighing rather heavily at the end of the stories, especially when the fair princess who fought to live under trying circumstances was rescued in the end by a dashing prince on a white steed." She looked at her friends. "That's what I want more than anything—a fairy-tale ending, and I'm no longer willing to settle for anything less than that."

Millie's eyes grew misty, she opened her mouth, but all that came out was one, lone hiccup before she drew in a deep breath and exchanged a glance with Lucetta.

Lucetta smiled. "You really are a romantic at heart, and you've achieved part of your dream, turning into a princess of sorts."

"And Oliver makes a nice prince," Millie said before she bit her lip. "Or maybe he's more the knight in shining armor, considering how he came to your defense at the ball." She smiled. "But whichever one he is, I do think he's a good man at heart."

Harriet returned Millie's smile. "You're right, of course, but the reality of our situation is that I barely know him, and I want a man to sweep me off my feet, and . . ." She shook herself. "Well, I'm sure both of you understand what I'm trying to say, but enough about my little romantic dream. We're running short on time, and we need to get these gowns packed up. Then I'm going to have to figure out what to do with them."

"Abigail said to tell you that you can store them at her house."

Harriet stood up. "I wouldn't want to dump all of these on her, and besides, it's not as if I'm ever going to open up my own shop now." She brushed aside the stab of pain that thought evoked. "Maybe we should have them delivered to another seamstress, one who could put them to good use."

"Do you have a seamstress in mind who might want them?" Lucetta asked.

"Well, no, but . . ." Harriet stopped speaking and tilted her head when she heard the sound of footsteps climbing up the outside stairs. "Are we expecting anyone?"

Millie frowned. "Not that I can think of. Your parents and Victoria are visiting with Abigail, and we know it's not your aunt, since she's in jail." Millie got to her feet and peered out the window right as the sound of footsteps stopped. She pressed her face against the glass. "I think your prince charming might have just shown up."

"What?"

Millie turned from the window and nodded toward the door. "Go see."

Unable to help herself, Harriet headed for the door. She walked out on the landing, her heart beating a rapid tattoo when she saw what was waiting for her . . . two flights down.

Oliver was clutching a huge bouquet of flowers, but petals were falling off at a rapid rate as he leaned over Buford, who seemed to be stuck once again on the second-floor landing.

"Did you forget he's terrified of heights?" Harriet yelled as she peered over the railing.

Oliver looked up, his expression decidedly grumpy. "Of course I forgot, otherwise I would never have brought him with me, but he's been missing you and your friends quite dreadfully, so . . ."

She leaned forward. "What are you doing here?"

A stiff breeze took that moment to blow around them, sending the flowers Oliver had just set down tumbling off the stairs and falling to the rubbish-strewn ground below. He straightened and ran a hand through hair that looked rather untidy even as he leaned over the railing, shook his head, turned, and sent her a charming, yet rueful smile. "I was hoping to present you with a bit of a romantic gesture, but that gesture seems to have gone horribly wrong since I'm now without any flowers."

Her pulse began racing through her veins so fast she felt a little light-headed. "You wanted to give me a romantic gesture?"

To her surprise, Oliver ignored her question as he returned his attention to Buford. The pathetic-looking pooch was frozen to the spot and, from what Harriet could tell, was intending to stay that way for quite some time.

"You're ruining the moment, Buford," Oliver said before he reached down and tried to tug the dog up a step to no avail. He glanced back up at her. "I could use a little help here."

Oliver's surly tone of voice was not exactly the romantic tone she'd been expecting, but . . . it made her grin even as she hurried down to him. "What would you like me to do?"

"Help me get him up the steps, of course." Oliver considered Buford for a moment. "You take his front, and I'll lift his behind, but be careful of those bandages. He's still a little tender from where that bullet grazed him."

Bending over, Harriet put her arms gently around Buford. "Now, don't worry, darling," she cooed. "We're going to be very careful with you, especially since you're the very bravest dog in the whole world."

"No, he's not, at least not at the moment," Oliver said with a grunt as he lifted Buford's behind. "And he's heavy."

"Make sure you watch his head," Lucetta called, her voice causing Buford to squirm.

"Yes, thank you for that, Lucetta," Oliver called, "but could you stop speaking?"

"Really, Oliver, there's no need to get testy," Lucetta called back. "I'm only trying to help."

"Stop talking. We're going to drop him if he doesn't stop wiggling."

Harriet grinned again when she glanced up and saw Lucetta disappearing through the door. Securing her hold on Buford, she began climbing backward up the stairs. It took them a good few minutes to reach the door, probably because Buford kept making pitiful little sounds that caused them to stop every other step in order to soothe him. When they finally made it to the top, Harriet was short of breath, as was Oliver. She edged through the door, set Buford down right as Oliver did, and wiped a hand across her perspiring brow. "There, that wasn't so bad."

"It completely ruined the mood. I have no idea what I was thinking, bringing Buford along. It's hardly the thing to have a mangy beast whimpering by one's side when one is intending to spout something of a mushy nature."

Pulse racing once again, Harriet could only stand there for a moment as she realized in all the commotion with Buford, she'd forgotten Oliver was here for a reason, and a reason that seemed to have something to do with . . . mushiness. A knot began to form in her stomach, but before she could actually think of anything to say, Millie stepped forward.

"You've got petals on you," Millie exclaimed after she gave Buford a pat on the head and plucked what appeared to be a red rose petal off Oliver's jacket. She handed it to him, and then plucked a few more petals off before she frowned. "Why are you covered in flower parts?"

Oliver looked at the rose petal in his hand, stepped around Millie, and held it out to Harriet. "For you."

Harriet took the petal, raised it to her nose, took a sniff, and smiled. "No one has ever given me a flower petal before."

"I was planning on giving you the whole bunch, but . . . best laid plans and all that." He took a deep breath and suddenly looked incredibly nervous. "May I have a glass of water? For some reason, my throat suddenly feels incredibly parched."

Harriet nodded but before she could take so much as a single step toward the kitchen, Lucetta brushed past her.

"I'll get it." She grabbed Millie's hand and began tugging her out of the room. "You can help."

"But it doesn't take two people to fetch a . . . ouch . . . Did you just pinch me? Because that felt remarkably like a pinch, and . . ." Millie's voice faded away as Lucetta hauled her into the hallway and toward the kitchen, shutting the door firmly behind them.

An odd silence settled over the cluttered room, broken only by the occasional grunts Buford was making as he stretched out on the floor and proceeded to bury his head underneath his massive paws.

Oliver sent her a grin. "I get the strangest feeling Buford feels I'm about to make a mess of things again. I might have gotten off to a rocky start, but since Lucetta has so very kindly granted me the chance to speak with you privately, I believe I'll do better from this point forward."

"I can't guarantee how long Lucetta will be able to keep Millie away."

"Then I suppose I should get right to what I need to say."

Heart racing faster than ever, Harriet turned and moved across the gown-strewn floor, dropping into the chair she'd recently abandoned. "Perhaps you should take a seat as well."

Glancing around, Oliver laughed. "I'm not certain that's possible, given that every spare inch of space seems to be taken up by gowns."

Harriet got back to her feet, shoved a mound of garments off a nearby chair, and gestured to Oliver. "That'll have to do, but I apologize for the mess. We've been trying to figure out what to do with all the gowns I've collected over the years, but so far, we haven't come up with a viable plan." She shook her head. "Lucetta suggested I store them at Abigail's for now, but that won't really solve the problem especially since I have no plans to return to the city."

"Speaking of returning to the city, that's actually why I'm here." Oliver scooted closer to her. "I've been doing some thinking, some soul-searching, if you will . . . and . . ."

Mouth immediately running dry, Harriet jumped to her feet. "I think I need some water too." She leapt over Buford, who didn't so much as twitch, made it to the kitchen door in a flash, opened it, and winced when the door connected with Lucetta's head. "What are you doing?"

"What do you think I'm doing? Eavesdropping, of course." Lucetta straightened and rubbed her head. "So, what did he say? Because that was awfully fast."

"He hasn't said much of anything yet, except for admitting he wants to speak to me about returning to the city."

Lucetta pointed a dainty finger at the door that had just walloped her in the head. "You need to get yourself right back out there and hear the man out. What were you thinking not allowing him a chance to finish what he had to say?"

"I need a glass of water."

"No, you don't. You need to hear what he has to say. Really, Harriet, you're not making this easy on the poor man, and he even tried to bring you flowers."

Harriet bit her lip. "That was somewhat romantic, wasn't it?"

Millie sighed. "It was completely romantic, especially when he handed you that single petal. Why, my heart just about stopped beating."

"Harriet, what are you doing in there?"

"Oh dear, he's getting grouchy," Lucetta said before she snatched up a pitcher filled with water, sloshed some into two cups and handed them to Harriet. "Off you go, and don't be nervous. This is a good thing, and I'm sure whatever Oliver has to say is exactly what you need to hear."

"I think the two of you should come with me for extra support."

Lucetta rolled her eyes. "We'll support you from behind the door. Now, go."

Harriet made her way out of the kitchen—but only because Millie pushed her through the door—and moved down the small hallway and into the receiving room, water sloshing over her dress when her hands started shaking. She handed one of the glasses to Oliver and retook her seat, taking a huge gulp of water before she finally raised her head and found herself pinned under his intense gaze.

"I'm sorry I lost the flowers," he began.

He looked so earnest that she couldn't stop her heart from giving a resounding lurch. "It was nice of you to even think to bring them to me, and I do have a lone petal left."

Setting his glass aside, Oliver moved closer to her. "I have some things I need to say."

Her hands immediately turned a little clammy, which made holding the glass somewhat difficult. She leaned over and placed it on the floor, smiling when Buford ambled over and began slurping from it. She gave him a quick pat, before lifting her gaze when Oliver cleared his throat in a slightly demanding way.

"May I continue?"

Harriet lifted her chin. "Not if you're going to keep speaking to me in that tone of voice."

To her surprise, Oliver laughed and sent her a sheepish grin. "I'm nervous."

Before she could think of anything to say that might calm his nerves, Oliver said, "I know we haven't been acquainted long, and I never expected when we entered into our agreement that we'd be involved in so much intrigue, but . . . I don't want to lose you."

"I have to go with my family, Oliver," she said slowly.

He beamed back at her. "I know. Which is why I've devised a plan."

"Your last plan almost got poor Buford killed and was on the verge of setting society against you."

"This is a better plan."

A small trace of disgruntlement settled over her. Where were the words of love and tender feelings? Oliver sounded somewhat businesslike and not romantic in the least. She leaned back against the chair. "I'm listening."

Oliver sent her one of his all-too-charming smiles. "Wonderful, but this might take a few minutes to explain, so I'm going to ask that you don't interrupt."

Her teeth clinked together, and it took everything she had to send him another nod and casually fold her hands in her lap.

Instead of continuing on, though, Oliver tilted his head and simply looked at her, amusement spilling from his eyes. She couldn't say she actually appreciated that amusement, but she refused to give him the satisfaction of speaking after he'd somewhat rudely demanded she not interrupt.

Getting to his feet, Oliver began pacing back and forth, his pacing hampered by all the gowns strewn on the floor. He finally stopped and simply gazed at her, until he let out what almost sounded like a grunt. "I don't know how else to say this, so I'll just get it over with—I'm in love with you."

Harriet suddenly couldn't breathe. "What did you say?"

"How could you not have heard him, Harriet," Lucetta called. "The man's standing right next to you and we caught what he said all the way from the kitchen. If you missed it, he was proclaiming himself in love with you, and far be it from me to give you some advice, but you probably should say something of a romantic nature back to him."

Harriet swallowed a laugh as she watched Oliver's eyes narrow right before he strode out of the room and toward the kitchen. The next second, she heard the kitchen door open.

"You might as well join us."

"We wouldn't want to intrude."

"Now."

A moment later, Lucetta and Millie marched into the room, followed closely by Oliver, who pointed to the chaise that was still covered in gowns. Both ladies jumped on top of the pile, and then Millie let out a snort. "I don't know about the two of you, but I had no idea Oliver could be so diametrical."

Silence was swift, and then Lucetta grinned. "And I have no idea, Millie, what word you should have just used, but I'm going to hazard a guess and say you might have wanted to choose *dictatorial*, but again, I'm not actually certain about that."

Millie opened her mouth but then snapped it shut when Oliver cleared his throat rather menacingly. "May I continue?"

Giving a dainty flick of her wrist, Lucetta nodded. "By all means, we're waiting with bated breath to hear what you'll say next."

Oliver's lips curled ever so slightly before he sent Lucetta a narrowing of his eyes. "Now then, since our little distractions—as in those two," he said with a telling look to Lucetta and Millie, "have been rounded up, I have a few more things

I'd like to say." He caught Harriet's gaze. "Because I've learned you're a somewhat suspicious lady, I need to be upfront with you and explain that I'm not in love with you because you've turned all respectable by being the daughter of a duke, which I know you'll think about sometime soon or maybe you've already considered, but . . . that isn't the case at all. I actually wish you weren't the long-lost daughter of a duke, because then we could just stay here in New York and settle down." He drew in a breath. "However, since that is the case, and I completely understand you need to be around your family, at least for the foreseeable future, I've decided to take a less active role in my business ventures and join you in England."

Harriet began shaking her head even before Oliver finished speaking. "I can't let you do that. Your happiness is directly connected with your business, and I won't be responsible for ending that happiness."

"While it is true that I did find a great deal of happiness—or what I believed to be happiness—in my business endeavors, the key word here is *did*." Oliver sent her a crooked grin. "I've recently discovered that *you* are my happiness, and the only way that happiness will end is if you refuse to stay with me."

"Oh, that was a good one," Lucetta sighed before she pressed her lips together when Oliver threw her a scowl.

Harriet sucked in a breath and then had to suck in another when she began to feel a little light-headed. "I don't understand how this happened. Our agreement never had us staying together."

Smiling somewhat tenderly, Oliver nodded. "I'm not exactly sure how this happened either, but I've already spoken with your father, and he's given me his blessing, as has your mother, if you're agreeable to what I'm about to offer."

"Of course she'll be agreeable," Lucetta said before Harriet could get a single word out of her mouth.

"And if I could just make the tiniest suggestion, Oliver," Millie added, "I do believe this is the point where you should get down on one knee."

"I know what I'm doing," Oliver said between gritted teeth as he tossed a glare to Millie before he was suddenly kneeling in front of Harriet, taking her hand in his. He pressed it to his lips and then, with his other hand, reached into his pocket and pulled out Abigail's ring. "She insisted I bring this with me and wanted me to tell you that you're the granddaughter she always wanted, which is why she thought this ring would truly make the perfect engagement ring for you." He leaned closer. "Miss Harriet Peabody, or rather Lady Harriet, as you are now formally known, would you do me the supreme honor of becoming my wife?"

She looked at him for a long moment. "No."

Lucetta and Millie began to sputter even as a look of shock entered Oliver's eyes. "You won't marry me?"

Harriet squeezed the hand that still clasped hers and felt a little giddy as she looked into the eyes of the gentleman she knew without a doubt she would love forever. "I won't agree to marry you unless *you* agree to remain living in New York."

"But . . . what about your family, and what about taking up your expected role as an aristocrat?"

"I'll never think of myself as an aristocrat, Oliver, no matter that my family bears a title. I'm simply Harriet, and I do believe my parents and sister would be fine with the idea of us visiting them for a few months every year." She smiled. "I also won't marry you unless you agree to continue on with your business—although not to the extent you've been doing in the past—and . . . I'd still like to open up my shop someday."

The smallest hint of a smile creased Oliver's lips. "Very well, I can agree to those terms, but you need to agree to some of mine."

"You might want to stop while you're ahead," Lucetta muttered, as Millie began nodding rather vigorously.

Harriet swallowed a laugh and looked back to Oliver. "What are your terms?"

"Well, for one, I'd like to help you produce and market that amazing bustle of yours."

Tapping her finger on her chin, Harriet tilted her head. "I could live with that, but you'll have to agree not to be bossy about it."

"Bossiness is part of my charm."

"And what else?" Harriet asked as she tried to keep from grinning.

"I'd like you to help me start up a charitable organization, one that will allow me to use my considerable funds to help the poor living in the tenement slums."

Tears blinded her for a second. "I could do that."

"I know you can, and . . . I think you should allow Abigail to help your mother plan our wedding—if you agree to marry me, that is."

"Of course she must help, but . . . where would we get married?"

"Good question," Millie said before she snapped her mouth shut when Oliver glanced her way.

Oliver returned his attention to Harriet. "Well, your parents are firmly entrenched within British society, and they've only recently found you, which means they're going to want to see the marriage take place in England, but . . . would you be comfortable getting married over there or would you prefer to have it done here in the States so that Reverend Gilmore could officiate at it?"

Lucetta raised her hand. "I do so hate to interrupt, but why don't you have two weddings? That way no one will be left out, such as me or Millie, since we might have a hard time making it over to England." She smiled. "The theater doesn't really like it when one of their main actresses takes off in the middle of a production."

Smiling, Harriet nodded. "That's a fabulous idea, Lucetta, and would make it so much easier on everyone here in the States, but . . . that might take quite a few months to plan, and I'm not certain . . ."

"You want to wait that long?" Oliver finished for her.

Heat flooded her face, but she was spared a response when Oliver, who'd been kneeling this entire time, got to his feet and squeezed the hand he was still holding. "While I would love nothing more than to marry you immediately, I think taking some time to get a wedding or two pulled together is a wonderful plan. It'll allow us the chance to really get to know each other. It will also allow you to get to know your family without all the pesky distractions of being a new wife. And I know my mother and father would be most put out if we got married while they were still over in India." He smiled. "My mother is going to adore you, as is my father."

She wrinkled her nose. "How do you know that?"

"Because my grandfather adores you, and he's a very good judge of character. I would have to imagine, if you accept my proposal—and this proposal being a real one this time—he'll send a telegram off to my parents immediately, telling them of my good fortune."

Happiness threatened to bubble out of her every pore. "It's so odd to think that I'm soon going to have more family surrounding me than I ever imagined."

"So you'll marry me?"

Finding it next to impossible to speak around the lump that clogged her throat, Harriet managed a nod.

Satisfaction settled in Oliver's eyes before they suddenly darkened, even as he squeezed her hand once again. "You have made me an incredibly happy gentleman, but I must ask you one more thing. . . . Do you think that, perhaps, you might hold me in a bit of affection? I certainly don't expect you to proclaim an undying love at this point, since we aren't well acquainted with each other, but I do hope that you have some type of tender feelings for me."

Tears stung her eyes again and blurred her vision. "Good heavens, Oliver, I do beg your pardon. Here I've been so diligent with my demands that I never even thought to tell you about my feelings."

She drew in a deep breath and released it in a rush. "I hold you in very deep affection, and even though, as you stated, we haven't known each other long, I must admit that I've fallen quite a bit in love with you, and—"

Before she could finish speaking, she suddenly found herself firmly held in Oliver's arms. He bent toward her, but just as his lips were about to claim hers, he stilled, lifted his head, and settled his attention on Lucetta and Millie, who were both watching them with their mouths gaping open. "Ladies, I think it might be for the best if you went back to the kitchen."

"But it was just getting good," Millie complained.

"The last thing I need is for the two of you to call out suggestions while I kiss my true fiancée for the first time."

"Maybe you *need* suggestions," Lucetta pointed out before she laughed when Oliver arched a brow her way. She grabbed Millie's hand, and they made a hasty retreat, their snorts of laughter drifting through the now closed kitchen door.

Anticipation shot through her when Oliver settled his full attention on her once again. He lifted both of his hands, cradled her face, and then drew near, his lips pressing against hers. She clutched the lapels of his finely made jacket and pulled him closer as tingles shot up her spine.

Buford's howl caused them to break apart, but Oliver kept his arm around her as he looked at his dog. "What in the world is the matter with you?"

Lumbering slowly to his feet, Buford took a moment to

stretch, apparently oblivious to the fact he'd interrupted a special moment. He released a yawn and then moved to the door, lifting a paw to scratch at it. When Oliver made no move for the door, Buford let out a yip and scratched it again.

Releasing a sigh, Oliver reluctantly stepped away from her. "I think he needs to go outside, but he has miserable timing. Perhaps, though, since this is his idea, he won't be so hesitant to move down the steps." Walking over to the door, Oliver opened it but then froze. "I almost forgot something." He looked back at Harriet. "You should come outside with me, but you'll need to close your eyes."

"You're not going to try and lead me down the steps with my eyes closed, are you?" Harriet asked as she went to join Oliver. "Because, though I'm not remotely in the mood to argue with you, those steps are tricky at the best of times, and Buford might need some assistance as well, and . . ."

Harriet stopped speaking when Oliver placed a finger over her lips. "Fine, don't close your eyes." He turned, stepped out on the landing, and whistled.

Curiosity had Harriet joining him. She looked over the railing and discovered Darren down below, leading a beautiful white horse away from Oliver's carriage.

Her breath caught in her throat. "You remembered."

Taking her hand in his, Oliver nodded. "Of course I remembered. I willingly admit I'm not exactly a knight in shining armor, or a prince charming, no matter that you claimed I was, but I am perfectly capable of riding off with you into the sunset." He frowned. "Although, now that I think about it, it's midafternoon and the sun still has hours left in the sky." Shrugging, he sent her a smile. "That won't ruin this for you, will it? I mean, I could always come back and whisk you off at sunset, but that might be a little anticlimactic."

"I think riding into the sunshine sounds just as lovely as riding into the sunset."

Oliver looked at her with eyes that were distinctly twinkling. "We're going to make a wonderful pair, you and I, and I promise you, I'll do everything within my power to make you happy."

"I should say so or you'll have to answer to me and Millie." Lucetta stepped out on the landing to join them with eyes that were suspiciously bright. She glanced down and smiled. "Well, it seems as if your fairy tale is just waiting to begin, Harriet." She stepped up to Buford and gave him a pat. "Millie and I will look after the pooch." She caught Harriet's eye. "Go."

Harriet gave Lucetta and then Millie a hug and, with anticipation flowing through her, took Oliver's hand and raced down the steep steps. He helped her up on the back of the white steed, and while she waited for him to join her, she realized that God had sent her more than just the something wonderful she'd requested. He'd sent her an entire family and a prince—if a rather surly one—and she knew without a single doubt that she was going to live from that moment forward happily-ever-after.

Epilogue

*T*aking a moment to simply enjoy the quiet that surrounded him, Reverend Gilmore settled into the pew he'd sat in when he'd counseled Oliver a few days before. He'd just returned from seeing Harriet and Oliver off to London on Oliver's yacht, their beaming faces giving testimony to the love they'd recently admitted they shared for one another. The duke and his duchess had been by their side, along with the delightful Lady Victoria, but Reverend Gilmore hadn't been sad to see Harriet leave the shores of New York. He knew she'd be back eventually, and then he'd be given the honor of performing their wedding ceremony in this very church.

Granted, the plan was for her to be married first in London, surrounded by her new family, but the second wedding would serve to honor the union God had so very expertly brought together.

He looked up at the cross hanging behind the pulpit and folded his hands. *Lord, I must thank you for granting me the prayer I prayed to you in regard to my dear Harriet. You sur-*

passed anything I could have expected for her, and for that, I'm deeply grateful.

He paused to gather his thoughts before a grin teased his lips. Bowing his head once again, he took a deep breath and slowly released it. *Now then, I'd like to discuss Millie, if you've got a moment.*

Jen Turano, author of *A Change of Fortune, A Most Peculiar Circumstance, A Talent for Trouble, A Match of Wits,* and *After a Fashion* is a graduate of the University of Akron with a degree in clothing and textiles. She is a member of ACFW and lives in a suburb of Denver, Colorado. Visit her website at www.jenturano.com.

More From Jen Turano

To learn more about Jen and her books, visit jenturano.com.

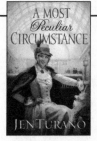

Private investigator Theodore Wilder is on a mission to find Miss Arabella Beckett. But this feisty suffragette may be more trouble than he bargained for!

A Most Peculiar Circumstance

When Miss Felicia Murdock stumbles into Grayson Sumner's life, he'll have to decide whether he wants to spend the rest of his life keeping this lively young lady out of trouble.

A Talent for Trouble

Zayne Beckett and Agatha Watson have always been able to match each other in wits. But will unlikely circumstances convince them they could also be a match made in heaven?

A Match of Wits

You May Also Like . . .

To fulfill a soldier's dying wish, nurse Abigail Stuart marries him and promises to look after his sister. But when the *real* Jeremiah Calhoun appears alive, can she provide the healing his entire family needs?

A Most Inconvenient Marriage by Regina Jennings
reginajennings.com

When a librarian and a young congressman join forces to solve a mystery, they become entangled in secrets more perilous than they could have imagined.

Beyond All Dreams by Elizabeth Camden
elizabethcamden.com

Charlotte wants nothing more than to continue working as an assistant to her father, an eminent English botanist, but he feels it is time for her to marry. Will she find a way to fulfill her dreams and her family's expectations?

Like a Flower in Bloom by Siri Mitchell
sirimitchell.com